A *USA Today* Bestseller

"A page turner! An innocent and a rake, both with dark secrets come together with explosive passion." - Kathy, *Goodreads*

"You will fall in love with Sinjin Pelham, Earl of Revelstoke and Miss Polly Kent. They are the perfect book couple....These two people come together and heal each other's soul and hearts. They take away the hurts they have received from the people of world and turn it into a passionate, protective and devoted love for each other." - Edwina, *Goodreads*

"Sinjin is one of my favorite Callaway heroes. He is deeply flawed and has struggled with his problems without much support. Like all good rakes, he finds something lasting and stabilizing about Polly—a man who has any vice he wants sees something necessary in a decent and honorable woman." -*Top 10 Romance Books*

"I loved this! Super insecure heroine who thinks she is plain and odd and fat... Overheard insult, misunderstandings, tormented hero; this book is right up my alley. Catered to my favorite tropes but still managed to be unique and multidimensional." -Rhiannon, *Goodreads*

ALSO BY GRACE CALLAWAY

LADY CHARLOTTE'S SOCIETY OF ANGELS

Olivia and the Masked Duke

Pippa and the Prince of Secrets (Fall 2021)

GAME OF DUKES

The Duke Identity

Enter the Duke

Regarding the Duke

The Duke Redemption

The Return of the Duke

HEART OF ENQUIRY (The Kents)

The Widow Vanishes (Prequel Novella)

The Duke Who Knew Too Much

M is for Marquess

The Lady Who Came in from the Cold

The Viscount Always Knocks Twice

Never Say Never to an Earl

The Gentleman Who Loved Me

MAYHEM IN MAYFAIR

Her Husband's Harlot

Her Wanton Wager

Her Protector's Pleasure

Her Prodigal Passion

NEVER SAY NEVER
TO AN
Earl

HEART *of* ENQUIRY

GRACE CALLAWAY

USA Today Bestselling Author

Cover Design Credit: Erin Dameron-Hill/ EDH Graphics

Cover Image Credit: Period Images

PROLOGUE

Floating on happiness, Miss Polly Kent decided to risk the censure of her chaperone and headed back through the dark garden in search of her lost slipper ribbon. She retraced her earlier steps, the gardenia-scented air wafting against her heated skin, the stars a scatter of diamonds overhead. She had a mad desire to skip along the winding maze of hedges.

Tonight, Lord Thomas Brockhurst had kissed her. Not only that, but she'd told him her secret—and although he'd been shocked, he hadn't pushed her away.

Can he truly accept me? Joyful heat nudged behind her eyes.

She still couldn't believe that Lord Brockhurst had any interest in her at all. She was a plain wallflower whilst he was a handsome, sought after young buck. Last month, when he'd first approached her as she stood at her usual place at the back of the ballroom, she'd been flummoxed. In fact, she'd looked left and right to be sure that he meant to ask *her* to dance and not someone else. Only when he'd asked again had she unknotted her tongue enough to say "yes."

Since then, he'd paid her attention—nothing to raise brows—but tonight he'd taken things a step further. He'd suggested that they meet out in the garden. And there, sheltered by flowering hedges, she'd received her first kiss.

Her heart sighed. It had been *beautiful*.

What was more beautiful was that he'd felt their connection, too. Polly wouldn't have believed this but for the fact that she could *see* his attraction to her... literally. For she had a strange and inexplicable acuity when it came to the feelings of others, a sort of sixth sense. When she was in close proximity to a person, she perceived a subtle glow around them. The aura—a play of color, texture, and light—revealed their emotional state.

Polly's perceptions had first begun after an accident at age five. Trying to follow her older (and more agile) sister Violet up a tree, she'd slipped, plunging head first to the ground. When she'd regained consciousness, she'd found herself in bed, her family gathered around her, and, to her dazed eyes, they'd literally *glowed* with relief.

Although her family accepted her odd new ability (they loved her unconditionally after all), they'd cautioned her not to disclose the fact of it to others who might not understand. Polly had promptly forgotten their advice and confided in her best friend at the time. The news of her freakishness had spread like wildfire through the village. Even now, her throat tightened as the childish jeers rang in her head.

> Watch out for Peculiar Polly,
> or she'll see what's in your head,
> Steer clear of Peculiar Polly,
> or she'll curse you in your bed.

No matter how she'd tried to explain that she couldn't read thoughts and certainly didn't have any magical powers—that all she could see were auras of emotions—the damage couldn't be undone. Peculiar Polly she was, and Peculiar Polly she'd remained.

An object of ridicule. An outcast.

By the time her family had moved to London five years ago, she'd long since adopted the habit of hiding her abnormality—and herself. She avoided attracting attention as much as possible. She'd succeeded too... until that ball when Lord Brockhurst had taken notice of her.

He's a miracle, she thought giddily.

Not just because of his handsome looks and polished manners, but because he'd listened without judgement as she'd falteringly confessed her dreadful affliction. Even though she'd been terrified of his rejection, her sense of honor made her tell him. Being a Kent, she believed that honesty and love went hand in hand, and since Lord Brockhurst had kissed her (which clearly indicated that he meant to court her), he deserved to know the truth.

Although his aura had reflected shock and disbelief, he hadn't rebuffed her. Relief had flooded her as he'd thanked her for telling the truth, kissed her hand, and told her, "Go in before anyone catches us. I promise to call on you tomorrow."

Now, as she turned the corner, she spied her red ribbon lying on the graveled path just ahead. *It really is my lucky night*, she thought with a smile. As she went over to retrieve the frippery, the murmur of conversation filtered through from the other side of the hedge. Her pulse gave a wayward leap at Lord Brockhurst's familiar tones—so cultured and smooth. She heard two other voices as well, which she identified as belonging to his cronies, Mr. Severton and Lord Eghart.

"It appears you've won the wager, Brockhurst," Severton's distinctively nasal voice pronounced. "I'll admit I didn't think you could peel that paltry bloom off the wall, but I was wrong. I'll have your blunt on the morrow."

The ribbon crumpled in Polly's fist, a cold seed planting in her belly.

"You'd have to pay me more than a hundred quid to consort with that quiz of a female." Lord Eghart gave a braying laugh. "Do tell, Brockhurst, what was it like? Was her kiss as odd as the rest of her—or do still waters run deep, eh?"

Icy vines twisted over Polly's insides.

"A gentleman does not kiss and tell," Brockhurst replied.

"What are a few details amongst friends?" Severton wheedled.

"My lips are sealed."

Numbness spread and spread. Dazed, Polly didn't know whether to be grateful for Lord Brockhurst's discretion or to weep at his betrayal. *He kissed me to win a wager. I'm the biggest fool...*

"Your lips are—but were hers?" Eghart sniggered.

Nausea surged, and Polly wished for the ground beneath her feet to open up and swallow her whole. The earth tremored; for a feverish instant, she thought her prayer had been granted. But no, it was merely the approach of newcomers on the other side of the leafy partition. She knew she should make her escape, yet her limbs remained paralyzed.

Severton's voice went from haughty to toadying. "I say, well met, Lord Revelstoke."

Despite her tumultuous state, Polly started at the name. What was the Earl of Revelstoke doing here? According to her sister Rosie, an expert in *ton* gossip, he was the most eligible bachelor in London, despite his marked disdain for polite society. It was a strange social paradox that the less he cared about the opinions of others, the more they revered him. Wherever he went, it was said that ladies pursued him and gentlemen wanted to *be* him.

In other words, Revelstoke was the polar opposite of Polly. He topped the social ladder whilst her place was on the bottom rung. In the special section reserved for feather-wits who deluded themselves into thinking that they could win a gentleman's love... when all they'd ever have was his scorn. Her throat swelled. *How could I have been so stupid?*

"Gentlemen." Revelstoke's deep, gravelly voice was impatient. "I believe you know Lady Langley?"

Hasty greetings followed, to which a languid female voice

replied, "The Kitburns ought to be congratulated on their consistency, if not talent. Their affairs are always the biggest bore."

"I couldn't agree more. Which is why we've had to concoct our own amusement," Severton said smugly. "A little wager, if you will."

"Oh, do tell," Lady Langley said.

Within her gloves, Polly's hands grew clammy.

"Severton," Lord Brockhurst said in warning tones.

"Don't be modest, Brockhurst. You won, after all. You succeeded in luring the most awkward chit of the Season into the garden and getting a kiss from her," Severton gloated.

"How *naughty*, Lord Brockhurst." Lady Langley's sultry laugh belied her reprimand. "With such exploits, you may give the God of Revelry here a run for his money."

"What do you say, Revelstoke?" Lord Eghart said eagerly. "Prime prank, eh?"

There was a pause, as if everyone was awaiting the earl's judgement on the matter of Polly's humiliation. Her fingers curled; her breath stuck in her throat.

"You'd do as well to kick a half-dead mongrel." Revelstoke's voice dripped with contempt. "Seducing a wallflower—what's the sport in that?"

The words branded themselves on Polly's brain, waves of pain and anger scorching through her. To be compared to a mongrel— a *half-dead* one—was the final straw. Revelstoke had reduced her shattered hopes to naught but *sport*... and not even a worthy competition at that. Right then, she didn't give a damn if he was the most popular rake in all of Christendom—she *hated* him. Despised the earl and his ilk with every part of her shamed and bleeding soul.

If only I could hate Lord Brockhurst, too. A sob rose suddenly in her throat; she pressed both hands over her mouth to contain it.

Lady Langley purred into the tense silence, "You have no interest in virgins, darling?"

"If I did, would I be with you tonight?" came Revelstoke's cool reply.

The ensuing titters and guffaws finally penetrated Polly's shock. She jerked back from the hedge. Cheeks wet, clutching her red ribbon, she dashed out of the maze, leaving the ashes of her dreams behind.

A YEAR LATER

As the carriage passed through the ironwork gates, Polly peered out the window. The rolling lawns and flowering hedges were pristine, stately elms lining the drive that led toward the main house. Fluffy clouds decorated the blue sky. If Mrs. Barlow's property had been the subject of a painting, Polly mused, it could have been entitled *Pastoral Picturesque*—as long as one didn't know about the purpose of the establishment.

"Isn't this place *perfect*? It's exactly as I imagined it."

At the bright tones, Polly turned from the window and smiled at Primrose, who occupied the squabs next to her. Known as Rosie to intimates, the beautiful blonde was two-and-twenty, the age Polly would be in two weeks' time. Although the girls were as different as night and day in looks and temperament, they were bosom companions and sisters in spirit—and nearly in blood, too, for Rosie's mama was wed to Polly's eldest brother Ambrose.

"I wasn't certain how a madhouse would look," Polly said honestly.

"Mrs. Barlow's isn't a madhouse, silly—it's a *retreat*," Rosie corrected. "The *crème de la crème* come here to take the waters. Why, with its Roman springs, it's practically a spa."

Despite the rather euphemistic description, Polly saw that the blonde's sunny aura was muddied by swirling nervousness. Polly exchanged a look with her older sister Dorothea, the carriage's third occupant and the girls' chaperone for the outing. Thea, whose glow was the soft, comforting white of fresh linens, regarded Rosie with gentle eyes.

"Having second thoughts about this visit, dear?" she said.

"Perhaps." Sighing, Rosie said, "I wish I had your charitable natures. You're both so kind to everyone. And Polly—you're a natural with those foundlings of yours."

Soon after her arrival in London, Polly had begun visiting the Hunt Academy, a unique school for foundlings. She adored working with the children, many of whom had once existed on the fringes of society. Through pure grit and pluck, they'd survived the harsh realities of the rookery, and at the school they were learning invaluable skills that would earn them a better lot in life. In truth, the academy was an oasis not only for them but her as well: it was the rare place where she felt a sense of belonging and purpose.

"I'm not sure who benefits more from my visits—me or the children," she said earnestly.

"Mayhap I ought to have stayed on with the foundlings myself, but children are so sticky." Rosie wrinkled her nose. "I do hope the lunatics have a better sense of hygiene."

Polly shook her head because the comment was just so... *Rosie*. People who didn't know the girl oft made the mistake of believing that flippancy was the beginning and end of her when, in fact, she possessed keen intelligence and a loyal heart.

"Instead of lunatics, it might help to think of them as people with ailments," Thea said mildly. "Folk who are doing their best to cope with a difficult illness."

Thea spoke with an empathy borne of experience. Once an

invalid, she'd fought an uphill battle to live a normal life, and her perseverance had paid off. Not only had her health improved, but she'd married her love, the Marquess of Tremont, and was the proud mama to a stepson and a pair of toddler twins.

Polly admired Thea's determination. At the same time, she felt a pang of longing. Unlike Thea, she couldn't rid herself of her affliction—which meant she'd never find love.

The memory of Lord Brockhurst wrung her heart like a wet rag. The only person she'd shared the experience with was Rosie, and she'd left out the part involving Revelstoke. That humiliation was too much to speak of to anyone. Being the object of a nasty wager was bad enough, but to be judged so unworthy…

For reasons she didn't fully fathom, Revelstoke's contempt clung to her like wet mud, harder to shake off than even the cruelty of Brockhurst's prank. *Seducing a wallflower—where's the sport in that?* Revelstoke's words had sunk into her, their fine grit settling uncomfortably into the crevices of her soul.

Still, she ought to count her lucky stars that her secret was safe. Brockhurst had kept her aura-seeing ability to himself—perhaps out of guilt or some belated sense of honor. She would never know because he hadn't approached her again, and she'd avoided him with equal fervor.

Not all that came from the incident was bad. She'd learned two important lessons, after all. First, the family tradition of marrying for love would not apply to her. No man would fall in love with a girl who was plain and peculiar. Second, it was a reminder that emotions were different from thoughts and actions. She'd glimpsed attraction in Brockhurst's aura, but his behavior spoke the truth: she'd been no more than a prank to him.

A way to prove his prowess to his friends… to win a hundred quid. Just because she saw an emotion didn't mean she knew its cause or meaning, and she'd be well served not to make assumptions in the future.

Seeing the worry that continued to flicker around Rosie,

however, Polly refocused her thoughts. The present trip was about Rosie's future. After everything the other had gone through this Season, she needed Polly's support.

Polly touched the other girl's sleeve. "We don't have to go through with this if you don't want to. But if you want to continue on, I know you'll do fine. You always do."

"You're a dear. And, no, I don't want to turn around. This was my idea, and I must follow it through." Rosie straightened her slim shoulders, her jade green eyes determined. "I'm going to prove that I'm not the flighty flirt everyone believes me to be."

"Everyone doesn't believe that," Polly protested.

"Half the *ton* does. The other half doesn't deign to notice me at all because I'm a bastard," Rosie said flatly.

Polly's chest tightened in sympathy.

Rosie had been born out of wedlock, the result of her mama Marianne's youthful indiscretion. Since then, however, she'd been publicly acknowledged by her paternal grandparents as well as her aunt, the influential Marchioness of Harteford. Moreover, Ambrose had adopted her after his marriage to Marianne, and the Kents had brought her unconditionally into their fold.

For the *beau monde*, however, none of this seemed to matter. Although they didn't give Rosie the cut direct, what they'd done was even crueler, to Polly's mind. They'd allowed Rosie the *illusion* of acceptance into their exclusive sphere. Since her debut, Rosie had enjoyed enormous popularity, her beauty and charm rightly winning her the admiration of countless gentlemen.

Yet in recent months it had become painfully clear that popularity was not the same as respectability. Flirtations had not led to offers, nor promises to proposals. Most unfair of all, Rosie's reputation had suffered from the men's fickle behavior: *she* had been the one labelled brazen—a flirt.

"It matters not. I've put it all behind me," Rosie declared. "Once I reform my image, I'll have eligible suitors *vying* for my hand. Which is why I must carry on with the visit today. To show them all that I'm charitable, respectable, and all the things a lady ought to be."

"And perhaps doing good will be reward in itself," Thea suggested. "You sing like an angel, Rosie. When we give our performance, I'm sure your voice will lift many a downtrodden spirit."

"I'll do my best." Rosie smoothed her hands over her skirts. "Well, since I'm to attempt to cheer up some cracked pots... how do I look?"

Rosie had inherited her mama's exquisite bone structure, corn-silk hair, and stunning green eyes. She had an unerring instinct for fashion as well, and her white sprigged muslin, with its *au courant* flounced butter-yellow underskirt and ribbon trim, set off her slender form to perfection. To complete the ensemble, she'd worn matching yellow kid boots, and a spray of buttercups adorned her bonnet.

"Beautiful as always," Polly said sincerely. "You do know how to put an outfit together."

"If that's the case, I do wish you'd let me dress you. That sack you're wearing,"—Rosie gave a shudder—"it's a *travesty*."

Since this was a familiar conversation, Polly didn't take offense. She knew Rosie had her best interests at heart, but what the other didn't understand was that Polly wasn't like her. Not everyone could be beautiful. And not everyone wanted to be noticed.

As if the fiasco of Lord Brockhurst hadn't been enough, Polly had suffered yet another indignity in the past year. For most of her life, she'd been a thin, slight girl, but Emma, her eldest sister, had correctly predicted that she'd be a late bloomer. Seemingly overnight, Polly had sprouted curves that strained the bodices of her dresses, and her lower half had undergone the same excessive expansion as well. Coupled with her short stature, her new form was awkward and ungainly.

How she wished she might be slender and lithe like Rosie. The

other was as graceful as a swan whereas Polly resembled the prover-
bial partridge—in figure and coloring. Her hair was a non-descript
shade, as if it couldn't decide whether to be blond or brown and
settled for something in between. Neither straight nor curly, the
thick tresses rebelled against pins and hot irons and were the bane
of her existence, trumped only by her aura-seeing queerness.

To Polly's mind, her only passable feature were her eyes. She
liked their clear, light shade of blue-green. Unfortunately, her gaze
had a tendency of making others uncomfortable and, thus, she
avoided making undue eye contact.

But as Em would say, there was no use crying over spilt milk.
Full skirts were in fashion, and Polly took full advantage of the
trend, obscuring her hips and bottom with layers of petticoats.
Against the modiste's protestations, she'd insisted on high neck-
lines, loosely cut bodices, and dull fabrics as well. A partridge's
best defense was camouflage after all.

"My dress is fine," she said.

"It's got yards of excessive fabric," Rosie pointed out. "One of
your dresses could make *two* of mine. That garment hides you,
Pols—which is a shame. You've a lovely figure."

"For a strumpet." She'd caught the way gentlemen ogled her
body parts, the animal lust staining their auras. *Like I'm a lump of
meat,* she thought with a humiliated shudder.

"For a *woman.* I wish my bosom was as nice as yours, and
you've the tiniest waist—"

"It only looks tiny in comparison to my vast hips." Polly set
her chin. "Leave it be, Rosie."

Rosie turned to Thea. "Lord above, can't you talk some sense
into her?"

"I think the most important thing is that one feels comfortable in what one wears," Thea said.

"You see?" Polly shrugged. "I'm perfectly comfortable."

Given the roomy design of her dress, it was hard not to be.

"When does comfort have anything to do with fashion?" Rosie said, clearly exasperated. "This blasted corset is squeezing the life out of me, and you don't hear me complaining."

"Why are you laced so tightly? You hardly need it."

"Try getting into this dress otherwise," Rosie grumbled. "But don't distract me from my point."

"Which is?"

"That you shouldn't hide behind drab and unflattering clothes. How are you going to husband hunt with me if you don't take advantage of your assets?"

"I don't want to husband hunt." *Because I've already found the perfect candidate.*

For Polly meant to use the valuable lessons she'd learned. Brockhurst may have destroyed her dreams, but her future was still hers to decide. She didn't want to be a burden to her siblings forever. She didn't want to be the spinster sister, shuffling between households with a menagerie of cats. If she couldn't have love, then she would have the next best thing.

Rosie rolled her eyes. "You cannot *possibly* be serious about Nigel Pickering-Parks."

As a matter of fact, Polly was. "Why not?"

"Um, because he's a pompous bore? Not fashionable at all? Besides, you cannot marry him for the simple fact that he's already married—to his *fossil collection.*"

It was true that Nigel had an avid interest in collecting old bones. Mammal, insect, fish, or amphibian—he was an equal opportunity enthusiast. If it could be dug up and placed in a display cabinet, then Nigel's interest was hooked.

To Polly, this was precisely what made him the solution to the problem of her future. In the two months of their acquaintance, he'd been so engrossed in his hobby that he'd never looked that closely at *her.* He was too wrapped up in his latest acquisition to notice her peculiarity or leer at her figure. He, himself, was comfortable-looking and a trifle pudgy—in other words, her perfect physical counterpart.

With Nigel, she would have a simple, convenient marriage. He could have his fossils; she'd have her foundlings. She'd devote herself to making their life together agreeable, and, God willing, they might even produce a child she could nurture and love. She would be content. If Nigel ever got around to offering for her, she knew what her answer would be.

"You could give Nigel more of a chance," Polly said.

"The fellow declined an invitation to your upcoming birthday supper in order to go looking for fossils. These are old bones we're talking about, ones that have been lying around for *centuries*. Why couldn't he wait until after your party to rush off?"

"Nigel says fossil hunters are a competitive lot," Polly said in his defense. "When he gets a tip, he must act."

Snorting, Rosie turned to Thea. "You don't approve of Nigel any more than I do, do you?"

Thea hesitated. "I don't know him well."

"But you don't *like* him, do you?" Rosie pressed.

"I don't dislike him," Thea hedged. "He's quite... unobjectionable."

"See?" Polly said.

"Quite. In fact, I can see his gravestone now: *here lies Nigel Pickering-Parks, unobjectionable husband and passable fellow to all those who knew him.*" Rosie huffed. "If you won't look for a more suitable match, I'll just have to find rich and handsome lords for both of us."

It was Polly's turn to cast her gaze heavenward. "How are you going to do that, pray tell?"

The other girl shrugged. "I buy you a bonnet whenever I buy myself one, don't I?"

"A husband is not the same as a bonnet!"

"I suppose that's true." Rosie's eyes widened innocently. "One can't replace them nearly as easily when they've gone out of style, can one?"

Polly's lips twitched, but she said severely, "So one better make the right choice the first time around. A title isn't everything, you know."

"Of course it is, silly." Rosie tapped her chin with a finger. "Who knows? Maybe there's a pair of twin *dukes* somewhere. Whoever came out first would technically be His Grace—but the other would likely have a courtesy title. Because I love you so, I'd give *you* the older brother."

"You'd make such a sacrifice for me?" Polly said dryly.

"What can I say?" Rosie's expression was angelic. "I'm a martyr."

A shared look—and they both burst into giggles.

A while later, Polly stood at the back of the salon waiting for Rosie and Thea's performance to begin. The room was stuffy, the heavy scent of perfume not entirely masking the underlying human smells. At first glance, the patients filing in appeared well-groomed and fashionably dressed, yet Polly saw the miasma that surrounded them like a fog and recognized it as... despair. Beneath that smothering cloud, bright and clashing colors flitted like desperate butterflies trapped in a glass jar. The suffocating atmosphere made Polly's lungs strain for air.

"Ah, there you are, Miss Kent."

Mrs. Barlow approached in a swish of chartreuse silk. The proprietress wore her dark hair in a simple twist, her jewelry sparse and tasteful. The widow of a prosperous factory owner, she'd purchased this once-ailing resort built upon mineral springs and transformed it into what her pamphlet described as a "haven for healing."

From the tour of the house Mrs. Barlow had given them

earlier, Polly could find no fault with the advertising. The main house had been redone in a crisp, Palladian style and boasted separate wings for male and female patients. There were spacious rooms for entertainment, including the present salon.

Although they hadn't yet toured the grounds or the famed baths, the windows near Polly displayed the manicured splendor behind the main house. Graveled paths wound past flower beds and leafy hedges. Mrs. Barlow had explained that the Roman springs lay just beyond the garden, along with small private villas reserved for her most distinguished residents.

Everything appeared first-rate, yet Polly couldn't quell her unease. A large part of it had to do with the proprietress, whose aura was the same color as her dress: a sickly shade of green.

"As you can see, my charges are on their best behavior," Mrs. Barlow said, her features schooled in a pleasant mask. "This performance is to be a reward for them."

Polly saw the patients filing like obedient schoolchildren into rows of hard-backed chairs. The charges darted nervous glances at the perimeter of the room where attendants, men and women dressed in severe grey uniforms, stood like sentinels. Behind them, sunlight glinted off the iron bars over the windows.

Polly suppressed a shiver. "I hope the residents will enjoy the selection of music."

"Oh, they will." Mrs. Barlow's smile had the sharp gleam of teeth.

A brouhaha suddenly came from the front of the room. One of the charges, a ginger-haired gentleman, shouted at a male attendant, "I do not wish to sit!"

"If you'll excuse me, Miss Kent?" Mrs. Barlow said brusquely.

The proprietress glided over to the resident. She spoke softly to him, her serene expression never changing, and yet the man turned ashen, his glow snuffed like a candle. He lowered himself into the chair, visibly shaking. Triumph wriggled like black snakes through Mrs. Barlow's aura; with a satisfied smirk, she headed off.

Polly's temples throbbed. Hopelessness hovered over all the patients like storm clouds, the feeling so oppressive that she couldn't breathe. Spotting a nearby door that looked to lead into the gardens, she headed toward it.

Once amongst the hedgerows, she lifted her face to the sun, willing its warmth to permeate her chilled insides. She sensed so much suffering inside that house—and yet she was helpless to do anything about it. She had no solid evidence, nothing to point to... except her own freakish intuition.

She kicked a pebble out of her path. She knew she would have to turn around soon, but her nerves were still jangled. Her gaze caught on a wooden structure just past the hedgerows, and curiosity nudged aside some of her unease. Was that one of the Roman baths? A distraction would prove welcome at the moment.

Drawing in another breath, she went to see what she would find.

Herbert Gerard St. John Pelham—known as Sinjin to anyone who didn't want a drubbing—dropped his robe and let it fall onto the stone floor. The sulphur-tinged steam curled upward from the hot spring, sheening his bare skin. The bathhouse had been modeled after the ancient spas at Bath, reproductions of Roman columns posted at the corners of the large rectangular pool, a wrought iron torch flickering upon each one. Smooth, golden stone paved the deck around the bath and the surrounding walls. The effect was cavernous, womb-like.

Sinjin descended the shallow steps into the glimmering blue-green depths of the pool. *Christ, that's good.* He waded deeper, nearly groaning as the warm, silky water lapped against the hard ridges of his torso. He was a man of sensual appetites, and Lord knew there'd been no earthly indulgences during the week he'd been trapped in this godforsaken place.

At least today all the lunatics had been herded to some musicale, and he finally had some peace and quiet. To be fair, he was the one intruding upon their territory: he was no resident, of course, but a special guest staying in one of Mrs. Barlow's private villas. His father, the Duke of Acton, had brought him here, and at the time, he'd been too disoriented, too bloody shaken, to take full note of his surroundings or ask any questions.

Shame rose like a tide. He told himself it was useless to think about the events of the night that had led to his arrival at Mrs. Barlow's. Even if he wanted to contemplate the sins he'd committed during those damnable hours, he couldn't.

Because all that came to him was darkness. The blackness of a hole punched from his memory. He'd tried and tried to remember what had happened, but all he saw was the end result.

Nicoletta's battered face and blackened eyes. The necklace of fingerprints around her neck. Her sobbing accusation and pointing finger. *He went mad and tried to kill me.*

Sinjin's stomach curdled, the contents of his lunch threatening to make a reappearance. Revulsion burned through his veins like acid; his fingers speared through his hair, gripping tightly, as if pain could somehow lessen his fear.

Why can't I remember? Am I going mad?

He'd have to be to hurt a woman. Sinjin did not pretend to be a gentleman of high morals, but *never* had he committed violence against a member of the gentler sex. The notion made him sick.

At six-and-twenty, he'd led a wild life and didn't give a damn what anyone thought of it. People came and went; in the end, he was the only one he could count on—and thus the only one whose opinion he cared to court. From the time he'd been expelled from Eton through the nightmare years at Creavey Hall, he'd stuck to that philosophy, and he'd survived, with the scars to prove it.

The idea that he would inflict similar abuse on an undeserving victim? *Not bloody possible.* As bedeviled as he was, he couldn't fathom it. Hurting someone less powerful than him went against what little he held sacred. But why couldn't he remember?

I'll teach you a trick, Sinjin, something I do to calm myself. I grab hold of something: a paperweight, a coin, anything. And I concentrate on that

one thing—the sensation of that object in my hand—until my mind is
steady again.

His older brother Stephan's advice surfaced in the vortex of
his thoughts. Wise, even-tempered Stephan had been his opposite, his anchor. The only one who'd given a damn about him. But
Stephan was gone, too; the familiar grief welled, and Sinjin tried
to escape it by plunging into the water for a swim.

The exercise calmed him, focused his thoughts. A week
without a drop of drink had been excruciating, but it had helped
to clear his head. With the raw, painful clarity of staring straight
into the sun, he'd begun to see that, in the two years since
Stephan's death, he'd let his devils get the better of him.

The black devil and the blue devil: that was how he'd come to
think of the two opposing sides of his nature. Since his early
adolescence, the bloodthirsty pair had staked his mind as their
battleground, and even now he could feel their presence, lurking,
waiting to make their next move.

The black devil who made him feel powerful and euphoric,
limitless. Who lured him with the rush of excitement, the thrill of
danger, the numbing high of recklessness. The fast crowd he ran
with revered this side of him; like the satyrs and Maenads of
myth, they erupted into an ecstatic frenzy at his exploits.

You race like the devil, old boy! his cronies would cheer when he
crossed the finish line first, nearly overturning his four-in-hand in
the process.

You carouse like a king, they'd crow when he won yet another
drinking contest.

You fuck like a god, the wench—or wenches—of the night would
purr.

Reaching the other end, Sinjin kicked off the stone wall,
propelling his body through the water. He fed off the adulation,
even when he knew it wasn't real. None of them—not his so-
called friends or the females clamoring for his attention—knew

him. The true him. Who he was behind the fearless stunts and brash confidence. How bedeviled he was by the black beast... and the blue.

What's the matter with you, boy? Get out of bed. You're pathetic, worthless.

The duke's contempt drove him through the pool, shame and anger churning the warm waves. As difficult as his black mood was to manage—in a heartbeat, euphoria could explode into irritability, recklessness into fisticuffs—the blue was infinitely worse. He hated that part of himself. How it turned him into a gutless prat, loaded his pockets with rocks and sunk him into the depths of despair.

Since he'd become the Earl of Revelstoke—Stephan's title, the one that he, Sinjin, had never wanted—the devils had become even more unruly. He'd tried to play them off each other, using black to stave off blue. All it took was more drink, more reckless feats. More sex. Which was why he'd gone to Corbett's, an exclusive and infamous bawdy house, a week ago. Why he'd tossed back a few drinks, played a few rounds of hazard, and then gone upstairs with Nicoletta, the club's newest light-skirt. Why he'd fucked her and then... what?

What bloody happened?

Frustration and anguish twisted his insides. Could the black devil have pilfered a chunk of time from him? In the past, orgiastic sprees had passed in a blur, and he'd drunk himself into oblivion more times than he could count, yet he'd always retained some memory of his escapades. Could it be possible that he'd beaten Nicoletta... and forgotten? There were cuts and scrapes on his knuckles, but since he'd gotten into a tavern brawl prior to visiting Corbett's, he didn't know if his injuries were the result of the drunken scuffle... or of beating her. A defenseless female.

His arms plowed through the water harder, faster, as if he could somehow outdistance himself from the reprehensible possibility. As if he could somehow outrace *himself*—get away from the sodding disaster that he was. From the possibility that he truly was mad.

Lungs burning, he told himself that he was nothing like the others at this "retreat." He didn't think a coat rack was a long-lost aunt, didn't see visions of angels telling him that he was the Savior reborn. He'd been dealing with his devils for more than half his life; he'd learned how to mask and manage them well enough.

Hell, the *ton* considered him a catch. What a bloody joke that was. Even more amusing was the fact that the more he shunned polite society, the more they wanted him—or, rather, his title and money.

Let them be blinded by status and wealth. By the cocky, good-looking bastard who stared back at him in the looking glass. At least he was no object of pity: he'd rather die than be that.

He'd seen how the hapless lunatics were treated here. He'd glimpsed behind the fashionable curtain of Mrs. Barlow's establishment to witness the dark underbelly. Despite the fancy trappings, this place was Creavey Hall all over again. Cold seeped in the depths of him, a place where no healing waters could reach.

By God, he did not belong here.

It'll only be temporary. The emotionless tones of his father, the Duke of Acton, echoed in his head. *You'll stay at Mrs. Barlow's until this catastrophe blows over. No one will recognize you there—and the waters will do you good. God knows you need to regain your equilibrium.*

At the time, he'd been too shaken to refuse his papa's help, and it had taken the past few days here to regain his footing. To take full stock of his situation and realize that he was hiding like a bloody bastard. His arms shredded the water, his feet kicking until the whole of him was burning. And still he couldn't shake free of the demons. Of the guilt and self-loathing and churning confusion.

Why can't I remember? What's wrong with me?

He forced himself into a more brutal pace. He swam until there was nothing left inside him. Only then did he haul himself out of the pool, flopping onto his back on the smooth stone. Chest heaving, he stared up at the wooden slats of the ceiling and tried to empty his head.

Yet the self-doubts wouldn't stop, rising in a choir of accusation. Tranquility became a cage, and he was trapped in his own skin with no comrades, no wenches, no mind-obliterating pursuits to distract him. Devil and damn, what was a fellow to do with himself?

He needed an escape. A release before his head combusted with all that was building inside.

Like a buoy in dark waters, a memory drifted to him. The afternoon he'd spent with Lady Evelyn De Ville and her maid... he couldn't recall the latter's name, but she'd been a buxom brunette with dark, prominent nipples. A rousing contrast to Lady Evelyn's delicate blond beauty.

He felt his blood heat, that welcome rush into his cock. He glanced at the closed door; that musicale would keep everyone occupied for another hour at least. Judging from the throbbing state of his erection, he wouldn't need more than five minutes at most. He wasn't a man meant for abstinence. The past week had been the longest time he'd gone without sex for as long as he could recall. Maybe releasing his seed would relax and calm him.

He lay back and fisted his cock. He couldn't recall the last time he'd frigged himself—why put in the effort when there was a surfeit of others to do it for you?—but if he closed his eyes, he could almost imagine it was someone else touching him.

Lady Evelyn's slender white fingers, for instance, circling the heavy up-thrust flesh.

He could almost hear her breathy, rather affected accents. *Oh, Sinjin, you've a monstrous large cock. The biggest rod I've ever seen.*

Considering the source, it was no small compliment. Despite

her ethereal looks, Countess De Ville was a connoisseur of the carnal arts. Her experience and appetite rivalled his own. Yet even her innovative bedroom antics had begun to bore him, and lately he'd had a strange yearning for something else. Something he couldn't name, but that was more than burying his prick in a convenient orifice, more than a fleeting release followed by that dark, unending emptiness...

Focus, he told himself. *Stay on the subject* literally *at hand.*

His biceps flexed as he stroked his thickening flesh. As he recalled, Lady Evelyn was an expert in fellatio, possessed of a voracious mouth. His breath quickened as she licked up and down his turgid shaft, tonguing the flaring dome before taking him deep. He tried to ignore her slurping and gagging; the lascivious sounds were meant to arouse, no doubt, but she took it a bit too far, sounding like she might cast her accounts.

Concentrate, you fool.

He shut his eyes. The maid—mustn't forget her. She joined in the fun, crawling between his legs and lapping at his bollocks while Lady Evelyn bobbed on his cock. Yes, this was more like it. Two ladies—one fair, one dark—intent upon his pleasure... and each other's. The maid abandoned him, her dark head slipping beneath her mistress. Lady Evelyn ground her sex against her servant's lusty mouth, moaning, the sound reverberating against his iron-hard shaft.

Right-o. Everyone to their fancy, as he always said.

His climax was nearing; he needed just a bit more to tip the scales. He pulled Lady Evelyn's mouth off the meat of his shaft and positioned her on her hands and knees. He plunged into her sopping cunny, riding her as she panted out encouragement. Not to be left out, the maid wriggled beneath her mistress, adding her lips and tongue to the lascivious joining. Apparently in the mood to return the favor, Lady Evelyn's head dipped to her servant's dark thatch.

His strokes quickened, his sac drawing taut, ready to fire—

A rustling sound tore him from his fantasy. His eyes snapped open, gaze shooting to the doorway. Through the haze of lust, he saw... a young woman? Small and prim, she was staring at him with enormous eyes.

In that moment, two incredible facts flashed through his mind. One, he'd been caught—red-handed, so to speak—by some virginal miss. Two, the lady's eyes were the exact color of the pool: a pure aquamarine, mesmerizingly clear... faultless. Her tongue darted out to wet her plump coral lips, and, devil and damn, he felt that swipe from his balls to his cockhead.

How long has she been watching?

An erotic buzz shot through him. Within his fist, his rod jerked, a droplet seeping from the bloated crown. The hot trickle over his knuckle shattered the remnants of his fantasy, reality crashing over him. With a curse, he released himself, made a grab for his robe. Before he could get the bloody thing on, he heard the rapid-fire retreat of footsteps.

He spun around; she was gone.

Heart thudding, he stared at the empty doorway. Who the bloody hell was she? Distracted by her startling eyes, he'd only gotten a vague impression of the rest of her: dowdy dress, neat little features. Was she a visiting relative of one of the patients?

He dragged a hand through his wet hair. If she was as prudish as her appearance suggested, he'd probably shocked her half to death. Although he didn't recognize her—he avoided innocent ladies like the plague—he wondered if she knew who *he* was...

By Jove, what if she *did* recognize him—and told someone about it?

Frost spread through him. His papa was working to control the damage he'd caused, asking only one thing in return: *stay at Mrs. Barlow's and out of sight.* His Grace had spread the fiction that Sinjin had hailed off to the Continent on a whim. If word got out that Sinjin was not abroad but housed at a lunatic asylum where he'd been caught *in flagrante* with *himself*...

His face burned. He had to nip this problem in the bud. He'd go find the chit—she'd likely come from the musicale—and ascertain whether she knew his identity. If she did... well, he'd come up with some plausible explanation for his behavior. Somehow.

Cursing, he strode off to get dressed—and to contain yet another scandal.

❧ 3 ❧

Polly hurried back to the musicale, her mind and senses awhirl. It was intermission, and under the watchful eyes of the attendants, the patients were docilely filing into a line in front of the refreshment table. Before Polly had a chance to collect herself, Rosie cornered her by the door.

"There you are. You missed the first part of my performance," Rosie said with a pout. "Where did you wander off to?"

"Sorry. I had to get some air," Polly mumbled.

"You're flushed." Rosie's pique faded. "Are you feeling unwell?"

She didn't know *what* she was feeling. Shocked, afraid... tingly all over. What she'd encountered in the bathhouse had been the most depraved thing she'd seen in her entire life. That man—what he'd been *doing*! Lying by the side of the Roman bath, he'd appeared like a young Bacchus come to life, wicked and entirely unabashed in his steam-glazed decadence.

The torchlight had burnished his mahogany hair, kissed the divinely handsome contours of his face. He had the body of a god, too: beneath his taut skin, sleek muscles had rippled with unmistakable power. His chest had resembled cut slabs of granite, no hint of softness save for the sprinkling of bronze hair. That trail of hair had drawn her gaze downward like a magnet toward the lean ridges of his abdomen, past the prominent vee of muscle girdling his hips, to his...

She swallowed, her mouth dry. She'd seen sculptures of the nude male form, but apparently they didn't accurately depict that part of a man's anatomy—at least not this man's. Heavens, his male equipment more resembled that of the mythical satyr: larger than life... beyond shocking! She saw again the wicked pumping of his fist, the animal pulsing of his aura, and a wave of dizziness washed over her.

"Gracious, now you look positively feverish. Shall I fetch you some lemonade?" Rosie said.

"No. I'm fine." Her quivering voice and insides contradicted her.

"It's me—your bosom chum and sister, remember?" Rosie's hands planted on her hips. "Out with it, Pols."

Polly gnawed on her lower lip. How on earth could she describe what she barely comprehended herself? How could she put into words the depraved behavior that she'd witnessed?

Then it occurred to her: the fellow must be *insane*. Of course. He was at Mrs. Barlow's for a reason after all. Perhaps he'd lost control over himself—over his animal impulses. Polly had heard tales of madmen barking at the moon. Might the poor man be afflicted with a similar canine delusion? Dogs, after all, were in the habit of licking themselves in unmentionable areas, and what he'd been doing was sort of similar, wasn't it?

He must be a lunatic, she reasoned with relief. It was the only plausible explanation for his unnatural behavior. And if he'd unleashed strange sensations in her—she felt shivery and shaky, a hot viscosity coating her insides—well, any *sane* person would feel discomfited.

Expelling a breath, she said, "I saw someone acting, um, oddly is all."

Rosie snorted. "Given the setting, that's hardly—"

A loud crash cut off the rest of her sentence. Polly started, her gaze jerking toward the refreshment table to their left. A wooden platter lay on the floor, cheese scattered around it, grapes rolling off like marbles. The cause of the disarray appeared to be one of the patients: the young ginger-haired man she'd noticed earlier.

"I don't want any cheese!" he yelled. "It's full of poison! You're trying to kill me!"

A murmur rose from the other patients. A few spat out their food.

"Calm yourself, Kirkham." A burly attendant approached him, hands raised. "You don't want to disrupt the party. Why don't you and I have a chat outside?"

"I'm not going anywhere with you!" Kirkham's eyes were wild, like those of a hunted creature. He grabbed a pitcher, threw it down, glass exploding into shards at his feet. "You don't want to chat. You want to throw me in the coffin and fill it up with water! You want to kill me, you want to kill all of us!"

Patients were looking at each other, nodding, whispers getting louder.

Someone shouted, "You tell 'em, Kirkham!"

Mrs. Barlow pushed her way through the crowd to stand next to the attendant.

"For God's sake, Lubbock," she snapped at the guard, "get a hold of him."

Desperation oozed from Kirkham in waves of yellow-brown. He suddenly crouched and came up with a large shard of glass in his hand. Blood trickled from his palm, matching the red aggression in his aura.

"Put that down," Lubbock ordered. "Don't make this harder on yourself."

"You want to murder me—well, I won't make it easy for you!" Kirkham swung the makeshift weapon in a wild arc.

Lubbock pounced. Kirkham managed to dodge the brawny guard, who flew straight into the table. Dishes and utensils went flying, the clatter mingling with the patients' shrieks and cheers. Other attendants entered the fray, but fear made Kirkham as slippery as a lamprey, and he evaded them all. He headed straight for the open door next to where Polly and Rosie stood transfixed, their hands gripped together. In the next breath, Polly felt Rosie's fingers being torn from hers and heard the other scream.

Kirkham had grabbed Rosie! He held her in front of him like a shield, the jagged glass blade pressed against her throat. Heart pounding, Polly took a step toward them.

"Please don't hurt my sister," she pleaded.

"*Stay back*." Kirkham edged his way backward toward the exit, keeping Rosie between him and the approaching battalion of attendants. "Try to stop me and she dies!"

"Let her go or it'll be the worse for you," Lubbock warned.

"It can't get worse than this place. I'm getting out of here, one way or another. Now stay back—or I'll cut her, do you hear me?"

Wings of panic thumped in Polly's chest as the guards ignored his threat, closing in on him as he backed toward the door. She stood helplessly, seeing the rising waves of aggression, the way the black energy fed off itself until it choked the entire room. One false move and...

Kirkham reached the exit—and in the next moment, he yelped, his face contorting with pain, his makeshift weapon falling from his grasp. He was yanked through the door and out of sight, and Rosie stumbled forward, *free*. Polly scrambled over, throwing her arms around the trembling girl while the guards rushed past them.

"Are you all right?" Polly said shakily.

"I most certainly am *not*." Rosie's jade eyes widened, her face pale. "Serves me right for trying to be a do-gooder. This is the *last* time I do anything charitable."

A relieved chuckle frothed up Polly's throat just as Thea came rushing over.

"My goodness, what happened?" Thea said with breathless

concern. "I returned from the retiring room to see Rosie being dragged away by some madman."

"He was using me as a hostage." Rosie shivered. "I don't know how I got free."

"It looked like someone grabbed him from behind," Polly said.

"Whoever that was saved my life. He's a *hero*. I must thank him."

Rosie dashed for the door, and Polly followed, Thea at their heels. Outside, the first thing Polly saw was Rosie's attacker: Kirkham was wrestled to the ground, his struggling form subdued by a gentleman whose back was turned to them. As the guards took over custody of Kirkham, the man rose, and even from behind, Polly could tell he was a top-of-the-trees Corinthian. Blue superfine clung lovingly to his wide shoulders and narrow hips, his trousers fitting his long, muscular legs like a second skin and tucking into Hessians.

In the sun, the thick waves of his hair gleamed like polished mahogany—and recognition struck Polly. *Dear God, not...* The man turned, and there was no mistaking that god-like face or the piercing midnight blue gaze. Her knees wobbled like an aspic.

"It's him." The whisper escaped unbidden from her lips.

"You know that gentleman?" Rosie's head swung in her direction.

Not wanting to lie, Polly stammered, "I-I don't know him, but I've seen him once—"

"And one never forgets the Earl of Revelstoke."

Rosie's declaration sent a jolt through Polly. That man... was *Revelstoke*? He was the cad who'd ridiculed her in the garden? Who'd compared her to a mongrel—called her *unworthy sport*?

Her breath turned choppy, her hands balling at her sides.

"I've only had one faraway glimpse of him at a party, but his is a face one never forgets," Rosie said knowingly. "'Tis no wonder they call him the God of Revelry: he is absolutely divine. All the debs want to land him, you know, but he's a confirmed rake who wants nothing to do with innocent misses."

"We'd better stay away then," Polly said tightly.

Or I might punch him in his perfect, popular nose.

"On the contrary." A determined light entered Rosie's eyes, her lips curving in a cat-got-in-the-cream smile. "I cannot *wait* to make his acquaintance."

———

A few minutes later, Polly watched the interaction between Rosie and Revelstoke with the grim fascination of one watching two shiny carriages on course for collision. They were all in a private drawing room that the proprietress had insisted they use to recover, Thea and Rosie flanking Revelstoke on a settee and Polly occupying an adjacent wingchair.

From a physical standpoint, Polly had to admit that the earl and her sister made a stunning pair: his dark, virile handsomeness was the ideal foil for Rosie's fair and slender beauty. Rosie was flirting; having witnessed the other in action countless times before, Polly recognized all the signs. The flip of the blond ringlets, the tinkling laugh, the way she was leaning forward as if to say, *You're the most interesting person in the world!*

Polly's posture, on the other hand, was stiff and rigid, her hands tightly clasped. Being face to face with the earl fanned the embers of her humiliation, memories bursting free, blasting the hinges off the box she'd locked them in. Suddenly, she was right back at that hedge, Revelstoke's derision piercing her like shrapnel.

You'd do as well to kick a half-dead mongrel. Seducing a wallflower— what's the sport in that?

She'd thought time would dull the pain of those words; she was wrong.

Before, he'd been a disembodied voice, but now that she saw

him—his utter perfection—it made his contempt of her even more despicable. Wasn't it enough for him to be the ultimate specimen of manhood? To be blessed with bounty in every respect? Why did he feel the need to be arrogant and hateful toward lesser mortals?

"You're a hero, my lord," Rosie was saying. "I owe you my *life*. How shall I ever repay you?"

"I did as any gentleman would have done," Revelstoke said. "Your well-being is ample reward, Miss Kent."

Apparently the cad could be gallant if he wished, Polly thought resentfully.

On his other side, Thea smiled and said, "You have my family's gratitude, my lord."

Rosie's eyelashes fluttered. "Surely there is *some* way I could express my appreciation for your bravery, my lord?"

Worry waded into the fray of Polly's emotions. Rosie was not only pouring on the butter boat, she was practically dousing the earl with it! Steely determination glinted in her aura—dear Lord, she couldn't have fixed her sights on the earl? With rising panic, Polly realized that, on the surface, Revelstoke fit Rosie's bill of a perfect husband: he was titled, rich, the most sought-after bachelor of the Season. Landing him would be nothing short of a social coup.

Polly had to do something before Rosie got herself entangled with the bounder. But what signal could she give her sister? She couldn't very well blurt out what Revelstoke had said about her or, God forbid, what she'd seen him doing in the bathhouse.

Then it struck her: *why* was the earl here?

She returned to the hypothesis she'd had before she'd learned his true identity. Could it be that Revelstoke was... mad? Heat seared her insides as she flashed back to his depravity. Surely even rakes didn't engage in such indecent behavior? Could it be that the celebrated earl was a few cards short of a full deck?

She surreptitiously studied his aura. She'd never seen one quite like his before. The dark, stormy blue matched his eyes, the outer layer so intense and opaque that she couldn't discern the feelings beneath, seeing only brief flashes of movement and color.

Regardless, the fact that he was a resident here spoke for itself. And even Rosie wouldn't carry on a flirtation with a madman, titled though he may be. If Polly experienced a smidgen of misgiving that she might be indulging in a desire for revenge, she pushed it aside. What mattered was ensuring that Rosie did not get caught up in Revelstoke's web of crazed debauchery. Lord knew her reputation couldn't take another blow.

Before she lost nerve, Polly blurted, "Have you enjoyed your stay here, my lord?"

The conversation came to a halt. Silence stretched between the ticks of the long-case clock. Rosie's silvery laugh ended the awkward moment.

"Dear Polly, you're so droll! I'm sure you meant to say the earl's *visit*—and not to imply that he, himself, is a resident here."

"I am staying here, actually." Revelstoke met Polly's gaze squarely. His vivid eyes had a swirl of darkness in them, like blue paint deepened with a drop of ink. "Though not as a resident, to be sure. Mrs. Barlow has kindly allowed me the use of the waters for my health. I find the springs here more convenient and private than those of Bath."

"Bath can get so crowded," Rosie agreed. "Why, one can hardly take a step without bumping into some acquaintance or another."

Come on, Rosie. See him for the lunatic that he is.

Steeling herself, Polly said, "What sort of ill health do you suffer from, my lord?"

"Dearest," Thea murmured, "that's hardly an appropriate—"

"'Tis quite all right, Lady Tremont. I thank Miss Kent for her concern." His voice was smoother than the finest wine. "My health suffers no ill effects save from the excesses of Town living.

I thought a week of the waters and country air might be restoring."

For a madman, he had an answer for everything, Polly thought darkly. His gaze met hers, and his lips quirked. He was amused... at *her*? A fresh wave of anger hit her.

"It must be difficult being so much in the public eye and in demand, my lord," Rosie chimed in. "Why, I daresay 'tis as difficult to get an audience with you as with His Majesty. Indeed," she added, dimpling, "up until today, I've only glimpsed you from afar."

"A most grievous oversight on my part. Forgive me?" he murmured.

Rosie's ringlets bobbed prettily as she nodded. The earl's manners were so polished, his aura so confident and controlled, that doubt crept though Polly. Was he not mad after all? But he'd been engaged in such *unnatural* behavior...

The door to the drawing room opened, and Mrs. Barlow swept in. Agitation sparked around her like fireflies. "My valued guests, I must apologize again for the dreadful incident," she began. "Rest assured that the patient has been dealt with."

A chill seeped through Polly. "Dealt with?" she said in a low voice.

"He is no longer a danger to others or himself."

As satisfaction slithered through the proprietress' aura, Polly shivered.

Turning to the earl, who'd risen at her entrée, Mrs. Barlow said, "Words cannot express my gratitude for your intervention, my lord. I deeply regret that the unfortunate incident interfered with your privacy and relaxation."

So he actually was a visitor—and, thus, sane. *Drat.*

"Making the acquaintance of present company was well worth any effort." For some reason, the earl wasn't looking at Rosie but at Polly, mocking humor in his eyes. It was as if he'd guessed what she'd believed about him and was *entertained* by it.

Once more, she was an object of ridicule to him.

Humiliation welled, flowing into tributaries of the past, all the other times she'd been treated with contempt. The village children's chants of "Peculiar Polly," melded into the smirks of the fashionable crowd, the laughing male voices making a wager of her emotions. A lifetime of being on the outside seared through her.

"Dear ladies," Mrs. Barlow said, "may I ask that you respect my policy on discretion? I have promised Lord Revelstoke a peaceful retreat from the furor of Town, and I should hate for his solitude to be ruined by interlopers."

"Trying to get away from the adoring hordes, are you?" Rosie said teasingly.

Revelstoke's broad shoulders moved in a careless shrug. "My companions can get a bit tiresome in their pursuit of revelry."

How trying it must be for you to be so popular, Polly thought with mounting ire.

Thea rose. "Well, we shan't interrupt your sojourn any longer, my lord. It was a pleasure to make your acquaintance."

"The pleasure was mine, Lady Tremont." The earl swept an artful bow.

"I do hope we'll see each other soon, my lord?" Rosie said.

"I will count the hours."

Beaming, Rosie added with a saucy twinkle, "Just so you know, my papa is London's *best* investigator. So I shall ask him to employ his skills and find you if you don't keep your promise!"

"Rosie," Thea said mildly. "Come along now."

As Thea and Rosie bade farewell to Mrs. Barlow, Revelstoke turned to Polly. She tensed as he bestowed a charming smile upon her.

"I hope we can put today behind us, Miss Kent," he said easily.

She knew he wasn't referring to the ruckus with the madman but to what she'd caught him doing in the bathhouse. His aura matched his eyes: the strong, confident blue of a man assured of his place at the top of the world. *Does being popular insulate him from all wrongdoing?* she fumed. She might be naïve, but he, not she, was the one who'd been caught in an ignominious act. *He*, not she, was the one who ought to feel mortified!

"I shan't think of it again," she said tightly.

If anything, his amusement grew stronger. His mouth quirked, the movement sinfully sensual and dashed *annoying* because he no doubt knew it was so.

"To think, I was going to apologize for causing you unintended shock," he murmured. "It seems you have more mettle than meets the eye, Miss Kent."

Did he think that just because she was plain and fat that she couldn't manage her reaction to him? That she'd be rendered insensate by his stupid depravity? That the mere sight of his godlike form would turn her into a wilting violet?

How. Dare. He.

"If by *mettle* you mean that I am capable of exerting self-control, then you have the right of it, my lord," she said in cutting tones. "I believe that one should be responsible for one's own actions."

Although his expression didn't change, the ominous flare in his aura made her breath lodge in her throat. Heart racing, she brushed past him toward the others. Even as she fled, the image of what she'd seen stayed with her: the moment when his glow had changed, flawless blue cracking... revealing the fresh red innards of shame.

4

That night, Sinjin hovered in the territory between dreams and wakefulness.

He'd left the shutters open, moonlight breaking upon the soft linens of his bed. The air was humid, warm, and he turned over again, unable to find a comfortable position. Perhaps it was the residual energy of subduing a maniac. Given some of the tavern brawls he'd participated in, the scenario hadn't been all that foreign to him, but it had felt good to put his skills to some meaningful use. The pretty blond chit had been grateful, certainly.

But it wasn't that Miss Kent who kept him tossing and turning into the night. Even as he sank deeper, farther away from the surface of consciousness, he couldn't escape that haunting aquamarine gaze. Those clear orbs followed him, and he was forced to look into them, to see himself reflected in the pure, unflinching light.

One should be responsible for one's own actions.

Nothing he hadn't heard before, and yet her voice threaded his dreams, stringing together a necklace of images and sensations. A beautiful, raven-haired Madonna, her laughter echoing down the hall, her voice softening into a song.

Bye, baby Bunting,
Daddy's gone a-hunting,
Gone to get a rabbit skin,
To wrap the baby Bunting in...

Velvet comfort against his cheek as he watched a gleaming pendulum, time ticking away in years rather than minutes, his hand reaching out, tangling in a flowing black mane. Scything hooves beneath him now, a pounding certainty in his adolescent heart. *I'm going to live forever!*

Back in the stables, he was a child again, his curiosity drawing him to the strange animal sounds, to the farthest stall where it wasn't a horse but the Madonna on her hands and knees, the groom bent over her, dirty hands gripping her hair like reins. Fear and anger propelled him forward, fists flying.

No, Sinjin, it's all right... don't tell, don't tell...

Tears sliding like pearls down her pale cheeks.

Mama's gone. Stephan's young face. *But we'll still have each other.*

Two stacks of trunks, one bound for Eton, the other Creavey Hall. As his brother slapped his back goodbye, the words sticking in his throat. *Don't leave me. I can't do this without you...*

Stephan's dead. The duke's voice floated through the ether. *It should have been you.*

He twisted, falling into darkness, an oblivion of deeper shadows. The seduction of pale curves against scarlet satin. *Name's Nicoletta, luv, and I'll make all your dreams come true...* The friction of skin against skin, the temporary lethargy, sweet viscosity relieving his parched throat. Tired, so tired. Voices filtering as if through a wall of water, the rise and fall of indistinct waves, a deep voice rumbling to the surface. *Hurry, we must act before he awakens...*

Sinjin bolted upright, a scream in his ears.

He sat there, chest thudding, disoriented. His clammy hands fisted the sheets. Even as he tried to sort dream from reality, he heard it again—that high-pitched wail—coming not from his dream but from somewhere in the distance. Human or animal? He strained to hear more, but only insects shrilled in reply.

Reaching over to the bedside table, he grasped his talisman. Squeezing the locket in his fist, he concentrated on its filigreed weight until his breath steadied, until he was certain this was no longer a dream. Only then did he loosen his grip. His lips twisted at the sight of the silver charm. No doubt Stephan would have approved of him using the calming trick, but what would his upstanding brother have said about the trinket in his palm, a symbol of all his excesses?

The locket had arrived on Sinjin's doorstep a few weeks ago. The appearance of the feminine trinket was not an unusual occurrence as his lovers (or those who wanted to be) made an annoying habit of sending him mementoes. What in God's name did women think he would want with a garter or jeweled hair pin, some perfumed handkerchief?

He usually let the servants take what they wanted, the rest going straight to the rubbish heap, but the locket had been different. Demure and modest, no note had accompanied it, no nause-atingly romantic verse. Its sender had chosen to remain anonymous, probably assuming that he would know who she was.

Bad assumption. Although the locket had kindled a faint sense of *déjà vu*, he definitely couldn't recall who it had belonged to. Hell, he couldn't recall the names of half the women he'd tupped, let alone what baubles they'd been wearing at the time. But for some reason he'd taken to carrying the thing around like a lucky... locket. A talisman of sorts.

Apparently, it worked. Calmer now, he tossed it back on the table and swung his legs over the side of the bed. He strode naked to the window, staring out into the shadowed landscape. Over-head the moon was an opalescent beacon, illuminating his thoughts.

Was the voice I heard real?

Not the scream—he'd slept enough nights here to know that

the residents were an unrestful bunch—but the other voice, the one in his dream. *Hurry, we must act before he awakens.* Deep and low, that distinctive bass belonged to a man.

Sinjin's nape tingled with recognition.

That voice was a *memory*... of that night with Nicoletta. He'd learned to trust his gut's reaction more than his mind for the latter could be held hostage by his demons. His primal instinct somehow managed to evade their devilish grasp, and if he could just hold onto it, hear its wisdom, it could lead him out of the darkness. To reality unfiltered by his frantic thoughts.

His instinct was speaking to him now about the scarlet satin sheets, Nicoletta's carnal offer... and the stranger's voice. His heart drummed against his ribs. Had someone else been in the room that night? A man—who'd witnessed what happened? Why hadn't Nicoletta mentioned him?

Why can't I bloody remember?

He gripped the sill in frustration. The dream—or memory—was already slipping from him.

With an oath, he pushed away from the window, prowling back and forth across the bedchamber. He couldn't stay here much longer. A sane man would be driven mad here. Nothing to do. Doing nothing but...

Hiding.

The fact had been festering in him like a piece of shrapnel. Stephan had always said he was too reckless, and, by Jove, he saw that now. But as wild and wicked as he'd been, he'd never hurt someone weaker than he—and, worse yet, run from it like the lowest of scoundrels.

He was no coward. He couldn't continue like this. Even if his father could snuff out the scandal, something egregious had happened that night—and Sinjin needed to know his part in it for his own peace of mind. To satisfy his honor.

We must act before he awakens.

Surely, that was a clue. A place to begin his quest for the truth.

Voices cut through his thoughts. He returned to the window, looking out. In the distance, he saw two attendants escorting a patient out of a gated villa, one that Mrs. Barlow had expressively told him was off-bounds. The resident was wearing a strait-waist-coat, a contraption that kept his arms strapped at his sides.

In the moonlight, the man's red hair was glistening wet. He was softly weeping.

A vise clamped around Sinjin's throat. The scars on his back tautened in instinctive empathy... at the same time that fear flooded him. He strode to the desk, lit the lamp with hands that shook. Fumbling for parchment and pen, he began to compose a letter.

Five days after Sinjin sent the letter, his papa had still not responded.

With each passing day, desperation mounted in Sinjin. A fear that he didn't want to give into but which clung to him like fine dust to a traveler. Dark thoughts burrowed themselves under his skin, digging deep, the roots spreading. *Papa's glad to be rid of you. He loves Stephan and Theodore, not you. He's going to leave you here to rot.*

He told himself the duke would come, but he couldn't convince himself. His thoughts built on one another, a vortex of suspicion that made it impossible for him to relax, eat, or sleep. In the looking glass, a stranger with shadowed eyes and a bristly jaw stared back at him. He knew he needed to rest, but he couldn't quiet his racing mind, the buzz of energy through his veins.

Bloody hell, he could handle this—but he needed a drink. A fuck. *Something.*

Perhaps the duke had been delayed because he was trying to locate the man with the deep voice whom Sinjin had written to him about. Sinjin tried to calm himself. Not even the locket helped. Frustrated, he flung the blasted thing across the room.

Time slowed, bogged down by restless waiting.

That night, Sinjin's patience snapped. If His Grace wasn't coming for him, then he would just bloody leave. At the gate, the two guards had the audacity to prevent his passage. He insisted that he was a guest, here of his own volition, but they wouldn't listen. When they tried to take his bag, he resisted. When they tried to manhandle him, he used his fists. The hours spent sparring at his boxing club hadn't been for naught. He took them down and made a run for it—only to be blocked by more guards.

They dragged him, thrashing and shouting, back to the villa and locked him inside.

He spent the night pacing like a caged animal. By dawn, the tide inside him had ebbed, but he could still feel its dark, churning energy. When the door opened a few hours later, he tensed, ready to fight his way to freedom.

His sire entered. Tall, immaculately dressed in iron grey broadcloth, Jeremy George St. John Pelham, the sixth Duke of Acton, emanated an air of command that had grown more imposing with age. Regal silver veined his dark hair, and time had honed the sharpness of his features.

"You look like hell," His Grace said.

Sinjin experienced a jumble of emotions. The anger and relief made sense but the longing? Pure stupidity. If he hadn't won the duke's approval in six-and-twenty years, he sure as hell wasn't about to do it now when he was accused of assault and hiding in a madhouse.

"Where the devil have you been?" he gritted out.

"I've been endeavoring to clean up your mess." His Grace ran a gloved finger along the table, his expression distasteful as he examined the clinging specks of dust. "I expected better of Mrs. Barlow."

"Damn Mrs. Barlow. And damn you. They wouldn't let me

leave last night—are you aware of that?" Sinjin injected his tone with scorn, hating the slight quiver beneath. "I'm not a prisoner here. I'm not a bloody lunatic. I never agreed to—"

He cut himself off as Lady Regina, the Duchess of Acton, crossed the threshold. She was followed by her son Lord Theodore Pelham. Both were slender and fair-haired, with high-nosed countenances. Sinjin could not claim an inordinate amount of affection for his stepmama and half-brother; the feelings, he knew, were mutual.

The duchess' ice blue skirts swirled as she sat in the chair that the duke held out for her.

"Hello, Revelstoke," she said with a cool nod.

"Your Grace," he said shortly.

Theodore, seven years Sinjin's junior, sauntered to his mama's side. His contrived air of *ennui* seemed to be the only thing he'd picked up thus far from his time at Oxford.

"*Aspice quod felix attracsit,*" he drawled.

Make that *two* things the prat had picked up: smug languor and a tendency to use Latin in a damned annoying way.

"Spare me the schoolboy doggerel," Sinjin snapped. "You're the one who showed up uninvited. Why are you here?"

"Perhaps I want to visit my *fratis ventrus?*"

"You can't. Stephan's dead," Sinjin said flatly.

Theodore's throat worked above his ostentatious cravat, grief shining for an instant through his foppish veneer. Sinjin knew a moment of grudging connection. Noble and caring, Stephan had been everyone's favorite, the glue that held the family mosaic together. Without him, the Pelhams were naught but disparate pieces, their sharp edges slicing relentlessly into one another.

"Enough, the two of you," the duke commanded. "Now, Sinjin, what's this about you trying to escape last night?"

"I wasn't trying to escape. I'm a guest here, remember?" Sinjin shot back. "I can leave whenever I want."

"That was not our agreement. You were to stay put until I sorted out your troubles."

"And have you?" Sinjin said evenly.

The duke's blue gaze—the one thing he and Sinjin had in common—held steely discipline. "These things take time. You've left me many fires to put out, and if you're seen traipsing about, you'll just add fuel to the flames—" He broke off in a fit of coughing.

The violence of the fit startled Sinjin. His father had always seemed impervious to the weaknesses of the human condition. Uncertain what to do, he took a step toward the duke, but his stepmama beat him to it and waved him aside.

She hovered next to her husband. "Are you all right, Acton?"

"I'm fine." His Grace blotted his mouth with a handkerchief.

"Perhaps you ought to sit and have some—"

"For God's sake, Regina, don't fuss," the duke said curtly.

Mouth pinched, Her Grace turned her pale gaze to Sinjin. She'd entered his life when he was six, a year after he'd lost his mama, and even then he'd known that she would never think of him as her own. For Stephan, she'd had the occasional smile, but for Sinjin, she'd reserved a reproving notch between her fair brows, which had since etched itself into a permanent line.

Serves her right for being a cold, judgmental bitch.

"Your papa has been working tirelessly to clean up your mess. He's lost sleep over it," she said in the customary tones of accusation that Sinjin despised. "The least you could do is hold up your end of the bargain. It is not so much to ask, is it? To spend a few weeks in the absence of dissipation?"

"That might be impossible for Sinjin, *mater*." Bending to the floor, Theodore straightened with a smirk on his face, the silver locket dangling from his finger. "In the time since he became Revelstoke, he's elevated himself to the status of a deity. They call him the God of Revelry, don't you know, and he has to fight off hordes of ladies and trollops alike."

The duke's gaze latched onto the swinging pendant, his mouth tightening. "Damnation, Sinjin, why must you insist on continually displaying such coarseness and depravity?"

Because it rattles your goddamned cage?

Their Graces had inquired about the locket when they'd first seen it, hoping, no doubt, that some witless virgin had given it to him and wedding bells were in his future. Sinjin had taken great satisfaction in informing them of the truth: that the locket was, in fact, a reminder that freedom held far more appeal than the shackles of matrimony.

Now he grabbed the trinket from his brother and slapped it onto the table where its presence could continue to offend. Petty... but satisfying.

"Really, Sinjin." His stepmama eyed the necklace as if it were a snake. "Flaunting rubbish given to you by some tart? Have you no respect for polite company?"

Her Grace had been the force behind getting him shipped off to an institution that housed the wildest boys in Christendom, and she'd barred him from his own childhood home... from having any semblance of a family. Yet she expected him to respect polite company—to even know what that *was*?

He was the God of Revelry *because* of her. Because of her, he'd had to fight for survival, to earn his place at the top of the rabid pack at Creavey. Because of her, he was more at home with rabble-rousers and whores than the strait-laced hypocrites of the *ton*.

"None at all," he said succinctly.

"Theodore, escort your mama to the carriage." The duke's tone brooked no refusal. "I wish to speak to Sinjin alone."

Her Grace looked as if she might argue, but after exchanging a glance with her husband, she sighed and took Theodore's arm.

When the door closed behind them, Sinjin bit out, "Tell that bitch to stay out of my business."

"Watch your tongue—she is your stepmama." Weariness

settled upon the duke's features, and he sat heavily in a chair. "Let us not argue about pointless matters. I came to update you on my progress. Suppressing the scandal you caused has not been a simple matter. The whore has agreed to maintain her silence, but Corbett is refusing to cooperate."

Andrew Corbett was the eponymous owner of the bawdy house where the trouble had taken place. Corbett's offered first-rate pleasures at commensurate prices, and its proprietor was known to be an exacting man who was ruthless when crossed. Anyone permitted entrée into Corbett's exclusive domain knew his rules—and that they would pay for any violations. That Corbett did not take kindly to one of his wenches being beaten half to death didn't surprise Sinjin.

Stomach churning, he said, "What does Corbett want?"

"To bring the matter to the magistrates. But there is no case without the whore's complaint. And I've convinced her to stay silent—at least for now."

In other words, the duke had bribed Nicoletta. The fact that Sinjin was party to yet another injustice made him feel ill. But was Nicoletta an innocent victim in all of this... or was there something more sinister going on?

"Did you get my letter?" he said abruptly.

The duke gave a terse nod.

"And you read it? The part where I remembered that someone else was in the room—a man?" *We must act before he awakens.* "That has to mean something," he went on eagerly. "Why didn't Nicoletta mention him?"

"What are you suggesting happened?"

"I don't know exactly." He raked a hand through his hair. "But I do know that something's not right. Why can't I remember anything? Believe me, if there's anything I excel at, it's holding my liquor. I've drank far more than I did that night and still remembered everything the next morning. I've been thinking perhaps that..." He expelled a breath and along with it the suspicion that had taken root in his mind. "It's possible, isn't it, that I was drugged?"

"You really believe that you were drugged?" The duke's eyebrows arched.

Sinjin hated that particular expression of his father's, which conveyed louder than words what His Grace thought of his second son. One would think that a lifetime of receiving such looks would make Sinjin inured to them, yet they never failed to draw his blood.

Fighting self-doubt, he insisted, "It's possible. I had three glasses of whiskey before Nicoletta and I went upstairs. Perhaps someone drugged one of my drinks."

"And even if it were true, this supposed drugging, to what purpose would this nefarious plot have been undertaken?"

"I have enemies," he said warily.

"Who?"

The list of potential suspects wasn't exactly short. His raucous lifestyle and make-no-apologies attitude had garnered him his share of detractors. Men he'd had disagreements or altercations with... women he'd refused or who'd wanted more than the casual bedding that they'd agreed to at the outset. But who hated him enough to try to make his life a living hell?

"Langley," Sinjin said. "He's had it in for me for some time."

"*Viscount* Langley?" The duke did not bother to hide his incredulity. "Why on earth would he want to see you tried for assault?"

Rubbing the back of his neck, Sinjin muttered, "A while back, I was paying a visit to his lady when Langley came home unannounced."

"Damnation, Sinjin," His Grace exploded, "you were bedding another man's wife?"

At the time, Sinjin hadn't thought anything of it. Audrey Langley had been the one to instigate the affair, after all. The sultry brunette had approached Sinjin at a ball, coyly informing him that she and her husband had an "understanding." As Langley kept a string of mistresses and had a legion of by-blows, Sinjin saw no reason to question her assertion. When Langley had returned home unexpectedly and caught them together, however, it had become blazingly clear that Audrey's understanding and her lord's were two different things.

What was sauce for the gander was *not* for the goose, after all.

Sinjin would have gladly sorted out the problem with pistols at dawn (it wouldn't have been the first time). But Langley, the blustering fool, hadn't called him out. About a week later, however, a wheel had come loose on Sinjin's carriage, and Sinjin's driving skill had saved him—just barely—from a dangerous crash. In examining the damage, he'd found that someone had tampered with the axle. Although he had no proof, his gut had told him who was responsible.

"I misunderstood the nature of the arrangement between the Langleys," he said finally.

"What goes on between the viscount and his wife are none of your business! Devil take it, Sinjin, since you took on the title, I have done everything in my power to reason with you. To make you desist with your degenerate ways. Yet you persist with it all: the wenching, drinking, and reckless behavior. Worse yet is the fact that you refuse to take any responsibility for your actions."

The lecture was as familiar as the twin surges of resentment and shame. "I *am* trying to take responsibility. That's what I'm telling you. There was a man there—"

"When Stephan was Revelstoke," His Grace cut in, "he knew his duty. What have you done? Have you even visited your estate?"

He hadn't—because the notion of taking his brother's place made grief howl inside him. He'd never wanted the title; it belonged to Stephan, the good brother. The brother who deserved to be alive.

"I'm not Stephan," he said tautly.

"No, you're not." A lifetime of disappointment dripped from the syllables, but His Grace had more insult to add. "We both know who you take after."

She who was never mentioned by name. Catherine Pelham, his mother and disgrace to the Acton name. The woman who'd cuck-olded her husband and abandoned her sons before meeting her end in the cold depths of the English Channel. As always, the thought of her caused a knife to twist in Sinjin's gut.

"I make my own choices," he gritted out, "and I don't give a damn if you don't like them."

"Your reckless behavior is a choice? What about these delu-sions that someone else is to blame for your actions? You haven't changed one whit. You've always lacked self-discipline and moral fiber. You've been given everything, yet you make nothing of yourself—"

"What have I been given, precisely?" Inside him, the black devil pounded its chest in sudden rage. "The years of hell at Creavey Hall?"

"That was your own fault. You set *fire* to the Headmaster's office at Eton, by God. No other school would take you after that. Creavey had a fine reputation for training boys of a high-strung nature—"

"By beating them into submission." Sinjin's hands balled. "You knew what was happening, and you kept me there. Wouldn't even let me come home for the sodding holidays."

"The school recommended pupils remain in a disciplined envi-ronment." Straightening his lapels, the duke said stiffly, "That is in the past. I will not stand here now and listen to you blame me and everyone else for your problems. I see now that the truth is your only hope of salvation."

"What the devil are you talking about?"

"I've consulted with Mrs. Barlow. She believes that you would benefit from the treatments here."

Blood rushed in Sinjin's ears. "Fuck what Mrs. Barlow believes. I'm not staying."

"If an affliction caused you to beat that whore, to behave as you've been behaving, treatment will help you." The duke's judgement fell like a gavel. "Once I've dealt with the Corbett problem, we'll revisit the issue. Hopefully, by that time, you'll have come to your senses."

"You're the one who needs to come to his senses. There's no way in *hell* I'm staying in this madhouse. And I told you: *I didn't hurt Nicoletta*."

"How do you know that?"

"Because I've never hurt a woman and never will!"

"You're out of control. Who knows what you're capable of? The fact that you want to blame some figment of your imagination—some nameless, faceless man whom no one else saw..." His Grace broke off, murmuring, "No, this is the only way. You need help, Sinjin, and perhaps all this was a blessing in disguise. You'll thank me for this one day."

He turned to leave.

Fear spurred Sinjin to grab the other's shoulder. "Papa, no—don't leave me here." He hated the pleading in his voice, the hoarseness he couldn't control. "I know I'm not perfect like Stephan, not good like him, but I can get better. I'll do better. Just... just believe me. I didn't do this. I know I didn't."

His father's eyes met his. They engaged in a silent tug-of-war, resolve pitted against desperation. The duke raised his fist and rapped on the door.

It opened, and two attendants appeared. One had a strait-waistcoat in hand.

"Get away from me." Sinjin backed away, shouting, "I will not be detained!"

"It's only temporary. For your own good."

With one last resigned look, the duke walked out.

❧ 6 ❧

A fortnight later, Polly was sitting in the well-appointed drawing room of her brother Ambrose's Mayfair home. She alternated between staying with her various older siblings, but for the past year, at Rosie's behest, she'd stayed on at Ambrose's to keep the other girl company. Tonight, Emma and Thea had brought their families over to celebrate Polly's birthday, and they were all enjoying a cozy visit before supper.

On Polly's lap rested the small blond head of Thea's girl, Francesca. The two-year-old had spent the last half-hour chasing her twin brother Samuel and her cousin Christopher around the zebrawood coffee table when she'd decided to stop for a break. She'd promptly passed out on the Aubusson, and Polly had scooped up the sleeping tot for a cuddle.

The cushions sank on Polly's other side, and she turned to see that Olivia, Emma's firstborn, had joined them.

"Aunt Polly," the pretty brown-haired cherub said, "what do you think of Christopher?"

"I like your younger brother very much."

"Would you like to have him for your birthday present?" Livy offered.

Emma, sitting nearby with a dozing Christopher, snickered.

Stifling a grin, Polly said, "I think your parents might want to keep him."

"Mama and Papa don't need him." Livy's green eyes flashed. "They have *me*."

"They have enough love for you and your brother," Polly assured her niece, "and I think you will grow to enjoy Christopher's company as well."

Livy crossed her arms. "He doesn't know how to do anything. He's boring."

"He won't be boring for long," Polly promised.

"Angel, how many times must I tell you that your brother is not for sale?" Livy's papa, the tall, dark, and wickedly handsome Duke of Strathaven, crossed the room to ruffle her dark ringlets.

"I'm not trying to sell him, Papa, I'm *giving* him away. Since Aunt Polly doesn't have a baby, I thought she might want one for her birthday," the little girl said virtuously.

Even as Polly smiled along with everyone, she felt a pang. *Out of the mouths of children...*

Today she'd turned two-and-twenty, and it made her acutely aware that, after being out for four seasons, she was still unwed, without a fiancé—let alone a babe—in sight. As much as she rejoiced at her siblings' happiness, loneliness stirred within her. Looking around the room, she saw the unique bonds shared between the married couples; over the years, she'd discovered that emotions such as anger and hate tended to be uniform, but love expressed its beauty in unique ways.

At the pianoforte, Thea was supervising as her stepson Freddy and Edward, Ambrose and Marianne's son, played a rousing duet. Thea's husband, the Marquess of Tremont, stood beside her, a possessive hand on her waist, adoration threading his aura with rich silver. The same silver flickered around her when she smiled at him. Strathaven, in the meantime, had joined Em, and the two were playfully bickering over something, attraction glittering between them like magenta confetti.

On a nearby settee, Rosie and Marianne were perusing the latest fashion plates from Ackerman's. They were debating the merits of various passimeterie choices when Ambrose came to sit with them, setting a casual arm around his wife's shoulders.

"Tired, sweetheart?" Ambrose said.

Marianne, a glamorous silver blonde, gave a rueful smile. "A bit. I don't recall being so peaked when I was carrying Edward. Pregnancy is a young woman's endeavor, I'm afraid."

It had come as a surprise to the entire Kent clan when the doctor had pronounced Marianne with child two months ago. As Marianne had explained it, she'd been feeling tired and achy and had thought she might have a touch of an ague. Instead, she'd discovered that she was expecting—fourteen years after she'd last given birth.

"You look the same as when we first married." Ambrose pressed a kiss against his wife's temple, his amber gaze and aura warm with love. "The most beautiful woman I've ever laid eyes upon."

Marianne laughed. "And you, my darling, have grown far more silver-tongued with age. I'm inflating like one of those hot air balloons. Soon I won't be able to hide it."

"I agree with Papa," Rosie said. "You have a ravishing glow about you, Mama."

"What a pair of flatterers." Contentment infused Marianne's emerald aura with radiant gold. "And how lucky I am to have you."

As much as Polly adored her ever-growing family, being with them sometimes made her feel more alone. She knew she'd always have a place with any one of her siblings, but she didn't want to be the tag-along sister forever. She wanted a home of her own. Of late, spending time with her nieces and nephews had also made her keenly aware of her own budding maternal instincts. Which meant she ought to focus on her plan of landing Nigel Pickering-Parks... but instead she couldn't stop thinking about Revelstoke.

At night, images of the earl's wickedness flitted through her dreams, and several times she'd woken to find herself sweaty and tangled in the sheets. Beneath her nightgown, the tips of her breasts had risen into stiff and tingling points. Lower, in the secret cove between her legs, she'd felt a pulsing ache and... a disconcerting glaze of wetness.

Dear heaven, what was happening to her?

She thought about asking her sisters, but the intimate nature of such questions—and what they might reveal about her—made her balk. The same thing occurred when she contemplated telling Rosie about how Revelstoke had mocked her in the garden all those months ago, and, more recently, what she'd seen him doing at the bathhouse. Just *thinking* about those events made Polly squirm with mortification, a rash of heat creeping over her insides.

Thus, her encounters with Revelstoke remained filed under the category of "Guilty Secrets." She rationalized to herself that it didn't matter: they weren't going to see him again anyway. Despite Rosie obsessing over him, he wasn't going to come calling. He was a cad and a rake, and as Lady Langley had pointed out (and he hadn't denied) that long ago night in the garden, he had no interest in virgins—*Praise Jesus.*

"When do you want to open your presents, Polly dear?"

Em's voice stirred her from her reverie. "Oh, um, whenever it is convenient," she said. "Maybe after dessert?"

"That's our Polly," her eldest brother said, "the easy-going and patient one of the family. Since you were a little girl, you've liked to save the best for last—even when the best wasn't much."

The Kents hadn't always lived in the lap of luxury. Mama had passed when Polly was six and Papa had fallen ill afterward, leaving Ambrose to provide for everyone and Em to run the household. As lean as times had been, however, the family had never been short on love.

"All of you have always made my birthday special," Polly said with heartfelt gratitude.

"I baked your favorite cake." A smile tucked into Em's cheeks. She was a marvelous cook, and the fact that she was now a duchess didn't prevent her from tinkering in the kitchen. "I doubled the icing since I knew Strathaven would insist on eating half of it."

"Being married to you has given me a sweet tooth," His Grace drawled, making Em blush.

"Chef has also prepared something special for dessert—" The opening door interrupted Marianne. Her brows lifted as Pitt, the butler, entered, his expression flustered. "What is it, Pitt?"

"Beg pardon, madam," Pitt said, "but there's a gentleman here to see Mr. Kent."

"I'm not expecting any visitors." Ambrose frowned. "What is his name?"

"He didn't give it, sir. He did claim, however, that he is here on a matter of some urgency."

Emma perked up. "Well, this sounds intriguing."

Before her marriage, Em had aspired to join Ambrose's private enquiry firm. Even now, she worked on the occasional case—with her duke's consent (and sometimes without his knowledge).

"Do you have any idea who it is, darling?" Marianne said to Ambrose.

"No, but I'll get rid of whoever it is." Ambrose unfolded himself from the settee and rose. "Tonight is a time for our family celebration…" He trailed off, his gaze going to the doorway.

Where the Earl of Revelstoke stood.

Awareness tingled through Polly as she stared at the man whose presence had invaded her dreams. Memory had dulled the reality of him. Standing at the threshold of the drawing room, he was even more virile, more startlingly attractive than she remembered. There was a slight dishevelment to him, but instead of detracting from his looks, it heightened his charisma. He looked as if he'd just come from a place beyond the civilized, some exotic place of untold pleasures, and Polly's female instincts told her why women would want to follow him there—or anywhere.

His stormy blue gaze circled the room, pausing on her. Like a captive bird, her heart dashed madly against its cage as the full impact of his presence slammed into her. Despite his controlled expression, a shield straining to hold back the emotions beneath, his aura blazed. Desperation, anger, and fear wriggled and pushed at the glowing cobalt wall like maddened worms.

Polly's lips parted. *What in God's name has happened to him?*

Rosie's chirpy tones broke the silence. "Lord Revelstoke!" She rose, her hands clasped at her breast, her face wreathed in smiles. "You kept your promise to call after all!"

7

S injin had not come to pay a social call.

Given Miss Primrose's welcome, however, it would have been rude to gainsay her invitation to sup. Thus, he found himself sitting beside her in the elegant dining room. The table was artfully set with a turquoise and gold Sèvres service, and he soon learned that the colorful hothouse arrangements were there to mark the occasion of Miss Polly Kent's twenty-second birthday.

He'd interrupted a family celebration. How bloody awkward.

Mrs. Kent was on his other side, at the hostess' end of the table, keeping a watchful eye on him. The subject of the fete was across the way, doing the opposite. Miss Polly avoided looking at him as if he sported a Gorgon's head and was capable of turning her to stone if she so much as glanced his way. Her posture was stiffer than one of Brummell's cravats.

What does she think I'm about to do—open my trousers and give her another display?

While he understood her antipathy, he didn't know why it bothered him. Usually he didn't give a damn what anyone thought of him, yet, for some reason, the judgmental little prude had attracted his notice from the start. He'd grant that she had her attractions—she was lovely in a quiet, unusual sort of way—but he'd been around plenty of beautiful women, and none of them had held onto his attention once he was out of their bed (and sometimes not even during).

He chalked it up to the novelty of encountering a female who wanted nothing to do with him. Who seemed wholly unimpressed by his looks, money, and title. Even if he didn't like her judgement, he supposed he couldn't fault it. Hell, she probably saw him more clearly than most.

At any rate, he had more important business to contend with than the offended sensibilities of some chit. Fortifying himself with a drink of wine, he remembered to smile at Miss Primrose, who was regaling him with witty anecdotes. He listened with half an ear, his mind whirling.

Do they know where I am? Will they track me down here?

It had been two days since he'd made his escape from Mrs. Barlow's. Since he'd fled that serene, soul-crushing hell. Although they hadn't dared to inflict physical abuses upon him, the deprivation of his personal liberty had been enough to trigger memories of Creavey. His black devil had awakened to a battle cry.

Never surrender.

He'd escaped with the clothes he was wearing and the coins that he'd found in the pockets of the two guards he'd knocked unconscious to make his escape. He'd made it back to London, half on foot, half as a stowaway on a farmer's cart. All the while, he'd kept a vigilant watch—every shadow, every flicker a potential threat to his freedom.

His father might think him delusional, but his suspicions had saved him. He'd sensed Mrs. Barlow's guards everywhere: following him, waiting to pounce and return him to that despicable prison. He'd gone to his townhouse first, but he'd waited outside. Waited and watched until he'd glimpsed shadows moving behind drawn shades. He'd been right all along. They were inside his home, readying to spring a trap.

He'd taken off, pulling his hat down low, disappearing into the crowded street.

He hadn't known where to go. They were after him, hunting him, and his family believed him mad. His so-called friends were out of the question. They might be good for a drunken escapade, but he wouldn't trust any of them farther than he could toss them. The ladies were no better, any help he received from them certain to come with unwanted strings. He didn't have enough money in his pockets to stay the night with a whore... and, after what happened at Corbett's, the last place he wanted to go to was a bawdy house.

Then it had struck him. *Merrick*—of course. His man of business was straight as a die and would surely know what to do. He'd gone directly to Merrick's office, but upon arrival, he was informed by the clerk that Merrick would be out of Town until after the weekend. Scrambling, he had gone from there to scout out his banking establishment where he'd spotted dark-garbed figures that could've been his enemies milling about the entrance.

They were everywhere he knew to go. His home, his clubs, his bank—all compromised. Without a safe harbor, he'd sought refuge in the darkest parts of London, cloaking himself in the fog and soot-choked air. Finally, when he could stay on his feet no longer, he'd found shelter in a flea-ridden inn that let rooms out by the hour.

He didn't know how long he'd slept—the first time he'd done so since his escape. But he must have fallen into a deep, restoring oblivion, for when he awoke, it was the next day and he found himself unexpectedly calmer. 'Twas as if the storm was passing, and the solution had suddenly shot like a star through the clearing clouds of his mind.

My papa is London's best investigator.

Primrose Kent's father was *Ambrose Kent*. Of course. The man was famous for all the cases he'd solved. Kent had helped powerful peers out of predicaments, and, through his sisters' marriages, was related to a few of them as well. With burgeoning hope, Sinjin had cleaned himself up and made his way over to Kent's offices. Finding them closed, he'd located the investigator's home address and gone directly there.

Which brought him to the present moment. From the head of the table, Kent watched over the proceedings like a hawk. Unlike his daughter, the investigator had clearly gleaned that this was not a social call. Strathaven and Tremont, seated beside their respective ladies, were also taking Sinjin's measure.

Desperation breathed down Sinjin's neck. He needed to speak to Kent in private, but dinner dragged on, course after course teeming with dishes. His stomach was too knotted for him to eat, so he drank more wine instead. Although it took willpower, he kept up the façade, bantering with Miss Primrose, her tinkling laugh scraping across his eardrums like a fork against china. He felt on edge, his grip on his equilibrium tenuous. A footman appeared at his elbow to refill his half-finished glass.

"My lord."

He started, his gaze meeting Miss Polly's over a plate of sweetmeats. She was actually looking at him now, and instead of the witless adoration or coy flirtation he was used to seeing in a female's gaze, hers was disconcertingly clear and unflinching. He felt as if he were staring at the surface of a pristine lake. He saw his own reflection in her eyes; it wasn't a pretty sight.

She gave the footman a subtle but firm shake of the head, and the servant backed away without replenishing his wine.

"Perhaps you'd care to eat something, my lord?" she said quietly.

Her underlying meaning could not be clearer: *Lay off the wine, you sot.* Beneath his collar, his neck burned. Who did she think she was? He'd never liked being told what to do—and by some puritanical slip of a miss, no less. Yet he was aware of the audience around them and the need to court Kent's favor, which he wasn't going to do if he issued an acerbic set-down to the man's youngest sister.

He lifted his glass, draining the remnants to prove his point. Only then did he aim a hard smile at the interfering do-gooder across the way.

"Since you've whetted my appetite, Miss Kent," he said silkily, "what tasty morsel do you suggest I sample?"

A slow blush rose beneath her porcelain skin. "The, um, pheasant is the chef's specialty."

"If you say so, then I must try it," he said coolly.

The dish in question was brought to his side. To his chagrin, his hands were not quite steady with the serving utensils, but he managed to get a portion onto his plate without embarrassing himself. He tried a forkful. The meat, accompanied by currant sauce, melted in his mouth.

"How is it?" she said.

"Young and tender, the way I like it," he drawled.

Her thick, gold-tipped lashes fanned against her reddened cheeks.

"If you like the pheasant, you must try the other dishes," Miss Primrose exclaimed.

More dishes were circulated his way. As he sampled the cuisine, he was keenly aware of the charged energy between him and Miss Polly, and he couldn't help surreptitiously observing her. Burnished by the chandelier, her hair was an intriguing mix of blond, bronze, and gold. Some of the heavy tresses had escaped their pins, wispy tendrils framing her face. It was the kind of sensual boudoir coiffure that ladies spent hours trying to achieve.

Miss Polly, however, seemed annoyed by her hair. She batted the fallen strands, and when that didn't work, she tried shoving pins at them. It was like watching someone try to catch water with a net. She seemed utterly unaware of her natural appeal: the undone locks made her look as if she'd just risen from a pleasurable romp.

The rest of her looked well suited for bed play as well, and God only knew why she'd chosen to disguise her assets behind the dowdiest dress he'd ever seen. But he wasn't fooled. A connoisseur of the female form, he'd bet his estate that she had curves that would make a courtesan weep with envy.

In fact, if she'd chosen to make a living in pleasure, her mouth alone would have secured her fortune. Even without paint, it was a coral shade and deliciously plump. The plush ledge of her bottom lip would be a perfect place for a lover to rest his tongue... or some other part of his anatomy.

Christ, why did his mind have to go there? But once thought, the notion could not be swept aside. The image of feeding his cock betwixt Miss Polly's sultry mouth, his fingers threaded through her bedroom hair, sent an alarming sizzle through his blood.

"Ah, here comes the dessert." Mrs. Kent's voice pierced his haze of unacceptable lust. "We are in for a treat. Not only do we have Emma's lovely cake, but Chef Lenôtre has prepared *les petites duchesses* for us tonight."

As the footmen arranged the desserts on the table, which included a large cake covered in fluffy white icing and a silver tier of pastries, Kent said with an Englishman's suspicion of all things foreign, "A *do-shess*? What's that?"

"A roll of pastry filled with cream. It's delicious. Do try," Mrs. Kent said.

"None for me, thank you." Miss Primrose gave Sinjin a coquettish look. "A lady must watch her figure, after all."

"I'll have cake *and* a pastry," Miss Polly said. "Where are the serving tongs?"

"A *duchesse* is meant to be eaten with one's fingers. That's why Chef has wrapped them in paper for us," Mrs. Kent explained.

With a shrug, Miss Polly reached out and selected one of the baked confections. It was about six inches long, and positively— there was no better way to describe it—*phallic*. With morbid fascination, Sinjin watched as she brought the icing-glazed length to her mouth. The tip of the pastry lingered on her bottom lip for the briefest moment—as he'd suspected, that luscious ledge made for the perfect resting place—before she slid it inside.

Goddamn. Sweat gathered beneath his collar.

She bit down, and before his disbelieving eyes, whipped cream squirted out the end. It splattered in thick, milky gobs on the tablecloth. When her tongue swiped out to catch a spot of filling clinging to her upper lip, he barely stifled a groan.

His trousers were suddenly, excruciatingly tight.

"Is it good?" the Duchess of Strathaven asked.

When Miss Polly gave an enthusiastic nod, the duchess and marchioness both reached for a pastry. As they nibbled away, their respective husbands watched on with transfixed gazes. Strathaven adjusted his collar repeatedly, his color high, whilst Tremont's eyes had glazed over.

Thankfully, the delicious torture of dessert ended before anyone unmanned himself, and Miss Primrose said merrily, "Time for presents!"

Brightly wrapped packages were duly brought in and placed in front of Miss Polly. As she carefully unwrapped each one to the smiles and exclamations of her kin, Sinjin felt his earlier awkwardness return. Not only was he intruding upon a family celebration, he had no prior experience with such affairs. His father and stepmama had never marked the occasion of his birth; in fact, that day was less than a month away, and he doubted that they would even remember.

Hell, sometimes he even forgot.

Now, watching Miss Polly's genuine joy as she thanked the Tremonts for a pretty music box, Sinjin felt a strange longing to... participate. To not be the uninvited outsider watching on.

"Let me guess who that is from."

Miss Primrose's dry comment made him look at the last of the gifts that Miss Polly had unwrapped. A door-stopper of a volume on... fossils? Egad. He might be a novice at birthdays, but even he... wait. He *could* do better than that.

"Miss Kent," he said impulsively, "I have a little something for you as well."

She blinked at him. "You, um, do?"

He reached into his pocket, dug out the locket. Slid it eagerly across the table.

"This is for me?" She picked up the necklace, the simple fili-greed pendant gleaming in the light of the candelabra. Her brow furrowed. "But how did you know to get me anything?"

Heat crept up his jaw. *You didn't think this through, you idiot.*

In the past, women had never questioned his gifts, but they'd been light-skirts and lovers, and Miss Kent was neither of those things. She fell in a category of female that he'd steered clear of—and obviously for good reason. Chits like her were naught but trouble. Faced with her question, he couldn't very well admit the truth: he'd given her a trinket that he'd happened to have in his pocket, a memento sent by some woman he'd tupped, whose iden-tity he couldn't even recall.

"It was my mother's," he heard himself lie.

"Then I couldn't possibly—"

"It's a trifle," he said brusquely.

"But if it belonged to—"

"Just take it." The words emerged filtered through his teeth.

Her eyes narrowed upon him... as if they could see *through* him. His face heated like that of a schoolboy caught cheating on a test. After a tense moment, during which he wished with every part of his benighted soul that he'd never given her the stupid thing, she slid his offering beneath her other gifts. As if she couldn't stand the sight of it.

The tinkling of crystal diverted everyone's attention to Miss Primrose, and not a bloody moment too soon. She set the fork down beside her glass and announced, "I'd like to propose a toast.

To Lord Revelstoke, the hero who rescued me from the jaws of death."

His embarrassment heightened. God knew he was the furthest thing from a hero.

"Quite unnecessary, Miss Kent," he muttered. "I was glad to be of service."

"You are far too modest, my lord. I owe you my *life*," she gushed. "If it weren't for you, I might not even be sitting here."

Kent's brows drew together at his daughter's pronouncement. During the locket incident, he'd looked distinctly disapproving, but now his expression shifted, conveying the depth of his love for his child. It was a look that Sinjin had never received from his own father.

"I am in your debt, Revelstoke," Kent said gravely.

"I did as any gentleman would have."

"If there is any way I can repay the favor, you need only ask," Kent returned with equal firmness.

The offer hung in the air; it was the opening Sinjin needed.

"There is no favor to repay," he said, "although there is business I wish to speak with you about, sir."

Mrs. Kent rose, and the gentlemen immediately followed suit.

"Ladies, shall we withdraw to the drawing room?" she said.

"Why?" Her Grace's brow furrowed.

Her reaction suggested that the family typically bucked the tradition of segregating sexes after dinner. Which wasn't all that surprising. From what Sinjin had witnessed thus far, this was no conventional family. Although he was hardly a stickler for convention, at the moment he wanted the women gone—and Miss Polly especially. She was too much of a distraction.

"Perhaps the men would like some privacy to go along with their port and cigars," Mrs. Kent said meaningfully.

"That is precisely why we ought to stay," the duchess protested. "Privacy is when all the interesting things happen."

Nonetheless, under Mrs. Kent's guidance, the ladies filed out.

Miss Polly brought up the rear. The last thing he saw before the door closed was her suspicious gaze upon him.

"Now, my lord," Kent said once the men were seated again, "I gather the purpose of your visit is not entirely social?"

Sinjin glanced at Kent's brothers-in-law.

"My family can be trusted," the investigator said.

In for a penny. He drew a breath. "I have come to retain your services, sir."

"For what purpose?" Kent looked curious rather than surprised.

Sinjin had the inkling that it would take a lot to disturb the other's equilibrium, and he found that stalwartness comforting. Also, he had nothing to lose.

He steeled himself. "I want to hire you to prove that I'm not mad."

8

"I'll finish up from here. Thank you, Nan," Polly said.

With a bob, the maid departed, and Polly continued with her evening ablutions. As she brushed her hair the requisite one hundred strokes, her thoughts kept returning to Revelstoke. Anger and humiliation smoldered, her gaze falling upon the locket on the vanity in front of her.

Does the dashed Lothario think I'll be fooled by his stupid tricks?

His mother's locket, indeed.

When she'd questioned him about the trinket, she'd seen the unease, the flash of guilt in his aura that labelled him a liar. He'd probably assumed that a wallflower like her wouldn't look a gift horse in the mouth, would simply be overjoyed to receive anything from the God of Revelry. Why he'd even bother trying to win her favor, however, was beyond her. Perhaps charming the opposite sex was a compulsion for him. Or maybe he wanted to impress her family with a seemingly thoughtful gesture.

Thoughtful. Hah. She'd wager he had dozens of those baubles, one in every pocket to use on unsuspecting females.

There was definitely something not right about the man. She shivered, thinking of the jumbled, agitated mass of his aura when he'd first arrived. Fear, anger... even desperation had been in the mix. He'd reached for his wineglass time and again, and whether or not he realized it, the alcohol had fueled his disordered state, making the emotions pulse like dark veins beneath the strained skin of his self-control.

Despite her dislike of the earl, she hadn't been able to stand by and allow him to go further down the path of self-destruction. He hadn't welcomed her interference—she flushed, recalling his innuendos which were clearly meant to put her in her place—but at least he'd stopped drinking, and the food had steadied his aura.

But why had he come? And what in heaven's name did he want with Ambrose?

The door opened, and Rosie slipped in. Dressed for bed, her blond tresses loose over her chintz wrapper, she had a dreamy look in her eyes. She flopped backward onto Polly's bed.

"Revelstoke is staying the night," she announced in dramatic tones. "I heard Papa tell Pitt to have the spare room in the mews readied."

The thought of Revelstoke spending the night sent a *frisson* through Polly. At the same time, she frowned in confusion. "Why would Ambrose put a guest in the mews?"

"Strange, isn't it? And terribly inhospitable, if you ask me. I don't know Papa's reasons, and the truth is I don't care." Rolling onto her belly, Rosie propped her chin in her hands. "The point of the matter is that Revelstoke said he would call and he did—and he's chosen to stay, even if it's in a room above the stables." She gave a swoony sigh. "Isn't it romantic? He must be truly smitten with me."

Seeing the sunburst of hope around her sister, Polly bit her lip. The last thing she wanted was to destroy Rosie's optimism after the disappointments of the last Season. Rosie had been through enough with gentlemen failing to come up to scratch and damaging her reputation in the process. By some miracle, the gossip labelling her a flirt had died as quickly as it had started, but the girl's self-confidence had been visibly shaken. Although Rosie tried to hide her reaction, Polly could see desperation and despair seeping in, dimming her sister's glow.

She didn't want to see the other hurt again. And Revelstoke was clearly trouble.

She sat next to Rosie on the bed. "You must have a care. There's more going on with Revelstoke than appears on the surface. Whatever he and Ambrose spoke about, I'm sure it's trouble."

"Did you... sense something?" Rosie said, her jade eyes wide.

Hesitating, Polly gave a nod. "His emotions are as dark and complicated as any I've seen—and don't ask me why," she said before the other could interrupt. "You know I can't read his mind."

It was yet another drawback of her ability. Just because she could see emotions didn't mean that she understood what elicited them. It made for frustrating guesswork, akin to reading a book with every other paragraph missing. Sometimes she was right, and sometimes she was wrong—the most prominent example of the latter being the case of Lord Thomas Brockhurst.

She'd made the assumption that the attraction in his aura had been for her, but obviously she'd been mistaken. Perhaps he'd been thinking of someone else when they were together. Or perhaps he had been attracted to her but not enough to overcome his repugnance of the flaw she'd so imprudently disclosed.

Why, oh why, did I tell him about my aberration?

There was no use regretting what could not be undone. Just as it was futile to try to understand Brockhurst's true motives. In the end, she knew one thing for certain: she would *never* share her secret with any man again.

"So what if Revelstoke has a few demons? Part of his attraction is how deliciously wicked he is. Just ask any of the ladies salivating after him." Rosie sat up, curling her arms around her raised knees. "And wouldn't it be grand if *I* were the one to conquer his demons?"

"Or he could ruin you utterly. He's a dangerous and degenerate *rake*," Polly pointed out, "and one of the wildest ones, according to you."

"You know what they say about reformed rakes making the best husbands. Why, look at Strathaven. He's utterly devoted to Emma."

"Yes, but that's different. His Grace was interested in Emma from the start—"

"Isn't Revelstoke interested in me?" A tremor entered Rosie's voice. "Did you see attraction in his aura, Polly? Tell me, *please*."

Polly's insides knotted. At the dinner table, she *had* glimpsed desire in Revelstoke's tumultuous aura; what man wouldn't find Rosie appealing? But the earl's glow had swirled with a host of other darker feelings, including the shame she'd seen back at Mrs. Barlow's.

What does he have to feel ashamed for—what is he hiding? Polly wondered with a shiver. Moreover, the fact that Revelstoke was attracted to Rosie didn't mean that his intentions were honorable. Polly herself knew from experience that a man might feel one way and act another. In the hierarchy of rakehells, Brockhurst probably fell somewhere in the middle; imagine the havoc that Revelstoke, the *god* of rakes, could wreak upon a vulnerable girl like Rosie.

Desperation spurred Polly to say, "The earl's aura was agitated, full of anger and fear. My best guess is that he's in some sort of trouble, which is why he sought out Ambrose—"

"But attraction *was* in his aura?"

Polly hesitated... and gave a reluctant nod.

Relief shone in Rosie's eyes, her uncertainty passing like clouds. "I just knew he liked me! Oh, Polly, I'm so happy. He's exactly the sort of husband I've been waiting for, and this time I shan't let the opportunity pass me by. Imagine me, a *countess*," she said giddily. "Those sticklers of the *beau monde* will have to eat their words, and can't you just see the looks on the other debs' faces? Why, they'll be pea green with envy that I landed the biggest catch of all!"

"Have you heard *anything* I've said?"

"If Revelstoke's in trouble, I'm sure Papa will help him out of it," Rosie said airily.

Polly struggled to find a foothold in Rosie's impenetrable adoration of Revelstoke. And she knew of only one way. As much as she dreaded dredging up the humiliation, she had to—for her sister's sake. "There's something else... something I haven't told you."

Rosie's head canted to one side.

Taking a deep breath, she said, "That night, when I overheard Brockhurst talking about the wager... Revelstoke was there, too."

"He *was?*" Her sister blinked. "Why didn't you mention that you'd met him before?"

"Because we didn't actually meet. Revelstoke was on the other side of the hedge with the others. And he said some... unpleasant things." Polly's throat clenched. "About me."

"I don't understand. How could he say such things if he doesn't know you?"

"Well, he didn't say them about *me*, as such," she was forced to admit. She related the incident in its mortifying entirety. When she was done, she was trembling.

Rosie said, "Oh, Pols," and wrapped her in a hug. As she soaked in the comfort of her sister's embrace, the other went on, "I'm so sorry you were subjected to that cruelty, I truly am. But you oughtn't take Revelstoke's words to heart, nor blame him for them."

Polly jerked. That was the *last* response she'd expected.

Pulling back, she whispered, "Pardon?"

"When gentlemen are around one another, they say stupid

things," Rosie explained. "And do stupid things. It's how they prove their manhood."

"By being... stupid?"

"Precisely. Now I'm not excusing that wretched Brockhurst or his friends, but Revelstoke wasn't part of the wager, was he?"

"No, but what he *said*—"

"He likely just said it to shut Brockhurst up. I daresay it's tiresome to have bucks constantly trying to join his herd," Rosie said complacently. "At any rate, his comment was in reference to some anonymous wallflower. I'm sure he wouldn't have said it if he knew *you* were the girl in question."

"But that's not the point! A true gentleman wouldn't say such things about *any* girl. He'd defend her honor and—"

"Pols, I hate to say this, but you are far too sensitive for your own good."

Her breath whooshed from her as if she'd been punched.

"The world is not a perfect place," her sister said matter-of-factly, "and neither of us are as naïve as we once were. Which means we must make the best of our situations. For you, that means getting over the business with Brockhurst—and by that I don't mean setting your cap for the likes of Nigel Pickering-Parks. You need to pull your head out of the sand, dearest, and see yourself as you truly are. You won't be happy until you do. As for me, I need respectability and status—which being a countess, and, eventually, a duchess will give me in spades. Therefore, Revelstoke is the answer to *my* happiness."

Polly felt as if her insides had been scrubbed with sandpaper, the other's observations leaving her raw. And that was before Rosie poured on the acid.

"Since Revelstoke is to be my husband, could you find it in yourself to be nicer to him? You were rather ungracious when he so thoughtfully gave you a gift," she said.

At the chastising tone, Polly could hold back her frustration no more.

"Because that gift wasn't meant for me," she burst out, "and it most definitely did not belong to his mother! He was lying. I could see it in his aura."

"I suspected as much," Rosie breathed, her glow... delighted? "He probably brought that locket for *me* but gave it to *you* because he felt badly about interrupting your birthday party. Oh, isn't he gallant?"

Polly didn't think she could feel further humiliated... but she was wrong apparently. Her sister's explanation made perfect sense. It also made her feel as if she'd been entered in a contest of pity against her will *and* handed the consolation prize.

To the fat, peculiar wallflower goes the locket...

"I don't want it," she said flatly. "Since it was meant for you, you take it."

"No, you keep it, dear. I'm sure Revelstoke will have other gifts for me in the future." Aglow with hope, Rosie danced to her feet. "Now you'll think about what I've said, won't you?"

Utterly deflated, Polly could only nod.

"Excellent, because I've exhausted my supply of seriousness for the entire year." Rosie flashed a saucy grin. "Now I must get my beauty rest if I'm to look my best for the earl." At the door, she paused. "And dearest?"

"Yes?"

"Once things are settled with Revelstoke, we'll find you a proper husband too."

"I don't need—"

But Rosie was already gone.

At half-past two in the morning, Polly gave up trying to sleep. Sighing, she tossed aside the bedclothes and sat up, rubbing the heels of her palms over her eyes. The conversation with Rosie had stayed with her, chasing sleep away.

Her sister had claimed she was too... sensitive. Was that her true problem? But who wouldn't feel hurt by what Revelstoke had said—what he'd done? Hurt swamped Polly, along with anxious bewilderment: Rosie had never dismissed her feelings before. The other was her best friend, her constant companion, the one who'd always understood. And now...

Anger bubbled up. This was all *Revelstoke's* fault.

From the moment he'd entered Polly's life, he'd wreaked havoc. He'd said those unforgivable things about her, mocked her when she'd caught him acting like a madman, and then added insult on top of injury tonight. Now he had Rosie in his thrall, so much so that the girl was taking *his* side over Polly's. And who knew what nefarious troubles had brought him to darken Ambrose's doorstep?

Her stomach rumbled noisily. On top of everything, she was hungry—*and that is Revelstoke's fault too*, she fumed. She'd been so distracted by the blasted man at supper that she'd hardly eaten anything herself.

Disgruntled, she tossed the coverlet aside and got out of bed. Perhaps warmed milk might soothe her ruffled state; she certainly wasn't going to fall asleep otherwise. She donned a chintz wrapper, lit a lamp, and made her way downstairs to the kitchen.

The cavernous basement room was warm, the air redolent of delicious smells. Embers glowed in the cooking hearth, the precisely hung rows of pots and pans glinting in the light of Polly's lamp. Making a trip to the larder, she returned with a jug of milk, a leftover slice of Em's cake, and a bowl of plump cherries. She nibbled on the fruit, pouring some milk into a pan to warm, when a faint rustling noise made her freeze.

It was coming from the dark corridor beyond the kitchen... the stillroom? Her muscles tensed, and she listened for more of the furtive sounds. She told herself it was just a mouse, but when more rummaging noises emerged, her pulse beat in a rapid staccato.

She grabbed hold of the closest weapon; with her hands wrapped around the handle of a cast-iron pan, she moved stealthily toward the stillroom. She'd do a quick reconnaissance, summon help if necessary. As she neared, she heard shuffling, glass tinkling... the sound of a clandestine search? She peered cautiously into the stillroom—and her breath clogged her throat. In the flickering dimness, she made out a large, menacing shape hunting through the shelves.

She gulped. *Time to get help.*

She began creeping backward down the hallway when a floor-board squeaked beneath her slipper. Through the pounding panic, she thought she heard a man's voice, and she turned to flee down the corridor. She made it to the kitchen when a vise-like grip closed around her arm.

"Let go of me!" She swung her weapon with all her might. She made contact, the force of impact vibrating up her arm.

"Hell and damnation," the burglar swore.

Panting, she raised the pan again—only to have it yanked from her grip. Even as she drew air to scream, a hand covered her mouth, her back colliding against a wall of muscle. Her hair in her eyes, she struggled blindly, kicking out, trying to escape by any means necessary.

"Desist, you Amazon," a low voice growled in her ear. "It's me. Revelstoke."

The words took an instant to penetrate.

"Rblsmuck?" Her words were muffled by his hand.

"Aye. Now if I release you, will you please refrain from waking up the entire bloody house?"

The instant she was free, she spun around, stumbled back. There was no mistaking the earl's sardonic features. In the dim kitchen, his eyes glittered like midnight sapphires, a night beard darkening his lean jaw. The scruff and his billowing linen shirt, which hung open at the collar, made him look like a dangerous pirate.

Wrapping her arms around herself, she struggled to calm the anarchy of her breath. "What on earth are you doing skulking about?"

He set her makeshift weapon down upon the kitchen trestle. "I wasn't skulking. I was looking for something."

"In the stillroom?"

"I woke up with a devil of a headache, if you must know. I didn't want to disturb anyone at this hour, so I came in to look for willow bark powder. My housekeeper always keeps some in the stillroom." He ran a hand through his dark hair and winced.

When he withdrew his hand, she saw that it had blood upon it.

"D-did I do that?" she stammered.

"It's nothing. I've a hard head, and trust me," he said wryly, "it has encountered harder surfaces than your pan."

Remorse percolated through her. She'd assaulted Revelstoke... made him *bleed*. Whatever she might think of him, she'd never wish him physical harm.

"Come with me," she said.

His brows lifted. "Where are we going?"

"To get you fixed up." Turning, she led the way back to the stillroom.

9

This was undoubtedly one of the most surreal moments
Sinjin could recall—and that was saying something, given
what he'd been through in the past month. There was a dream-
like quality to the scene: sitting on the edge of the work table, he
felt as if he'd landed in a magician's laboratory.

Lamplight illuminated the bottles of potions lining the shelves
of the stillroom, showing off their rainbow hues. A large apothe-
cary's cabinet dominated one wall, and the magician's daughter
was there, rummaging through the cupboards. She had her back
to him, and he couldn't deny that it was a lovely view. Free of its
usual confines, her hair fell in a thick, wavy cascade to her hips,
the mix of gold and bronze as lush as a Titian painting.

When she bent over to search in another drawer, he was met
with another revelation. As prim as her wrapper was, it clung
faithfully to what was inside. The belt cinched around a ridicu-
lously tiny waist. The robe flared to accommodate sweetly
rounded hips and, as she leaned over more, the material stretched
over her derriere for a taut and transcendent instant.

By Jove. He'd been right about her figure. Her dowdy frocks
hid a fortune of feminine bounty.

A buffle-headed sensation stole over him. He must be woozy from the injury... or from the enforced celibacy. Yes, that must be it. Blood loss combined with pent-up seed would make any man crazed.

Get it together. You need Kent's help, and you're not going to get it by ogling his sister like some randy schoolboy.

Although it hadn't been easy, he'd laid out his situation to Kent, asking for help. The investigator, to his credit, had seemed to take the story in stride. Perhaps it was the fact that he considered himself indebted to Sinjin for rescuing his daughter. Either way, he jotted down the information in a notebook, stopping Sinjin now and again to ask for clarification.

Kent's neutral posture and patient questioning had made it easier for Sinjin to talk about that night. He'd divulged every detail he could think of, including his belief that his whiskey had been drugged and the distinctive male voice that had surfaced in his dream. He supposed some might think that he sounded like a lunatic, yet Kent had lived up to his reputation as a fair and deliberate man who didn't jump to conclusions.

He'd refused to take a retainer fee, saying that he needed more facts before deciding whether or not there was a case to take on. He'd agreed to interview Nicoletta on the morrow to get her side of the story. He'd also taken Sinjin's concerns about being followed seriously and allowed him to stay the night.

Sinjin was grateful to his host, even if his guest quarters were situated above the stables. He understood the other man's caution. If he were a husband, papa, and brother, he wouldn't want himself spending the night under the same roof as his womenfolk either.

By the time Miss Polly returned bearing a tray, his somber thoughts had helped to rein in his wholly unsuitable reaction to her. She set the tray down next to where he was sitting on the table and handed him a paper sachet.

"Here you go. Willow bark," she said.

Unfolding the paper, he downed the contents in a practiced gulp. When she offered him a glass, he took it, the cool water washing away the bitterness.

"Thank you," he said.

She regarded him with pursed lips. "I'll have a look at your head now."

"That's not necessary—"

"Hold still."

Ignoring his protests, she reached up, tugging his head down gently. She ran her fingers lightly through his hair. At her probing touch, he felt a line tighten from his gut to his balls.

"Oh, dear," she said with obvious remorse. "There's a bump forming already."

Luckily, his untucked shirt covered his loins, where the bump was growing larger by the moment. Seeing her worried expression, however, he felt an odd twinge in his chest. Perhaps it was the novelty of a female evincing concern over his welfare. He was not used to being coddled. His fleeting memories of his mama's tenderness were tainted by the fact that she'd abandoned her own sons. Whenever he chanced to hear the lullaby she'd sung to him, the longing that welled was bittersweet.

As for his stepmama, he hadn't received an ounce of kindness from her. He'd been a rough-and-tumble boy, and she and His Grace had treated his injuries with scathing lectures, eventually packing him off to Creavey Hall when they no longer wished to deal with him. At the school, his feats had earned him beatings from the staff and respect from his wild cronies, who crowned him their leader. His scars became badges of honor, a symbol of neck-or-nothing rebellion. The females he later consorted with claimed that the rough marks enhanced his virility.

But Polly Kent, the odd creature, seemed genuinely disquieted by, what was for him, a negligible hurt. He could only imagine what she'd say if she saw the scars on his back... not that she ever would.

Gruffly, he said, "'Tis but a scratch."

"You're dripping blood onto the table."

"I have plenty to spare."

"Hold still, or you'll only bleed more." As appeared to be her wont, she showed no sign of deferring to him. She fussed with something on the tray, returning with a handkerchief. "This may sting a bit."

"What are you—*bloody hell*." The sudden burn blurred his vision. "What in blazes is that?"

"Spirit of witch hazel. Our physician recommends it for cleansing wounds."

"Does your quack happen to be employed by the devil?"

"Lean your head down, if you please." There she went, paying him no mind *again*. She might try to disguise herself as a wallflower, but nothing could hide that stem of steel. "It'll only take me longer to finish if you don't."

He yielded, gritting his teeth as she proceeded to set the rest of the wound on fire. He tried to distract himself... and found it absurdly easy. For in her quest to have her way with him, dictatorial Miss Polly had ended up standing between his splayed thighs. The scent of her hair—apple blossoms and honey—wafted into his nostrils, his mouth watering. With his head pulled down and her hands raised as she fussed with his wound, he had an unobstructed view of her bosom, and *what* a bosom it was.

Her modest bodices were a crime. The lapels of her chintz wrapper, however, confessed the true story: like the Red Sea, they parted to the holy power of her breasts, which were undoubtedly divine. The fine muslin of her nightgown couldn't hide the shape of those magnificent bubbies, perfectly round and full, made to fill a man's palms. As she moved about, swabbing his scalp, the lovelies gave a saucy bounce for which he'd endure a hundred other injuries for the privilege of seeing.

Christ Almighty, Polly Kent has a fine pair of tits.

His cock, that randy beast, twitched with interest. He was no stranger to lustful thoughts, but what was foreign to him was this sense of... curiosity. Over a female, of all things. Women were hardly a novelty, and reading their signals was a skill he'd honed over the years. They usually wanted one (or more) of the following from him: money, sex, or marriage. He was generous with the first two and never with the last.

Miss Polly, however, remained an enigma, a bundle of contradictions. Why did she care about his injury when she obviously couldn't stand him? And why would she choose to cloak her loveliness with dowdy clothes? Was she as prudish as she made herself out to be—or as passionate as her body's promise?

Not that he'd ever find out. He needed to get involved with a virgin like he needed to get shot in the head. The only honorable outcome of dallying with an innocent was wedlock, and God knew he wasn't equipped to be a husband. Marriage, intimacy, emotional entanglements of any kind—he wanted none of it. *Especially* not with an interfering little prude who'd made him feel like a fool more than once, who wouldn't even accept a damned gift without questioning it.

The subject of his musings took an abrupt step back, and against his will, he found himself in the thrall of her clear, blue-green gaze. For an odd, prickling instant, he fancied she could see through him—through the twisted maze of his inner workings to the devils at his core...

She jerked her wrapper closed, tightening the belt. "You're patched up. Now why are you here?"

He gathered himself. "I told you. The headache."

"I meant what is the purpose of your calling here tonight? And, please," she said with a dismissive shake of her head, "don't say it is social. Why did you wish to speak to my brother?"

It was her damned acuity, he decided, that had bothered him from the start. She had a way of making a man feel transparent—laid bare. Her perceptiveness had the opposite effect of flirtation: it felt unmanning and unpleasant. If she wished to ward away suitors, her keenness was a better shield than her frumpy get-up would ever be.

"If I have business with your brother, it's not really your concern, is it?" he said.

"Anything that involves my family involves me." She crossed her arms over her chest, and he'd wager his stables that she was oblivious to how that gesture thrust her tits up, emphasizing their spectacular size and heft. Of course, that led him to wonder about her nipples, if they would be plump or shy, fair as her skin or rosy as her lips... which were, unfortunately, still moving.

"... especially when your actions raise the hopes of my sister," she was saying. "She doesn't deserve to be dallied with by a hardened rake. I know the type of man that you are, my lord, and I doubt you have an honorable bone in your body."

Her last words cut his lustful musings short. Normally, he didn't give a damn what people thought, but her judgmental assumption got his back up.

Therefore, he drawled in a tone designed to annoy, "Ah, the fair Miss Primrose. She is a side benefit of this visit, isn't she?"

"She's not a side benefit to you or any other man." Her eyes weren't so calm and clear any more. *Good.* "Are your intentions toward her honorable?"

Up until this point, he'd had no intentions whatsoever concerning Primrose Kent. But he wasn't going to give this holier-than-thou miss the satisfaction of knowing that.

Bridling his anger, he quirked a brow. "I thought I was a hardened rake, Miss Kent. What would I know about honor?"

"I will not allow you to hurt my sister. If you don't treat her as she deserves, I... I will expose you." Her cheeks flushed, her small hands forming fists. "I'll tell my brother what I saw you doing."

So they'd circled back to the bathhouse. He'd wondered if that would come up again. If she hadn't said anything yet, however, he doubted she would do so now. It would take even more bravado than this little termagant possessed to confess she'd watched a man frigging himself. The idea that she thought she could shame him—*blackmail* him—was laughable.

Didn't she know who he was? The God of Revelry answered to no one.

"You'll admit to your brother you spied on me during a private moment?" he inquired.

"I did not spy on you!" Her blush deepened. "I didn't know anyone was in the bathhouse."

"But you didn't exactly avert your gaze, did you?" By the nervous way she wetted her lips, he knew he had her. "How long, precisely, were you enjoying the show?"

"I was not... enjoying anything! It was disgusting, *despicable*," she sputtered. "Only a madman would do such a thing!"

He had to laugh. God, her naiveté. In truth, he might have found it charming had it not been coupled with the sort of prudish self-righteousness he despised. He'd been judged and found lacking by moral pundits all his life. The best way to deal with sanctimony? Being exactly what they accused him of being—and *more*.

"If that were true, then all of mankind is mad," he said.

Her eyes rounded. "Don't be absurd."

"Only one of us is being absurd, and, alas, Miss Kent, it is not I. Here's the rub. Your brother strikes me as a fellow who disdains hypocrisy. If you tell him I belong in a madhouse because you saw me behaving like a healthy, red-blooded man, well,"—he shrugged—"he's going to have to check into Bedlam, too."

"Ambrose would never... how dare you accuse him of..." She gaped at him, her cheeks afire.

He reached out and casually chucked her under the chin. "You can thank me later," he said in a kindly, superior tone, "for educating you about the facts of life."

"I don't need any *educating* from the likes of you! Why, you're worse than a... a tomcat! You couldn't keep your trousers buttoned if you tried."

He gave her a sardonic smile. "I wouldn't know. I haven't tried."

He could see her struggling to come up with a rejoinder, and, in spite of his irritation, he found himself entertained. She was like a kitten, spitting mad and boldly swiping her claws at a panther; she seemed to have no idea that she wasn't his match, not by a long shot. Yet he had to admit that her spitfire attitude was adorable. Her flashing eyes and heaving bosom didn't hurt matters either.

She suddenly stilled, those lush, gold-tipped lashes blinking at him. "You're enjoying yourself? You find me *amusing*?" she said incredulously.

He did, actually. It almost made up for how much she'd provoked him. But he'd allowed this little minx to get too far under his skin. Time to dig her out and make nice: he had to stay on her brother's good side after all. His future depended upon it.

Before he could establish a truce, she choked out, "You think I'm naïve, too much of a ninny to see what you really are?"

"I never said that." He had thought it, though.

"You're a heartless *bastard*." At her scathing words, his humor evaporated, leaving the fine grit of annoyance behind. "You think that because you're a top-of-the-trees fellow you can get away with anything. You ridicule others, amuse yourself at their expense. You rakes—you're all the same."

Her unjust indictments flared his anger. "You don't know a goddamned thing about me."

"Don't I?" Her eyes narrowed, and their alert focus caused a prickle of unease again. 'Twas as if she could see past his surface to all his ugly secrets. "With the life you've led, I wouldn't be surprised if your misdeeds are catching up to you."

He controlled a flinch. Hers was merely a good guess. Since she knew that he'd consulted with her brother, it wouldn't take much to surmise that he was in some sort of difficulty.

"One man's misdeed is another man's pleasure," he said nonchalantly.

"Your devil-may-care façade doesn't fool me. I know how you feel. You're ashamed, desperate... and *scared*."

Her words landed with the surety of arrows. *Thunk, thunk, thunk*, they tore through the chinks in his armor, plunging into his unguarded self. How in blazes had she managed to guess...?

Heart thudding, he managed a derisive tone. "You don't know what you're talking about."

"Don't I?" Her chin lifted. "Then why are you even *more* scared now?"

"I am not bloody scared," he snapped.

God's teeth, why was the chit pushing him? Baiting him? Was the *entire* bloody world out to get him? Memories gathered: Nicoletta's bruised face, the man's voice, the strait-waistcoat. Fear was a squall inside him, threatening the barriers of his self-control.

You're not a lunatic. You're in control. You answer to no one.

She took a step closer, her red-cheeked, apple-scented outrage inflaming his senses. A vein throbbed at his temple. His fingers curled as invisible threads of energy spun tautly around them.

"You're right. You're not scared." She had the audacity to jab a finger at him. "What *you* are, my lord, is terrified."

"You're dreaming, sweeting, because it's past your bedtime," he bit out.

Her eyes flashed. "Do not treat me like I'm a child, you bounder!"

"You wish to be treated as a woman? I'll oblige you, then."

He yanked her into his arms and slammed his mouth over hers.

10

Polly's gasp of shock and outrage was muffled by Revelstoke's lips. His kiss swept over her like an inferno, sucking the air from her lungs, sealing her lips to his, making it impossible to pull away. His heat and smoky male flavor invaded her. In some distant part of her mind, she knew she ought to be struggling, protesting... but her will gave way to a mightier force.

Curiosity and craving rolled into one.

Yearning surged from the deepest recesses of her being, battering her defenses from the inside. Lord Brockhurst's kiss, the only other she'd known, had been *nothing* like this. As Revelstoke's lips roved masterfully over hers, any comparison vanished in a sultry haze. With a sigh, she surrendered to instinct, her lips parting, seeking the life-giving force the way a flower turns to the sun.

The moment she softened, the kiss changed. The charge of anger morphed into something even more potent. His tongue pushed inside, and she jolted at the shocking foray. His palms caged her jaw, held her steady as he continued the silken plundering. The hot, slick plunges caused a melting at her core, and her hands fisted in the fabric of his shirt as she held on, not knowing what else to do.

When he licked her tongue, she whimpered. He did it again and again, enticing an instinctive reply. Her tongue shyly met his, and he growled, the kiss deepening. He left no part of her cove unexplored, igniting sensations that linked her entire body. She felt his kiss on her lips, in the stiff, throbbing peaks of her breasts, in the damp fluttering between her thighs.

She moaned, needing more.

In the next instant, she was soaring through air, her bottom planting against the hard surface of the table. She clutched at the tough sinew of his shoulders as he invaded the space between her thighs, spreading them. Her head tipped back to receive the deep thrusts of his tongue. She felt his hand sliding up her ribcage and then—*heavens*—cupping her breast. Shock burned into pleasure as he found the hardened peak through her nightclothes.

He rubbed and circled the stiff bud, and her core trembled. Her entire being became his fingers caressing her breast, his lips hot and hungry upon hers. He pinched her nipple as he licked inside her mouth, and she responded with blind need, sucking eagerly on his invading organ.

A raspy sound came from his chest, and his hand left her breast, clamping on her bottom. He yanked her closer, and her legs parted naturally to accommodate him, her knees pressing against his lean hips. Her breath hitched as her softness met his hard edges—and one hard edge in particular.

Heavens again. Despite the layers between them, there was no mistaking the jutting ridge of his arousal. The image shot forth from her memory: of that erect pole of flesh, so long and thick, his pumping fist barely containing its veined girth. Wetness trickled between her legs, and she squirmed, moaning when that small friction set off exquisite sensations. His hands molded to her bottom, urging her movements, creating an alignment of soft and hard that stole her mind.

Her fingers dug into his granite-hard shoulders as their kiss raged on, as her hips moved in desperate counterpart to his heavy thrusts. *Yes, dear God, yes...* Desperation climbed and climbed and then his hardness dragged against some magical peak, and she flew over the edge. She cried out as bliss buffered her fall, a cloud of pleasure catching her.

Boneless and witless, she floated... until his hoarse oath pierced her dazed state. She tipped her head back to look at him, blinking at what she saw. Her haze vaporized in the scorching midnight blue of his eyes, in the storm of energy around him. Her entire being stiffened as she was confronted by his emotions.

Lust tangled with anger... and disgust.

He was *disgusted* by her?

Reality slapped her back to her senses. *Dear God, I've acted like the veriest trollop!* Appalled, she shoved at his chest, and he moved out of her way. She jumped off the table, stumbling in her haste and pitching forward.

He caught her. "Easy, there——"

"Let me *go*." Beyond humiliated, she slapped away his attempt to steady her.

He took a step back, hands raised. "I was just trying to help."

"You've done quite enough," she said, her face flaming.

"I must apologize," he said grimly. "It was a mistake. I should never have——"

"Think nothing of it." She forced the words past the tight ring of her throat. "As I most certainly intend to."

His eyebrows drew together. "You're just going to... forget this?"

Anger butted against mortification. *The arrogant bastard.* Wasn't it bad enough that she'd succumbed so easily to his seductive prowess? Did he believe that he was so unforgettable that she, a paltry wallflower, would never get over being granted the God of Revelry's inimitable favors?

"It was hardly a memorable event." She was proud of her

composure. "It was not my first encounter of this nature,"—he didn't have to know that the other one had comprised of one chaste peck from Lord Brockhurst—"and I daresay it won't be my last."

His jaw hardened. "Pardon. I had no idea what a little hussy you are."

"There goes the pot calling the kettle black," she shot back.

He sketched her a livid bow. "I believe I shall bid you good night then."

"Good night." Her tone wished him otherwise.

His mouth opened... and shut. Tight-lipped, he gave her a wordless glare before stalking out of the kitchen.

She waited until the door shut behind him, his steps fading into the courtyard. Only then did she sag, shivering, against the kitchen table. Why had she acted like such a wanton? The disgust in his eyes when his lust had faded to the awareness of who he'd been kissing—and another thought struck, piercing her to the quick.

Dear God... Rosie, she thought with horrified remorse. *What have I done?*

11

I made her come with a kiss.

Awareness permeated Sinjin as Polly entered the breakfast parlor the next morning. He was seated between her sister and sister-in-law at the table, and they continued to chatter away, not yet aware of her presence. But for him everything faded; his senses focused entirely on her.

She looked ill-rested, her eyes smudged with shadows. She'd tried to contain her hair in a severe knot, and she was wearing one of her usual drab gowns. But he barely registered her unflattering trappings because he knew the treasures that lay beneath them.

Cherry-sweet lips. Feminine curves that overflowed his palms.

The purest, most wanton heat he'd ever experienced.

He rose as she approached the table. It was a damned good thing he was wearing a frock coat and not a cutaway that would have revealed the extent of his body's reaction to her. Christ, what was it about her that made him, a worldly rake, feel like the veriest greenling?

It might have something to do with her going off like a Roman candle from just a kiss.

Goddamn. That had been a first, even for him.

"There you are, Pols!" Next to him, Miss Primrose gave a dazzling smile. "I was telling the earl that you're usually the first at the breakfast table."

"I, um, slept later than usual," Polly said.

Seated on his other side, Mrs. Kent said with sympathy, "Restless night?"

"Something like that." Rosy color suffused Polly's cheeks.

When he bade her good morning, she mumbled a reply, avoiding his gaze. How did she manage to look both wretched and adorable at once? he thought broodingly as she conversed with the other ladies. And why in God's name did he think she was adorable when he knew, for a fact, that she was the most frustrating female he'd ever met—and a virgin, to make matters worse?

When it came to sex, he had only one inviolate rule: stay away from the uninitiated. Seducing an innocent meant marriage, which would be nothing short of a catastrophe for a man like him. What proper lady could accept his dark demon's insatiable appetites? When that side of him took over, he craved fucking, could do it for hours; more than once, he'd worn out a trio of wenches and still hadn't been satisfied. What sweet little virgin could put up with that? Or his irritability and devilish temper?

Then there was his other side. His gut tightened in shame. The thought of exposing that wretched, pathetic part of himself sickened him. One time, the blue devil had struck during a weekend of debauchery at a friend's country house. He'd woken from the high of the previous evening to find himself suddenly plunged low into the abyss of his own private hell. One of the strumpets, clearly wanting to reap the most from her invested time, had made advances upon him... and he'd been unable to respond.

Can't get a stiff breeze blowin', luv? Lie back and let me take care o' you...

Even her experienced wiles couldn't compete with the boulder of despair crushing him. Her paid touch had amplified the gaping emptiness inside him, and curled on his side, he'd lay there like a mule... a bloody dull knife. Finally, she'd given up with a disgusted huff, leaving him steeped in humiliation and self-loathing.

Last night, however, his iron-clad rule had been blown to smithereens. Polly's wanton innocence had inflamed him as nothing ever had. A simple kiss with her had been more titillating than an orgy with a bevy of whores. He'd let things go too far with her, and, when he'd regained his senses, he'd been disgusted at himself. Angry and appalled at his lack of self-control—that he'd started something he knew he couldn't bring to an honorable conclusion.

When he'd tried to apologize, Polly had thrown it back in his face. She thought nothing of their "encounter," did she? And it hadn't been her first?

Who the bloody hell kissed her before me?

A foreign emotion gripped him. It took him a moment to recognize it as... jealousy? Christ, he'd never felt possessive of a woman before, and that did *not* bode well. He savagely shoved the feeling aside as he watched Polly head over to the sideboard. He needed to rid himself of his mad fascination with the chit. Things hadn't ended well last night—in large part due to her—but he would be the bigger person. He'd apologize again, patch up any damage, and wash his hands of her entirely.

A capital plan.

As soon as he judged it not too obvious, he excused himself from the table to join her at the sideboard. By the way she stiffened, he knew she was aware of his presence, but she continued to peruse the silver-domed dishes lining the buffet as if they contained the key to the mysteries of the universe.

Mindful of the passing servants, he said in a low voice, "We ought to talk."

"There's nothing to talk about." She lifted a lid and scooped coddled eggs onto her plate without sparing him a glance.

"I owe you an apology for what happened last night."

"Fine. You've apologized." A rasher of bacon joined the eggs.

Dealing with the blasted chit was proof positive of why he'd always avoided her kind. Nonetheless, he gritted his teeth and said, "I made a mistake—"

"You can say that again." She snatched up a roll.

"Ordinarily, I wouldn't go near a lady such as you, but it was late and I'd had too much to drink—"

"A lady such as me?" She skewered a sausage with enough force to make him cringe. "For your information, *I* would never go near a man such as *you*."

His irritation mounted. It was one thing for him to judge himself unfit to touch her, quite another for her to do so. She didn't know the first thing about him. Besides, he'd never given enough of a damn to apologize to anyone before, and here she was not only refusing his olive branch, but slapping him in the face with it?

To hell with this.

"Pardon, but your tongue in my mouth suggested otherwise," he said scathingly. "Then there's the small fact that you climaxed, fully clothed, in my arms."

She turned crimson. Casting a skittish look around, she whispered furiously, "You are no gentleman to say those things."

"And you are a lady to do them?"

"*You* started it."

"And I ended it. Which you seemed loathe to do, sweeting," he drawled.

"Why, you arrogant *rake*—"

"Better a rake who knows himself than a self-deluding virgin."

"How *dare* you." Her eyes flashed. "I know exactly who I am."

"Do you? Then why the masquerade?"

She paused for a tray-bearing footman to pass by before saying hotly, "I don't know what you're talking about."

He lifted an eyebrow. "It's a costumed event where people disguise their true identity."

Reaching the end of the buffet, she marched to the other side of the Oriental screen where the beverage service was laid out. The exotic panels of birds and blooms didn't offer much privacy but did partially shield them from the view of those at the table.

"I know what a dashed masquerade *is*," she said between clenched teeth. "I simply don't know why you're blathering on about it."

"Because I see through that camouflage of yours, and you're not the lady you pretend to be," he said succinctly.

A loud ringing sounded in Polly's ears. Her respiration shallow and choppy, she stared at Revelstoke. Dear Lord, he couldn't have gleaned her freakish ability...

"I b-beg your pardon?" she whispered.

"Do you think that your dowdy gown and holier-than-thou attitude can hide that you're a hot-blooded wench through and through? Well, they don't," he said coldly. "All they do is make you a hypocrite."

In a blink, her relief that her defect remained a secret turned to an anger so intense that scarlet seared the edges of her vision. *He* was lecturing *her* on hypocrisy? After he'd torn her to pieces behind the hedge with his friends for the sake of entertainment?

Resentment shattered her self-restraint.

He wants to talk about duplicity? Then, by God, we will.

"I know who I am. A plain, fat, and peculiar wallflower." As she said the words, she felt a strange, painful satisfaction—like that of lancing a boil. It hurt, but it also felt good to release the festering inside. "If you try to say otherwise, you're the hypocrite. Because I heard you—heard you say *I'm not worth the sport*."

For an instant, he just stared at her. "What the devil are you talking about?"

"Don't bother denying it. I *heard* you," she repeated with quiet vehemence.

"Then you ought to have your hearing—and your head—examined," he clipped out. "I never said that."

"You don't even remember, do you?" she breathed in outrage.

Impatience flared around him. "Remember what?"

She leaned in, her plate nearly poking into his waistcoat. "A year ago, in the Kitburns' garden. You and Lady Langley were talking with Lord Brockhurst and Mr. Severton."

He frowned. "What of it?"

"Severton told you about their wager. That Brockhurst had won because he'd gotten a kiss from a wallflower. And you replied that he'd do as well to kick a half-dead mongrel because there was no sport in seducing a wallflower." Pain and vindication made her voice tremble. "Well, *I* was that wallflower."

She didn't know what she expected as a response. Embarrassment. An apology, perhaps. Instead, his eyes darkened, as did his aura, his anger filling and vibrating in the sliver of space between them.

"That's it?" His voice was menacingly soft. "This incident... it explains why you've been a judgmental shrew toward me since the moment we met?"

Her jaw slackened. "How dare you—"

"How dare I what? Accuse you of being something that you're not?" His fury whipped through her. "The shoe doesn't feel quite as comfortable on the other foot, does it?"

Oh no, he didn't. He wasn't going to shift the blame onto her.

"*I* am not the one at fault. I'm not the one who said unforgivable things—"

"Did it ever occur to you to ask me about that night? Instead of holding a grudge, of blaming me, did it ever cross your mind to just bloody *ask*?"

"And what would you have said if I did? That I misheard the entire incident?" she said scornfully.

"You didn't mishear anything. I did say there's no sport in seducing a wallflower,"—he said, his tone furious—"because it is a *damned dishonorable activity*. There's no pride to be had in taking advantage of a female—of anyone who is vulnerable. That is the despicable act of a coward. The same kind of bastard, incidentally, who would kick a hapless mongrel."

She blinked at his thunderous expression—at the righteous wrath blazing around him. He believed his words... he wasn't lying. His explanation prickled through her like the painful, sensations of a reawakening limb. Her lips numb, all she could manage was a faint, "Oh."

"How *serious* the two of you appear!" Rosie's cheerful tones sliced through the thick tension. Poised by the screen, she was giving Polly and Revelstoke a quizzical look. "What scintillating topic are you discussing so intently, and may I join in?"

Polly wetted her lips, guilt warring with mortification.

Turning his back to her, Revelstoke bowed to Rosie. "It's nothing of import." His smooth words were a sharp contrast to his smoldering aura.

Rosie gave his arm a coquettish tap. "Are you certain you two aren't keeping secrets from me?"

"Not at all. It is just that your charming presence eclipses my memory of the inconsequential conversation," he drawled.

If a hole were to open up in the parquet floor, Polly would have leapt right in.

"Well, never mind, then." Dimpling, Rosie said, "Mama has agreed to chaperone a tour of the garden, my lord. Will you come, too, Pols?"

"No." Heat nudged horrifyingly behind Polly's eyes. Setting her untouched plate down on the nearest table, she blurted, "That is, I, um, just remembered I have something to do after breakfast. If you'll excuse me."

Before the tears could fall, she turned from them both and fled for the door.

Behind her, she heard Revelstoke say, "Shall we, Miss Primrose?"

12

An hour later, after a good and cleansing cry, Polly sat at her escritoire. She was trying to compose a letter to her sister Violet. The closest sibling to her in age, Vi was married to Viscount Carlisle and lived most of the year in Scotland with her husband and their young son.

Pen poised above the parchment, Polly tried to collect her thoughts.

Dear Violet,

~~*I hope the weather is fair in Scotland.*~~ (Too mundane.)

~~*I can't wait for you to visit at the end of summer.*~~ (Too desperate.)

I'm a horrible person. I labelled Revelstoke a bounder when, in fact, I misjudged him badly. On top of that, I wronged Rosie.

A droplet of ink dripped off the nib, bleeding into the parchment.

"Dash it all," she muttered.

The door whipped open, and Rosie burst into the room. "We must hurry!"

Balling the paper, her heart pounding, Polly said, "Are we, um, late for something?"

"Papa's home." Rosie hooked her by the arm, pulling her to her feet. "Mr. Lugo and Mr. McLeod are here as well, and they're all in the study with Revelstoke."

At the mention of Ambrose's business associates, a cool drop of premonition slid down Polly's spine. "What does that have to do with us?"

"We're going to eavesdrop, of course," her sister said, tugging her toward the door. "Don't you want to know what is going on?"

Polly did... and didn't. She needed to stay as far away from Revelstoke as possible. He was the ultimate threat to her equilibrium, bringing her to the heights of untold pleasure—she'd never experienced anything like that magical release in the stillroom—before dropping her like a stone into an ocean of guilt and misery. He was too dangerous a temptation, and, moreover, he brought out the worst in her.

You've been a judgmental shrew toward me since the moment we met.

She swallowed painfully. He wasn't wrong. And it shamed her.

While she might not be pretty or popular, she'd always thought of herself as a nice sort of girl. Not one who harbored unfounded hostilities—and definitely not one who'd kiss the gentleman her sister fancied.

Guilt spiking inside her, she dragged her heels. "The earl's affairs are none of my business."

"Of course they are, silly." Like a determined tugboat, Rosie towed her along, out of the room and toward the curving staircase. "Anything that involves Revelstoke involves me, and anything that involves me involves *you*."

Her shame and remorse ballooned. The hours before dawn had indeed been dark as she'd contemplated whether to tell Rosie about her encounter with Revelstoke. Her mind had teeter-tottered between possible courses of action. On the one hand, the wrong she'd done was festering inside her. She hated herself for betraying Rosie and, to make matters worse, concealing the truth.

On the other, the possibility of angering Rosie gnarled her insides with anxiety. She'd never fought with Rosie over anything before. Typically, Polly was the easy-going one, the tag-along who was happy to let the other take the lead; she rarely gainsaid her sister, let alone interfered with the other's wishes. Bewildered, she *still* didn't understand how she and Revelstoke had wound up kissing when animosity simmered between them.

Polly dreaded angering Rosie—almost as much as she dreaded triggering the other's hopelessness. For even now, she could see the feverish desperation in her sister's aura. Rosie was walking a tightrope between hope and despair, and Polly couldn't bear to tip the other into the dark abyss.

And who knew what could happen between Rosie and Revelstoke? she acknowledged with an odd little spasm. Now that she knew Revelstoke wasn't the heartless cad she'd believed him to be, maybe he wouldn't be such an unsuitable match for her sister after all. In the breakfast room, she'd seen attraction in the earl's aura —which had to be for Rosie, who looked stunning in her raspberry-striped morning dress, matching ribbons in her hair. At any rate, his desire clearly couldn't be for Polly, not when he'd told her their kiss was a mistake... twice.

Maybe Rosie was right. Maybe he had come to court her. Maybe her beauty and charm could reform him—and Polly had merely gotten in the way.

Polly's throat constricted. She'd made such a muddle of things, and after wracking her brain, the best solution she could come up with was to conceal her wrongdoing. To pretend the kiss—meaningless, anyway—never happened. It was the coward's way out, she knew, but she couldn't think of a better alternative. She vowed to herself never to repeat the transgression.

Rosie led the way to the main floor. They crossed the marble foyer toward the hallway, following the gilt-framed landscapes until they reached the library. Smelling faintly of leather and firewood, the room boasted stately bow windows that looked onto the street, the other walls covered in bookshelves. As Rosie closed the door silently behind them, Polly heard the murmur of male voices coming from the adjacent room—Ambrose's study. Although she couldn't make out the words, the somber undertone sent a *frisson* through her.

"We shouldn't be doing this," she whispered.

Rosie was already at the wall shared by the two rooms, busily removing books from a shelf. "Pish posh, give me a hand, will you?"

With a sigh, Polly took the leather-bound volumes from her sister, creating neat stacks on the floor. When enough space was cleared, Rosie leaned in and Polly followed suit, both of them pressing their ears against the smooth wood. She made out Mr. McLeod's voice, which had the lilt of a Scottish brogue, and Mr. Lugo's baritone, which bore the rhythm of his native Africa. Revelstoke's low rasp responded to Ambrose's measured syllables, yet she could only discern the occasional words—"interview" and "club" amongst them.

"I can't make out what they're saying," Rosie whispered in frustration.

"Perhaps that's a sign that we ought to—"

The door opened. Heart racing, Polly whirled around.

Edward, Ambrose and Marianne's lanky fourteen-year-old, stood in the doorway, his dark head tilted. "What are the two of you doing?"

"Nothing." Straightening hastily, Rosie shot her younger brother an annoyed look. "Don't you have anything better to do than to skulk around startling people?"

"I wasn't skulking. I just came to find a book," he protested.

"Well go find one elsewhere," Rosie said imperiously. "Polly and I are using the library at the moment."

Edward's green gaze travelled from the empty shelf to the pile of books on the floor. "Are you two eavesdropping on Papa?"

"*Hush*, for heaven's sake." Rosie hurried over, dragging her brother inside and closing the door behind him. "Must you announce it to all the world?"

"Why are you trying to listen in on Papa and his partners?"

"It is none of your business," Rosie said loftily.

"It's because of the earl, isn't it?" Edward's eyes turned speculative.

Precocious as a child, Edward was now an adolescent possessed of a startlingly keen intelligence. Marianne had ruefully called him the "Little Professor" until he'd contradicted her, saying that he didn't plan to become a scholar but an investigator like his father. In fact, he and his cousin Freddy planned on establishing their own private enquiry firm one day—a venture Violet had humorously dubbed, "Fredward & Associates."

Rosie said crossly, "Don't you have anything better to do than to torment me?"

"Not really. I'm at loose ends until Freddy comes over." Going over to the bookcase, Edward stuck his ear to the wood paneling. "Can't hear much this way, can you?"

"Will you *please* be quiet?" Rosie said with a touch of desperation.

"All right." Shrugging, Edward strolled back toward the entrance. "Seeing as you aren't interested in listening to what is going on in the study, I'll just be on my way—"

"Hold up." Rosie's gaze narrowed. "Do you know a better way of eavesdropping?"

Pivoting, Edward nodded.

When he added nothing more, Rosie demanded, "Well, spit it out."

His brows lifted. "I thought you wanted me to be quiet?"

Edward might be a genius, but he was still an adolescent, Polly thought ruefully. Like any self-respecting younger brother, he couldn't resist trying to get his sister's goat.

Seeing Rosie's rising color, Polly intervened. "Be a dear, Edward, and tell us how to do it."

"Since Aunt Polly asked so nicely,"—Edward flashed an impish grin—"I'll be right back."

He loped off. When he returned a few minutes later, he had a pair of gadgets in hand. Each device consisted of two metal funnels, one larger and one smaller, connected by a length of metal tubing.

"What on earth are those?" Rosie said.

"*Ears of Stealth*," her brother said proudly. "Freddy and I invented them for the purpose of clandestine monitoring. They're even collapsible for easy portability." He shortened and lengthened the metal tubing with clear relish. "We were inspired by Mr. Rein's ear trumpets, you see, which operate on the principle of collecting sound waves and intensifying their impact on the eardrums, thereby—"

"Never mind the science lesson," Rosie said, rolling her eyes. "How do you *use* them?"

"It's quite elementary." Edward led the way over to the bookcase. Pulling the funnels apart, he positioned the larger funnel against the wood and fitted the smaller end to his sister's ear.

Rosie's face lit up. She whispered, "I can hear what they're saying. You're a blessed *genius*."

Beaming, Edward handed Polly the second pair. Before she could try out the device, the doorbell rang.

"That must be Freddy," Edward said. "You two all right without me?"

Rosie waved him away, and he ambled off, closing the door behind him. Joining her sister at the wall, Polly placed the larger funnel against the wood, and voices flowed with startling clarity from the contraption into her ear.

"... located Miss Nicoletta French at Number 12 Castle Street, a townhouse owned by her employer, Corbett." The somber tones belonged to Ambrose. "During my interview with Miss French, she denied the presence of another man that evening. According to her, you'd been drinking heavily all night, and after the two of you, ahem, completed your transaction, you went mad and assaulted her. She claims you stopped only when you lost consciousness."

Dear God, Revelstoke beat a woman? Polly exchanged shocked, wide-eyed looks with Rosie.

"Fearing reprisal for reporting the matter to the authorities," Ambrose went on, "Miss French instead sent a message to your father, the Duke of Acton, to come collect you. This was against the wishes of the club's owner, Corbett, who wanted to have you hauled off to the nearest gaol. But Miss French refused to testify against you, and thus he has no case to bring before the magistrates. That, my lord, is the summary of our interview."

A heavy silence ensued, during which Polly was acutely aware of the ringing in her ears. Was it possible, what Ambrose said? she thought dazedly. Could Revelstoke be a *brute*?

Her gut balked at the possibility. Despite the antipathy between her and the earl, she couldn't fathom him abusing a woman. She knew first-hand that he could lash out with scathing words and sarcasm, yet he had not, in any of their interactions, showed any propensity toward violence. His words returned to her.

I did say there's no sport in seducing a wallflower because it is a damned dishonorable activity. There's no pride to be had in taking advantage of a female—of anyone who is vulnerable. That is the despicable act of a coward.

His aura had burned with angry veracity; he'd meant what he said.

Further, with an embarrassed twinge, she had to admit that when they'd kissed in the stillroom, he'd been the one to put a stop to it. She'd been so lost in passion that, if he'd chosen to, he could have progressed things much further. Taken advantage of her, if he wished. But he hadn't. He'd apologized for his actions not once but twice—owning up for his "mistake."

There was also the fact that he'd rescued Rosie from the patient at Mrs. Barlow's.

"I didn't do this." Revelstoke's hoarse words poured into her ear, the listening device magnifying his pain and frustration. "I cannot explain how it happened or why Nicoletta would lie. But I am certain the voice I heard was no dream. There was a man in the room—her accomplice is my guess. Why else would he say, *Hurry, we must act before he awakens?*"

"So you are saying this is some elaborate set-up?" The wall didn't filter out the skepticism in Mr. McLeod's voice.

"I am saying I believe I was drugged. Believe me, it takes more than three drinks for me to reach oblivion. There are people who have an axe to grind with me. I could give you a list of suspects—"

"There is no indication of a ruse. The victim points her finger at you." Mr. McLeod's brogue underscored his blunt words. "You ken why we canna go interrogating these so-called suspects without any evidence? We'll be laughed out of their homes—or thrown out, as we'd well deserve."

"That's a circular argument." Polly could picture Revelstoke dragging his hands through his hair. "Because you have no evidence, you cannot go searching for the truth?"

"What my partner is saying is that perhaps you are better off doing as your father says. Miss French stated that she has reached an agreement with the duke. She does not intend to press charges." Ambrose's tone was cool. "If we look into the matter for you, you risk scandal, perhaps worse. We are of the professional opinion that you stand to lose less by allowing His Grace to handle the situation for you."

"I refuse to hide behind my father's name. And I'd rather die than go back to that bloody madhouse," Revelstoke said, his voice gritty.

"Mr. Kent told me of your fears that you are being followed," Mr. Lugo's baritone cut in. "The law protects sane men from being detained against their will. No one can force you back to Mrs. Barlow's—or any asylum—without the certification of physicians. So you see, my lord, you are quite safe."

"Damnit, I am *not* safe. Someone is out to get me."

"I'm afraid there's little we can do to help," Ambrose said.

After a terse pause, the earl bit out, "Then I'll find someone else who can."

"Oh no, he's *leaving*," Rosie whispered.

Before Polly could react, the other grabbed the listening devices, stuffing them behind a chair. She dashed to the door, wrenching it open just as Revelstoke strode by.

"My lord?" Rosie called. "You're not leaving already?"

The earl halted, pivoting. Polly's breath caught at the frustration, helplessness, and pain roiling around him. Not the emotions of a man who was lying... but of one fighting to be believed.

Revelstoke believes in his own innocence—even if no one else does.

"I'm afraid so. Thank you both for your hospitality." His bow was stiff.

When he lifted his head, his gaze met Polly's. The intense blue flames seemed to suck the air out of her lungs. Energy pulsed between them: unspoken words, feelings too complicated to disentangle.

"If I have caused any inconvenience, you have my most sincere regrets," he said.

Somehow she knew that the gruff apology was intended for her.

"Your presence was an *honor*, my lord," Rosie said, sounding rather desperate. "I do hope you'll call again soon?"

Polly felt Revelstoke's gaze on her. She knew she ought to say something, but her tongue was a lead weight in her mouth. Thoughts swarmed in her head. *How can Revelstoke believe one thing*

—and the victim say another? Why do I believe him? How can the God of Revelry be so... friendless?

Because she saw his loneliness, oozing from him like tar.

"Good day, ladies." Another leg, and Revelstoke turned to go.

Polly watched his solitary retreat down the hallway, her heart clenching. She heard the front door close, and, numbly, allowed Rosie to pull her back into the library. The muffled sound of Ambrose and his partners conferring filtered through the wall.

"Can you *believe* what just happened?" Though hushed, Rosie's tone vibrated with outrage.

Polly moistened her lips. "I don't think the earl is capable of such a despicable act, but I—"

"Of course he isn't! I'm an excellent judge of character, and I can tell you Revelstoke would never hurt a woman," Rosie said fiercely. "He saved *my life*. What flummoxes me is the fact that Papa didn't even give him a chance."

"Ambrose is afraid of making matters worse for the earl. Besides, his conclusion is based on evidence—on the victim's testimony." Yet Polly just couldn't imagine Revelstoke being a brute toward women; if anything, the man was a Casanova. "Unless... do you think Miss French could be lying?"

"I'd wager my pin money on it. If there were only some way we could convince Papa of the fact..." Rosie's gaze widened.

Polly frowned. "Why are you looking at me like that?"

"Because you are my dearest sister and most bosom companion. I would do anything for you—and you'd do the same for me, wouldn't you?"

Comprehension hit her with the force of a hammer. "You can't mean—"

"I won't ask you for another favor for the rest of my *life* if you'll help me prove to Papa that Revelstoke is telling the truth. *Please*, Pols,"—Rosie's hands clasped as if in prayer—"you're my only hope."

13

Three days later, Polly stood in the aisle of a sun-filled classroom, which bore the pleasant scents of beeswax polish and fresh ink. A field of children surrounded her, their bright heads bobbing over their desks. As nibs scratched diligently against paper, Polly found her thoughts wandering. Her visits to the Hunt Academy for Foundlings typically absorbed her full attention, but today was no normal day.

It had begun with Rosie cornering her in her room after breakfast.

"Everything is set," her sister had said excitedly. "Today we carry out our plan!"

Polly bit her lip. "So many things could go wrong—"

"We've gone through this before. In order to interview Miss French and get proof that she's lying, we need to be free of chaperonage. Your visit to the Hunt Academy today will provide the perfect opportunity."

Although a chaperone or maid always accompanied Polly to the school, during the visits she moved about as she pleased, helping the children with various activities. The Academy was home to more than a hundred children, milling around in over a dozen classrooms, so she had ample opportunity to slip out without anyone noticing.

"Given that the Academy is a mere two blocks away from Miss French's address on Castle Street, 'tis as if we were destined for the undertaking," Rosie went on gleefully. "The trickiest part will be getting *me* free. I vow Mama watches me like a hawk."

"I wonder why."

Rosie rolled her eyes. "We can't *all* be paragons."

"I'm not a paragon," Polly protested. "I've just never had a reason to get into trouble."

Until Revelstoke came along, her inner voice reminded her, and guilt flickered.

"*As* I was saying, it would rouse suspicion if I suddenly developed a fondness for foundlings when I never have before." Rosie tapped her chin. "So I'll just fake a megrim this afternoon and come out to meet you. What could go wrong?"

Only about a million things, Polly thought now. *Why on earth did I agree to this?*

It was a rhetorical question because she knew why. Part of the reason had to do with Rosie. She found it difficult to refuse her sister in the first place, and, after the wrong she'd done, the least she could do was agree to the other's entreaty. But the more compelling reason, she admitted, was her debt to Revelstoke.

She'd misjudged him horribly. In truth, she was guilty of judging him harshly and unfairly—the very thing she'd condemned him for all these months. She'd believed he'd denigrated her because she was a wallflower when, in fact, he'd been *defending* her. She was the one who'd jumped to conclusions about him because he was a rake. The truth was shameful and humbling.

But now it was in her power to help him. To protect an innocent man—which her gut told her he was—from a terrible accusation.

"Um, Miss Kent? I'm finished."

The timid voice penetrated Polly's tumultuous thoughts.

Seeing the freckled, brown-haired girl who had an ink-smudged hand shyly raised, she put a lid on her thoughts. It wasn't right to neglect her charges just because she was about to participate in the most risky, hare-brained scheme of her life.

Summoning a smile, she headed over to the desk. "That was quick, Maisie. Let's have a look, then, shall we?"

Maisie handed over her notebook, gnawing on her lip all the while.

Polly scanned the page. Her smile deepened as she inspected the rows of cursive, which were painstakingly tidy and precise. "What beautiful penmanship, Maisie," she said warmly.

The girl flushed to the roots of her shiny brown plaits. "Thank you, Miss Kent. I've been practicing. Like you told me, '*If at first you don't succeed…*'"

"*…try and try again.*' That was my papa's favorite saying," Polly said with a reminiscent smile. "As a scholar and schoolmaster, he said his work never got any easier—he merely got more used to trying. Well, your efforts have certainly paid off, Maisie. I'm very impressed, and Mrs. Hunt will be as well at your remarkable progress."

"Do you think so?" Pleasure warmed the girl's glow.

Like all of the foundlings, Maisie Cullen adored the school's benefactress, Persephone Hunt. The academy had been established by Mrs. Hunt's husband, Gavin Hunt, a powerful and affluent businessman. A product of the stews, Mr. Hunt aimed to give the children of the rookery opportunities that he, himself, had lacked. The Hunts were long-time friends of the Kents, and it had been Mrs. Hunt who'd first suggested that Polly might enjoy volunteering at the academy.

"What will I be impressed by?" The lady in question approached, a questioning smile on her heart-shaped face. Mrs. Hunt's slender figure was clad in a sky blue walking dress that matched her eyes, her upswept golden curls bouncing with each step. Her loveliness was more than skin-deep: she glowed with the vitality of her spirit.

"Maisie completed her lesson." Polly showed Mrs. Hunt the page.

"Well done, Maisie!" Mrs. Hunt said. "We shall celebrate with cake at lunch, shall we?"

Maisie turned even pinker. "Miss Kent's been 'elping me with my q's."

"Then Miss Kent shall have some cake too," Mrs. Hunt declared. "Now, run along, Maisie, and get some fresh air before the lunch bell rings. You've earned it."

The girl bobbed a curtsy and scampered off, plaits flying.

"She has bloomed, hasn't she?" Mrs. Hunt said with satisfaction.

"Indeed," Polly said fondly.

She could still remember when Maisie had arrived at the school a year ago, a malnourished ten-year-old dressed in rags. Unlike London's Foundling Hospital, the Hunt Academy took in children of all ages and regardless of the circumstances that had forced them to seek refuge. Maisie and her older brother, Timothy, had been abandoned by their mother, a prostitute whose addiction to blue ruin had taken away her ability to care for her offspring.

"Now if only Tim would set roots down here as well," Mrs. Hunt murmured.

While Maisie had adapted to her new home, her brother, unfortunately, had not. At fifteen, Tim was a wild and unruly boy who ran with a band of mudlarks, children who scavenged the banks of the Thames collecting anything of value. Given the desperation of their situation, mudlarks who managed to survive into adulthood oft found themselves apprenticed into the world of thieves and cutthroats. Only Tim's love for his sister kept him coming to the academy for visits and, Polly suspected, from succumbing to the darkness of the rookery once and for all.

"I wish there was some way to convince him," she said.

"One can only bring a horse to water," Mrs. Hunt said with a sigh. "But enough of that. I have something to show you in my office if you're free?"

Polly nodded. She had an hour before she was to meet Rosie around the corner from the school. They'd chosen that time because the children would be transitioning from lunch to recess; in the hullabaloo, no one would notice Polly's absence.

Polly followed the other out of the classroom. Occupying a large plot on the boundary between the stews and Covent Garden, the academy had once been a warehouse for spices, and the barest traces of cinnamon and saffron still tinged the air. The Hunts had redesigned the cavernous space, adding windows and walls to create large, bright rooms that branched off the arterial hallway.

As Polly kept pace with Mrs. Hunt's lively stride, she glimpsed children learning various trades in those rooms, everything from shoemaking to sewing to cookery. The Academy's unique philosophy was to provide students not only with food and shelter, but with the tools—including literacy—with which they could build successful lives.

"You've made quite an impression on Maisie," Mrs. Hunt said.

"And vice versa. She's a bright and capable girl."

It was one of the reasons Polly loved working at the academy. The students had so much potential—and at the same time, little in the way of conceit. Because of their humble beginnings, the children knew the pain of living on society's fringes, and their auras shone with hope and determination to make better lives for themselves.

"She was in dire need of a mentor and friend. Maisie talks about you all the time. How you've helped her with her letters and her sewing."

"She's a prodigy with a needle. Even Madame Rousseau is impressed," Polly said with a smile. Through their circle of influence, the Hunts had been able to recruit experts to apprentice the children. Madame Rousseau, the famed and long-time modiste of the Kents, had taken Maisie and several girls under her tutelage. "I've hardly done anything."

Mrs. Hunt sent her a quizzical look. "You do know Maisie adores you, don't you? As do all of the children you've worked with."

"I think it is you whom they admire, Mrs. Hunt."

"Well, we all have our blinders," the other murmured, somewhat cryptically. "Never mind. One day you'll recognize your own value, my dear."

"I'm just happy to contribute as much as I can." *And to find a place where I belong.*

Turning the corner, Mrs. Hunt led the way into the offices that housed the academy's staff. She said a cheery hello to the secretary stationed at the front desk and ushered Polly down another corridor. They passed by an immaculate chamber outfitted in dark, masculine tones. A painting of Mrs. Hunt and her three golden-haired offspring hung over the large mahogany desk, lending a bright note to the otherwise stark decor.

They reached Mrs. Hunt's personal office, an airy space marked by an eyebrow-raising amount of clutter. Mrs. Hunt made a beeline for her rosewood escritoire. The desk's legs creaked as she shuffled through the piles on its surface.

"Make yourself at home, dear," she muttered absently. "Now where is the dashed thing?"

Eyeing the seating options, Polly hid a grin. The chairs and settee were also covered in books and papers—the tools of a writer's trade. For in addition to her charity work, Mrs. Hunt wrote wildly popular novels under her pseudonym P. R. Fines.

Polly was discreetly clearing a stack of newspapers off a chair when Mrs. Hunt exclaimed, "Aha. Here it is!" Waving a book like a flag, Mrs. Hunt came over and held it out.

Polly took the handsome leather-bound volume. Reverently,

she ran her fingertips over the title embossed in gold. "Is this your newest book?"

"I received it yesterday," Mrs. Hunt said with a happy nod, "and I'm going to unveil it at our charity ball, less than a fortnight away. I'll be auctioning off signed copies to raise funds for the academy."

"What a brilliant notion."

"That is what Mr. Hunt said." Mrs. Hunt looked quite pleased with herself. "Now on the topic of the ball, have you decided what you're going to wear?"

Polly hadn't given it much thought. In truth, she was not particularly thrilled at the notion of enduring yet another social crush, but she would go, of course, to support the children and the Hunts' excellent cause.

"I'll find something suitable," she said off-handedly.

"Actually, I was hoping you'd do me and the academy a favor."

She tilted her head. "Of course, if I can."

"As you know, all the classes are working on projects to display at the ball. Seeing the fruits of the children's hard work always encourages our donors to reach more deeply into their pockets. This year, Madame Rousseau has been working with Maisie and the other girls to design a ball gown for the occasion—and they'd like for you to model their creation."

Tendrils of dread crept over Polly. She shook her head. "I wouldn't do their work justice—"

"On the contrary, you'd be the *perfect* model," Mrs. Hunt argued. "Madame Rousseau already has your measurements from gowns she has made you in the past, and Maisie and the girls are so excited over the project. Indeed, they're likening it to the story of the Girl in the Cinders—not that you're dressed in rags, of course," she added hastily. "They would just like to create a different style for you."

"But I don't want—"

"It would mean ever so much to Maisie and the other girls,"

Mrs. Hunt said. "It would show them that you have faith in their abilities. That you're proud of them and their handiwork."

Polly gnawed on her lip. How could she refuse such a request? It was just a dress, after all. The truth was that she'd wear a sack if it would prove to the children how proud she was of them.

"All right," she said. "I'll do it."

"Marvelous! You shan't regret it," Mrs. Hunt said, her eyes sparkling.

Polly hoped the other was right.

———

A little shy of an hour later, Polly stood around the corner from the academy at a busy intersection of passing carriages, wagons, and people on foot. She tried to blend in as she waited anxiously for Rosie to arrive. She'd purposefully worn her most concealing cottage bonnet, its large straw brim hiding most of her profile.

"Miss Kent?"

She started, her head twisting in the direction of the strange voice. Her bonnet had worked too well, preventing her from seeing the street urchin who'd approached her from the other side.

"Yes, that's me," she said, perplexed.

"I 'ave a message for ye." The gap-toothed boy held out a missive.

Polly took the note. Breaking the wax seal, she scanned it quickly.

Dear Pols,

Mama has had a spell—don't worry, the physician says she just needs bedrest. But of course Papa rushed home, and now it will be impossible for me to slip out. Because time is of essence, I must ask you the greatest favor. Will you, my dearest sister, carry out our mission on your own? My future depends upon it.

R.

P.S. Please tell the messenger the month in which you were born. That way I can be sure you received this, and he will get his other half-crown.

With trembling hands, Polly folded the note.

"Well, miss?" The urchin cocked his brown-capped head. "Wot's your reply, then?"

She inhaled. "June. And you may tell her my answer is 'yes'."

❧ 14 ❦

Sinjin stared broodingly out through the slit in the carriage curtains. From his vantage point on a cross street, he had a clear view of Number 12 Castle Street, a tidy building just north of the Covent Garden market. Come sundown, the block would grow raucous due to its taverns and gaming hells, yet the three-storey residence maintained an elegant Palladian façade, well-tended flower boxes blooming beneath spotless windows.

It would take a generous employer indeed to put an employee up in this abode. Which led Sinjin to wonder if Corbett's relationship with Nicoletta was more than professional. Why would the owner of a bawdy house give a damn about one of his wenches? Could it be a lover's fury that drove Corbett to pursue justice on Nicoletta's behalf? Or could Corbett have some other, more sinister involvement in the affairs of that night?

Whatever the case, Sinjin would discover the truth.

Since leaving the Kent residence three days ago, Sinjin had accepted that he would have to rely upon himself to get out of his current predicament. It was not a new state of affairs. With Stephan gone, he didn't have anyone to take his back. He recalled one of his dark periods when his older brother had come to find him in his apartments. As he'd shut everyone out, including the servants, the place had turned into a pig sty. He hadn't washed for two days, hadn't eaten—unless one counted the copious amounts of whiskey he'd poured down his throat.

Stephan had forced Sinjin to bathe and eat. He'd stayed until the fog lifted a few days later.

I won't always be here, Stephan had said. *You have to learn to pull yourself up by the bootstraps. Find some way to beat these monstrous moods.*

As Sinjin watched the passers-by on the street, he felt the truth of his brother's words. Of course, it was always easier during the periods when the devils were sleeping. When he was calm and himself. He had to take advantage of his clear head and advance his plan.

In retrospect, he'd realized that the escape from Mrs. Barlow's had unbalanced him, the black devil quietly whispering in his ear, seducing him with delusions that sounded like facts. Now that he was thinking rationally, he could see that he had no solid proof that guards were after him—and even if they were, what could they do? Kent's partner was right. A man couldn't be locked in an asylum without documented proof of his insanity. He had no cause to worry, he assured himself.

Thus, after leaving Kent's, Sinjin had returned to his town-house. Predictably, there'd been no one there but his skeleton crew of servants. He'd been so relieved that he'd laughed at his own folly. His humor died a quick death when he read the letter sent by his father. The terse paragraphs had outlined a threat: return to Mrs. Barlow's or be cut off financially.

So be it. Crumpling the letter into a ball, Sinjin had tossed it into the fire. He didn't need the duke's money. To be certain, he'd paid a visit to Randolph Merrick, his man of business, earlier this morning. He'd inherited Merrick along with a sizeable portion from his mama on his twenty-first birthday.

Catherine Pelham had come from a family of wealthy

merchants, and her marriage contract had provided bequests to both her sons, with the stipulation that one would inherit all if the other should pass; if none of her children survived, all would go to one of her distant male relatives. After Stephan's death, Sinjin had found himself in possession of some four hundred thousand pounds.

Merrick's job was to ensure that Sinjin kept that fortune—and the man was exceedingly good at what he did. He'd worked for two generations of mama's family, outliving his clients but ensuring that their financial legacy lived on. A slight, bespectacled fellow with a ring of grey hair, he was unprepossessing in looks and manner and a bona fide genius when it came to money, a fact proved once again when he'd provided a current review of Sinjin's portfolio.

"That's an impressive showing, old boy." Filching the glass paperweight from Merrick's desk, Sinjin had idly tossed it from hand to hand. "Even I couldn't fritter that fortune away."

"Your expenses last quarter did not even make a dint in the interest, my lord, let alone the principle," Merrick said calmly. As usual, attempts at levity went over the professional man's balding pate. "My clerk informed me that you paid a visit when I away. Was there something particular you wished to discuss, my lord?"

Sinjin hesitated, the smooth weight heavy in his palm. He'd met Merrick five years ago and owed much to the other. Back then, he'd been living on a meager stipend from His Grace and spending most of it on a trifecta of sin: spirits, gambling, and tarts. He'd lived in a hellhole, had creditors breathing down his neck, and basically let his demons run roughshod over his life. After the years at Creavey Hall, he hadn't given a damn about anything beyond the gratifications of the moment.

The appearance of Merrick had changed Sinjin's life. The day after his twenty-first birthday, Sinjin had returned to his dilapidated lodgings, drunk and bleary-eyed, to find the stooped grey man waiting patiently by the door. Merrick had introduced himself, and when Sinjin had let him inside, the man of business had glanced around and said, "We shall ensure that you never live like this again."

Merrick had lived up to his words. The man not only took care of the money, but he quietly made countless life arrangements for Sinjin as well. In truth, Sinjin was quite certain he could not have managed half as well without the other. Yet as reliable and stalwart as Merrick was, the man kept to a strictly professional role. The closest they had to a personal conversation was when the other reconciled Sinjin's expenses.

Once, Merrick had queried him about two identical bills received from a jeweler on the same day. The man of business had been certain that an error had been made. When Sinjin explained that he had, in fact, sent identical baubles to a pair of twins in whose company he'd spent the night, Merrick's eyebrows had inched slightly upward. He'd settled the receipts without further comment.

Today, Sinjin had found that his desire to confide was uncharacteristically strong. Thus, he'd related his present circumstances, battling shame and fear. Setting the paperweight back on the desk with an uncomfortable click, he said, "Well, what do you think I should do?"

Reaching over, Merrick straightened the paperweight. "This is not my area of expertise, my lord."

"But surely you have some suggestion?" He hoped that the other would not second Kent's advice for he refused to be a bloody coward and hide behind his father's coattails.

"You believe you are innocent of this crime?" Merrick said after a pause.

"Yes," Sinjin said firmly. "I've never hit a woman. I never would."

"Money can provide independence, but it is the truth that sets one free." Merrick's bespectacled gaze did not waver. "If I were in your shoes, I would not rest until I had the liberty that only peace of mind can bring."

Gratitude and relief rolled through Sinjin. One person, at least, didn't reject the possibility of his innocence. "I see. Thank you for your input, Merrick."

"You are welcome, my lord. And money is never without its uses," the man of business had said in brisk tones. "Shall I look into retaining the services of the Bow Street Runners on your behalf?"

It had been an excellent suggestion, and Sinjin had decided that he would hire the Runners himself. He'd been on his way to Bow Street when some impulse had directed him to Nicoletta's residence instead. Which brought him to his present vigil. The door of Number 12 remained stubbornly closed. People and carriages passed by. A lady on the other side of the street snagged his attention, drawing him closer to the window. Her face was concealed by a large bonnet, but something about her triggered thoughts... of Polly Kent.

Anger still simmered at the chit's unjust accusations, her damned assumptions about him. Yet, oddly enough, as time had passed, it was her assessment of *herself* that niggled at him more. *I know what I am. A plain, fat, and peculiar wallflower.* Was she cracked? Had she never consulted a looking glass? A part of him wanted to shake her, make her see the truth.

Another part of him wanted to hunt Brockhurst down. He'd thought the bastard cowardly back then; now, he wanted to call the tosser out. His fierce protectiveness was as novel as it was alarming: he'd never felt that way about a woman. Ever.

So why in blazes did he experience it toward Polly, who had made it clear that she wanted naught to do with him? Part termagant, part kitten, she was wholly a confusing, complicated chit— and a temptation he could ill afford. The Fates had done him a favor by putting her out of his reach.

His gaze sharpened as he followed the journey of the mysterious lady who'd triggered his unwelcome thoughts, who'd now rounded the corner onto Castle Street. Damn, she reminded him of Polly. She had a curvaceous figure that her frumpy brown dress couldn't hide, and the determined set of her shoulders was unnervingly familiar. The hairs prickled on his nape when she headed up the steps to Number 12.

The door opened, and a servant appeared, obviously inquiring as to the visitor's purpose. The lady replied, and, as she did so, her head tilted to one side, revealing a clear glimpse of her profile.

Sinjin's blood turned to ice as he watched Polly Kent traipse into his enemy's domain.

"Didn't you lot come by earlier this week?" the maid said as she led the way down a tastefully decorated hallway.

"I'm, um, here to conduct the follow up," Polly extemporized, her heart thumping.

Thankfully, the maid didn't ask any further questions, her aura corroborating her indifference. She left Polly to wait in a small parlor and said her mistress would be in shortly. The instant the door closed behind her, Polly jumped up and paced around the room. She didn't know what she was looking for, but any clues concerning the mysterious Nicoletta French might prove useful.

The parlor was elegantly appointed, with buttermilk damask covering the walls and an Aegean blue Aubusson upon the floor. The furnishings were upholstered in brushed saffron velvet. Finding nothing of note in the seating area, Polly spied a secretaire in the far corner and hurried over to investigate.

A filigree tray of writing implements, a crystal inkwell, and a book rested on the blotter. Casting a nervous glance at the door, Polly picked up the volume and flipped through it. A comedic play—her brows lifted—and a rather risqué one at that. She was about to replace the book when a scrap drifted from between the pages, fluttering into the shadows beneath the desk. Simultaneously, footsteps approached in the hallway.

Panicked, she put the book down, dropped onto her hands and knees. She had to stretch to reach the fallen paper, her fingers closing around it just as the footsteps reached the parlor. Without a second to spare, she hastily stuffed the scrap into the hidden pocket of her skirts and dashed toward the sitting area. Her bottom collided with a chair cushion just as the door opened.

"Apologies for keeping you waiting, Miss Kent, but I wasn't expecting visitors." An ebony-haired beauty glided toward her. "I'm Nicoletta French. What can I do for you?"

Polly couldn't help but stare. Tall and statuesque, Miss French wore a rose silk walking dress that looked sewn onto her hourglass figure. Her skin seemed too pale for her dark hair, creating a dramatic look, and her hazel eyes had a feline cast. Polly saw no lingering evidence of the assault on the other's face, which was subtly enhanced with paint.

Even more than Miss French's looks, Polly noticed the other's aura: the woman shimmered with confidence... and not a little conceit.

Swallowing, Polly said, "I'm here to follow up with some questions concerning the Earl of Revelstoke. On, um, behalf of my brother." She sent a silent apology to Ambrose.

Miss French seated herself. "I said all I had to say to your brother."

"It won't take but a moment," Polly said quickly.

"I don't like to speak of the incident." A quiver entered Miss French's voice, and she shuddered. Both gestures struck Polly as odd given that there was no sign of fear in the other's aura. Just that eerie, unwavering self-assurance.

"I'm certain it must be difficult," she began tentatively.

"*Difficult?* You have no idea what I suffer." Moisture gathered in Miss French's eyes, trickling over her high cheekbones. She dabbed at the tears with a handkerchief before saying with a sniffle, "It haunts me nightly in my dreams. The last thing I want is to relive it during the day as well."

Polly's nape tingled. Not because of the other's tears but because Miss French's glow remained utterly unchanged despite her apparent distress. If anything, her confidence grew stronger... as if she were enjoying the performance she was giving.

"I have only one detail to clear up, and then I'll be on my way," Polly said.

Miss French gave a weak wave of her handkerchief. "If you must."

"Why are you trying to frame Revelstoke?"

Alarm slashed through the woman's aura, but her expression didn't alter. Instead she said tearfully, "I don't know what you're talking about."

"Who is paying you to smear the earl's reputation?" Polly said evenly. "My brother is London's best investigator, and he *will* track down the other man who was in the room that night. It'll go better for you if you confess now."

Before Polly's focused gaze, the woman's alarm gave way to anger... and then her aura took on the hard, superficial glitter of paste jewels as smug confidence reasserted itself.

Nicoletta French stood, her bottom lip quivering, freshly manufactured tears—for Polly was certain that they weren't genuine—leaking from her eyes. "How dare you come and make such horrid accusations. I want you to leave!"

Before Polly could reply, a commotion sounded beyond the room. Pounding footsteps, the maid's raised voice, "Ye can't go in there—"

The door flung open, and the air whooshed from Polly's lungs.

Revelstoke stood in the doorway. He strode forward, his anger filling the room. A second later, his hand closed like a manacle around Polly's arm.

"Let's go," he clipped out.

"*You.*"

At the gasped word, Polly's gaze swung from Revelstoke's livid face to Nicoletta's pale one. The woman's eyes were wide, her lips visibly trembling, her hands clasped to her breast. Despite those dramatic gestures, the woman's aura shone not with fear, but...

Avarice. Thrill. Triumph.

This is a performance for her. In that moment, Polly knew it for certain.

"Why can't you leave me be?" Nicoletta cowered against the settee although Revelstoke made no move toward her. "Haven't you done enough?"

Polly saw a flash of real pain. Not from Miss French—but from Revelstoke. He still had a hold on Polly's arm, and she felt him flinch, anguish and uncertainty ripping through his aura. Yet he didn't respond to the accusation, instead hauling her out of the room.

"Have a care, Miss Kent,"—Nicoletta's sobs followed them down the corridor—"or the devil will have his way with you, too!"

Revelstoke stiffened as if he'd been shot, but he didn't halt, dragging Polly out the front door, down the steps, and tossing her into the waiting carriage.

"Drive and don't stop until I tell you to," he barked to the driver before vaulting inside, slamming the door behind him. As the carriage swayed into motion, he planted his hands on either side of her. Caged by his body, his engulfing rage, she stared at him.

"What the bloody hell do you think you're doing?" he thundered.

15

Polly's heart pounded in her ears. If she thought she'd provoked Revelstoke before, she now knew she'd been mistaken. His emotions whipped around him like a primal storm, the colors wild, dazzlingly intense.

"H-how did you find me?" she stammered.

"Answer my bloody question." His pupils expanded, black crowding out blue. "Why in *blazes* did you go to see Nicoletta French?"

She searched for a plausible explanation... but there was none. None but the truth. Besides, her sense of self-preservation warned her not to risk more of Revelstoke's wrath by lying.

In a small voice, she said, "I was questioning her."

"The *devil* you say."

Unnerved by his unrelenting stare, she rushed on, "I, um, overheard your discussion with Ambrose and his partners. I know about your... situation, and I wanted to help."

"You know about my situation and wanted to *help?*"

His incredulous repetition of her words ramped up her unease. That and the fact that he still had her pinned against the carriage cushions. In truth, she might have been terrified had she not been able to see his aura. Beneath the anger was vivid, pulsing worry.

He was worried... for her?

The knots in her chest eased slightly. "I thought that if I spoke to Miss French, I might be able to..."—she warned herself to tread lightly, for the last thing she wished was to let slip her freakish ability—"...figure out the truth and convince my brother to help you. My sister Emma has oft had success interviewing female suspects, so I thought I might give it a go. Ladies have a way of speaking with other ladies, if you know what I mean."

"I most assuredly do not know what you mean. Why don't you explain to me why a well-bred virgin marches into the den of a whore and carries on as if she's an investigator? While you're at it, why don't you clarify why you risked your neck—never mind your reputation—doing the most asinine thing in the history of asinine things?"

His question ended on a roar, and Polly supposed she really ought to have been frightened. But she wasn't, not of him, this man who feared for her safety, who'd recoiled at Nicoletta's false accusations. Despite his domineering stance, waves of agitation poured off him, his heat and spicy male scent flooding her senses, the bleakness in his eyes pulling the truth from her.

"I went because I misjudged you," she said quietly. "You were right: I was wrong to assume the worst of what you said that night in the garden, and my behavior toward you since has reflected my unfair prejudice."

His brows snapped together. "So you went to Nicoletta's out of obligation?"

She could have left it at that. A part of her wanted to. But something in his fierce gaze would not allow anything but the complete truth. Her hand seemed to lift of its own accord. He jerked at her touch, his hard jaw ticking with tension against her gloved palm.

"No, I went because I believe you," she said steadily. "I believe that you're not the type of man who would beat a woman—who would hurt someone less powerful. And after speaking with Miss French, I believe that she is lying, and you were framed, although I don't know the reasons behind her evil scheme. But I vow I will convince my brother to take on your case."

He stared at her as if he'd never seen her before. His brows-drawn expression was strangely vulnerable. "You... believe me?"

"I believe you," she reaffirmed, "and I'm sorry I misjudged you in the first place."

The yearning in his gaze, in his aura, was mesmerizing. A magnetic force seemed to vibrate between them, breath-stealing, irresistible, entraining her heartbeat to its ungoverned pulse. Every part of her felt innervated, thrumming with anticipation.

"You feel it, don't you?" he said hoarsely. "This wanting between us."

Their gazes held as a heartbeat ticked by. Then another. The world outside faded to the primitive drumming in her ears, and her chin dipped in a nearly imperceptible nod. After that, she didn't know who made the first move, but the last thing she saw was smoldering blue before their mouths met in a crushing kiss.

———

There would be consequences, but he was too far gone to give a damn. Had been from the moment he'd clapped eyes on her. A part of him had always known the risk she posed, but he'd never been good at denying what he wanted. And, by Jove, he wanted her.

I believe you.

The words hit his bloodstream like an aphrodisiac. Roaring need met with the heady relief that she was safe, and it was a combustible combination. Hunger roared through him, the rush as strong as that of the black devil, the bastard stirring but remaining asleep.

The need he was feeling was all for Polly. All because of her.

Pressing her into the corner of the carriage, he feasted on her mouth, her sweetness a drug and he an addict who'd been craving it since his last taste. He licked into her honeyed cove, coaxing her to kiss him back, and when her tongue brushed against his, that shy swipe travelled all the way to his groin. His bollocks swelled with pent-up seed. His cock was harder than a fire iron—Christ, from just a kiss.

But kissing with her was different than with other women. It wasn't just a prelude to fucking. It was... more. Her wanton innocence was, for him, the essence of pleasure. The way she received his questing tongue as if it were the sweetest treat—as if she would accept anything he gave her.

As if she could want all of him, everything that he was.

Ravenous, he left her mouth for her earlobe, tugging the plumpness between his lips. Her breath hitched, and he did it again, flicking wetly, suckling the soft lobe until she squirmed with ardent insistence against him, her little gloved hands pawing at his shoulders. He nuzzled her throat, her apple blossom scent making his mouth water. Speaking of ripe, delicious fruit...

He nimbly searched out buttons and laces, loosening and undoing them until he could tug down the bodice of her gown and petticoat. His nostrils flared at the sight of what he'd revealed. Although he'd seen his fair share of racy boudoir wear, her modest white unmentionables were the most erotic garments he'd ever seen on a woman. Nearly transparent, her fine linen shift was cut low, draping over the lush upper mounds of her breasts, the lower half hidden in the pleated cups of her corset.

He traced a fingertip over her kiss-reddened lips, her delicate chin, down the silken arch of her throat. As his touch wandered lower, over the deep, linen-covered crevice between her heaving tits, he marveled, "How beautiful you are."

"I'm not beautiful." Her denial was immediate, no trace of coyness in her clear eyes.

He would show her how wrong she was. He traced the delicate slope of her collarbone, her skin softer than swan's-down beneath his fingertips.

"Beautiful," he repeated.

"I'm not—"

She broke off with a gasp when he hooked his index finger beneath the neckline of her shift, dipping into the cup of her corset. He found the taut bud of her nipple, slowly flicking the velvety tip back and forth. He held her gaze, hunger surging in him as her aquamarine eyes grew unfocused, a soft whimper leaving her.

"Satisfy my curiosity, kitten: are your nipples a shy pink to match your creamy skin," he murmured, "or a naughty coral like your incomparable mouth? I've always wondered."

Rosy color climbed her cheeks—God, he'd never found blushing to be such a charming habit until her. "You've wondered about the color... of my..."

When she trailed off with mute embarrassment, he gave a soft laugh. "I suppose I'll have to find out for myself."

Given that her chemise was trapped in place by her corset, his only recourse was to pull down the quilted cup. There wasn't a lot of give, just enough for her linen-covered nipple to peep over the rim of stiffened fabric. Even so, the sight of that plump, erect bud made his gut seize with want.

"Coral," he said huskily. "I should have known."

He bent his head to sample the inviting morsel.

Polly jolted with shock as Revelstoke's lips closed around her nipple. Her hands shot to his head, intending to halt the scandalous caress, but she felt the curl of his tongue, the decadent lapping through the linen, and instead of pushing him away, her fingers threaded through the rough silk of his hair, gripping tightly as a moan rustled from her throat.

In a swift movement, he lay her fully across the bench, kneeling beside her on the carriage floor. She had the dissonant thought that his position couldn't be comfortable, but then he bent over her again, and the hot, wet suction of his mouth drained her of all thought. She became a creature of sensation, writhing as he licked and suckled, going from breast to breast.

"You have the loveliest breasts. See how pretty your nipples are?" He blew softly on the damp linen, and she shivered at the exquisite sensation and wicked words, the vibrant desire in his eyes. "Like the ripest cherries, so red and plump, they make me want to eat you all up..."

She moaned helplessly as he made good on his words, lavishing her breasts with kisses. Never had she imagined such decadent pleasure, his clever mouth wreaking havoc on one breast, his long, agile fingers at the other. The heat and friction twined in a blazing trail from her breasts to her sex. She squeezed her thighs together in an effort to relieve the throbbing between them. Her respiration grew fitful, the constriction of her stays growing tighter, the stimulation too much to bear.

"Revelstoke," she pleaded.

His head lifted, his gaze searing down into hers. "Sinjin, love. Say my name."

"Sinjin..." Despite what they were doing, the intimacy of those two syllables quivered through her. Wetting her lips, she said, "Sinjin, please stop. I can't stand it anymore."

His beautiful mouth twitched, his gaze dancing with the devil's merriment. Before she could question his amusement, he kissed her again until her mind emptied, her senses overwhelmed by his virile skill.

Against her lips, he murmured, "You don't want me to stop, kitten. Because if I did, you wouldn't get to see what comes next."

"What comes next?" The words popped out before she could stop them.

His sensual smile stole her breath. He dropped kisses on the corner of her mouth, the surging slope of one breast, her bound, fully-clothed waist. As his head descended farther and farther, she heard the rustling of her skirts and petticoats, felt a startling waft of air against her stockinged legs...

"What are you doing?" she gasped, levering herself up on her elbows.

"Answering your question of what comes next." He continued to sweep her skirts up, bunching them at her waist. His large hands landed above her garters, on her bare and trembling thighs. "In a nutshell, my sweet? You do."

When she tried to close her legs, he held them spread. He stared intently at her most private place while she squirmed with mortification.

"Look at you, by Jove," he murmured.

Steeped in shame, she squeezed her eyes shut.

"You're a work of art."

She peeped at him. Was he... making fun of her? "That's not amusing."

"Who's laughing? You're a bloody masterpiece."

Reverence threaded his tone and, she saw with astonishment, his aura.

"Gorgeous tits, legs, not to mention the prettiest pussy I've ever seen." His sincerity was as jarring as his wicked turn of phrase. "It's a good thing I don't have time to get you fully naked: I might expire on the spot. We'll have to build up to it—give my heart time to adjust. Now let's see if your pussy feels as nice as it looks..."

She shuddered as he brushed a finger through the silky thatch that guarded her feminine secrets. When he nudged against her damp folds, a strangled sound rose up her throat. Then he was stroking her... *there*... a wicked and thorough exploration that reduced her breath to choppy pants. He delved higher, touching that hidden peak that sent sparks up her spine. He stroked, circling and circling, and the sparks blurred into a fiery streak. Suddenly, she caught fire: bliss exploded through her, forcing his name from her lips.

"Christ, that looked sweet," he said thickly. "Was it good then, kitten?"

Good? It was even better than their last kiss, beyond anything she could have imagined. Before she could gather her wits to answer, moisture trickled from her core, dampness slickening his fingers, which continued to leisurely stroke her. Mortified, she tried to clamp her legs together again.

"No, don't hide. I love how wet you're getting for me," he rasped.

Flushing, she whispered, "You... do?"

"Bloody hell, yes. It tells me you like what I'm doing, so I'm going to do more. Let me, sweeting. Let me kiss it better..."

Kiss? Surely he didn't mean to—

Shocked, she felt his hot, strong licking at her center. Her hands went to push his head away... but instead her fingers curled in his dark hair. His kiss was relentless, undeniable, searching out all her secrets. When his lips closed over the sensitive peak of her sex, a sob caught in her throat. He suckled with tender insistence at the same time that his finger circled the entrance to her body. She felt a foreign stretch, then a stunning fullness that eased the aching inside her. Her hips lifted for his decadent kiss, for the plunging necessity of his touch...

"That's it, sweeting," he growled. "Come again for me. Coat my tongue with your honey."

At his command, a deep wave of ecstasy rolled over her. Smaller tides followed in its wake, and he buoyed her through the aftermath with murmured praise, languid strokes of his tongue. As she floated, he came up, kissing her softly. The wicked, forbidden taste of herself on his lips made her stiffen.

He pulled his head back; to her relief, there was no sign of disgust this time. Arousal dilated his eyes, colored the high crests of his cheekbones. Against her bare thigh, she could feel the hot, heavy bar of his arousal straining against his trousers. His aura roiled with need, and yet it was contained by steely restraint.

The intensity of his gaze made her heart pound, reality returning in a rush.

Dear God, what have I done... again?

16

Sinjin knew the instant that Polly recovered from the climax he'd given her. She pushed at him, and he let her go, grimacing as, in her efforts to scramble away, she joggled his throbbing erection.

Shoving her skirts into place, she blurted, "I have to get back to the Hunt Academy. Before anyone realizes that I'm gone—"

"We'll send a message, let them know you're fine."

Which was more than he could say about his own damned state. In the past, he'd never made love to a woman without finding release himself; what would be the point of that? With Polly, however, he'd done so not once but twice, and, as frustrated as his physical state was, he also felt a bone-deep sense of satisfaction.

She was his. Her sweet honey on his fingers and lips proved it.

"But how will we explain—" she began.

"We'll go speak to you brother straightaway."

She blinked at him. "Speak to Ambrose? About... what?"

"Isn't it obvious? I'm going to offer for you," he heard himself say.

Of the two of them, he didn't know who was more shocked by

his words. As she continued to stare at him, slack-jawed and definitely not overjoyed, his satisfaction fizzled. Reality reared its ugly head, bringing agitation in its tow. How the hell was he going to handle *marriage*?

You have no choice. You compromised her. You have to marry her now.

Even in the face of panic, he couldn't wholly regret what had happened. *I believe you.* Sweeter words he'd never heard, and her passion had exceeded his wildest imaginings. God, the *fire* in her. In this, at least, they were well matched. As for the rest... his heart thudded. He'd have to figure out some way to hide his devils from her. To make sure that his future wife never saw him as he truly was... for the rest of their married lives.

Cold sweat broke out beneath his cravat. "Wife" and "marriage" were two words he'd believed would never enter his personal vocabulary, and Polly's continued, wordless scrutiny wasn't helping his jangled nerves. Why was she staring at him as if he'd proposed that they take a short stroll off Westminster Bridge together? Why wasn't she gratefully accepting his offer as any other miss in her shoes would have done?

"It isn't necessary," she said firmly.

If her silence had irked him, then her words furthered the trend. "Like hell it isn't. I've compromised you."

"Nothing unalterable happened. Technically speaking, I'm still, um... untouched."

The slight hitch in her sentence betrayed her uncertainty about the status of her virginity—*and well it should*, he thought on a surge of indignation.

"My fingers are still wet with your dew. I can bloody *taste* you," he pointed out ruthlessly. "Are you saying you don't feel my touch inside you?"

Her cheeks rosy, she said, "What happened was a mistake. We got carried away, but we can just put it behind us. No one has to know."

"I don't give a damn what anyone else knows. *I* know. And if you think I'm the sort of man who would shirk his obligation—"

"That's just it," she burst out. "I don't want to be married out of obligation—out of some misplaced sense of honor. You don't want to marry me, and don't try to tell me otherwise because I can see it in your aur—*eyes*, I mean." Her gaze flashed, her bosom heaving. "Which is just as well because I don't want to marry you either."

His palm itched for his calming locket, which of course he didn't have because he'd given it to her. Yet another thing she'd tried to refuse from him. Goddamnit, he was worried enough about his potential shortcomings as a husband. He didn't need the added burden of having to convince her of the sodding obvious: wedlock was no longer a choice.

"It doesn't bloody matter what either of us wants because I compromised you. You may not take stock in my honor, but I do. I seduced you in a carriage in the middle of the day, by God, and I'm going to do what is right!"

He hadn't meant to shout, but his intentions seemed to have little impact on his behavior where the infuriating chit was concerned. She sat there, blinking at him, and he wanted to punch the wall in frustration. God, what would it take to convince her that, right or wrong, she belonged to him now?

Because, he fumed, she bloody *did*.

"I do take stock in your honor as a gentleman," she said quietly. "That's not the issue."

He released a breath, one that he hadn't known he was holding. He didn't know why her faith in him should matter, but it did. "Then what is?" he pressed.

"I don't want you to marry me just because you have to."

"That's not the only reason." As the words left him, he realized they were true. He reached for her gloved hand, saw how small and fragile it was. Bringing it to his lips, he murmured, "You can't deny the attraction between us. The pleasure you've felt in my arms."

"That's just... desire." She drew her hand away, the movement shaky. Rather like her arguments. "It's not enough to overcome our differences."

Seeing the sensual awareness in her eyes calmed him, renewed his confidence. "Desire can make up for a lot of things, kitten. Let me prove it to you."

Pulse racing at his smoldering intent, she planted her palms against the bulwark of his shoulders. "That is what got us into trouble in the first place!"

"We were rubbing along just fine before we started talking. As I recall, you enjoyed my rubbing so well that—"

"That's not the point," she said desperately. "There are barriers between us. Ones that cannot and *should* not be ignored."

To her surprise, he backed away. Gave her a measuring look. "All right. Have at it. Tell me all the reasons bouncing around in your pretty head."

"You're going to listen?"

"Are you going to let me make love to you?"

"No!"

"Then I have nothing better to do." He shrugged, settling back against the cushions. "But you had better get on with things. We're not leaving this carriage until we settle the matter, and that means the longer you tarry, the more you risk getting caught with me."

Her head whirling, she blurted out the first reason that came to mind. "You're Rosie's."

"I beg your pardon?" He blinked at her.

"She had hopes where you're concerned, and I've betrayed her." Guilt cinching her throat, she looked down at her lap. How could she have done this... *again?*

"You must be joking."

Her head snapped up. "I am *not*. I have a sense of honor too. Rosie is my bosom chum, my sister in every way that counts—"

"For God's sake, do I look like a sodding hair ribbon to you?" He sounded thoroughly disgruntled. "I'm not an object one can lay claim upon with a word. I haven't given your sister any reason to believe that I have intentions toward her because I don't and never will. She has nothing to do with what goes on between you and me."

"It's still my fault for betraying her." Self-recrimination weighed like a sodden cloak.

"Bollocks."

She started at his expletive. "Pardon?"

"Your reasoning—it's shit," he said with stunning bluntness. "You and I acted on our impulses, and we'll both be paying a price. But not because of your sister. If she cannot relinquish some stupid fantasy—which, seeing as she knows nothing about me, is all it could possibly be—then that is not your problem. If she cannot forgive you for something that has naught to do with her, then she does not deserve your affection." Before Polly could absorb his words, he said, "Do you know what your trouble is?"

"What?" she said uneasily.

"You care too much what others think."

The second time hearing that message—the first time being from Rosie—didn't make it sting any less. Hurt wove a cocoon inside Polly, protecting her most vulnerable secrets. He knew *nothing* about her. He had never walked in the shadow of ostracism, had never known the pain of being rejected time and again. If her experiences had made her acutely aware of others' opinions, it was justly so.

He cocked a brow. "There you go again. Stewing on what I just said."

"I'm *not* stewing," she lied irately. "At any rate, it's easy for *you* not to care what others think because you're so popular. You know that you're a perfect specimen of manhood—the stuff of female fantasies!"

His expression turned fascinated. "Do *you* fantasize about me?"

Argh. Her head was going to explode. "That's not the point—"

"Kitten, it *is*. When it comes to our future, all that matters is you and me. As for other women," he said, his tone dismissive, "I don't give a damn because they don't know me. And do not, for an instant, mistake popularity for anything real. Before I came into my title and money, not a single well-bred miss wanted anything to do with me. As for the other sorts of females, all they are after is a meaningless escapade. Status, wealth, or a temporary diversion: that's what I am to women."

She couldn't believe that he thought that. "Women want you for far more than those things."

His brows lifted. "What else is there?"

"Well, you're intelligent and witty. You possess a keen sense of honor. You can be amusing when it suits you and..."

She caught his lips quirking and realized that she'd been had. She would have been piqued—had she not also seen his yearning. His glow intensified as he absorbed her compliments, a hunger gleaming in his eyes as if he were starved for her positive regard.

That he should care what she thought of him melted her insides like butter. Still she muttered, "You hardly need yet another female to extol your virtues."

"You're not just any female." He curled his finger under her chin. "Just so you know, you haven't provided a single valid reason for why we shouldn't get married."

"We're too different. And you just said you thought I'm too sensitive."

"I think you're adorable. You just need to grow a thicker skin, kitten, and I can teach you how, if you like. Trust me, I've had practice: my hide's thick as an elephant's."

She didn't know what flummoxed her more: the fact that he

had just called her *adorable* or that he, the confident, charismatic God of Revelry, had had to learn to protect himself from criticism.

But she mentioned neither of those things. Instead, she blurted the question foremost in her mind. "Why do you call me kitten?"

"Because you remind me of one with your big clear eyes. Then there's your hair, as soft and tawny as a newborn tabby." Just as his words battered at her defenses, he added, "Not to mention that sweet, furry little patch of yours that I want to pet again and again—"

"You shouldn't say such things," she choked out.

"Why not? It's the truth. Might as well get used to hearing it since we're to be married."

She could feel herself weakening, wanting what could never be. How could she even imagine wedding this vital, tempestuous man? With Sinjin, her secret would not be safe—nor her heart, she was honest enough to admit to herself. If they married and he discovered her abnormality... She shivered. The pain of his rejection would be too much to bear.

She had to put a stop to things now.

"I'm not the kind of woman you want for a wife," she said resolutely.

"I say you are."

"You don't know me. I... I'm not suited for the usual sort of marriage."

He regarded her with hooded eyes. "What sort of marriage do you want?"

She decided to give him part of the truth to throw him off her scent. "One that doesn't require intimacy. I'm a... private person." *Because I have to be.* "I have my own interests, and I want to lead my own separate life without my husband's interference."

What she described wasn't what she wanted at all but a necessary arrangement to protect her secret. It was the sort of match that would have been possible with Nigel Pickering-Parks. But Sinjin was the opposite of Nigel: he was too astute, too intense, too dashed attractive to make a comfortable spouse. And given the primal edge to his nature, she suspected wistfully that he'd be possessive and protective of the woman to whom he gave his name.

"Actually, the marriage you described *is* the usual sort amongst the *ton*," he said.

"Well, it's not usual for my family." She studied her hands, feeling even more forlorn.

When he didn't speak, she looked up—and realized that he was studying her. Thin golden strands wove through his aura, bolstering and steadying the roiling blue. He felt... hopeful?

Why?

"As it happens, I'm a private sort myself. Intimacy only leads to disappointment—and love? Even worse." He held her surprised gaze. "I'm not a man who wants entanglements. The kind of marriage I desire would be simple, easy. Both partners would be free to come and go as they please. We wouldn't have to answer to one another."

His reason for wanting a marriage of convenience hit home, and her heart gave a painful spasm. Which was ridiculous. She knew that he was a rake. A man of his appetites wouldn't settle for one woman when he could have a bevy of them at his beck and call. Extramarital affairs weren't uncommon in high society; love matches were far rarer. She supposed she ought to be thankful that he was simply more honest than most men about how he intended to carry on after he wed.

The idea of other women knowing his touches and kisses, enjoying the warmth of his attention, twisted her insides into jealous knots. Good heavens, imagine how she'd feel if they were *married*. It was one more reason why she and he did not suit.

"You misunderstand. I believe in fidelity," she said firmly. "I have no intention of having lovers, nor would I countenance my husband doing so."

"You're bloody right you won't be taking any lovers."

Her breath caught at the possessive heat simmering in his words. "But you just said... I'd be free to come and go as I please." She frowned. "Or did you mean that would apply only to you? Because that would be the most hypocritical—"

"No lovers for me either." His tone was unequivocal. "I meant that we would respect each other's interests and need for privacy. If I wanted time alone for my pursuits, you would grant it to me with no fuss. No demands or questions. And I would extend you the same courtesy. But those pursuits would not include violating the vows of marriage."

Recalling their conversation in the stillroom, she looked at him doubtfully. "But you said before that you've never been faithful."

"I said I've never *tried*. I've also never been married."

"You would try... for me?"

He yanked her onto his lap, startling a squeak from her. "It would be no sacrifice, given what I'd be getting in return. I have a feeling you'll wear me out and then some." Then shadows crept into his gaze, dimming the playful sensuality. "In all fairness, however, there's something else you ought to know about me."

Her head was spinning. "What is it?"

"I'm not... an easy man to deal with. I vow that I'd never hurt you, but I can have a devil of a temper, and my moods can be... unpredictable."

Having seen the stormy nature of his aura, she was hardly surprised by his admission. His moods were indeed mercurial and as intense as any she'd ever seen. But given her intimate acquaintance with emotions, she wasn't intimidated by his, and she'd never, not once, feared that he would do her harm.

"That is not a problem for me," she said honestly.

Relief forked like lightning through his gaze, along with a

yearning that spurred her heart into an unbridled pace. "Then what a time we'll have of it, kitten," he murmured, "enjoying the best of life without the complications. Say you'll have me."

Desire warred with her instinct for self-preservation. In theory, his proposal of an "easy" marriage sounded ideal, but could she actually carry it through?

Maintaining emotional distance from Nigel Pickering-Parks was one thing, Sinjin another altogether. What if she fell in love with him, only to have him spurn her when he discovered the truth of what she was? In hindsight, she knew that her heart had merely been bruised by Brockhurst; being rejected by Sinjin would shatter that organ irrevocably.

Opposing forces tore at her. "I... don't know."

"Then I'll court you until you do." Steely determination was back in his aura. "Give me a chance to convince you that a future is possible for us. Give me that at least."

Despite the looming pitfalls, she didn't have the willpower to refuse what she so dearly desired.

"All right," she said tremulously.

"Thank you, sweet." He brushed his knuckles against her cheek, the tender gesture weakening her defenses further. "The timing of our courtship is less than spectacular, given my situation, but I plan to hire Runners to follow Nicoletta. I'm certain they'll clear up the matter—"

"Heavens, I forgot!" In all the turmoil, the clue she'd found at Nicoletta's had slipped her mind. She dug into the pocket of her skirts and fished out the scrap of paper. "I found this."

He took it from her. "An old ticket from a play?"

"It fell out of a book on her desk." Peering intently at the lettering on the ticket, Polly said, "I've never heard of The Cytherea Theatre, have you?"

"It's a third-rate place near Drury Lane. The players' skills in bed are more of a draw than their abilities on stage."

"And how would you know that?" The words slipped out

before she could stop them. Dash it all, they weren't even engaged, and she already sounded like a jealous fishwife.

His lips curved in a lazy grin. "Sheath your claws, puss. I have no interest in third-rate wares—especially now that I've found myself a prime article."

She didn't know whether to be annoyed or flattered. Apparently, he found her reaction amusing, his smile deepening.

With a huff, she said, "As I was saying, I found this in one of her books—a rather ribald play, actually. Now we have a ticket from this theatre." She recalled how Miss French's aura hadn't matched the emotion she'd supposedly been feeling... which was what one might expect of a third-rate actress. "Put that together with the fact that Miss French was lying, as if she were playing a role, and I think we may have a lead."

"You think Nicoletta is an actress? That she staged the scene that night?" As Sinjin spoke, excitement blazed around him. "By Jove, that makes sense."

Polly nodded. "And that mysterious man whose voice you recalled had to be her accomplice. Perhaps he was the one who gave her the injuries, not you."

"Yes," Sinjin said hoarsely.

Seeing the relief percolating through his glow, Polly placed her hand on his. "The Cytherea is a clue, a place to start. We'll bring this new evidence to my brother. I know he'll help."

"Because you believe in me." His fingers engulfed hers in a tight grip. "Let's go speak to him now."

She bit her lip. "Can we wait until tomorrow?"

"Why?"

"I have to talk to my sister first," she whispered.

Her chest constricted at the thought of what she had to do. Of the only right course of action now. And she prayed for a miracle.

17

"You kissed the earl—*my* earl—*twice?*" Rosie said.

"I'm so sorry. I don't know how... it just happened," Polly said helplessly.

The two of them were sitting beneath the damask canopy of Rosie's bed. After supper, Polly had gone to her sister's bedchamber. The short distance had felt like a walk to the gallows, and, once there, she'd confessed everything, sparing only the most intimate of details.

She now waited, her heart thudding, for Rosie's response.

"How could you do that to me? You've been *lying* to me this entire time." Rosie jumped up, the ribbons on her nightrail fluttering, her stare accusatory. "Why, you've been acting no better than a strumpet behind my back!"

Riddled with guilt and shame, Polly rose as well, held out a beseeching hand. "I know what I did was wrong. Please believe I never meant to hurt you. I'll do whatever it takes to earn your forgiveness—"

"Give him up."

Polly's throat convulsed. Her hand fell slowly to her side. "I... can't."

"You mean you *won't*," Rosie said icily.

"I don't know if he and I will have a future together, but I have to give the possibility a chance." She tried to think of an explanation that wouldn't alienate her sister further. Some way to explain how, despite the differences between her and Sinjin, they were like iron and lodestone, drawn together by some irresistible, elemental force. "He wants the same thing as I do, Rosie. A marriage in which we would each have privacy. I'd be able to keep my affliction to myself and—"

"So you're lying to him like you've lied to me."

Rosie's words sliced into her, but she shook her head. "I'm not lying to him. Sinjin wishes to have a marriage free of entanglements. He neither expects, nor wants, us to share emotional intimacies."

She'd sensed that he had his own secrets he wanted to keep, but that was fine by her. Indeed, in this regard, they were an ideal match.

"*Sinjin?*"

At the fury behind Rosie's whisper, Polly knew her mistake immediately. Her pulse skittering, she said, "I know I deserve your anger—"

"You took the one thing that I wanted." Rosie's hands bracketed her hips. "You know how much this match meant to me!"

Polly swallowed. Hung her head. "I know."

"I would have never done the same to you," Rosie raged on.

"I'm sorry," she said wretchedly.

"He was the answer to all my problems, and you stole him away!"

Polly didn't know what else to say. Yet in the midst of her spiraling self-recrimination, Sinjin's words came to her.

If your sister cannot relinquish some stupid fantasy... seeing as she knows nothing about me... that is not your problem. If she cannot forgive you... then she does not deserve your affection.

Harsh words and ones that Polly did not agree with—at least,

not entirely. She *was* at fault for hurting Rosie. But Sinjin's asser-
tions did make her think: how well *did* Rosie know him? It wasn't
as if she had spent a great deal of time with him. And, as he'd said,
other than the usual courtesies, he hadn't shown any intentions
toward her.

Inhaling, Polly said, "What I did was wrong, but I didn't steal
him."

"Yes, you *did*. You knew I wanted him." Rosie's arms crossed
over her bosom.

"I did know, and, for that, I can only ask for your forgiveness.
I was wrong not to be honest with you from the start. The truth
is, I didn't understand my own feelings, and I didn't know that Sin
—the earl had any interest in me."

"How could you bloody not know?" her sister snapped.

"Because no one's been interested in me before," she said
quietly. "Not truly."

Something flitted through Rosie's eyes, but her chin remained
lifted. "That doesn't excuse what you did. You stole the man I
love—"

"*Do* you love him?" Polly studied her sister.

"He's handsome, rich, *and* a peer. Everything I wanted. I
would have fallen in love with him eventually—if you hadn't
snatched him from under my nose!"

Rosie's words confirmed what Polly believed. And gave her
courage to say what was in her heart.

"I'm not trying to excuse my behavior. It was my fault for not
sharing my feelings about the earl, confused as they were."
Releasing a breath, Polly went on, "But I didn't take anything
from you, Rosie, because the truth is he wasn't yours to take. You
may have been infatuated with him, but you don't know him.
Sinjin is more than a stepladder to social success; he *deserves* to be
seen as more." The truth flowed from her like water released from
a valve. "I don't know if he and I have a future together, but I'm

going to stand by his side now. To help him through his present troubles because I believe in him—in the man he wants to be."

The room fell silent. Polly didn't know what else to say. She'd let it all pour out in a way she'd never done before, and now there was nothing left for her to do. Except wait.

"Get out," Rosie said flatly. "I don't want to see you or speak to you ever again."

Anguish gnarled her insides. Heat pushed behind her eyes, but she pushed it back.

"I'm sorry," she whispered.

"Just go!"

She did as her sister asked.

18

At one o'clock the following afternoon, Sinjin strode into Kent's study. His gaze circled the room, noting the presence of the Strathavens and Kent before landing on Polly. Despite the undercurrent of tension in the room, the sight of her calmed him, his apprehension replaced by a swell of possessiveness.

He'd never known that sense of... rightness about a woman before—hell, about anything in his life. When he'd proposed to her, he'd done so on blind instinct, with a gut-deep hope that somehow he could make a marriage work. But then she'd told him the kind of union *she* wanted, and the truth had struck him: she was exactly what he needed and never thought he could find.

A gently bred lady who saw him as more than a fashionable catch. A sweet wanton who aroused both his body and his mind, showing him pleasure unlike any he'd experienced before... and he hadn't even had her yet. In truth, everything with her felt new and different, giving rise to a heretofore dormant sense of optimism: could his future be better than his past?

Although he didn't fully comprehend the reasons behind her need for privacy, he didn't care. As far as he was concerned, it made her the *perfect* match for him. They would have passion and, he hoped, a kind of... friendship.

I believe you. Her three simple words had rocked him to the core.

But he would have to have a plan for when his devils attacked, to shield her from who he became under their influences. The black devil was the lesser of his worries. In the past, women were drawn to him in this state: his euphoric energy and neck-or-nothing confidence, his insatiable sexual appetite. When the pendulum swung in this direction, he could fuck for hours—couldn't get enough—and his gut told him that, with Polly, this would not be a problem.

Hell, she'd come *twice* with him in the carriage, fully clothed. Imagining what he could do to her naked in a bed, he'd had to relieve himself several times last night. Even so, seeing her now, with her plump coral lips and big kitten eyes, he felt a hot stirring in his blood.

He would still have the blue devil to contend with, but for that he could fall back on their agreement about privacy. The freedom for each to do as he or she wished with no questions asked. Thus, when his spirits took that despicable plunge, he would retreat somewhere—an apartment he could keep for such purposes. He would commit to going there if he was low... or if his high turned to ill-temper. He wouldn't emerge until he was himself again. He'd make sure she never saw him at his pathetic worst.

As long as he kept Polly's expectations low and his devils hidden, there was no reason why he couldn't make a go of marriage with her. Of course, he had to convince her family that he would make a worthy husband and hence his presence in Kent's study.

Judging from his future in-laws' expressions, he realized the task would not be easy. Kent stood, glowering at him behind his desk. The Strathavens flanked Polly, the duchess beside her on the settee, the duke posted like a sentinel behind the ladies.

Whether they liked it or not, Sinjin was going to make Polly his; for her sake, however, he would prefer their blessing. It was clear that she shared close relationships with her kin, and he didn't want her to feel the strain of opposing loyalties.

He bowed. "Thank you all for seeing me."

"Polly told us you would be calling." Kent's scowl conveyed his feelings about the visit. "You'll understand why I am not best pleased to learn of your escapade with my sister yesterday."

The man didn't know the half of it. Polly had said that she would tell her brother about her meeting with Nicoletta but not the rest of what had transpired—*thank God*. Heat crept up beneath Sinjin's collar. He'd never gone courting before, hadn't imagined he would need more than his title and wealth to recommend him. But Kent clearly saw through those trappings, and Sinjin felt like a schoolboy called to the carpet by an exacting schoolmaster.

As he fumbled for an excuse, Polly spoke up.

"As I explained, it wasn't Lord Revelstoke's fault," she said steadfastly. "He didn't know that I intended to interview Miss French. I did that all on my own."

"You were alone with him in his carriage," her brother bit out.

"The earl was only trying to protect me. Get me to safety," she insisted.

Her defense of him affected him the way her belief in him had. It was like being struck by a blast of sunshine during a rain shower: unexpected and stunning, its warmth glimmered through him. With the exception of his brother, no one had ever stood up for him, and she was certainly the first female to do so.

Yet as much as he savored his kitten's loyalty, he was a man who could speak for himself.

"Sir, I regret the circumstances that brought Miss Kent and I together," he said, "but I do not regret the consequences. She came to my aid when no one else would, and you may rest assured that I will do right by her."

"You embroiled my sister in your affairs. You've *compromised* her." Kent's palms slammed onto his desk, and he leaned forward, his expression foreboding. "How the devil will you rectify that?"

"By requesting your permission to court her."

"You want to *court* my sister?"

"I want to marry her, actually. But she wanted more time to be certain of her feelings." He nodded at Polly, who was blushing, looking so damned adorable that he ached. "Although the circumstances of how I met your sister are admittedly less than fortuitous, I give you my word as a gentleman that my intentions are honorable. I will woo her until she consents to be my wife."

He directed the last part at Polly. Despite her stated ambivalence about their future, she was looking at him as if he could hang stars in the sky for her. He wanted her to look at him thus *always*. Beside her, the duchess let out a heartfelt sigh.

"Out of the question." Kent's peremptory tone dispelled the moment. "You are not wooing, much less marrying, my sister."

Sinjin wasn't surprised by Kent's stance, nor was he cowed by it. "I am, sir, unless she tells me no. Even then, I will move heaven and earth to convince her to be mine."

"How romantic," Her Grace whispered to Polly. "Strathaven was the same way, you know."

Behind his wife, His Grace aimed his gaze to the ceiling.

"Need I remind you, Revelstoke," Kent went on grimly, "that you stand accused of a heinous crime. In all good conscience, I cannot allow my sister to be associated with a man who is quite possibly a brute."

A muscle leapt in Sinjin's jaw. He might deserve Kent's righteous scorn, but he wasn't a fellow used to standing down to anyone. As he struggled to control his rising temper, Polly popped up from the settee and came to his side, so that they faced her brother together.

"That is why you must help clear his name, Ambrose," she said earnestly, "because he didn't commit that crime. As I told you earlier, I am *absolutely certain* Miss French was lying. You know you can trust me on this."

Evidently, Kent took uncommon stock in his youngest sister's judgement, for he said in terse tones, "Be that as it may, he's still not good enough for you. He is the architect of his own troubles. You know his reputation. And the fact that he was at that den of iniquity in the first place—"

"I'm sure Strathaven was no stranger to such places before our marriage," the duchess chimed in. "And look at him now."

"Why am I being dragged into this?" the duke said, raising a brow.

His lady twisted around to look at him. "Because you were a rake just like Revelstoke here, and look how well you turned out."

"I'm glad you think so." The duke's gaze dropped to her throat, and he slipped a finger beneath her choker of pearls, the touch more than a little proprietary. He smiled faintly. "I couldn't have done it without your reformatory efforts, pet."

Color stole up the duchess' cheeks. "Nonsense, you were always a good man. You just needed the right motivation to change your ways. And the earl appears to be in much the same situation."

Sinjin didn't know what to make of the fact that Her Grace apparently was taking his side. He cast a questioning look at Polly; she gave him a small smile in return.

"You cannot be serious, Emma," Kent protested.

"I am," the duchess replied. "Recall how you didn't approve of Strathaven, either, and yet he's turned out to be the best of husbands. Why shouldn't Revelstoke be given the same chance to prove his worth? He seems to be genuine in his suit, and *Polly* believes him." Her brows lifted with a significance that Sinjin didn't fully understand. "Of all of us, Polly is the most equipped to judge true from false—and to make decisions about her own future."

Looking disgruntled, Kent crossed his arms over his chest. "I cannot condone our youngest sister being involved with a man with Revelstoke's past—and that's to say nothing of his present troubles."

"I'm hiring Runners," Sinjin intervened swiftly. "To look into the clue that Pol—I mean, Miss Kent, found. Thanks to her ingenuity, we now have reason to believe that Nicoletta French has a connection to..."—he darted a glance at Her Grace—"a theatre. Of sorts."

He had no problem being frank, but the last thing he wanted was to offend the one member of Polly's family who was championing his cause. Nor did he think that Strathaven would take well to his bringing up a brothel poorly disguised as a theatre in front of the duchess.

"Oh, we're familiar with The Cytherea," Her Grace said cheerfully. "We've been there."

Sinjin's brows shot up, his gaze veering to Strathaven.

"Be forewarned, my lord," the duke said wryly. "Marrying a Kent is not for the faint-hearted."

"Pish posh. You know I did a marvelous job interviewing that actress at The Cytherea when we were busy clearing *your* name." Turning to Sinjin, Her Grace added, "As to Runners, we'll not hear of it. This matter concerns your future, which now concerns Polly's future, and therefore the future of this family. No one but the best will do. Which is why Ambrose will take on the case himself, won't he? With my assistance, of course."

"You've always said that everyone is deserving of justice, Ambrose," Polly put in. "Surely you cannot stand by and let a man you know to be innocent be accused of a crime he did not commit? Whoever concocted this reprehensible plan may have

other schemes planned against him. You must help him. Please—
for my sake."

Kent's mien was one of aggrieved resignation. Sinjin even felt
empathy for the man. It couldn't be easy being faced with those
wide-eyed feminine pleas.

"Bloody hell." The investigator dropped into his chair. To no
one in particular, he muttered, "Why couldn't I have had
brothers?"

"You have Harry, and he's more trouble than us by far," Her
Grace said.

"My brother Harry is a genius and a scientist, but he has a
penchant for blowing things to smithereens," Polly said in an
undertone.

Sinjin wondered why she didn't seem like she was jesting.

"Thank you, Ambrose," Polly went on softly. "And you as well,
Emma."

Her sister beamed; her brother just shook his head.

"Now that that's settled, we ought to work out a plan of
attack," the duchess said.

Kent drummed his fingers on the desk. "At this point, we have
naught but hunches concerning Miss French. We need evidence
of her true identity before we consider other suspects. The place
to begin the search appears to be The Cytherea."

"No time like the present," Her Grace said. "Shall we take
your carriage or ours?"

"I'm coming too," Polly said.

"I appreciate the offer, sweeting, but The Cytherea is no place
for you," Sinjin countered.

"On this, we agree," Kent declared.

"Polly could prove useful." Her Grace delivered a meaningful
look to her brother. "After all, she's the one who discovered the
connection to The Cytherea. Strathaven and I will escort her."

"I won't be any trouble at all," Polly promised, "and I'll be
perfectly safe with all of you present. Please. Let me help."

She turned big, beseeching eyes first to her brother, then to Sinjin. God help him, Sinjin couldn't be the one to refuse her. Besides, everyone in that room would protect her—he, himself, would do so to his dying breath.

"Fine. Polly goes with Em and Strathaven. The earl,"—Kent jerked his chin in Sinjin's direction—"rides with me."

19

Descending from the carriage, Polly spotted Sinjin and Ambrose standing at the entrance of a rickety building. Over their heads, a painted sign boldly proclaimed, "Welcome to The Cytherea: Where Every Performance Guarantees a Happy Ending."

Polly hurried over, accompanied by Em and the duke.

"There's an entrance around the corner," His Grace said. "It'll take us directly backstage."

"Lead the way," Ambrose said.

As they all moved on, Polly whispered worriedly to Sinjin, "How was the ride over with Ambrose?"

"You've heard of the Spanish Inquisition?" came the wry reply.

"Oh *no*. I'm so sorry—"

"Kitten, I'm teasing. Be at ease."

Searching his vivid midnight blue gaze and aura, she saw that he *was* teasing. Partly, anyway, for faint annoyance did speckle his glow.

"Did Ambrose ask a lot of intrusive questions?" she said.

"He asked me questions that any good brother would ask. In his shoes, I'd do the same."

"Thank you for understanding," she said softly.

"You're welcome. Thank you for believing in me."

Basking in the warmth of his regard, she returned his words. "You're welcome."

His lips formed an almost boyish curve. He was always handsome, but when he smiled at her this way, his mouth a gentle contrast to the wicked slash of his cheekbones and hard line of his jaw, he was undoubtedly the most beautiful man she'd ever seen. He tucked her gloved hand in the crook of his arm and guided her through the entryway, bending his head to avoid the low-hanging beam.

Inside, her eyes slowly adjusted to the windowless gloom. She saw a host of cluttered vanities, dark islands around which some dozen or so actresses gathered. The women were laughing and chatting as they primped themselves in the cracked looking glasses, their auras flittering around them like bright butterflies.

Polly's eyebrows rose at the cast's skimpy attire. Most of the ladies wore short filmy robes, paint... and very little else. She glanced at Sinjin to gauge his response.

He was scanning the crowd impatiently. "Who should we talk to first, I wonder?"

"Well, knock me down with a feather! If it isn't my fair lady." A bespectacled blond fellow came rushing over, and, to Polly's surprise, stopped before Emma. His waistcoat was ink-stained and his cravat raggedy, but he made a leg with remarkable flourish. "Miss Kent, how smashing of you to pay me another visit," he said with a dazzling smile.

"She's the Duchess of Strathaven now." His Grace came to stand behind Em, his icy green gaze narrowed on the newcomer's face.

The blond fellow's enthusiasm dimmed. "Oh... you brought *him* back as well."

"Everyone, this is Mr. Dunn," Em said briskly. "He's the resident playwright, and we made his acquaintance during the course of another case. Mr. Dunn, I'm afraid we need your help again."

"I live to be of service to you, lovely lady," the playwright declared.

From the look on her brother-in-law's face, Polly predicted that if Mr. Dunn continued in this vein, his days of being of service would be numbered.

She spoke up hastily. "Mr. Dunn, we're looking for information concerning Nicoletta French. We believe she may have some connection with this theatre."

The playwright's bespectacled gaze shifted to her. He jolted as if struck by a thunderbolt.

"You," he breathed.

"Um... pardon?"

He advanced, stopping just short of her, and, to her shock, dropped down on one knee.

"Daughter of Zeus, just *look* at your eyes," he said ardently. "Erato, Calliope, Thalia—you are all the muses and more wrapped up in one divine package. You, fairest maiden, are the inspiration I have been searching for."

"Thought I were your inspiration, Dunny," a blond actress called out good-naturedly.

"Then 'e 'ad you and 'is inkwell ran dry," her friend snickered.

"A pen wot keeps a hard nib ain't easy to find," the first one agreed, and they fell into each other, laughing and snorting.

"Dilettantes. Ignore them, my sweet one." Dunn reached for Polly's hand.

"Touch her, and you'll regret it."

Sinjin's low warning dispelled Polly's bemusement at the whole exchange. Her head swung in his direction; his aura was afire with possessiveness. A warm, tingling sensation spread in her belly.

Sighing, Dunn rose and dusted off his trousers. "He belongs to you, I suppose?"

"Um..." She darted a look at Sinjin's predatory countenance, uncertain how to respond.

"She's mine." Sinjin's reply was unequivocal. "Stay away from her."

"Where do you ladies find such troglodytes?" Dunn held his hands up when Sinjin took a menacing step forward. "Easy there, big fellow. No need to make mincemeat of me over a jest."

Polly laid a staying hand on Sinjin's upper arm. Beneath the navy superfine, she felt the bulging power of his muscles... and her pussy gave a shocking, moist flutter. At the same time, she realized that her nipples had risen, stiff and throbbing, beneath her bodice. She blinked, wetting her lips. Sinjin's gaze followed the path of her tongue, and his gaze grew heavy-lidded, as if he could sense her arousal.

Satisfaction smoldering in his aura, he took the hand she touched him with, pressing a brief yet proprietary kiss over her gloved knuckles before letting her go.

"See here, Dunn." Ambrose took over with authority. "Do you know Nicoletta French?"

"No," the playwright said sulkily.

"She likely went by another name," her brother said. "She's about five and a half feet tall, black hair, hazel eyes."

Dunn pushed his spectacles up. "That describes half the doves that nest in this place, not to mention the flock of fly-by-nights who roost here now and again. You need to be more specific."

"Her voice was on the lower end of the register for a female. She had a habit of twitching her skirts—a likely sign of nerves. Her accent is polished but from elocution lessons, I believe, as the Cockney is discernable beneath—"

"Egad, are you some sort of human magnifying glass?" Dunn stared at Ambrose. "You can't expect that I would notice such obscure details."

Frowning, her brother said, "You requested more specifics."

"I meant about her, ahem,"—he cast a hasty glance at Polly and Em—"physical attributes?"

Ambrose inhaled, as if for patience. "Her build is on the voluptuous side."

"Oooh, lovey, you got to be more precise than that. Most all o' us fit that bill." An actress with brassy ringlets sauntered over, her short pink dressing gown leaving little to the imagination. "The name's Sweet Pea, an' bein' a warm-'earted sort, I'd be willing to 'elp you out." She held out a hand, palm up. "For a small donation, o' course."

With a sigh, Ambrose took out his coin purse.

The money disappeared into Sweet Pea's pink robe, and she emitted an ear-splitting whistle. "C'mon, doves, let's show these nobs what The Cytherea 'as to offer!"

Like whirling dervishes, the actresses moved in a flurry of motion and color. When the dust settled, Polly saw that they'd arranged themselves in a line of impressive precision. Their poses were identical: each had their hands on their hips, their right legs jutting saucily forward. The women were so synchronized, so uniform in the front that they presented, that it took Polly a moment to recognize the principle by which they'd organized themselves.

A shocked giggle rose up her throat.

"They call it the, ahem, buffet queue. Everything on the menu, organized from a bite-sized aperitif,"—Dunn gestured to the woman with the scantest curves at the start of the line—"to a full-fledged entrée." The woman on the other end wriggled her remarkably generous bosom and rump.

"So which o' us does this Miss French o' yours most resemble?" Sweet Pea called from the middle of the line.

Ambrose lifted a brow at Sinjin. His tone cool, he said, "Well, my lord?"

Sinjin's cheekbones were stained a dull red. He slid a glance at Polly, who gave him an encouraging nod. He'd never hidden who he was before they met, and she wasn't about to hold his past against him now. With marriage as a possibility between them, she wanted them to be honest with one another—as honest as they could be anyway.

When still he hesitated, she took the bull by the horns. Gesturing toward two curvy brunettes, she said, "From my recollection, I'd say Miss French fits between those two ladies."

"But not as buxom as you, luvie, eh?" Sweet Pea said with a friendly wink. "Got a fortune 'iding 'neath that nun's 'abit, I'd wager."

Blood rushed into Polly's cheeks. Although the woman's compliment appeared genuine, its frankness took her aback.

"Kindly refrain from addressing Miss Kent in that manner," Sinjin said coldly.

"Oo, protective, ain't you, guv?" the woman cooed. "Not to worry, just making a comparison to get a clearer picture o' the dove you're looking for."

"I'd concur with Miss Kent's assessment, shifting one position closer to the end," Sinjin muttered after an instant.

Sweet Pea and Dunn looked at each other.

"Nymphea," they said.

"Pardon?" Polly said.

"This Nicoletta French o' yours—could be our Nymphea Flott," Sweet Pea explained. "Now 'er 'air weren't dark like you said. It were a sandy brown, but changin' the color o' one's coif, well, that's as easy as switchin' out a frock for us trained professionals." She preened, flipping a lock over her shoulder. "But 'er shape, no changin' that, and 'er place in the buffet queue was right where the toff says, 'twixt Hyacinth and Orchid."

"Miss Flott no longer works here, I presume?" Ambrose said.

"Worked 'ere for l'il o'er a year, then moved on 'bout two months ago," the actress replied. To her colleagues, she said, "Back to work, doves," and the other players scattered like bright marbles.

Ambrose whipped out his trusty notebook. "What else can you tell us about her?"

"Nymphea wasn't a friendly sort. Always 'ad airs an' thought she was better than she ought to be." Sweet Pea sniffed. "But she 'ad 'er share o' nightly patrons."

Polly noticed a flicker in the woman's aura. A spark of ambivalence, doubt... as if she recalled something but didn't think it important enough to share?

"Whatever you remember, Miss Sweet Pea, no matter how minor, could prove useful," Polly coaxed. "Please tell us anything that comes to mind."

"Now that you mention it, I did see 'er wif a fellow once. A follower, I mean—not a customer."

"Tell us more about him," Sinjin said intently.

Twirling a curl around her finger, Sweet Pea said, "Don't know 'is name or much else. Only saw 'im that once, mind, and I weren't paying much attention. First rule o' The Cytherea: don't poach on another's territory," she said virtuously. "But wot wif 'im being as big as a 'ouse, 'e was a 'ard one to miss. Black 'air, night beard afore noon, eyes mean as a snake. And 'is voice was so deep it was more o' a rumble."

Polly saw the excitement radiating from Sinjin. Sweet Pea's description was a spot-on match for the male voice he'd heard that night. This had to be Nicoletta's accomplice.

"The cove came 'round right afore Nymphea left. 'Eard the pair o' 'em kicking up a dust in the alley. Dunno wot it was about." Sweet Pea shrugged. "And that's all I know 'bout im."

"You mentioned Nymphea's patrons earlier," Ambrose said, his pencil poised. "Could you name them?"

"Ain't enough pages in your book, luv," Sweet Pea drawled.

"Could you provide us with a list?" Sinjin said to the playwright.

Dunn nodded. "Would take a bit of time to question the girls and go through the ledgers, but I reckon I could come up with something."

After further questioning, it became apparent that Sweet Pea and Dunn had disclosed all they knew. Thanking the pair, Polly and the others returned outside where their carriages stood waiting.

"That was productive," Polly said brightly.

"Indeed." Hope was fierce in Sinjin's gaze.

"What next?" Em said to the group at large.

"Strathaven will take you and Polly home," Ambrose stated.

From her brother's tone of voice, Polly knew that he would not be swayed. Evidently, Em knew this as well for she said merely, "What about you, Ambrose? Where are you going?"

"Revelstoke and I are paying another visit to Nicoletta French, Nymphea Flott, or whatever the blazes her name is," he said grimly. "We're going to get to the bottom of this."

20

G iven the proximity of the theatre to Nicoletta's lodging,
Sinjin and Kent arrived at their destination within
minutes. Throughout the ride, Kent had seemed preoccupied, his
focus clearly upon what they'd just learned. Sinjin, for his part, felt
a mix of relief and anticipation.

At last, there was proof that he hadn't made up the mysterious
man—that Nicoletta French was not what she seemed. Proof that
he'd been framed and wasn't the brute that she and her accomplice had tried to make him out to be. And now, with the help of
Polly's family, he would soon unravel the sinister web and clear his
name and conscience.

Then he could go to Polly a free man.

As they headed up the front steps of No. 12 Castle Street,
Kent said curtly, "Let me lead the interview, my lord. It's critical
to strike a balance: if we intimidate her too much, she won't talk."

"All right. But if I…"

Sinjin trailed off at the same time that Kent stilled beside him.
The front door was ajar.

"Stay behind me," the investigator ordered.

Sinjin followed the other man inside, his neck prickling at the eerie stillness of the foyer. Sunshine shafted in through the transom above the door, gilding the dancing dust motes, the only movement in the room. No sounds of domestic activity, no voices... His ears twitched at a faint shuffling noise, and he tried to discern its origin. He gestured toward the hallway.

Kent jerked his chin, and the two of them advanced stealthily down the corridor, deeper into the heart of the house. The rustling grew louder, coming from the room up ahead—the parlor where Sinjin had found Polly the other day. He and Kent were almost within the line of vision of the open door. With their backs against the wall, they consulted silently. The investigator hiked his thumb at his own chest, then made a staying motion at Sinjin.

His gestured instructions were clear: *I'm going in, you stay here.*

Like hell Sinjin would.

Kent was already moving, swiftly rounding the doorway into the room. His voice emerged the next instant, calm yet commanding. "Stay where you are. I just want to talk."

"*Buggering hell.*" The deep bass voice was straight out of Sinjin's nightmare.

He didn't pause, sprinted inside. A startling tableau greeted him: Nicoletta lying on the carpet, a scarlet bloom on her chest, a hulking black-haired man standing over her with a pistol in his fist. The gun was aimed at Kent. Instinct coiled Sinjin's muscles. He sprang forward, diving for Polly's brother as the shot went off in a deafening blast.

21

Three days later, Polly stepped into the sunshine, her hand on the sleeve of Sinjin's jacket. His gleaming phaeton stood waiting in front of the house, the pair of matched bays bridling in their harnesses and stamping their hooves.

"I can't believe we're going for a ride together," she murmured. "It seems so..."

"Ordinary?" When she nodded, he placed his hand over hers, giving it a light squeeze before handing her up into the equipage. "After everything that has happened, I'd say we've earned a little normality, kitten."

She couldn't agree more.

Three days ago, Sinjin and Ambrose had found Miss French shot through the heart, her killer standing red-handed over her. The blackguard had tried to commit murder yet again, but Sinjin had foiled his attempt. He'd pushed Ambrose out of harm's way, and, thankfully, the shot had missed them both. Unfortunately, the villain had gotten away, but the truth of what had happened at Corbett's had finally come to light.

Ambrose had discovered a blackmail note on Nicoletta's desk. Signed by the dead woman, it had been addressed to Sinjin and contained a nefarious demand: pay five thousand pounds or she would bring charges of assault against him. She'd stated that she'd convinced Corbett of her story and would use the powerful businessman as a corroborating witness. She'd threatened to spread word of Sinjin's brutality to the gossip rags and destroy his reputation unless he paid for her silence.

The extortion attempt had been well planned, but something must have gone dangerously awry between Nicoletta and her accomplice. Ambrose hypothesized that they'd had an argument, over the money perhaps, and, in a fit of rage, the man with the deep voice had shot his lover dead. At present, Ambrose and his partners were on the hunt for Nicoletta's co-conspirator and murderer.

Although questions remain unanswered, Ambrose no longer had any doubt that Sinjin had been the victim, not the perpetrator, of a heinous crime. The evidence found at Nicoletta's lodgings had compelled him to revise his assessment of Sinjin—that and the fact that he owed his life to the other man's bravery.

Hence, Polly was allowed on this, her first drive, with Sinjin. It was all very proper, an unchaperoned ride in an open carriage deemed permitted behavior. For Polly, it was a thrill nonetheless to spend time alone with Sinjin, even if only for a short journey through Hyde Park.

He vaulted into the high perch, settling beside her. With the dreadful business over, it became clear to Polly just how much of a strain he'd been under. 'Twas as if a dark cloud had passed, his true brilliance now shining through. Goodness, she didn't know how it was possible, but he was even *more* devastatingly handsome than before.

Shadows no longer hung beneath his vivid eyes. His chiseled features were smooth and rested. His deep blue jacket, striped waistcoat, and biscuit-colored trousers clung to his muscular physique. He exuded male power, his virility undeniable.

Although she'd worn her best promenade dress—a white

dotted Swiss muslin with ruffles on the high bodice—she wished she was more his match. Perhaps she ought to consider trying a more daring and fashionable silhouette. Then again, how could she ever compare with his perfection? If she tried to, she might draw more attention to her flaws and end up looking even more foolish... like a partridge masquerading in a swan's feathers.

With a practiced snap of the reins, he set the spirited horses into motion, the smooth ride dispelling some of her doubts. She told herself to focus on the beauty of the moment, which had been hard-fought for. The usual city brouhaha—clattering vehicles, shouting hawkers and tradesmen—made it difficult to do more than make small talk until they passed the gates of the park. Once within the leafy enclosure, they found an oasis. Frenzy gave way to birdsong and the muted conversations of the fashionable crowd on horse or on foot.

Polly noted the curious looks aimed in their direction—not surprising, since Sinjin caused a furor wherever he went. By supper, word would be all over Town that he'd been seen in her company. Anxiety surged; she had enough concerns about the feasibility of marriage to Sinjin without the added pressure of being placed in Society's fishbowl.

"We'll avoid Rotten Row," Sinjin said as if gleaning her thoughts. "Too crowded by far."

He navigated them toward a quieter, winding path that took them along the banks of the sparkling Serpentine. Polly couldn't help but admire the way he handled the reins. Unlike many sporting gentlemen, Sinjin showed no unnecessary flourishes. He didn't need to: his masterful driving said it all. His horses clearly knew who was in charge for they responded with exquisite precision to his maneuvering.

Having experienced the strength and skill of Sinjin's touch, Polly understood the horses' reaction. The memory of his love-making in the carriage momentarily fogged her brain. Shameless wanton that she was, she'd relived that magic more than once in the privacy of her own head.

"Penny for your thoughts?" Sinjin said.

Her cheeks warmed. Since she couldn't very well tell him that she'd been having lustful fantasies of him, she said the next closest thing on her mind. "I was wondering how you're faring now that the nasty business with Nicoletta French is over."

"I'm relieved," he said, "and I will be more so once your brother apprehends her accomplice. Questions remain that I want answered." He frowned. "I still don't understand, for instance, why she and her co-conspirator didn't try to extort me sooner, why they waited as long as they did."

"Perhaps because they couldn't locate you at Mrs. Barlow's retreat?" Polly suggested. "Or perhaps they thought they'd take your father's br—money first. Drain him of what they could before they moved onto you."

"There's no need to sugar coat: my father did pay her for her silence," he said flatly, "and you've likely hit the nail on the head with the rest of it as well."

His expression didn't change, but she saw the dark pain seeping into his light. She wondered, not for the first time, about his family. Her own would support her through anything, and she didn't understand why the Duke of Acton wouldn't believe in his own son's innocence. In the past, Sinjin had proved reticent about his kin, but now they had the opportunity for deeper conversation.

Proceeding with caution, she said, "Have you spoken to him about the latest developments?"

A muscle jerked in Sinjin's jaw. "I sent him a note."

"Did he reply?"

He gave a curt nod.

When he said no more, she prompted, "What did he say?"

Sinjin's broad shoulders hitched in a careless shrug. "That he was glad the business was over and hoped I wouldn't besmirch the family name again."

"You didn't in the first place," she said hotly. "It wasn't your fault that the villains targeted you. You were an innocent victim. How could the duke blame you?"

"I wouldn't say I was innocent, exactly." His tone was wry. "As for my father blaming me, that's nothing new. I'm the black sheep of the family. My eldest brother Stephan was the golden child and deservedly so. He was so damned perfect he ought to have been annoying—except he wasn't. He was the most decent fellow I've ever met."

Seeing his grief, she said softly, "You miss him."

"Yes."

"You have a half-brother, don't you?" she ventured.

"Theodore's a prat." His mouth formed a cynical line. "No surprise, coming from the womb he did."

Heavens, Sinjin truly did not get along with his family. Wanting to know more of his past, she said carefully, "What about your own mama? Were you close to her?"

"She died when I was five." Emotions clashed, an ambivalent tangling. "She wasn't mourned. Catherine Pelham was a blight on the Acton name, you see. Not only was her family in trade—my father married her to replenish the family coffers—but she also had a scandalous habit of collecting lovers. In fact, she was running away with one when their ship went down off the coast of Dorset."

Beneath the jaded words lay sorrow... and yearning.

"No matter what she did, she was your mama," Polly said gently.

They passed beneath a leafy canopy, a lattice of shadows crossing his face. "I don't remember her much, but what I do remember is mostly good," he admitted in gruff tones. "She laughed a lot. Sang to me. *Bye, Baby Bunting...* I can still recall her voice soothing me to sleep."

"My mama sang that lullaby to us as well. She died when I was six, and I still miss her."

"Tell me more about your family."

His genuine interest made it easy to talk about herself. She recounted what life had been like back in Chudleigh Crest while carefully omitting any mention of her peculiarity. She described the cozy cottage, the creek where she and her siblings had liked to swim, and the schoolhouse where her papa had imparted wisdom to generations of children. She shared some of her family's good times as well as some of the difficult ones.

She avoided mention of Rosie; their continuing estrangement was too painful to address. He seemed to understand and didn't press her on the topic. There were plenty of other things to converse about, and he seemed vastly entertained, even laughing aloud as she related some of the Kents' adventures.

When he asked about the large age difference between her and Ambrose, she explained, "Ambrose is actually my half-brother, as his mama was Papa's first wife, but he's as kin to me as my other siblings. In fact, he's more like a father to me in some ways. He's provided for the family since I was a little girl, when our father first fell ill."

"That's why he's so protective of you."

She nodded. "Ambrose is the best of brothers—and of men. He won't stop until he sees justice done. I know he'll settle your case before long."

"I hope that's true as I have important matters I'd like to get on with."

She tipped her head to one side. "Such as?"

"You and me, kitten. More precisely—us."

At his lazy, sensual smile, her heart took on a giddy cadence. A carriage came from the opposite direction, interrupting their banter. Sinjin exchanged greetings with the occupants of the other vehicle, whose gazes followed them even as they drove on.

"I vowed to myself that I'd come to you with a clean slate—at least one unsullied by blackmail and murder," Sinjin amended. "The rest of my past isn't subject to change, unfortunately."

"I wouldn't want you to change your past," she protested. "It's made you who you are."

"And you like me the way I am? You believe in me?"

Although his tone was playful, flirtatious even, she again sensed an underlying vulnerability. It amazed her that this dazzling, god-like man truly cared what she thought of him. Although, given what he'd disclosed about his family, it ought to come as no surprise that he should want her positive opinion. Either way, the boyish longing in his aura made her heart squeeze.

"Of course I believe in you," she said firmly.

"Then will you fetch something from my left pocket? My hands are full at the moment."

She blinked at the non sequitur but did as he asked. When she pulled out a velvet-covered box, she stilled. The box might contain a ring, something she wasn't certain she was ready for. Or —she flashed to the locket—it might contain a meaningless trinket. And she didn't want that either.

"Open it," he said.

Halfheartedly, she did... and her next breath whooshed from her lungs.

It wasn't a ring inside but a necklace. One that had clearly been chosen with care. Nestled in white satin, the piece was exquisite in its simplicity: a flawless aquamarine cabochon set in a delicate frame of gold. When she lifted the necklace by its fine gold chain, the stone's pristine, watery depths glimmered in the sunlight, its beauty unique and utterly breathtaking.

"It reminded me of your eyes, though nothing matches their splendor, of course," he said huskily. "Happy belated birthday."

"You already gave me a present," she blurted—and immediately wished she hadn't. She didn't want to ruin the moment by bringing up that unpleasant incident.

"That gift was an unworthy one. And I think you and I both

know it didn't belong to my mama." Cheekbones reddening, he said, "The locket was sent to me as an, ahem, memento. By whom, I don't know. I happened to have it on me at the time."

Relieved by his honesty and candor, she said curiously, "Why did you give it to me?"

"It was an impulse." His brows drew together. "I'd intruded upon your private celebration, and I suppose I wanted to... join in. Contribute in some way. An ill-conceived notion, obviously."

The sincerity of his explanation warmed her. She was also aware that she'd misjudged his motivation with the locket, believing his gesture to be the scheming of a seasoned Lothario when the truth was far simpler. He'd just wanted to feel included. To be part of a family celebration—something, she understood now, that he'd had little experience with.

With aching remorse, she said, "The gesture was thoughtful. And I'm sorry I responded with such poor grace."

"You can't help being acute, Polly." He studied her intently. "Do you know, sometimes I fancy those eyes of yours can see through anything. Through twisting passages and false ends, straight to the heart of the matter."

Watch out for Peculiar Polly...she'll see what's in your head... Steer clear of Peculiar Polly...

Panic knocked her heart against her ribs. "I'm not acute. Or different in any way. I'm perfectly ordinary—"

"That you most definitely are not. You, kitten, are special."

The warmth of his regard gradually dissolved her alarm. Somehow, Sinjin managed to make her *feel* special—in a good way. As unique and beautiful as the necklace he'd given her. And therein lay her conflict. She needed a marriage of convenience to protect her secret, yet Sinjin made her yearn for intimacy. If she married him, how would she be able to safeguard her heart?

Yet how could she resist the elemental force between them?

"You're special, too," she said softly.

"In that case, did I mention that the necklace is part of a set? There's a matching ring, for instance."

At his unsubtle hint, she had to laugh. "The necklace will do for now. Thank you, Sinjin, it's lovely beyond words." She admired the treasure once more before carefully stowing it away in her reticule.

"I promised to court you, and court you I shall. But the truth is, sweeting,"—his gaze grew heated, a ragged edge in his voice— "I cannot wait to make you mine. I've been going mad, reliving our time in the carriage."

"I've thought of it, too," she confessed.

"Have you now?" he rasped. "Did you do anything about it... the way I did?"

Blood surged into her cheeks. She was grateful for her coal-scuttle bonnet, its deep, ribbon-trimmed brim hiding her flaming face from the occupants of another oncoming carriage.

"That's wicked," she managed after the conveyance had passed.

"Aye, but did you?"

"I most certainly did *not*."

"Would you consider doing it?" Smoldering challenge entered his gaze. "Because the thought of you petting your soft, wet little pussy while I touch myself, thinking of you... Devil and damn, I'd give everything I own for that to be true."

His naughty suggestion ignited her own forbidden yearnings. In truth, it had been a torment thinking of him—of his hot kisses and masterful touch—without being able to do anything about it. Ache had bloomed inside her, the same throbbing awareness that spread through her now. Would it be so bad to relieve that tension... to share something that only he and she would know about?

"All right," she said slowly.

"Holy hell." His eyes widened. "You mean it?"

Seeing him actually *shudder* with lust dispelled her lingering doubts. It thrilled her that she could elicit this reaction in a man as worldly as Sinjin. It dawned upon her that, when she was with him, she felt less inhibited, more comfortable in her own skin. It seemed his bold nature was rubbing off on her... and she liked it.

"I go to bed at midnight," she informed him.

"I'll be there. In my own bed, I mean." His grin was downright wolfish. "So what will you be thinking about when we're together yet apart?"

"About... you kissing me." She may have shed some of her inhibitions, but that was as brazen as she could manage.

"Where?"

"Sinjin," she protested with a laugh, "I already gave you an inch. Don't take a mile."

"I shall give you a pass this one time." He winked. "But I'll expect a full report tomorrow. When I take you driving again."

"Oh... I can't go for a drive." Flustered, she said, "I mean, I would like to very much, but I have a prior engagement."

She was dreading the event, which Thea's note—asking if she still needed a chaperone for the Pickering-Parks' picnic—had reminded her of just this morning. Not only was it too late to send regrets, but Polly felt she owed it to Nigel to make matters clear between them. Although no promises had been made, she'd sensed that he'd been considering offering for her. She wanted to let him know in person (hopefully, in some subtle and adroit manner) that such an offer would no longer be welcomed.

"What event are you attending? Perhaps I've been invited as well."

The last thing she needed was for Sinjin to show up at the picnic. His presence would only complicate the already delicate situation.

"The Pickering-Parks are hosting a picnic at their Hampstead estate," she said reluctantly, "but I'm certain you won't want to go. It won't be your sort of entertainment at all."

"My sort?" His brows rose.

"Mostly wallflowers and dowagers will be attending. And gentlemen willing to sift through the dregs of the marriage mart. So it won't be a fashionable crowd, and I'm sure the entertainments will be exceedingly dull—"

"The lady doth protest too much, methinks." His gaze was all too keen. "Why do I have the distinct feeling that you don't want me there?"

"I think you'd be, um, bored is all." Realizing that further protests would only deepen his suspicion, she adopted a tone of indifference. "But go ahead and attend, if you like."

"As it happens, I don't have an invitation."

"You won't be missing much," she said lightly.

Thankfully, he let it go at that, and the ride home was spent in lively banter. He escorted her all the way to her doorstep, bowing over her hand.

"Until tonight, kitten," he rasped, "when we meet in our dreams."

She floated, rosy-cheeked, through the front door.

T he next day, Polly and Thea arrived to find the picnic in full swing. The Pickering-Parks' Hampstead estate bordered on the picturesque Heath, and the al fresco event was being held behind the sweeping Italianate manor house. The two were greeted by their hostess, Mrs. Pickering-Parks, a rail-thin woman whose preference for the color pink was shown not only in her wardrobe but that of her only son as well. Nigel stood beside his mama, perspiring in pink and brown plaid worsted, his protruding midsection highlighted by a fuchsia waistcoat.

"We've recently restocked the Chinese Pond with carp," Mrs. Pickering-Parks was saying. "After luncheon, you must allow my son to guide you ladies on a tour."

"Indeed." Nigel addressed Polly. "Have you finished the book I sent you for your birthday?"

She hadn't even started it. "Um... not quite yet. But it was very thoughtful of you to—"

"It's unfortunate that you haven't read the treatise," he interrupted, "for it would help you to understand the significance of my latest acquisition—"

"Leave off the old bones for now, dearest," his mother said

hastily. "I'm sure Lady Tremont and Miss Kent would like to refresh themselves first."

"Perhaps we could, um, talk later?" Polly said to Nigel.

At his beaming smile, her discomfiture grew. She hoped that he wouldn't take the news she had to share badly. On the other hand, it was possible that he wouldn't care at all. The passion in his aura seemed exclusively linked to his favorite hobby.

A footman led Polly and Thea to the picnic area, where cloth-covered tables had been set up beneath a flowing pink tent. A quartet provided serene accompaniment to the sweltering summer day whilst perspiring servants delivered trays of refreshments. The stations of games—everything from archery to a ring toss—stood empty, failing to entice guests made lethargic by the heat, food, and their own restrictive finery.

Finding a quiet table, Polly sat with her sister, sipping on iced lemonade and nibbling on sliced fruits and tiny sandwiches. Scanning the crowd, Polly saw there were quite a few gentlemen at the event, and more latitude than usual was given for the mixing of the sexes. Perhaps the impending end of the Season had persuaded mamas and duennas to sacrifice strict chaperonage for a potential eleventh-hour catch.

With a pang, Polly said, "I wish Rosie would have come. The place is teeming with eligible *parti*."

"She'll come around eventually." Beneath the flower-strewn brim of her bonnet, Thea's hazel eyes held gentle empathy. "You two love each other far too well for this rift to continue indefinitely."

Polly wished she shared Thea's optimism. It had been five days, and the shoulder Rosie presented to her was colder than ever. Polly had begun to regret her assertive words to her sister, but she didn't know how to make things right. It was the one dark spot in her burgeoning happiness.

"What if what I've done is unforgivable?" she said forlornly.

"It's hardly that, my dear. The fact of the matter is you could not have predicted the connection between you and the earl. And you are fond of Revelstoke, are you not?"

Fond wasn't the right word. Thinking of what she'd done in the privacy of her bed last night whilst thinking of him doing the same thing, she flushed. "I do like him. Perhaps too much."

"Too much?"

Unable to resist her sister's gentle inquiry, Polly shared her fears that she might not be able to safeguard her heart or her affliction if she were to become Sinjin's wife.

"But why would you wish to hide your true self from the man you marry?"

Astonishment glimmered around Thea, and Polly understood why. Her sister, like the rest of her married siblings, shared uncommonly intimate relationships with their spouses. Thea and Tremont were so close that their auras were oft attuned, mirroring the others' glow.

"Because I'm no stranger to rejection," Polly said frankly, "and the thought of experiencing it at Sinjin's hands—oh, Thea, it would be too much to bear."

Thea studied her. "I could tell you again that you don't have an affliction—that you are perfectly lovely as you are—but you wouldn't believe me, would you?"

Of course her sister thought that. Polly's family loved her unconditionally, which meant they didn't see her as the rest of the world did.

"No," she said honestly, "but thank you for thinking that."

"And I could also say that, if Revelstoke truly cares for you as I believe he does, he wouldn't reject you for any reason... but you wouldn't believe that either?"

She wished she could believe it. She shook her head.

"Then only time will tell, little sister. But if I may pass on something I've learned? Love, like anything worthwhile, involves taking a risk. You'll have to decide if Revelstoke is worth that risk to you. But in the meantime,"—Thea's gaze went over

Polly's shoulder—"the purpose for today's visit is headed this way."

Polly turned to see Nigel lumbering toward her.

"Miss Kent." He bowed, the movement straining the buttons of his waistcoat to an alarming degree. "I believe we are promised for a tour of the pond."

He led the way across the scythed grass toward a wooded path at the end of which, he promised, lay the pond. By tacit agreement, Thea performed her chaperonage at a distance, staying several paces behind so that Polly could have the privacy to address the uncomfortable topic.

Before Polly could begin, however, Nigel launched straightaway into a discourse about his favorite subject. "As you know, I recently returned from an expedition in Sussex, where I purchased the most remarkable specimen."

"Oh?" How could she subtly inform him that she was no longer interested in a courtship? If, indeed, they had ever engaged in one. The ambiguity of their relationship made her task all the more challenging, but she wanted to end whatever was between them in a respectful manner.

"An ichthyosaurus. A complete set, no less." Excitement radiated from his sweat-sheened face.

"How, um, thrilling." Gathering her courage, she said, "Mr. Pickering-Parks, I've recently made a discovery myself, and it concerns my future—"

"I beat out two other collectors in order to attain it. It was the highlight of my life," he crowed.

"Speaking of highlights, I've recently made the acquaintance of—"

"But the ichthyosaurus pales in comparison to the new lead I received," he said as if she hadn't spoken at all.

The truth was that he'd always had the tendency to carry on his own conversation. Whereas she'd once welcomed his self-absorption—because it meant less of a focus on her—now she found it... exasperating. It wasn't his fault that her preferences had changed, but she couldn't deny that they had. She was no longer content with a one-sided relationship. A convenient and passionless match. She wanted... more.

Because of Sinjin.

From the start, even when she and he had butted heads, she'd felt that she had his undivided attention. Whenever they were together, even in a roomful of people, invisible filaments of awareness seemed to connect them. It was more than just physical attraction, though Lord knew there was plenty of that between them. He made her feel special, cared for—and, at the same time, she suddenly realized, *terrified.*

She was a girl who'd spent most of her life trying to avoid notice. Yet now she had the attention of the most compelling and attractive man she'd ever met, and he wanted to marry her... and all she had to do was say "yes."

Love, like anything worthwhile, involves taking a risk, Thea had said.

Was Sinjin worth the risk of rejection and pain?

In the midst of Nigel's droning, her heart gave the unequivocal answer. In truth, she didn't know why it had taken her so long to come to the inevitable conclusion. Beneath her bodice, his pendant was warm and vital next to her skin.

I'm falling in love with Sinjin.

The knowledge flowed through her even as she realized there was really only one answer to her dilemma. It was too late to guard her heart where Sinjin was concerned—that ship had sailed—but she could marry him... as long as she kept her affliction hidden.

She appreciated Thea's advice, but any risk she took would have to be calculated. She didn't have a normal ailment like her sister; she, Polly, was a freak. One who'd already experienced the consequences of revealing her flaw to a man. Reminded of her folly with Brockhurst, she felt a quiver of fear; she prayed that he would take her secret to his grave.

If the notion of marrying Sinjin without telling him about her anomaly caused a stab of guilt, she reminded herself that he didn't *want* intimacy. In fact, he'd insisted upon privacy for both of them... so really she was just going along with the rules that he'd set, wasn't she? Sinjin had also said that he didn't want love, so she would strive to keep her feelings to herself, to not make any emotional demands upon him.

She couldn't deny that having Sinjin for a husband would bring more happiness than she'd dreamed possible... and they might one day have a family as well. The image rose of a little boy with mahogany hair and devilish blue eyes, and her chest constricted with longing.

"As you know, I am a member of the *Society for the Study of Antiquities and Historical Artifacts*," Nigel was saying, "and from there I heard rumblings of a new find in Dorset. Now can I trust you with a secret, Miss Kent?"

She tried to focus on him. "Er, yes?"

"Apparently this new set of fossils is of a mammoth creature *never before catalogued*," Nigel said ardently. "A giant biped with a massive tail. Whoever discovers the bones will be feted by collectors throughout the kingdom!"

"But didn't you say someone already found the fossil?" Polly said in confusion.

"Well, if you must nitpick, some local clergyman found it, but the man who *owns* and displays the specimen as part of his collection is its true discoverer, naturally. Everyone knows that." Nigel swatted irritably at an insect. "I should think that obvious, Miss Kent."

Thankfully, they'd reached the Chinese Pond, the loveliness of the spot softening her increasing aggravation with her escort. The water was dotted with waterlilies, surrounded by trailing willows and rippling screens of cattails and rushes. Carp darted in bright flashes beneath the murky surface. In the distance, Polly spotted a golden spire, the rest of the structure obscured by surrounding greenery.

Just then, a figure materialized, rounding a bend in the path and heading toward them. There was no mistaking the graceful, predatory stride, the virile physique in the merlot jacket and tan trousers, the devilishly handsome face.

"Who on earth is that?" Nigel muttered.

"Revelstoke," Polly breathed.

Sinjin exchanged introductions with Nigel and greetings with her and Thea, who'd just caught up to them.

"What are you doing here, my lord?" Polly said in disbelief.

"Just happened to be in the neighborhood. I was taking air in the Heath and was lured over by this scenic pond." To Nigel, he said easily, "Jewel of a place, sir."

Nigel mumbled a reply. Polly did not, for a single moment, buy Sinjin's innocent tone. But she was so happy to see him that she didn't care.

Thea shot her an *I-told-you-so* glance. "If you'll excuse me, I believe I'll take a little rest on that inviting bench over there." A hint of mischief danced in her eyes. "You three go on and enjoy yourselves."

Thea headed off, and Sinjin said, "May I compliment you on your exceedingly fine looks today, Miss Kent?"

His gaze caressed her like a touch, her body responding helplessly. Her breath quickened, nipples rising into tingling stiffness. As if he knew his effect on her, his eyes grew heavy-lidded, satisfaction deepening the blue of his aura.

"You must be counting your lucky stars to have such charming company, Pickering," he added.

"It's Pickering-*Parks*." Nigel mopped his brow with a handkerchief, a rivulet of sweat escaping and catching in his limp cravat. "As it happens, Miss Kent and I were enjoying a chat—"

"I hope you won't mind if I join in, then." Tucking her hand into the crook of his arm, Sinjin guided her along the path. His eyes smiled at her. "What were we talking about?"

"Miss Kent and I were discussing fossils," Nigel huffed, trying to get alongside them. The graveled walkway was just wide enough for two to stroll comfortably side by side, and Nigel swore as he snagged his jacket on some thistly brush, falling behind them. "I doubt our conversation would interest you, my lord. I am a noted collector, you see, and the level of my discourse may not be suitable for amateurs. In fact, I'm in the process of acquiring the largest bones—"

"I'm no stranger to big bones," Sinjin said smoothly. "Indeed, I'm certain Miss Kent will vouch that I've been in possession of a rather large, hard specimen in her presence."

Polly choked back a horrified giggle.

"Is this true, Miss Kent?" Nigel said suspiciously. "You've seen this fellow's bone?"

She couldn't form a reply, not if her life depended upon it.

"Do you have it with you now?" he demanded to Sinjin.

"I only show it under the most intimate circumstances. You understand."

"I do indeed," Nigel said with an air of importance. "Fossil collectors can be a shifty, unscrupulous lot, not to be trusted. In fact, that is precisely what I was telling Miss Kent before you came. Between you and me, my lord, I'm in negotiations to obtain one of the most important finds in Dorset—"

"Dorset, you say?" Sinjin shook his head, making a *tsk*-ing sound.

Nigel paled. "What have you heard? Is someone else after the find? I *knew* I should have set off immediately when I received the news—"

"It's not too late now."

"By George, you're right." Nigel thumped his fist into his palm. "I don't care what Mama says. No stupid picnic is more important than those bones."

"You're still here," Sinjin said.

"Farewell, sir. And you as well, Miss Kent." Nigel doffed his hat hastily before trundling off.

Polly wondered in bemusement if she'd ever see him again.

"Care to explain what you're doing with that fribble?"

She turned to Sinjin—and was shocked to see the banked fire in his eyes.

❧ 23 ❧

Polly blinked at him. Shaded by the brim of her straw bonnet, her aquamarine eyes were so huge and clear that Sinjin could see himself reflected in them, and he didn't like what he saw. More to the point, he didn't like what he *felt*.

Could he, the notorious God of Revelry, be jealous over some windbag fossil collector?

The idea was laughable. Absurd. There was no way in hell he felt threatened by Pickering-Parks. He told himself that he just didn't like the fact that Polly had hidden whatever was going on between her and that popinjay. Because she *was* hiding something: he'd sensed it yesterday and now, catching her on a jaunt with the bone-chasing buffoon, he was sure of it.

"I wasn't, um, doing anything," she said.

Her answer, the nervous way she wetted her lips, did not improve his disposition. Taking her firmly by the arm, he led her along the path and a safe distance away from her chaperone. He took her to the Chinoiserie style pagoda he'd passed on his way to find her. The rectangular structure was made up of four columns holding up a double-tiered roof and was topped by a golden spire. The longer side overlooked the pond, the shorter sides shielded by dense walls of rushes. He backed her up against the nearest column, which was hidden from view of the path.

Leaning in, he said, "If it was nothing, then why did you lie about it?"

"I didn't lie," she protested. "I told you I would be here."

"Not about that. About why you didn't want me here. Does it have something to do with that stuffed shirt?"

A notch formed between her brows. "You can't possibly be jealous... of *Nigel?*"

Wrong bloody thing to say. On two counts.

"Nigel?" he said acidly.

She flushed, mumbling, "It's easier to say than Mr. Pickering-Parks."

"You'd best take that into consideration, then. Polly Pickering-Parks—that's quite a tongue-twister. You'd give old Peter Piper a run for his money."

"There's no need to be sarcastic." Frowning, she added, "And you're making a mountain out of a molehill."

Rationally, he knew she was right, but she'd stirred the devil in him. Even as he strove to keep the monster in check, he was swayed by the powerful emotions and roaring thoughts. *Why is Polly dragging her heels over marrying me? Does she think that I won't make a good husband? Does she think that that paltry bone collector would make a better one?*

Sinjin's molars ground together. This burning possessiveness was new to him. He didn't like her power over him: how easily she could unbalance his equanimity, add momentum to his inner pendulum.

"Tell me what's going on," he bit out.

With a sigh, she said, "In the past several months, Mr. Pickering-Parks and I have spent some time in each other's company. Nothing happened between us, but there was the unspoken possibility that something might. I came today to let him know that the possibility was no longer there."

"Did he kiss you?"

"Nige—I mean, Mr. Pickering Parks?" She made a sound of amusement. "Can you imagine him being moved to do so with anything other than a fossil?"

He knew she was right. Still...

"Did you want him to kiss you?"

Her head rocked side to side against the column.

"Then why was there even a 'possibility' with that prat?" he said flatly.

She chewed on her bottom lip, and he couldn't blame her. He wanted to nibble it, too. And other parts of her—

"Because I thought he might make a suitable husband." Her words pierced his lustful trance. "Socially, we're equals. And, physically speaking, he's my male counterpart."

The pressure in Sinjin's veins shot up at her using the phrase "suitable husband" to refer to that fool—to any man but him. At the same time, he couldn't help but stare at her.

"You believe he's *your* counterpart," he said incredulously.

"It's the truth. We're about the same height and similarly nondescript." Her chin lifted a fraction. "We're both plump."

Holy hell, she couldn't be *serious*. Yet he could tell from her resolute expression that she was. That she truly thought of herself in this distorted manner. Seeing the slight quiver of her lower lip, he felt his anger abruptly fade. Understanding took its place... along with a rush of tenderness.

"Apparently, I've failed to convince you of how desirable you are," he said after a moment. "And here I was thinking that I'd done a rather thorough job of it during that carriage ride."

Roses bloomed in her cheeks. "You were seducing me. Of course you'd use flattery."

"You didn't think I was sincere?"

"I'm sure you were but..."—she frowned, and he could practically see the gears of denial turning in her head—"... you were being kind. A gentleman."

"You think I'd make love to a woman I didn't find genuinely attractive?" He shook his head. "Kitten, I'm not that much of a gentleman."

"Maybe you're less... particular when it comes to carnal matters." She must have gauged his scowl for what it was, for she added hastily, "I don't mean that you're indiscriminate, just that you're, um, open-minded. About what constitutes beauty, I mean."

"It doesn't take an open mind to see your attractions, just a bloody pair of eyes."

As he spoke, he took in her outfit—yet another high-necked, dull frock—and the realization suddenly struck. He didn't know why it hadn't sooner. Probably because he'd been too distracted by what lay beneath to duly ponder the reason behind her wardrobe choices. Before, he'd attributed her concealing frocks to modesty or a lack of interest in style, but now...

"Is that why you dress the way you do? Because you think you have something to *hide*?"

That little chin angled up more. "Not all of us can be perfectly formed, you know. We can't all look like dashed Greek Gods— what are you doing?"

He finished untying her cherry-colored bonnet strings and tossed the head covering aside. "Seeing as I can't convince you through words, I'm reverting to my other method." He nuzzled her ear, savoring her apple blossom freshness. "And if that doesn't work, at least I'll have fun trying."

"We can't—*ohh*."

As he sucked on her plump earlobe, she melted against him. He moved on, hunting for her scent above the high, ruffled edge of her bodice. When her lips parted on a sigh, he swooped in, claiming the mouth that he'd been hungering for since he'd last tasted it. He threaded his fingers in her silken curls, holding her in place.

"I fantasized about this last night," he murmured between plundering kisses. "Did you?"

In answer, her hands clutched at his shoulders, pulling him closer. He obliged, pressing her against the column, reveling in their perfect fit. Their mating tongues, his hard edges against her delectable curves—they went together like pieces of a damned jigsaw puzzle. It was ridiculous that he had to convince her of so obvious a fact.

Wedging his leg boldly between her thighs, he tore himself away from her luscious mouth long enough to say, "What did you think about while you touched yourself?"

She made a whimper of embarrassment. "I... I can't talk about it."

"But you did do it?"

Her lower lip caught beneath her teeth, she gave a little nod.

Fire swirled through him at her admission. "All right, my shy puss, I'll start us off. Alone in my bed, I thought about you looking at me the way you are now."

He saw her surprise, as if that wasn't what she expected him to say. Drawing his thumb along the slope of her cheekbone, he murmured, "Aye, you were looking at me just so, your eyes so clear and pure, the color of wonder itself. And when I kissed you,"—he couldn't resist dipping his head for another quick taste—"I could see that in your eyes too. The way they are now, darkened and desirous, telling me you want me as much as I want you."

"You thought about my eyes?" Her lashes fluttered like the wings of a tawny butterfly. "When you were, you know... doing that?"

"Yes," he said huskily. "I also thought about the way your lips have the slightest curve, even when you're not smiling, as if you know secrets we mere mortals do not. And when you do smile at me,"—he ran the pad of his thumb over her bottom lip—"it warms me down to the marrow."

"Oh, Sinjin," she said tremulously.

"There's more, of course. I'd be lying if I said I didn't also imagine stripping you layer by layer, until there was nothing separating us." Imagining doing that very thing, he slid his palms over her shoulders, down her arms, cupping the generous swells of her breasts. He squeezed gently, savoring the erotic heft. "And these beauties—do you know what I did to them?"

"What?" The word was a sensual puff from her lips.

"I kissed and licked them all over. Especially here." He circled the center of her breasts, found the jutting tips beneath the layers. "Are your nipples hard for me, kitten? Do they throb for my touch, my kiss?"

"Mmm hmm." Her head fell back against the column.

He'd take that as a yes. "You taste so sweet here, like a ripe berry against my tongue. Just the memory of licking you, suckling these tight little buds, arouses me—can you feel that?" Fisting her skirts, he tossed them up, grinding the clothed ridge of his erection against her bare thigh. "Can you feel how hard you make me?"

Her eyes were dazed with longing. "Oh, Sinjin, you make me feel so... awash."

He knew the feeling. But he didn't want to give in, not just yet. Not until he was certain that she saw herself the way he did. "Do you also feel desired?" He flexed his hips again to drive the point home.

"Yes," she breathed.

"And beautiful?"

"I feel that way... when I'm in your arms."

Her smile made him ache, not just in his cock, which was throbbing like the devil, but in his chest. In some deep and essential place.

"That's a start, at least," he said huskily. "Now be a love, and hold your skirts up for me."

When she hesitantly complied, he went down on one knee. With the reverence of an acolyte—which was no less than she deserved—he ran his hands up her dainty, stocking-covered ankles, over the sweet curves of her calves, all the way to the satiny skin above her ribbon garters.

He honed in on the treasure that awaited him at the apex of her thighs. As he ran a fingertip through that soft tawny thatch, he whispered, "You're so damned gorgeous, Polly. Not just in your physical charms—which God knows you possess in abundance—but in your passion. How generous and full of life you are. How wet you get,"—he swallowed, feeling that dew ease his exploring touch—"how you melt at my touch... my kiss."

So saying, he leaned in and gave her the kiss that had featured in his fantasies.

Her taste was as he remembered: honey and woman, all Polly. Parting her plump folds, he licked hungrily along her pink slit, fueled by the primal need to dispel any doubt that she belonged to him. To the man who was her true match. Who not only saw her beauty but *felt* it—in her shivers of delight, the rain of dew upon his tongue, the ardent way she arched herself into his kiss.

When his tongue delved upward to her pearl, her knees buckled, and he steadied her, swinging one of her legs over his shoulder, bracing her against the column. With this improved access, he returned to his interrupted pleasure. He suckled on her little knot, then tickled it with his tongue. She reached her pinnacle with a sudden soft cry that made his turgid member jerk against his smalls.

Her indescribable sweetness made his senses spin. Not ready to give up his seat at the feast, he continued to tongue her pearl as she came down, drawing out her voluptuous pleasure. He traced her drenched furrow with his middle finger until he found her tight entrance. Slowly but surely, he worked his way inside.

The fit was snug, her sheath dewy but unaccustomed to invasion. Once he passed the initial resistance, however, her virgin muscles tugged at his digit, that erotic pull drawing a spurt of pre-spend from his cock. He lapped at her pearl as he screwed his finger inside, steadily and all the way, until her nest feathered across his knuckles. He was rewarded by a fresh gush of her ambrosia.

"Yes, kitten," he growled. "Spend for me again. Give me more of your sweet honey."

Afire with lust, he redoubled his efforts, stabbing her clit with his tongue, her tight cunny with his finger. Her hips bucked wantonly against his mouth, and when he judged her ready, he gave her more, adding another finger to the mix. His excitement surged as she took it readily, her pussy clenching lushly around his thick digits, her cream rich upon his tongue.

"*Sinjin.*"

In her moment of crisis, she called out his name—a summons that could not be denied. Aroused beyond reason, he surged to his feet, crushing her lips with his, their kiss flavored with the wild beauty of her pleasure. The intimacy of what they were sharing pushed him over the edge: he ground his hips against her, rubbing his trouser-confined erection against her thigh, finding the essential friction. When his release slammed into him, he buried his shout of satisfaction in her hair.

When he regained his senses, he lifted his head—to see Polly smiling at him. She looked adorably... smug.

He chucked her under the chin. "Pleased with yourself, sweeting?"

"I can't help it." With a mischievous twinkle in her eyes, she said, "I suppose it's nice to know that I'm not the only one who can, um, climax fully clothed."

"Touché," he said with a wry grin. He examined the front of his trousers, gingerly buttoning his jacket over the stain. "I don't relish handing this over to my valet. He'll think his rakehell of a master was replaced by a fifteen-year-old greenling. Which, incidentally, was my age when I last disgraced myself in this manner."

She clearly tried to hide her smile, so dazzling that it could have lit up a ballroom. "I'm sorry. I know I shouldn't find it amusing," she said between giggles. "It's just that I never thought that *I* could... that the wallflower could turn the tables on the *rake*..."

"If you need further proof, I'd be happy to provide it." Intently, he said, "You're beautiful, Polly, but more than that you've got so much passion to share. You are my match—and then some. Never doubt it."

"You're right." Regaining her composure, she took a deep breath. "And I will."

He cocked his head, not following. "You will...?"

"I will marry you," she said.

24

"How much longer?" Polly's lashes brushed against the blindfold.

"Just another minute, Miss Kent," a voice—which she identified as Maisie's—called out. "Now 'old still—we're almost finished!"

Hearing the girl's excitement, Polly smiled and complied. She was in one of the classrooms at the Hunt Academy, where Madame Rousseau had set up a changing area to mimic the one she had at her exclusive boutique. Screens provided privacy around the dressmaker's dais upon which Polly stood, the modiste and her pupils bustling around her, making adjustments to their masterpiece which would be debuted at the charity ball in two days' time.

Maisie had tied the scrap of silk over Polly's eyes, saying that they didn't want Polly to see the dress until it was perfectly in place.

Although Polly couldn't see the ball gown, she felt the swish of fine fabric against her skin... and the waft of air against the places the garment left bare. Which, she could already tell, were far more than what she was accustomed to. But instead of apprehension, she brimmed with anticipation. A readiness to try something more daring when it came to fashion... and life.

This was Sinjin's effect on her, of course. He gave her the courage to take risks, the ultimate one being her decision to commit her future to his. Yet from the moment she'd pledged her troth to him, she'd had no regrets. Her focus was now on the future, which held such promise... as long as she kept her deformity and love hidden. And she would. She *would* make this work.

Sinjin, for his part, had wasted no time in making their engagement official. The day after the Pickering-Parks' picnic, he'd paid a call and presented her with a ring. She rubbed her left thumb against it now; she didn't need her eyes to see it since she'd committed every detail to memory. The ring matched the necklace Sinjin had given her, with a flawless aquamarine cabochon set in a frame of sparkling white diamonds and mounted atop a delicate gold band.

Her sisters had agreed that the ring was perfect for Polly, and Ambrose had given his blessing to the marriage, which would take place eight weeks hence. Marianne, an expert at wedding planning, had said that two months was the minimum time necessary to properly execute such an event, and Ambrose had seconded the notion, although for different reasons.

After a week, the search for Miss French's accomplice had gone surprisingly cold. The scoundrel seemed to have vanished into thin air despite the fact that Ambrose had had a sketch made up of him and was circulating it far and wide with the promise of a reward. Ambrose wanted to clear up the business before the wedding, to give Polly and Sinjin the ultimate gift: peace of mind.

Thus, in two months' time, she, Polly Kent, was going to become the Earl of Revelstoke's wife. The wallflower was going to wed the rake. Recalling the way Sinjin's powerful body had shuddered against her when they'd made love by the pond, the way he'd growled her name in his throes, she was filled with a heady sense of wonder and power. He had claimed she was his match—and she was finally beginning to believe it.

"*Attends*, Annie," Madame Rousseau's accented voice said sharply. "The bow by the hem has come undone. Details, no matter how large or small, must not be overlooked. *Comprends?*"

"Yes, Madame," her pupil replied in a chastened voice.

Polly felt a slight tug as the girl worked on the overlooked ribbon.

"Maisie, straighten the train at the back," Madame Rousseau instructed. "*Alors*, stand back, *mes filles*, and I will perform the final inspection."

One could hear a pin drop in the silence that followed. Even Polly's heart sped up as she heard the dressmaker's slow, precise footsteps circling her. Finally, an instant before the tension became unbearable and Polly was about to tear off the blindfold herself because she couldn't stand the anticipation any longer, Madame declared softly, "*Bien*. Have a look, Miss Kent."

The silk slipped from Polly's eyes. She blinked, staring at the image in the looking glass.

"Don't you like it?" Maisie said.

Polly couldn't summon up a single word.

"It's so much prettier than your other frocks, miss," Annie piped up.

"The color may take getting used to, *chérie*," Madame Rousseau interjected, "but I assure you it is all the rage in Paris and—"

"It's perfect." In a voice that wobbled, Polly said, "Thank you, all of you—I couldn't have imagined a more perfect dress. I truly do feel like the Girl in the Cinders. And I'm so honored to showcase your creation at the ball tomorrow night." Polly smiled tremulously at the beaming faces. "I expect your handiwork will bring a flood of donations to the academy."

As the girls squealed, clapping their hands, Polly's gaze was drawn back to the image in the glass. It was amazing how different a dress could make one look: she felt as if a stranger was looking back at her.

The lady in the mirror wore a gown that was neither blue nor green but some extraordinary, shimmering shade in between. The silk chiffon flowed like water over her figure, highlighting lush curves and a nipped-in waist, the full skirts cascading to the floor. The bodice was cut daringly low off the shoulder, edged with frothy, sea-green lace that emphasized the purity of the skin above.

In the reflection, Polly saw herself standing taller, her carriage imbued with a new confidence. Because of the dress... and because of Sinjin. Because of how he made her feel: wanted and desired, no longer a wallflower but a lady coming into bloom.

Then and there, she made a decision.

"Madame, I'd like to come by your shop to have a few new dresses made," she said.

"*Sacré dieu,* my prayers have been answered," the French-woman said fervently.

A rueful grin tucked into Polly's cheeks. The beleaguered modiste had campaigned tirelessly for Polly to consider more fashionable garments. Had her sisters not been amongst the modiste's most favored patrons, Polly was certain that Madame would have refused to make the frumpy dresses she'd insisted upon.

After helping Polly back into her old clothes, the girls trooped out of the classroom—except for Maisie, who lingered to help Madame Rousseau tidy up. Seeing the flicker of uncertainty around the girl, who'd become quite subdued, Polly wondered what was amiss. She didn't have long to wonder.

"Miss Kent... may I ask you something?"

"Of course you may."

Maisie's brown eyes slid to Polly's ring. "Is it true that you're to be married?"

"*Alors*, Maisie, that is not your concern," the modiste chided as she rolled up a measuring tape.

"It's all right, Madame. I don't mind answering." Turning to Maisie, Polly said gently, "Yes, it's true. I'm engaged to the Earl of Revelstoke."

"Oh." The girl's bottom lip trembled, and she turned quickly to the worktable, her small hands fumbling at she organized the dressmaker's tools. Fear glowed around her brown plaits.

"Maisie," Polly said with concern, "what's the matter?"

"N-nothin'," came the quivering reply.

Seeing the girl's distress, Polly murmured to the dressmaker, "Would you mind giving us a moment, Madame?"

With an understanding nod, the Frenchwoman departed.

"We're alone now," Polly said. "Won't you talk to me, Maisie?"

The girl's shoulders hunched. She turned around, her small face aged by resignation. "There's naught to talk about."

"I think there is. I think something is troubling you, and I'd like to help, if I can."

The girl's gaze was trained on the floor. "And if you can't?"

"Then at least you'll have spoken about your concerns to someone who cares." Polly set her hands lightly on the girl's shoulders. "That is something, I think."

Maisie raised her eyes and blurted, "But it won't matter because you'll still leave. The other girls said once you're married, you'll 'ave a family o' your own, and no time for us foundlings." A tear leaked down her freckled cheek. "You won't come by 'ere no more. You'll leave—like everyone does!"

Taken aback by the fact that *she* was the cause of the girl's distress, Polly was at a momentary loss for words. The girl shook free of her touch and returned to sorting pins into boxes.

"Maisie, please look at me."

"Go away," the girl sniffled.

"Maisie," Polly repeated.

The girl pivoted slowly, her expression defiant and at odds with her affable nature.

"Just because I'm getting married doesn't mean I'll stop coming here," Polly said gently.

"That's not true. The other girls said—"

"It doesn't matter what they said. I'm telling you what is true."

Maisie's hands curled into fists at her sides. "The girls said that even if you *said* you would keep coming, your new 'usband might 'ave something different to say in the matter. And because e's your 'usband, you'll 'ave to mind 'im. So you couldn't come even if you wanted to."

"Goodness," Polly murmured, "the other girls have rather a lot to say, don't they?"

Maisie gave a fierce little nod.

"Well, I can tell you that my future husband won't try to inter-fere with something that is important to me." Sinjin had agreed, after all, that they would respect each other's interests. "And I have no intention of stopping my visits here."

Hope sparked in the foundling's aura, a tiny flame fighting against the dark gloom. Having survived so many travails, was it any wonder that the girl expected the worst?

"You're marrying a nob," Maisie said in a quavering voice. "'E won't want you associating with the likes o' me. 'E'll want you to do other things—like eat bonbons or 'ave tea with the King."

Would Sinjin object to her work at the academy? Polly doubted it. Despite his title and wealth, he disliked pretensions and snobbery. She was learning that he was his own man, one who lived by his own rules and code of honor, and she respected him for it. In fact, he was teaching her to care less about what others thought—and she believed that he would support her in the endeavors that were important to her.

"You'll have to trust me on this, Maisie," she said. "I haven't lied to you before, have I?"

The girl gave an adamant shake of her head, her braids whirling.

"Then I won't do so with this. I like being here," Polly said earnestly, "being with you and the other children. I plan to continue my work here for the foreseeable future. And if there came a time when I couldn't... well, I'd be honest about it. I'd tell you straight to your face, Maisie, so you never have to worry that I'll just disappear one day."

"Ma did." The words emerged in a whisper. "One day I woke up, and she was gone. Tim said she weren't coming back, but I didn't believe 'im. I thought she'd want to come back. For us. I was wrong."

There it was. The root of Maisie's worry. And, by God, Polly knew from her own experience that it was not an easy fear to eradicate. Nonetheless, she had to try.

"I was six when my mama left us," she said quietly. "She was taken away by a fever. We thought she'd taken a bit of a chill, but she was gone within the week."

Even after all these years, she felt tiny reverberations of that shock. Of discovering that her warm, full-of-life mama had gone to be with the angels, leaving the rest of the family stricken with grief. Papa had never fully recovered from the loss.

"I'm so sorry, Miss Kent," Maisie said, her eyes wide.

"Thank you, dear, but my point is only that I understand how difficult it is to lose someone."

"But my ma... she didn't 'ave an ailment." The girl's shoulders drooped. "She just left us—on account o' the drink, Tim said."

"Which is an illness of a sort, when one thinks about it. But whatever her reason, it doesn't have anything to do with you," Polly said, giving the girl's arm a light squeeze. "Bad things happen in life, and we might not understand why, but we have to have faith that good things will happen too."

Maisie fell silent. As Polly struggled to come up with some

other way to offer comfort, the girl said in a thin voice, "I'm worried... about Tim."

"Your brother?" Another surprise. Polly's head tipped to one side. "Why?"

"'E used to visit me every week, but this last time, 'e didn't come for an entire fortnight. And now it's been nearly three weeks since I seen 'im last." The words rushed out in a torrent, as if they'd been dammed up far too long. "What if 'e tires o' me... the way Ma did?"

Polly's heart wrenched at the girl's despair. "Your brother loves you very much. He would never tire of you." At fifteen, Timothy Cullen was already a rough-and-ready sort of fellow, a survivor of the stews, but during his visits, Polly had seen his bright and unfaltering devotion to his younger sister. "I'm sure other matters are detaining him. Have you asked him about it?"

Maisie's chin dipped. "'E said since the old Prince o' the Larks cocked up 'is toes, the gang's been all mingle-mangled. Different coves 'ave tried to take charge, but Tim says all o' 'em are driven by greed and care only for themselves." Pride crept into the girl's voice. "My brother says 'e 'as to stay on and keep an eye on the l'il ones—'e won't leave 'em high and dry."

Even as Polly admired Tim's noble instinct, she felt a sense of foreboding. The life of a mudlark was tumultuous enough without adding a struggle for power to the mix. She prayed Tim would not be endangered by his desire to do the right thing. She didn't want to worry Maisie further, however.

"Then you must take him at his word rather than casting about for other reasons," she said.

"You're right." Relief flared around the girl. "I believe Tim. He wouldn't leave me."

"I'm very glad you told me about this. You can talk to me about anything. You know that, don't you?"

The girl nodded.

"Good." Inspiration struck. "Now I have a favor to ask."

Curiosity formed a halo around Maisie. "You do?"

"I'm in need of a head flower girl for the wedding. My nieces will be happy to toss petals—seeing as they love to toss just about anything—but they'll need someone to keep them in order. Someone older and more responsible. I know it is a lot to ask, but what do you say, Maisie? Will you do it?"

"Me?" Maisie's brown eyes were huge in her small face. "You mean it?"

"Of course."

"Yes!" The girl shrieked. "Wait until I tell the other girls!"

Chuckling, Polly held out her hand. "Excellent. Then let's find Madame Rousseau, shall we? We'll need her to measure you for a dress for the occasion."

Maisie's hand shot out, her fingers gripping Polly's very tightly.

25

S injin inspected his image in the chevalier glass. His shave was precise, the dark waves of his hair gleaming, his attire the epitome of Corinthian perfection. Strickley, his valet, was a genius with the restrained style; he'd wager even Brummell couldn't find a single fault.

Seeing the valet's habitually impassive expression, however, Sinjin couldn't resist trying to get a rise out of the other. It was an old game between them, one he never tired of.

"I was thinking of adding a few accessories, Strickley," he said innocently. "A pair of gold fobs, perhaps. What do you think?"

"Might as well carry coals to Newcastle," came the valet's succinct reply.

Sinjin turned this way and that, pretending to study the folds of his neck cloth. "But the cravat—don't you think it needs a pin of some sort?"

"Like one needs a blow to the head."

"Maybe jeweled cufflinks?"

"When pigs fly," Strickley returned calmly. "Is there anything else, my lord?"

Sinjin couldn't hide his grin. "You win, my good fellow. That'll be all."

After the valet departed, Sinjin went to look out the window. Carriages passed on the street below, parasols and fashionable hats in abundance upon the paved walk. The day was bright and filled with promise. He'd awoken this morning feeling refreshed, brimming with good cheer. He was certain it was because of Polly —because she now wore his ring on her finger.

In eight weeks—what seemed an interminable amount of time —she was officially going to be his. Personally, he would have happy with a trip to Gretna, but of course he wanted Polly to have the wedding of her dreams. She'd make a beautiful bride... *his* bride.

The thought filled him with elation. He'd be meeting her at some charity ball this evening, the first time they would be out together in Society as an engaged couple. He didn't give a farthing what the tossers of the *ton* thought, but her family would be there, and he wanted to make a good impression on his in-laws to be. To reassure them that their trust in him was not unwarranted: he would be a good husband to Polly. The best. No less than she deserved.

By God, it had been a long time since he'd had something to look forward to in his future. He descended the stairs two at a time. Finding that he wasn't hungry, he eschewed breakfast for a pot of tea in his study. He idly sorted through the mounting pile of calling cards on his desk, noting the names of his former companions without enthusiasm.

The last month had changed him. The near-disastrous affair with Nicoletta was a sign of just how contemptible his existence had become. He'd been made a target, a pigeon, because his behavior had been reckless and out of control, even by his own standards. He had invited disaster into his life.

Well, no longer. He was no longer going to be that aimless fellow. He wanted nothing more to do with his previous existence and the debauchery that had never brought him any true satisfaction. Although he didn't know yet what to do with his life, he did know that he wanted to live better... to accomplish something. To be a man deserving of a woman like Polly.

Thinking of her, he looked around his study: like the rest of the house, it was a decidedly masculine space designed to suit a bachelor's lifestyle. After he and Polly were married, they would find a new place to live, he decided. He'd let her choose whatever she wanted because the Countess of Revelstoke would have only the very best. Besides, they would need more space as a couple—and a family, if it came to that. The notion of Polly growing ripe with his child stirred a hot, primal satisfaction. At the same time, uncertainty niggled at him.

What kind of a father would he make? What kind of husband?

With his spirits so buoyant today, however, he was able to cast those doubts aside. He and Polly had agreed upon their terms of privacy. As long as he kept to his plan of retreating to an apartment when the devils took over—of never letting her see him in a sorry state—he would be fine.

Filled with restless energy, he was about to call for his carriage and start hunting for an apartment when the doorbell rang. Harvey, his butler, brought in the visitor's card, and Sinjin's eyebrows snapped together.

What the devil does Andrew Corbett want?

Sinjin hadn't seen the proprietor since that fateful night in the other's club. Kent had informed Corbett about Nicoletta's death, handling matters on Sinjin's behalf. Per the investigator, Corbett had appeared genuinely stunned when shown the blackmail note written in Nicoletta's hand. Apparently, he'd had no idea that he'd been used as a dupe, that Nicoletta had played on his sympathies in order to extort Sinjin.

Sinjin rose as Corbett entered the study. Strangely, it was almost like looking into a mirror. The other man shared his height and build, and they might have shared a tailor as well given their similar taste in fashion. The main difference between them was coloring. Corbett's hair was a lighter shade mixed with bronze, and he had a swarthier complexion. The fine lines on his countenance suggested that he had a few years on Sinjin.

It was rumored that the man had once been a stud for hire for the ladies—not only that, but he'd made a bloody fortune at it. Yet nothing about Corbett betrayed his past as a prostitute or, indeed, his present as a procurer. His accent and manner were polished. From the precise cut of his tobacco brown coat down to his polished Hessians, he appeared, outwardly at least, every inch the gentleman.

"Thank you for seeing me, my lord," Corbett said.

Finding it difficult to ignore that this man had believed him a brute, Sinjin said coolly, "This is an unexpected visit."

"And an unwelcome one, too, I expect. But I won't take up too much of your time." The club owner gestured to the chair opposite Sinjin's. "May I?"

He shrugged. "Be my guest."

Once they were both seated, Corbett met his gaze directly. "I'll cut to the chase. Since Kent informed me of the truth, I've struggled with the knowledge that I played a role, albeit inadvertent, in the plot against you. I felt compelled to come today to offer my sincere apologies."

"A conscience, have you?" Sinjin drawled. "Isn't that a hazard in your line of work?"

Color appeared on Corbett's slashing cheekbones, but his tone remained politely neutral.

"Any man of success has standards. It is my mission to ensure a first-rate experience for everyone involved in my business, from the customer to the whore to the footmen serving the champagne. My patrons won't be happy if my employees aren't: that is my philosophy. Thus, I am concerned about everyone and everything that happens in my club. Call it a conscience, if it suits you. I call it good business sense."

"I really hope that is not your version of an apology."

"No, it is simply an explanation for why I took Nicoletta at her word. She is—was," he corrected, "one of my employees, and the wenches are the most vulnerable to uncouth clientele. I do not tolerate mistreatment of those who work for me—"

"Only those who patronize your business," Sinjin said acerbically.

"Point taken." With a nod, Corbett acknowledged his blame. "It was my fault for not investigating the matter more thoroughly. There's no excuse for it, but when I saw the state that she was in, the way she was weeping..."—something dark and dangerous flashed in Corbett's gaze—"I believed her lies. My error led me to treat you inhospitably."

"You wanted to have me hauled off by the magistrates. If that is your version of *inhospitable*, I wonder what your behavior is like when you're actually being rude."

"As I have said in various ways, I am sorry for my mistake. I hope you will accept my apology."

Sinjin brooded over his options. He could tell the other to go to hell—which would be satisfying but childish. The man had made an honest mistake; hell, for a brief while, Sinjin had doubted his own innocence. It would be churlish to refuse an apology so freely and sincerely given.

"I suppose I can't blame you for being duped by the same villainess who duped me," he muttered.

"Quite generous of you, my lord. Thank you." The lines around the other man's mouth eased. He leaned slightly forward. "And now for the second reason for my visit: I would like to offer you something for the trouble I've caused."

"That is unnecessary. I'm done with your establishment," Sinjin stated.

To his surprise, Corbett gave a light laugh. "And for more than one reason, I understand."

"Beg pardon?"

"May I congratulate you on your engagement to Miss Kent?"

News travelled quickly. Then again, Corbett was a legendary fount of information. Given that his club was as prime a hub of gossip as White's or Boodle's, it wasn't surprising that the man knew of Sinjin's engagement. Well, in this instance, Sinjin had naught to hide. He wanted to shout it from the rooftops that Polly belonged to him.

"Thank you," he said with pride.

Corbett nodded. "Now what I want to offer you is information. Kent left me a sketch and description of Nicoletta's accomplice, and I've interviewed every one of my staff personally, from my most popular wench down to the boot-blacking boy. And I have some news that might interest you."

Sinjin sat up in his chair. "I'm listening."

"One of my girls, Angelina, recalled seeing that man in the club the night you were poisoned. I don't know how he slipped in —the guards at the door didn't see him—but Nicoletta could have let him in through one of the back entrances. At any rate, Angelina passed him on the stairs, and it stayed with her because he looked familiar to her. She used to work near the West India Docks and thinks she might have seen him in one of the area's taverns. It was his voice that she remembered most clearly: 'deep as a foghorn,' she said."

The hair prickled on Sinjin's neck at the spot-on description.

"Unfortunately, she couldn't recall which tavern she saw him in," Corbett said, "and I reckon there are at least two dozen or more by the docks, but I hope this will provide a useful lead in your search for the true culprit."

"I'm certain it will," Sinjin said with anticipation. "Thank you."

"It was the least that I could do, my lord." The other man stood and bowed, and Sinjin returned the courtesy. "May I offer my felicitations again? I understand Miss Kent is a fine young lady, the apple not falling far from the tree. I have great respect for her family."

"You have a personal acquaintance with the Kents?" Somehow, Sinjin had difficulty imagining Ambrose Kent being chummy with a cock-bawd—or allowing one near his kin.

"I cannot claim that, no. A man like me would hardly belong in their circle." The other's mouth had a self-deprecating curve. "But from what I've heard, the family is a good one and devoted to one another. A true rarity."

Corbett departed, leaving Sinjin to muse at the fleeting and strangely wistful look he'd glimpsed on the pimp's face.

———

"Are you certain you don't want to go to the Hunts' ball tonight?" Marianne said from their bed. "You needn't stay with me, darling; I feel perfectly fine."

Ambrose finished tying his dressing gown and strode over to the canopied tester. "Let me see: spend the night shoulder-to-shoulder with a bunch of noisy strangers or in bed with the most beautiful woman in all of London. Yes, a difficult choice."

His wife smiled. "They're not all strangers. Since the Hunts are hosting the event, the Hartefords and Fineses are certain to be there as well."

"Much as I like our friends," Ambrose said, settling onto the mattress and gathering her into his arms, "there's nothing I like better than being alone with you." He looked into her emerald eyes, brushed a moonlight-colored curl off her cheek. "You're certain that you're feeling better?"

"I haven't had a spell since the last one, and that was merely due to fatigue." She kissed his jaw. "Don't worry so, darling."

"I can't help it. You're doing all the work,"—he splayed a hand over the small, satin-covered bump of her belly—"whilst I stand by twiddling my thumbs."

"You've hardly been idle. Any new developments on Revelstoke's case?"

He hesitated. Typically, he shared most everything with his wife—not only because he trusted her, but because beneath her dazzling beauty lay one of the cleverest minds he'd ever encountered. But the news that he'd received from Revelstoke earlier today would disturb her peace.

When he hesitated, she said, "Whatever it is, you can tell me, you know. I may be *enceinte,* but I'm not made of glass."

Clever, like he said.

"Revelstoke sent me a note." He paused. "He had an unexpected call today from Andrew Corbett."

She stiffened against him. "What did Corbett want?"

Ambrose wasn't surprised at her response. Corbett was part of a past she wanted forgotten—for their daughter's sake. Rosie had been taken from Marianne as an infant, and fourteen years ago, Corbett had provided critical information that had eventually led to the girl's recovery.

The journey to find Rosie had been dark, the villain who'd taken her a twisted, evil man. Not a moment passed without Ambrose feeling grateful that the bastard hadn't had a chance to put his degenerate scheme into action—hadn't harmed Rosie, beyond spoiling her and catering to her every whim—before they'd defeated him. To protect Rosie from further trauma, Marianne had insisted that the girl be shielded from the villain's real and despicable motives.

Thus, Rosie had been told that the scoundrel had taken her because he'd wanted a daughter. At the tender age of eight, she'd accepted this explanation without question—or looking back. She'd joyfully moved onto her new life with Marianne and him and the rest of the clan.

But Ambrose had not missed the recent changes in his daughter, and although he was not a superstitious man, he could not deny that the reappearance of Corbett seemed portentous. An omen of troubles ahead. Even so, he didn't want to cause his beloved unnecessary worry.

"Corbett brought some useful information regarding Miss French's accomplice," he said. "Apparently, the man frequented taverns near the West India Docks, so starting tomorrow we'll focus our search there."

"And that is all Corbett wanted?" Marianne pressed.

"I believe so."

"He didn't ask... about Rosie?"

At her whispered words, Ambrose tipped her chin up. Looking into her fear-darkened gaze, he said firmly, "Not a word. I thought he might when I went to inform him about Miss French's death, but our business was professionally conducted; he made no mention of you or Rosie." He paused before adding, "I must say, for a man in his line of work, Corbett carries himself like a gentleman."

"I suspect that he is," Marianne said somberly, "at least that is all he has ever been in my presence. But he is one of the few people who knows the truth of Rosie's past: that she'd been sold to that blackguard for... a reprehensible purpose." Her voice quivered. "Our daughter must be protected from that horror. For that reason alone, I don't want Corbett anywhere near her."

Ambrose's hand moved in soothing circles over his wife's back. "We'll keep her safe, my love. You have my word."

"I trust you, Ambrose, but I'm worried about her. Since her disappointments this Season, her behavior has become increasingly... desperate. It's not helping her quest to find a suitable husband." Marianne bit her lip. "And her behavior toward Polly— frankly, I expected better of her and told her so, which is why she is now giving me the cold shoulder as well."

"I'll speak with her," Ambrose said, frowning. "That is no way to treat her own mama."

"I can handle Rosie. After all, who do you think she gets her willfulness from? But poor Polly." Marianne sighed. "She's had a hard time of it, and I cannot believe Rosie would begrudge her the chance at happiness with Revelstoke. Especially when you and I both know that Rosie's heart was never engaged with the earl. She merely wanted him for his title."

"Whereas Polly wants him for reasons I still cannot fathom," Ambrose muttered.

His wife's lips curved. "Can't you, darling? She may be your youngest sister, but she is also a woman."

"Pray do not remind me." There were things an older brother never wanted to contemplate. "Although I concede that he is not the bounder that I thought him to be and I have no reason to stand in the way of his suit, I still don't understand why a good girl like Polly would want a man with his past."

"You could ask Emma or Thea the same question," Marianne teased. "It seems your sisters have an attraction to tortured rakes."

He grunted. "At least Violet chose a decent chap for herself."

"That's because she's the wild one in that relationship." Leaning up, she murmured in his ear, "Personally, I've never understood the attraction of rakes. I prefer a good, upstanding man myself. Especially,"—her hands wandered, the delicate caresses setting fire to his blood—"the *upstanding* part. Mmm... it seems I'm in luck."

Even as desire surged through him, he managed, "Are you certain it's safe?"

"The doctor said I could resume my regular activities." Her smile was sultry. "Which means you had better see to your husbandly responsibilities, darling."

Never a man to shirk his duties, he obliged.

26

For the first time in her recollection, Polly was enjoying herself at a ball. Accompanied by Em and the duke, she made the rounds of the Hunts' flower-festooned ballroom, determined to do justice to her beautiful new gown. Whenever she received compliments—which was often—she gave credit to the girls and their hard work.

"You ought to see how clever the children are," she'd say. Or, "I've never encountered such diligent and inquiring minds."

To her surprise, others responded well, even expressing interest in visiting the academy, which Polly knew was a thing the Hunts encouraged. She felt a sense of achievement, of burgeoning self-confidence. For once, she wasn't a wallflower but a young woman with purpose, and she couldn't wait for Sinjin to arrive so that she could share her successes.

The only awkward note of the evening thus far occurred during a crush of new arrivals. Someone bumped into her, and she turned to find herself face to face with Lord Brockhurst.

He gawked at her; her face flamed. It was their first meeting since the incident in the garden.

"Miss Kent," he stammered. "You look... different."

He, she noted, did not. He still had the look of a storybook prince—and was about as flat and lifeless as a drawing in a book. Perhaps Sinjin had changed her taste in men, but Brockhurst was a mere shadow compared to her husband-to-be. He had none of Sinjin's masculine vitality, none of his wit or warmth. And why hadn't she noticed how weak his chin was?

"Good evening, my lord," she said stiffly.

"Well... this is dashed awkward, isn't it?" he said, his tone rueful.

Once, she would have found the way his hand disarranged his golden curls charming. Now she felt only gnawing anxiety and anger at herself that she'd let this man know her secret. That she'd given her trust to someone who was unworthy of it.

But what was done could not be undone. By some miracle, he hadn't shared her affliction with the world, and if he hadn't done so in over a year, she reassured herself, then there was no reason for him to do so now.

"My sister and brother-in-law are waiting for me," she said.

"Before you go," he said in a rush, "I heard about your engagement. Is it true?"

Was he asking because he couldn't believe someone would want to marry her? Bitterness nipped at her, making her tone curt. "Yes, it is. Now if you'll excuse me—"

"I think of you, Polly." His low, urgent words stunned her. "We made a connection, and I regret deeply that I did not pursue it."

Flummoxed, she saw that his aura was sincere and could only stare at him in riotous confusion. Once upon a time, she'd have done anything to hear those words from him. But now... they meant nothing.

"Let us leave the past where it belongs. Good evening, my lord." Turning on her heels, she went over to Emma, who was waving at her by the dance floor.

A while later, she stood beneath the ubiquitous potted palm, sipping her second glass of champagne. Once the shock of encountering Brockhurst had worn off, she'd found herself in a strangely celebratory mood. The intersection of past and present had shown her how much she'd changed, and she vastly preferred her new self. She was watching Em dance with the duke when Marianne's best friends swooped upon her. The trio of beautiful ladies were like aunts to her.

"Oh, Polly, you look simply ravishing!" Mrs. Hunt declared, herself a vision in sapphire crepe de chine.

"That color is the perfect match for your eyes." Lady Helena Harteford, a lovely brunette in amethyst-colored silk, beamed at her. "And for your stunning ring."

"May I offer felicitations?" This came from Charity Fines, a slender lady who wore her locks in a short, stylish crop. Her shot silk gown brought out the unique opalescence of her eyes. "I am not acquainted with the Earl of Revelstoke, but I was delighted—and a bit surprised—to hear the news of your engagement."

Polly blushed. "Thank you. It all happened, um, rather quickly."

"That is the way of love," Mrs. Hunt said cheerfully. "It's a whirlwind."

"Speak for yourself." Lady Harteford's gaze rolled heavenward, and for some reason this made the other two ladies burst into peals of laughter.

"I agree with Helena," Mrs. Fines confided. "I was in love with Mr. Fines for years before he noticed."

"That's because your husband is a numskull," Mrs. Hunt said.

"Oh ho, are you talking about your favorite brother again?" Mr. Fines, a raffish blond fellow, strolled up. He was followed by Lord Harteford and Mr. Hunt, who each took a proprietary stance by their ladies.

"Since you're my *only* brother," Mrs. Hunt retorted, "I suppose that's true."

"I may be a numskull, but I still managed to land myself an exceptional wife, didn't I?" He kissed his lady's hand, grinning when she blushed. "Honestly, my love, I'll never understand how a woman with your sweet disposition could be bosom friends with my hoyden of a sister."

"Watch your tongue, Fines." The warning came from Mr. Hunt. With his looming, muscular build and scarred countenance, he was an intimidating presence. But, to Polly, his glow when he looked at his wife softened his rough edges.

"Yes, Paul, watch your tongue," Mrs. Hunt said impishly.

"Easy for you to taunt when you've got Goliath at your back," her brother shot back.

Lord Harteford, who had his arm around his lady's waist, muttered to her, "These two squabble worse than our boys."

"And that is saying *a lot*," Lady Harteford said with a sigh.

Having spent time in the company of the Hartefords' four heathens, Polly couldn't disagree. She was about to inquire after the boys and the other couples' broods when she felt a slight stirring sensation on her nape. Her head turned—and her heart stuttered.

Sinjin was here. And he was prowling—there was no other word for it—toward her.

He was a riveting man on any occasion, but tonight he made her heart thump at an ungoverned pace. His mahogany hair gleamed beneath the chandeliers, his chiseled countenance the ideal of male beauty. In his stark evening wear, he exuded power and predatory grace. But even more than his physical perfection, his vibrant charisma drew all eyes as he passed. Whilst others could not see his aura, Polly reckoned they could feel its pull.

She didn't know what caused his flame to burn so brightly tonight; it was more intense than she'd ever seen it. He glowed with vitality, confidence, and sensuality beyond the civilized. His animal energy triggered a visceral reaction in her. Her nipples went taut. Her pussy dampened.

"Is *that* your earl?" Mrs. Fines whispered.

"Oh my," Lady Harteford breathed.

"Well done, Polly!" Mrs. Hunt winked at her.

Sinjin halted before her. His eyes, the deep vivid blue of a dream, were focused entirely, exclusively on her, and the world faded away. There was nothing but him, the warmth of his lips permeating her glove, scattering sparks over her skin.

"So my wallflower has shed her disguise at last, and there you are," he said huskily, "in full, glorious bloom. Your beauty devastates me, Miss Kent."

His admiration made her *feel* beautiful. It always had.

"You look rather wonderful yourself," she blurted.

His smile was slow, dazzling. "May I have the next dance?"

Until that moment, she hadn't been aware that the orchestra had started up again, but now she heard the lilting first bars of a waltz.

"Yes, please," she said breathlessly.

Belatedly, she looked to the other ladies for permission.

Their heads were bobbing in unison, their faces beaming.

Sinjin offered her his arm, and, giddily, she stepped with him onto the dance floor.

Sinjin had danced with many women, too many to count. But Polly, as always, transformed the experience for him. Dancing was no longer a matter of stepping to music or making chitchat to pass the time or thinking about other things he'd rather be doing. Holding Polly in his arms, staring into her unparalleled eyes, he felt a rightness that he'd never felt before. The moment consumed him: the need to be close to her, to inhale her unique scent... to make love to her.

She'd always been beautiful, but tonight she mesmerized him.

Christ, the way she looked in that dress. Her loveliness made a chaos of his mind. He wanted to have her painted, immortalized. He also wanted to strip her bare, to be horizontal with her, to bury himself in her giving warmth. She laughed breathlessly as he took her into a spin, and he caught other men staring at her, clearly entertaining lustful thoughts—and that made him want to plant a facer on any bastard who dared to look at her twice.

When the dance ended, it required all his willpower to let her go. He wasn't ready to relinquish their moment of privacy, public as it had been. The need to be with her felt urgent, overwhelming.

As he escorted her to her chaperones, he said in low tones, "Meet me on the balcony, kitten."

She stared at him, and for an instant he feared she would say no.

"Which one?" she said.

"The one in the corner, with the curtains drawn." Away from the buffet tables and entertainments, the spot might offer a bit of seclusion. "In ten minutes?" His breath held; he felt as if his life depended on her reply.

Her nod was shy, but her eyes were shining.

Euphoria rushed through him.

Polly made her excuses to her sister, saying that she was visiting the retiring room. Instead, she made a furtive escape toward the appointed balcony where Sinjin was waiting. She didn't know if it was the champagne or the dance with Sinjin or the successes of the night, but she felt freer, more *alive* than she ever had.

She wanted to be with Sinjin more than she wanted her next breath... and *he felt the same way*. She'd seen his desire, felt its wild energy. His pumping need fed her own restless yearning.

She approached their designated meeting place. Luckily, the refreshment tables had just been replenished, attracting a swarm of guests, leaving the present area deserted. She slipped through the velvet panels and out onto the balcony, closing the glass doors behind her. The darkness enveloped her the moment before warm, strong arms did.

27

The feel of her, warm and pliant, made Sinjin's head reel. The pale crescent moon reflected in her luminous eyes, and her smile held all the secrets of the universe. The rest of the world disappeared: there was only the two of them, man and woman alone in a midnight garden, the energy pulsing between them as ancient as time itself.

"God, you're beautiful." He ran his hands reverently over the shoulders left bare by her gown, savoring her silken skin, how she shivered at his touch. "I've missed you, kitten."

"I've missed you too," she said shyly.

Her sweetness undid him. Palming the back of her head, he took her mouth. Her taste hit him like a shot of fine whiskey, a long, smooth burn in his gut. Craving more, he deepened the kiss, his tongue plundering her sweetness and fire; when she licked him back, his mind went black. He backed her into a corner where the balcony met the house, lifting her onto the wide balustrade, propping her back against the wall.

Raging impulse took over. The need to taste, touch, *claim* every part of her.

Wedged between her spread, dangling legs, he consumed her

mouth. She kissed him back with inflaming ardor. Soon, kissing wasn't enough—he had to have more. His lips roved to her right ear, sampling the succulent lobe. She shivered, pressing herself against him, and when he cupped her large, firm tits in his palms, her nipples jutted pleadingly beneath her bodice.

His cock, already rock-hard, jerked in his trousers. He reached for her skirts, tossing them up, wanting nothing between them. When his fingers encountered her slick, hot flesh, he reached a new state of frenzy.

"Christ, you're dripping for me." With pounding lust, he diddled her pearl, painting it over and again with her own dew. "You want me, don't you, love?"

"Yes," she gasped. "So much."

The last vestiges of his control vanished; he became impulse. His fingers went to the hidden buttons of his waistband, freeing his heavy erection. Fisting himself, he ran the blunt tip along her plush slit, moans escaping both of them at the rapturous contact. He slid his turgid shaft against her love knot, stoking both their fires, building the burning crisis. When she came, she chanted his name, and it was a Siren's call he could not deny.

With wanting so intense it was a pain, he notched his cock-head to her entrance.

"I need you, Polly." The guttural words tore from him.

Her eyes held his; the longing and acceptance in them stole his breath.

"I'm yours," she whispered.

With a groan that seemed to come from the depths of his soul, he drove home.

Polly jolted at the incursion. At the exquisitely tight stretch of Sinjin... inside her.

The sensation felt shocking yet right. From the moment

they'd met, he'd filled her humdrum existence with his larger than life presence, and now he was filling her body too... with his larger than life presence. Her intimate muscles instinctively resisted the thick intrusion.

"Kitten?" Need was a blazing halo around him. His pupils were dilated, black edging out blue. Even so, he held himself still. "Should I stop?"

Tenderness flooded her. The discomfort was already fading, a strange but not unpleasant fullness taking its place. She gave a cautious wriggle of her hips, and he suddenly slid in farther. His groan was pained.

"Did I hurt you?" she said anxiously.

"You've confused the text, I think." His brows were drawn, as if he were enduring exquisite torture. "You're so tight. Small and snug. It's you I'm concerned about."

"I think... I'm getting used to it."

"I'll go slowly, love. Tell me if you want me to stop."

He began to move, slowly as promised, even though she could see the effort it cost him. Soon his surges became more than tolerable, her sex tingling with each plunge and withdrawal. Her excitement returned, along with a burgeoning ache in her lower belly, one that, unlike the earlier discomfort, increased when he left her and eased when he returned. Instinctively, her legs circled his hips to draw him closer.

"God, yes." His eyes smoldered into hers. "Can you take more of my cock, little one?"

When she whimpered in reply, he drove in, and only then did she realize how much he'd been holding back. His next thrust took him deeper than he'd gone before. The one after that hit some transcendent place inside. Her fingers dug into his shoulders, her head rocking against the stone wall as his possession tested her very limits. The aching pressure built and built, and then... the release took her by surprise, and she came on a sudden blissful cry.

"Bloody fuck, I can *feel* you coming. So wet and hot, gripping me like a fist..." His mouth covered hers, his groan reverberating in her throat at the same time that his cock exploded inside her. He shuddered, thrusting deeply, drenching her insides with heat.

Music suddenly blared, and for one disoriented moment, she wondered if it was part of the wondrous aftermath.

"What in heaven's name is going on here?" a stranger's voice shrilled.

"Well, I *never*," another declared.

Sinjin jerked. He moved in a blur to pull down her skirts, fasten himself. He turned, keeping her shielded behind him. But catching a glimpse of the matrons' scandalized expressions, the titillated delight in their auras, Polly knew it was far too late.

28

A week later, Polly stood before the looking glass in her bedchamber as her older sisters helped her get ready for her wedding. In two hours, she and Sinjin would be getting married by special license; given the scandal they'd caused, there'd been no other choice. She was riddled with nerves, and her family's presence was a great comfort.

Her brother Harry had arrived last night, and Ambrose would be walking her down the aisle of the drawing room, which Marianne had decorated with a plethora of hothouse blooms. Maisie, Olivia, and Francesca would be tossing rose petals in her wake.

And her sister Violet was here as well.

Looking at Vi, who was adjusting the train of her gown, Polly said tremulously, "I still can't believe that you made it in time. Carlisle must have driven like Helios himself."

Violet's husband, Viscount Carlisle, was an expert horseman, his breeding program one of the most sought after in the nation. Thanks to his elite driving skills, he'd managed to get Vi and their son Jamie here from Scotland to London on exceedingly short notice.

"Actually, Carlisle let *me* do half the driving." Violet grinned at their combined reflections in the mirror. A lithe brunette, Vi had always been a pretty hoyden, but since her marriage, she'd gained a maturity that tempered her golden aura without sacrificing its unique energy.

"What doesn't he allow you to do?" Em observed. "The man indulges you to no end."

"He just likes to pick his battles," Vi said blithely. "But never mind me—our Polly is the one getting married today. Gadzooks, look at you! Our baby sister all grown up."

"You do make a beautiful bride, dear." As Thea added ivory rosebuds to Polly's hair, she said dreamily, "I hope your day is every bit as special as mine was."

Polly managed a smile, even as the knot of doubt tightened in her stomach. The uncertainty had been there for the entire week, and it wasn't over her own feelings. She was certain she wanted to marry Sinjin: it was why she'd agreed to wear his ring... and why she'd given him her maidenhead.

She didn't regret what she'd done. Experiencing the bright intensity of his passion had been like touching an electrifying machine. He'd sparked an elemental response in her, a desire every bit as strong as his. There on the balcony, she'd known that she wasn't falling in love with him: she was already there. She loved him. And, because she was a Kent, she did so in a head-over-slippers, wholehearted, and forever sort of way.

What she was far less certain about was *his* feelings for her. His odd, distant behavior during the past week had only ratcheted up her fears. Was he regretting what they'd done? Had his mind changed about wanting to marry her? For her, their love-making had been the most pleasurable experience of her life... but what did she know? She didn't have his experience. What if she didn't measure up to his previous lovers or disappointed him in some way—

"What *is* the matter, dear?"

Finding herself under Em's scrutiny, she tried to drag herself out of the vortex of panic. "Um, nothing's the matter. Nothing at all."

Given the scandalous reason for her hasty nuptials, she knew that her siblings had reservations about Sinjin. She'd tried to explain that it had been as much her fault as his—that she'd been just as carried away by the moment—but that didn't overcome her family's doubts entirely. The last thing she wanted was to give them any more reason not to welcome him into the fold.

"Then why are you as pale as a sheet? And if you gnaw on your lip any more, there'll be none of it left." Em placed her hands on Polly's shoulders. "I may not have your acuity, dear, but I have known you all your life. You can talk about whatever is troubling you, you know."

Faced with those maternal brown eyes, Polly could bear it no longer. She burst into tears.

Em held her until the storm passed. Afterward, she sat on the bed, surrounded by her sisters, and spoke haltingly of her fears.

"He d-didn't even c-come see me for three days," she sniffled into the handkerchief that Thea had handed her. "And when h-he did, he was so... s-somber." At the memory of the darkness shrouding him, fear skated through her. She'd never seen him look so *grim*.

"Did you ask him what the matter was?" Em said, frowning.

Nodding, she said, "He apologized profusely for what happened. For his, um, lack of self-control." His remorse and disgust at himself had been evident, but there had been more to his gloomy aura... a despair that she didn't understand. "He denied that anything else was wrong, but I could *see* that wasn't true. Why wouldn't he tell me what was truly bothering him? Unless what he's upset about has to do with..."—her hand balled the linen—"me?"

"I wouldn't jump to that conclusion," Emma said prosaically. "You mustn't forget that the day after the ball, he sent you that note explaining why he didn't come straightaway. That he was busy making arrangements for the special license."

That was true.

"And he did send you tokens of his esteem every day." Thea gestured to the extravagant bouquets that perfumed Polly's room.

"Thunder and turf, I'd call that king's ransom she's wearing more than a *token*," Vi put in.

Polly brushed her fingertips over the diamond and aquamarine bracelet and earbobs that he'd sent. The jewels had been accompanied by a brief message.

Kitten,
    To match the ring and necklace but never your peerless eyes.
    —S.

She'd slept with that note under her pillow all week. Still...

"Why does his manner seem so distant?" she said miserably.

"Maybe he's trying to keep up appearances," Vi suggested. "Crumpets, Polly, he compromised you on a *balcony*. I'm sure he doesn't want to give the tongues more to wag about by showing up daily on your doorstep like an overeager bridegroom."

Heat bloomed in Polly's cheeks... but embarrassment felt better than despair.

"Despite Vi's indelicate way of putting it,"—Em aimed an exasperated look at Vi, who responded with an unrepentant grin —"she does have a point. Revelstoke probably wanted to observe the proprieties and forestall any further gossip." She paused, then muttered as if she couldn't help herself, "Bit late to shut the barn doors, if you ask me."

"There may be other reasons for his distance as well." Thea patted Polly's hand. "Before Tremont and I got married, he was behaving in a similar fashion, and I, too, interpreted it as a sign that he was having second thoughts about me. In fact, I believe I felt much as you are feeling right now."

"You did? What made you feel better?"

"Tremont and I talked," Thea said simply. "He made me understand that his aloofness wasn't about me but his past. His uncertainty had to with himself, the sort of husband he'd make. Might that be true of Revelstoke?"

Polly thought about it. He had told her that he wasn't an easy man to live with. He'd said that he disliked intimacy because, in his experience, it had led to disappointment. From what she'd learned about his family, she could understand his feelings. After all, he'd lost his brother and mama, the two people he'd been closest to.

And it was sadly telling that his other family members would not be in attendance at the wedding ceremony. She'd persuaded Sinjin to send invitations to the Actons, and he'd done so with clear reluctance. They'd sent terse regrets.

Given his history, would it be surprising if Sinjin felt uneasy committing his future to another's? With a blaze of insight, she saw how similar they were. How, from the very beginning, his loneliness had resonated with her own. Whilst she undoubtedly had the advantage of a loving family, her affliction had taught her what it was like to be an outsider. To be rejected and abandoned.

Although Sinjin had been mobbed by adoring hordes, he himself had said that he'd only been sought after for his money and title, a night's distraction. He'd never felt valued for himself— for who he truly was. For the intelligent, passionate, and honorable man Polly knew him to be.

"Sinjin is so popular and self-assured that sometimes I forget that he might have uncertainties, too," she said with remorse. "That he is as human as I am."

"Gracious, you're *every* bit as good as the earl," Em said tartly. "Your trouble is that you've always underestimated your own worth. Indeed, if you have any doubts about *him*, Polly, it's time to speak now." Worried eyes searched her face. "I know you're marrying under exigent circumstances, but if you've changed your mind, we'll support—"

"I want to marry him." Polly said quickly. "I'm sure of it."

A knock sounded on the door, and she was relieved for the interruption. Vi went to open it, and Rosie entered. Polly's heart beat in a rapid staccato at the sight of her sister, who was wearing a pretty white muslin and an uncertain expression.

"Polly... may I have a word?" Rosie said.

She nodded.

"We'll let you two girls chat in private," Thea said with a smile.

After the others left, silence descended. As Polly wracked her brain for what to say, Rosie blurted, "I'm sorry, Polly. I've been the most awful person *ever*. I've wanted to apologize for days, but I was so ashamed of my behavior and—"

Polly ran over and hugged her. "No, I'm the one who's sorry," she said and was fiercely glad when her sister hugged her back. "I hurt you and—"

"You didn't do it on purpose. I know that. But I was just so angry and frustrated at my own situation that I took it out on you. I envied your happiness when, in reality, it was never at the expense of my own. *That's* how petty I was being." Pulling back, Rosie said tearfully, "Can you ever forgive me?"

Relief made her throat swell. "There's nothing to forgive."

"There is. I've been absolutely horrid to you. I ought to have been there for you, to listen or talk things over or just to share in your joy. No, don't you start crying, too." Rosie dabbed at Polly's cheeks with her own handkerchief and then steered her back in front of the looking glass. "It's the most important day of your life, and you must look your absolute best. Bosom chums and sisters do not allow each other to get married with red eyes and a runny nose."

The return of the old Rosie made happiness leap in Polly's heart. As the blond girl fussed over her, she said with a pang, "I've missed you so. And I can't believe... this is good-bye." It struck her that after the wedding, she'd be leaving her old life behind and taking her new place with her husband.

"It's not as if you're moving to the Outer Hebrides, silly. You'll be a five minute carriage drive away." Despite her teasing, there was a hitch to Rosie's voice. "We'll see each other all the time— even more, now that I'm finished acting like a spoilt brat. Don't argue, dearest," she said, forestalling Polly's protest, "because it's true. What's also true is that we both have to grow up sometime. And maybe we have to do some of that growing up on our own."

The words hit like pinpricks on Polly's heart. Because she knew they were true. As painful as her separation from Rosie had been, the time apart had also been a catalyst for her to carve out her own future.

Rosie made a few more expert adjustments to the gown and stepped back. "And speaking of growing up, will you please explain why, after I nagged you forever to change your wardrobe, you do nothing, but when I don't speak to you for a fortnight, you suddenly turn into a fashion plate?" She gestured at the looking glass.

Obediently, Polly peered at her reflection. She'd chosen the cerulean blue silk because it reminded her of Sinjin's eyes. Although Madame Rousseau had made the frock on a rush order, artistry was apparent in every detail. The gown flattered Polly's figure, its jeweled belt emphasizing her narrow waist and V-shaped neckline displaying her high bosom. Fine blond lace trimmed the bodice, gigot sleeves, and tiered underskirt.

"The time seemed right to try something different," Polly murmured.

"It's because of Revelstoke, isn't it? Because you love him?"

She bit her lip, not wanting to open up wounds so recently healed.

"You can tell me, Pols." Rosie's jade eyes were solemn. "I may have fancied him for his title and looks, but my heart wasn't involved—you and I both know that. So not only do I hope you've found what I'm too shallow to look for, I want more than anything for you to be loved as you deserve."

"You're *not* shallow. After everything you've been through, it makes perfect sense that you'd want a husband who can give you security."

"You see the best in everyone." Her sister squeezed her hand. "Now we'll see if you can do the same for yourself. So you love Revelstoke?"

"Yes," Polly whispered.

"Does he love you?"

She shook her head. "But it's all right. He was honest about it from the start. He doesn't believe in emotional entanglements—and that will be best, anyway, given that I..."

"That you don't plan on telling him about your ability?" her sister prodded gently.

"My curse, you mean." Sighing, Polly said, "Don't look at me that way, Rosie. I've made up my mind about this."

"Is that why you turned down Papa's offer to spend your wedding trip at the cottage?" Rosie said, proving yet again how astute she was.

Ambrose and Marianne had suggested that Polly take a brief sojourn with Sinjin to the cozy cottage they maintained back in Chudleigh Crest. She'd declined politely, giving the excuse that she wanted to stay in Town until Sinjin's case was solved. It wasn't a lie—she and Sinjin had discussed the matter, preferring to post-pone a honeymoon until Nicoletta's accomplice was apprehended—but, as Rosie had surmised, it also wasn't the full truth.

"Sinjin thinks I'm beautiful. I don't want him to see me... the way the villagers do." Polly's voice cracked a little. "I don't want to be Peculiar Polly all over again."

"Oh, how I wish I could give those clodhoppers and busy-bodies a good tongue lashing!" Rosie fumed. "Listen to me, Polly—that was a long time ago. You cannot let the cruelty of children and ignorance of adults haunt you forever."

"It doesn't... at least not the way it used to," she said falteringly, "but that doesn't mean I want to expose myself to ridicule or rejection. I just want to leave the past in the past. Please understand, Rosie."

"I do, of course." Her sister huffed out a breath. "And seeing as how it is your wedding day, dearest, I'm not going to plague you further. Just promise me one thing, will you?"

"Yes?" she said cautiously.

Taking her hands, Rosie said, her eyes glimmering, "If you must leave me, do it for a good reason. Be happy, my dearest sister."

"I'll do my best." Polly's heart welled with love—the same emotion she saw glowing around her bosom spirit. "As long as *you* promise to do the same."

29

Freshly bathed, Sinjin dismissed his valet and poured himself a scotch. Elation hummed inside him. This had to be the best day of his life. Not because it happened to be his birthday, an occasion he wasn't accustomed to celebrating and didn't care all that much about, but because, on the other side of the door, Polly was completing her evening ablutions in her bridal bower.

Soon, he'd join her—his *wife*.

I've done it. Polly's mine.

Somehow he'd managed not to bollix things up... although it'd been a close call.

It was the nature of his devils to creep up on him. Not only did they pilfer his will, they could perform sneak-thievery upon his judgement and awareness. At the ball, he ought to have recognized the signs, but he'd attributed the euphoric feelings to Polly... which wasn't entirely inaccurate. Seeing her so radiant, brimming with sensual confidence, had aroused him immeasurably. In retrospect, however, it had also magnified the black demon's seductive whispers to take what was his—to claim his mate.

So he had. On a bloody balcony.

God, she deserved so much more for her first time.

The familiar remorse and self-recrimination tightened his gut. The last week had been a test of things to come. For after the high of the ball, he'd plunged immediately into the abyss. The blue monster had been relentless, filling his head with loathsome thoughts.

You're a bastard for ruining Polly. What will you do when she discovers how pathetic, how gutless you truly are? She'll despise you. Leave you.

He took another sip of whiskey to dispel the tendrils of his inner chill. His head was clear again, and, as unpleasant as the episode had been, he felt a spark of triumph because, through the worst of it, he hadn't lost sight of what was important. For the first time, he'd had a purpose to anchor him: Polly. Thoughts of her had buoyed him through dark waters.

The morning after the ball, despite his plummeting spirits, he'd dragged himself to the Archbishop of Canterbury to attain a special license. Next he'd made arrangements for flowers to be sent to Polly every day. He'd written her a note, making an excuse for his absence; there was no way in hell she could see him in the state he was in. In a stroke of luck, he'd already had that set of jewels ready for her. He'd been waiting for the right moment to give her the remaining pieces. While he was curled up like a bastard in bed had seemed as good a time as any.

The important thing, he told himself, was that the two of them had weathered his storm. After three days, when the worst of it was over and he was at least marginally fit for company, he'd gone to see her. He could tell she was hurt by his behavior, but she'd stayed the course with him.

That was what counted.

Gratitude and wonder warmed his chest. His new countess was loyal, would stick with him through thick and thin. She wouldn't be like his family whose absence had been palpable at the intimate wedding ceremony and breakfast that followed. It was what he'd expected from them; he told himself it didn't matter. With Polly, he finally had more than empty chairs in his future.

Through the walls, he heard Polly's maid bidding her good night. His bride was alone now, waiting for him. Anticipation simmering, he paused in front of the chevalier glass.

As his habit was to sleep in the buff, he wore nothing beneath his silk robe. He hesitated, wondering if he ought to don a night-shirt. Light-skirts might not blink at the scars on his back, and worldly ladies had found them titillating... but Polly fell in neither of those categories. She was no casual tumble. She was his wife, and this was their wedding night.

In the reflection, his lips curled in self-derision. *You are who you are.* Unless he meant to hide his back from her forever, he might as well begin as he meant to go on. Besides, he thought dryly, of all the things he needed to keep from her, his back was a damned low priority.

He'd neither hide nor bring attention to that part of himself; her reaction would be what it had to be. Setting down his empty glass, he tightened the belt on his dressing robe, went over to the door between their adjoining chambers. He gave a brisk knock.

"Come in." His wife's sweet summons beckoned like a dream.

Watching Sinjin enter her chamber filled Polly with a giddy sense of unreality.

In truth, the entire day had had a dream-like quality. Sinjin had been back to his old self, his aura once again vital and bright. He'd lavished such attention on her that she'd begun to wonder if her earlier apprehension had just been a case of the bridal jitters.

And as much as she loved her family, she'd loved them even more when, in the absence of Sinjin's kin, they'd made extra efforts to welcome him into the fold. He and her brother Harry, in particular, had seemed to hit it off; the two were of a similar age and apparently shared a fanatical love of boxing. Between the toasts and general hilarity, the wedding "breakfast" had gone on until nearly suppertime, when Ambrose had announced that the newlyweds should be allowed to leave.

Now Polly was at her new home with her new husband, and all she could think was, *I'm married to this god-like man?*

Sinjin's dark hair was still wet from his bath, the ends damp and curling. His sinfully handsome face was freshly shaved, and his eyes gleamed in the light of the lamps. He wore a black silk dressing gown that clung to the broad planes of his chest, revealing a vee of virile chest hair. Beneath the hem, his calves bulged with muscle.

His male sensuality was raw and uncivilized, and every part of her responded to his wild energy. Her breath quickened. Her nipples stiffened. Her pussy moistened in a damp rush.

He strode over to her. When he'd knocked, she'd had a sudden panic about how she ought to pose herself. Sitting on the bed might appear too forward—on the chair by the fire too prim. How should a bride greet her new husband? Paralyzed by indecision, she'd wound up where she was, frozen at the foot of the bed. Gawking at him, she realized belatedly, like a feather-wit.

He curled a finger under her chin. "What's going on in that head of yours, kitten?"

"I understand why they call you the God of Revelry," she blurted.

His brows lifted.

"The only thing you're missing is a leopard skin and a thyrsus. And maybe a few Maenads and Satyrs following in tow," she babbled on like an idiot.

"This room isn't all that large. I'm not sure we could fit in a procession." His lips quirked. "What's a thyrsus?"

"It's a kind of staff. With a pine cone on top. It's supposed to be a symbol of fertility," she said and immediately wished she hadn't. What a time to mention the issue of fecundity... on her wedding night! It was as if her tongue had a mind of its own.

"You have an awful lot of knowledge in that pretty head," he commented. "From your papa the schoolmaster, I take it?"

She nodded, deciding it might be better if she didn't talk. Ever again.

Sinjin lifted a tendril of her loose hair, rubbing it between finger and thumb. "So if I'm Bacchus," he murmured, "does that mean you're my Ariadne?"

His words sparked an uncomfortable connection—not the one he obviously intended. She *was* like the mythical Princess of Crete in that she'd once been duped by a man. Before being discovered and rescued by Bacchus, Ariadne had been dumped on an island by Theseus—the supposed hero whom she'd helped to slay the Minotaur and escape the labyrinth. Polly had known a similar betrayal: Brockhurst had used her to win a wager, then tossed her aside like yesterday's newspaper.

Why was she thinking about that now? It was in the past and had no place in the present. In the future embodied by her outrageously attractive husband whose aura blazed with desire for her. *Her*—Peculiar Polly Kent. She could hardly believe that destiny had been so generous.

"I'm no goddess," she managed.

"Aren't you? You could have fooled me." He released her hair to cup her jaw, and her breath caught at the fierce tenderness in his gaze. "From the moment we met, I thought that you had divine wisdom in those eyes of yours. That you saw in me something no one else had before. I must have recognized my own fate."

He kissed her, and some of her nervousness fled. Passion nudged doubt aside. Heavens, she'd missed this—missed him. The reassurance of his firm lips moving over hers, the taste of him saturating her senses like the finest wine. He was intoxicating, real, and all hers. When the kiss ended, they were both breathless.

He traced the curve of her cheek with his thumb. "I'm a scoundrel, but I can't bring myself to regret what happened on the balcony. For it led to this, to you being mine—even though you deserved much more for your first time."

"More?" She blinked. Recalling the riotous bliss, she said doubtfully, "I'm not certain I could have handled more."

"Oh, you can, sweeting." His lazy, wicked smile made her heart stutter. "I've never met a woman with your passion. There hasn't been a time when you haven't come at least twice for me—and I haven't even had you on a bed yet."

Her cheeks warmed. Was her response... normal? "Do you think me wanton?"

"Yes, love." Before she could start to fret, he kissed her again, whispering against her lips, "You're wanton and sweet, and I'm damned lucky I found you before someone else did."

"I'm the lucky one," she said earnestly.

"I'm glad you think so, but you're wrong." His gaze was solemn. "You're a gift, sweetheart, the sort I never thought to have in my life, but I'm not a fellow who looks a gift horse in the mouth. I'd rather spend my time unwrapping you." He toyed with the sash of her chintz wrapper. "No doubt a considerate husband would douse the lamps... but I'd prefer to see you, Polly."

She realized that he was giving her a choice. And she loved him for it.

She also knew how she wanted to reply.

Taking a step back, holding her husband's gaze, she reached for the belt that held her wrapper together. She inhaled for courage, gave a sharp tug, and pushed the modest covering off her shoulders, letting it pool at her bare feet. Pulse skittering, she felt his gaze traveling over what she wore beneath.

"Devil and damn." He sounded stunned.

Those three guttural words—along with the leap of lust in his aura—boosted her confidence. Her sisters had been right in suggesting this particular choice for her wedding night. At first, she'd balked at the notion of wearing something this risqué: the white satin negligee dipped low over her bosom, leaving her upper back bare, its lace-trimmed hem ending just below her knees. The garment was held up by a single cherry-red bow tied at her nape.

She stood there, debating her next move, when he spoke up.

"There's no need to be shy or embarrassed with me, kitten. Or anything but bloody proud of everything that you are." His gaze raked hotly over her. "You do know that, don't you?"

"I'm not embarrassed." How could she be when confronted by his vivid admiration? "I was just wondering since you said that I'm, um, your gift... if you would like to do the honors?" Blushing, she gestured to the bow.

The fierce approval in his eyes told her she'd made the right decision.

He reached out, her pulse quickening as he slid his fingers under the ribbon. The faint rasp of his callused fingertips chased thrills over her nape. Her breath lodged as he pulled on the end of the bow, the action as slow and deliberate as a boy who is striving to make a treat last. He let the ribbon fall, his gaze following the fluttering strip as it obeyed gravity's call, bringing the garment with it.

Polly felt the sensuous slide of silk over her breasts, the fabric hitching slightly over her taut nipples before it shed from her like an unnecessary skin. Seeing the flare of Sinjin's nostrils, she knew the sight pleased him, and it made her stand taller, proud indeed that she could have this effect on a man as worldly as him. She waited, breath held.

"You are the finest birthday gift I could hope to receive," he said.

The reverence that lit his aura was so dazzling that it took her a moment to register his words.

"It's your *birthday*?" she burst out. "Today? Why didn't you say anything?"

"I just did." He sounded distracted—perhaps because he'd cupped one of her breasts, his gaze focused on his thumb as it circled her erect nipple.

Even as his touch released shivers of pleasure, she persisted, "But you didn't mention anything earlier. We could have celebrated properly. I didn't even get you a present—"

"I've never celebrated my birthday." Before she could question that, he said huskily, "Polly, do you know what I really want?"

"What?" Whatever he wanted, she was determined to get it for him.

He moved, quick as lightning. One instant she was standing, the next she was on her back upon the feather mattress, her husband lying on his side next to her, looking at her like she was a feast and he a man starved. He ran a finger between her breasts, the possession in his touch unmistakable.

"You. My wife. Mine." Blue flames leapt in his eyes.

Then his lips claimed the arch of her throat. Even as pleasure overtook her, she made a mental note to return to the topic of his birthday... later. He cupped her heaving breasts like a pirate weighing his treasure, licking back and forth between the stiff peaks, tormenting her with his mouth. Turbulent pleasure gathered as he cupped her between her legs, his fingers plundering the depths of her giving flesh. Again and again, he touched deep inside her while his palm ground against the sensitive crest of her mound.

The storm broke, flooding her with bliss.

"By Jove, you're a sight to behold in the throes." His earthy praise didn't help her heart's erratic thumping. "I wonder if your pleasure tastes as good as it looks..."

The mattress shifted as he kissed his way downward, between the valley of her ribs, the soft rise of her belly. Like a playful panther, he nipped and nuzzled, making her giggle when his tongue tucked into her belly button, tickled the back of one knee. Then he made himself a place between her thighs, and all laughter fled at the first lush swipe of his tongue along her cleft.

"Mouthwatering." At the burning hunger in his eyes, her satiated nerves sprang back to life. "I love the way you taste, Polly. Love eating this sweet, juicy part of you. Spread your legs further, love, show me you want this too."

With a moan, she did. He mouthed her exposed sex, his tongue delving between her swollen folds, teasing the entrance to her sheath. Her fingers found the rough silk of his hair, holding on as he ate at her tender flesh. It was more than the sensations that rocked her: it was *him*. The way his cheekbones were flushed, his brows drawn with pleasure. Knowing that she could affect him thus brought her to the brink—and then he suckled her pearl, his tongue strong and flicking, propelling her over.

As she came with a cry, he surged upward, yanking at the belt of his robe. He didn't even bother to remove it completely, his mouth latching onto hers as the broad crown of his cock prodded her entrance. She sighed against his lips as he pushed into her, a thrust that was exquisitely filling... but not painful.

"Polly?"

"Yes," she murmured, knowing what he was asking. "It's good, Sinjin. *So* good."

With a groan, he began to move. His hard, hair-dusted chest scraped against her nipples, setting off shocks of pleasure. She slid her palms beneath his parted robe, touching wherever she could, clinging to the bulging strength of his shoulders as he moved within her. His big, powerful shaft caressed her with stunning tenderness. It was more than a connection of bodies, it was a closeness unlike any she'd experienced. A closeness she'd craved without even knowing it.

Apparently, he felt it too, for he growled, "Wrap your legs around my hips. I want to get in deeper. To have all of you."

Her calves fitted in the lean, hard grooves of his hips as if they were meant to be there. His big palms cupped her bottom, tipping her hips up, and she gasped as that altered angle dragged fiery friction against her pearl. The steel-hard root of his cock grazed against her with each pass, triggering tremors deep in her pussy.

"Sinjin," she moaned, "it's happening again..."

"Yes, love, *yes*." His eyes burned, his hips thrusting harder and faster. "Come for me once more, take me with you."

The tremors built and built and then something inside her *snapped*. The convulsions shook her very core, rippling outward in ecstatic waves. As bliss rolled through her, she felt him seize her hands, planting them onto the mattress as his hips pounded her fiercely. His fingers laced with hers, he exploded inside her, their shared cries of fulfillment ricocheting off the walls.

🦋 30 🦋

Polly was having a wondrous dream. She was cocooned in warmth, in feelings of safety and belonging, her body lax and satiated. But something was tickling her nose, and though she tried to move away, she couldn't. She was trapped.

Awareness drifted over her, and she surfaced groggily, her lashes blinking at the unfamiliar sight that greeted her. The muscular planes of a male chest, the glinting bronze hair on it the culprit of her nose's discomfort. Beyond that, bulging biceps. And beyond that, a strange room, a line of watery light peeping through a slit in the curtains.

Then it returned to her that this wasn't a dream—this was her *reality*—and joy inundated her. She lay quietly for a few moments, savoring the beauty of waking up tucked next to Sinjin. Even in sleep, he kept an arm curled possessively around her... as if she'd want to be anywhere but where she was at the moment! Then she recalled what he'd told her last night.

I've never celebrated my birthday. The notion filled her with sorrow—and indignation on his behalf. How could his family be so cold toward him? She resolved to make certain that, from here on in, every birthday of his would be marked with proper festivity.

Nature soon interrupted her musings, and not wanting to wake Sinjin, she eased herself carefully from under his heavy arm. She found her wrapper tangled up with his dressing gown on the floor, the entwining of chintz and black silk making her smile. As she got dressed, she couldn't help but admire her sleeping husband.

She thought Sinjin was even more handsome with his features relaxed, the faintest curve on his sensual lips, as if he were enjoying a good dream (was it greedy to hope it was of her?). Lying on his back, the sheet down to his waist and baring his defined torso, he was the very picture of muscular virility. Beneath the sheet, she saw the prominent outline of his member against his thigh, and her well-used inner muscles fluttered.

Goodness. Even at rest, her husband's potency could not be denied.

Chiding herself for being a shameless wanton—and feeling giddy because she had cause to be—she quickly went to use the adjoining bathing room. When she returned, she saw that Sinjin was still asleep, though he'd turned over onto his side. She removed her robe, put her knee on the bed, and her gaze hit his bare back for the first time.

A gasp left her. She stumbled backwards in shock, bumping against the bedside table, rattling the glass shade of the lamp.

"Polly?" He turned over, his blue eyes slumberous, a mahogany lock falling over his brow. He radiated lazy male satisfaction. "Why are you standing all the way over there?"

She couldn't erase what she'd seen. The white scars criss-crossed over his muscled back. The evidence of untold abuses.

"What happened to your back?" she whispered.

His languor vanished. He sat up, his expression hard, his eyes like chips of ice.

"It's nothing," he said curtly.

"Who did that to you?" Her voice shook.

"I said it's nothing. I'll put on a shirt if the scars bother you. Now come back to bed."

"Of course the scars bother me—because someone hurt you! I want to know: *who?*"

Jaw set, he stared at her. Anger ripped through his tranquil aura, along with a host of other dark emotions that she was too distraught, too *furious* to pay heed to.

"Was it your father?" she persisted.

She'd had cause to dislike the duke before, knowing that he hadn't believed in his own son's innocence... hadn't even bothered to attend the wedding. The notion of him abusing Sinjin as a child —for those scars were as old as they were plentiful—made her feel fit to kill. Her hands balled.

"His Grace couldn't be bothered to discipline his spare," Sinjin drawled—yes, *drawled*, as if they were talking about the blessed weather!—"so he paid someone else to do it. After I was expelled from Eton, he sent me to another school. Creavey Hall prided itself on being an academy that reformed problematic children."

"Did he know what they were doing to you?" she whispered.

"My stepmama and I did not rub along, so I was rarely allowed home. I did, however, write His Grace about it. He wrote back saying that whatever happened was my fault and that he hoped I would learn some self-discipline to prevent further punishment." Mouth twisting, Sinjin gave a shrug. "He wasn't wrong. I was a troublesome child. At Creavey Hall, they had their ways for dealing with rabble-rousers. Spare the rod, spoil the boy and all that."

Was he actually *defending* the bounders who had beaten him? "There is nothing you could have done to deserve such treatment," she said vehemently. "*Nothing.*"

"You don't know what I'm capable of. Self-restraint—it has never come easily to me." Though his tone was light, she saw the tangled morass of anger, despair... even resignation in his aura. "I fought with the other boys. I played truant on a regular basis. One time, I locked the tutor in his room so he couldn't get to class—"

"And none of that warrants being abused," she burst out. "My papa taught an entire generation of children in our village, and he never, not once, beat a child. Nor any of us, and my siblings and I made more than our fair share of mischief." Desperate to convince him, she rattled on, "Violet was always ruining her clothes with her acrobatic antics, Harry blew things up constantly with his scientific experiments, and even Em lost track of the cat one time and set the cottage on fire—"

"That's enough," he said.

His tone—quiet and girdled with steel—halted her chatter. That and his aura, pain and loneliness oozing through the thick layer of anger. Her heart wept for what he'd suffered as a boy, alone, abandoned to the cruelties of the world without anyone's protection. A boy whose birthday hadn't even been recognized.

"You didn't deserve it," she insisted. "You were just a child. And, furthermore, your father should have put a stop to what was going on. He ought to have protected you and—"

"Polly, enough. I get the picture. I didn't deserve to be beaten."

"No, you did *not*."

"And you don't find the sight of the scars repellant, just the fact of how I got them."

"I could never find you repellant," she said, appalled that he could even think such a thing.

"Then why are you still all the way over there?" He crooked a finger at her. "Come here."

Uncertain of his mood, the welter of emotion in his aura, she nonetheless didn't hesitate to do as he asked. She didn't want him to think, for even a second, that she could be repulsed by him. That she could think of him as anything but the most attractive and wonderful man in the world. She opened her mouth to say so, but all that emerged was a whoosh of air from her lungs because his arms closed around her like bands of steel, pulling her onto the bed, locking her against him.

His face buried in her hair, he whispered, "Thank you. For being in my corner."

In those words, he conveyed a world of feeling, similar to when he'd thanked her for believing in him. Now she understood even more why that was so important to him. That even a god could be besieged by inner monsters and be in need of reinforcements. And she vowed to herself that she would never let him down.

"I'll always be in your corner." She hugged him back. "I'm your wife. I... care about you."

She caught herself in the nick of time. She knew his views on love and intimacy, but surely he wouldn't mind having her affection? After all, *he* showered her with affection all the time. With his gifts. His endearments. The way he made her feel like the most desirable creature in all of Christendom.

His fierce words rumbled into her ear. "And you're loyal, devoted, and protective of those you care about, aren't you?"

"You make me sound like a well-trained spaniel," she said, wrinkling her nose.

His hold loosened enough for him to look down at her. Although his pain hadn't faded entirely, something else bloomed in his aura: hope. Blue and so beautiful it made her throat convulse. And something else beneath that, dim yet glimmering, something that she didn't quite recognize but which made her heart pound...

"Not a spaniel." He smiled slowly. "You're more of a... guard kitten."

She huffed out a breath. "That's hardly intimidating."

"I don't know. At certain points last night, I felt your little claws biting into me."

"I didn't hurt you, did I?" Worriedly, she searched his shoulders for marks.

He laughed and kissed her soundly on the nose. "No, you didn't hurt me. God, Polly, as if you could. I'm teasing, of course. Although, if you want to kiss it all better"—he waggled his brows —"I wouldn't stop you."

The heavy moment had passed. In its place was a different sort of tension, one that made her pulse quicken, her body blossoming with awareness of him. Of his addictive male scent, his strong and virile form, his eyes radiant with sensual heat. Desire soared in her, tempered by the need to show him how much he mattered.

He made her feel beautiful, and she wanted to return that gift. To make him feel every bit as *wanted* as he made her feel. Thus far, she'd been content to let him take the lead in their lovemaking. Could she be bold enough to try something different?

When he bent his head to kiss her, she ducked out of his way.

"Polly?" he said, his brows knitting.

In answer, she placed her hands on his shoulders and pushed. She saw his look of surprise the second before he fell back, his head landing on the pillow. Before she lost her nerve, she clambered atop him, straddling his hips.

"All right," she said.

His brows shot up. "Er... all right?"

"All right, I *will* kiss it all better," she clarified, "so don't stop me."

What kind of an idiot did she think he was? Of course he wasn't going to stop her.

He would never look a gift horse like this in the mouth—and, ah, God, what a *mouth*. Sinjin's gaze honed hungrily on his wife's ripe lips at they descended toward his. She kissed him with a tenderness that made his head spin, her tongue lapping at the seam of his lips. He invited her in, relishing her newfound boldness, the sensual confidence he knew he'd had a part in unleashing.

Her tongue swirled against his, and arousal sang in his blood. *Christ*, the passion in her. That itself made her the most tempting woman he'd ever known, but she gave him even more. Something he'd never had and never thought he'd find.

I'll always take your side. I care for you.

His chest tightened; his prick throbbed. He speared his fingers in her hair, kissing her with greedy desperation. He blinked when she slapped at his arms.

"I'm doing the kissing, remember?" she said.

She was clearly trying to appear stern. Since she was sitting naked atop him with her hair a silken curtain to her waist, her red nipples playing erotic peek-a-boo through the tawny tresses, and her cunny wetly kissing his abdomen, he couldn't say he was much intimidated.

Randy as hell, yes. Intimidated, no.

But, as he'd said before, he was no idiot.

"Yes, my lady." He managed a contrite tone. "I'll keep my hands right here at my sides where you can see them."

Her glorious eyes narrowed, as if she suspected he might be teasing her, but he kept his look innocent, and, with a little huff, she continued on with her game. Praise Jesus. She nuzzled his earlobe, flicking and sucking it like he'd done to her, making his blood hum. His neck arched as she kissed his throat, licking the bump, working her way down to his chest.

Like a frisky little feline, she rubbed her cheek against the muscled planes, seeming to enjoy the scratch of his hair against her smooth cheek. Seeing her enjoyment in her explorations amplified the pleasure of what she was doing. He watched with interest as she approached his right nipple. She gave the flat disc a tentative lick, and then her gaze shot to his, the question in those aquamarine depths making his teeth ache—that was how sweet he found her. How bloody cute.

"It feels good," he said huskily, "though I'm probably not quite as sensitive there as you are."

"We'll just have to find your special spots then," she said decisively.

"Special spots?'

"The places that make your toes curl." Her tongue traced the valley between his pectoral muscles. "Here, maybe?"

He shivered. "That feels nice, though not toe-curlingly good."

"What about here?" She peppered kisses over the flexing ridges of his abdomen.

"Getting warmer." Aroused as hell, he wondered just how far she would go with this.

His breath held as her lips neared his rod, which was already hard and throbbing. She hadn't touched that part of him yet—except with her pussy, of course, and just thinking of that wet, wringing caress made seed dribble from the slit in his cockhead. Thus, he couldn't blame her for bypassing the drooling, one-eyed monster to nuzzle his thigh instead. He had to bite back a groan when her hair slid like silk over his turgid length as she kissed her way down his lower half, inquiring now and again as to whether or not she'd hit a "special spot."

By the time she made her way back, settling between his thighs, he was afire. Primed as a pistol ready to fire. And *dying* for her to touch his cock.

"Hmm, what could I be missing?" Her eyes sparkled at him; he *loved* this playful side of her. "Could you give me a hint?"

"It's big, thick, and about to go off like a firecracker."

Her smiling mouth hovered a hairsbreadth above his prick, by this time an engorged and throbbing bar across his stomach. "How warm am I?"

"Very." He dared her with his eyes.

She leaned over, and, to his ecstatic disbelief, pressed a soft kiss on his erection. "And that?"

"Hot," he breathed. "So damned hot."

He was so aroused that she had to use both hands to pry his cockstand away from his abdomen. He loved the way she handled him, her small hands working together to surround his thickly veined shaft. She pumped him between her palms and took note when he urged her to do it harder. Even so, her exquisitely gentle frigging threatened to make him lose his mind.

And then she decided to use her lips. She proceeded to kiss her way up and down his pole, the butterfly touches of her lips nearly his undoing. When she licked the tip like an inquisitive kitten, he let out a tortured groan.

"Are your toes curling yet?" she whispered.

"I love what you're doing, sweeting." *Understatement of the year.* "But there's more you could do, if you want to."

"I want to," she said immediately.

God's teeth. Could she get any more delightful?

"Then take as much of my cock into your mouth as you can. Suck on me, love, and watch your teeth. Also, the tip feels especially good—sensitive, like your pearl."

Her eyes widened as she absorbed the blunt facts he'd delivered. He wondered if he'd gone too far. As naturally sensual as she was, her virginity wasn't far behind her, and, moreover, she was a gently bred lady. And here he was explaining in graphic detail a pleasure that he'd engaged in with experienced lovers or whores he'd paid extra coin.

Just as he was about to turn it into a jest and let her off the hook, she bent her head.

His entire being shuddered as wet fire engulfed his prick. "*Christ.*"

Her reply—garbled by a mouthful of his cock—shot fire up his spine. The sight of her pretty head bobbing on his rod was almost too much to bear. She could only manage to take about half of his length, but, holy hell, it was enough. He wound his fingers into her hair, gripping a silken handful, using it to guide her movements.

"Breathe through your nose, love," he instructed hoarsely, "and relax your throat if you can. God, *yes*. Just like that."

Watching her, *feeling* her, he was struck by how different this was from anything he'd known before. This wasn't just a woman performing fellatio—this was Polly, making love to him. Lavishing his cock with selfless affection because that was what she felt for *him*. She cared for him. She'd said so, and now she was showing him so.

The realization ricocheted through him. His bollocks pulsed, shooting a hot spurt of pre-spend betwixt her lips. She choked a little, and he shuddered: it was too much, he couldn't take any more, would surely unload his cannon if this continued. Though no expert in etiquette, he was quite certain that a man did not spill in his lady's mouth. Thus, he clamped his hands on her shoulders, hauling her over him. He had a brief instant to enjoy her shocked expression before he fisted his erection, notched it to her dew-slickened petals, and pushed her down at the same time that he drove his hips up.

Moans exploded from them both.

"So bloody perfect," he groaned. "Ride me, Polly."

He guided her hips, showing her what he meant. It didn't take long for her to catch on. Slowly at first, then with growing confidence, she worked herself on his erection. Rising up to the tip and then wriggling her way down, she sheathed him to the balls in her snug, hot pussy.

"Oh, I like this," she sighed.

"Faster," he urged. "Harder."

She obeyed. The sight of her—her cheeks flushed and eyes sultry, her cherry-tipped tits bouncing as she impaled herself on his cock—was so bloody magnificent that he wanted it to go on forever. At the same time, he had to grit his teeth against the pressure roiling in his stones. He was determined not to find release until she did. Fingers digging into her hips, he helped her fuck him, shoving his hips up as she came down. The air filled with the sounds of their panting, of the deliciously lewd slapping of their meeting flesh.

"*Sinjin*," she chanted.

"Right here, love," he groaned. "I love feeling you come around me. The way your pussy hugs my prick like you never want to let me go—"

She gave a sharp gasp, and he shouted out as her convulsions milked his length. Cupping her shoulder blades, he pushed her down against his chest, his hips thrusting fiercely as his climax raged through him. Pulse after pulse of heat shot up his shaft, and he emptied himself completely into his wife's giving depths.

Afterward, he lay there, suffused in bliss, trying to catch his breath. Polly was still sprawled over him. She was so quiet that he thought she'd fallen asleep until she mumbled something.

"What, love?" he said huskily.

"Happy belated birthday." Her drowsy words sent a bolt of warmth through him. "I'll be better prepared next year, but just so you know: when it's your special day, you can have anything you want."

Something elusive flitted through his chest, a feeling beyond the reach of words. He just cuddled her closer until her breathing evened out, and she fell asleep curled atop him.

His adorable, protective... sex kitten.

Five days later, Sinjin stayed on the balls of his feet as he and his opponent circled one another in the practice ring at Apollo Fines' Boxing Club. He dodged a front hook, feinting left, then went in with his own combination of punches. His boxing gloves made satisfying impact, and his adversary stumbled back against the ropes, grunting.

He dashed sweat off his brow. "Ready for a break, old boy?"

Harry Kent grimaced, rubbing his midsection. Polly's dark-haired brother was an unusual mix of scholar and athlete. During the sparring, he'd removed the gold-rimmed spectacles which gave him a studious mien, and his large, rangy build moved with natural athleticism.

"I may be done for the day," Harry said ruefully. "Devil and damn, you generate momentum with that jab of yours."

Grinning, Sinjin reached for a towel and slung one at his brother-in-law. They headed to the benches next to the ring, where beverages awaited on a silver cart. Founded by Apollo Fines, a gentleman and retired prizefighter, the club rivalled Gentleman Jackson's in popularity, and the practice rings teemed with fashionable young bloods. Several of them came by to congratulate Sinjin on his recent nuptials. When they tried to lure him into their rakehell escapades, he firmly declined.

In truth, as much as Sinjin enjoyed manly pursuits, he'd have preferred another activity this afternoon—namely a session betwixt the sheets with his new bride. But Polly had insisted that he spend time with her brother, who would be returning to Cambridge soon. Sinjin had caved, not just because he did like Harry, who was a solid, sporting chap, but because he found it difficult to say no to his wife.

After five days of marriage, he found himself wondering why he hadn't gotten leg-shackled earlier. He knew the answer, of course: because he hadn't met Polly. She was the necessary ingredient to his marital bliss.

When he'd heard marriage being discussed at the clubs, men typically joked about one of two things: the expense of the endeavor and/or its necessity in the producing of an heir and a spare. What gentlemen didn't talk about—at least, not in public —were the grace notes that marriage added to everyday life.

For the first time, Sinjin was waking up to the same body in his bed every morning, and he adored it. Not just because he could start the day with one of his favorite activities—and by Jove, those early lovemaking sessions were fine—but because seeing Polly the first thing when he woke gave him a sense of rightness he'd never known before.

He was feeling... settled. Anchored by his new role as a husband.

There were countless other delights as well. He liked having a wife to care about his preferences, from how he took his tea to his favorite foods to assorted household decisions he'd never paid any mind to before. It soothed him knowing that she was close by; if she wasn't, the lingering trace of apple blossoms reminded him that she would be back soon. He enjoyed their conversations, which addressed everything from mundane matters to more private ones.

He'd never liked to talk about his past or his family, but with Polly it was different. Sharing with her came naturally. All in all, their union had the easy camaraderie and affection he had hoped for. And, as much as he liked Harry, he found himself missing his new bride already.

"This has been grand," he began, "but I really ought to—"

"Let's go another round." Harry sent a harried glance at his pocket watch. "Polly doesn't expect us back until three, so there's still time... that is, if you can bear being parted from her?"

Accompanied by a beatific smile, Harry's words were a downright challenge.

Sinjin had never been one to back down. "All right. One more round."

They returned to the ring, and as Sinjin's body took over, defending against attacks and issuing them, his mind wandered. He wondered if Polly's feelings for him could ever run deeper than affection. As he delivered a jab and hook combination, he told himself to be grateful with the marriage he had and not to rock the boat, especially when his new wife hadn't yet weathered one of his storms. He'd leased an apartment to go to when the devils took over, but he had to remain vigilant to their reemergence. At the first sign of one of his moods, he would have to beat a hasty retreat.

The notion, though necessary, struck him as wholly unappealing. It also distracted him from the oncoming attack. Harry's uppercut snapped his head back.

"Sorry, old boy," the other called cheerfully.

Once the stars cleared, and he saw one version of Harry, rather than two, he muttered, "My fault for woolgathering." He declined the other's offer to have a rest, and they continued sparring, with Sinjin giving as good as he got.

By the time the two of them returned to the townhouse an hour later, they'd both undergone a battering. Sinjin felt limber and relaxed as he stepped over the threshold, inquiring after Polly's whereabouts.

"The countess is in the drawing room, my lord," Harvey said.

The old retainer, who was as stoic as Strickley, looked as if he was trying to hide a smile. Sinjin's face heated as he could well imagine the cause of the other's good humor. He probably appeared like an overeager bridegroom. Not wanting to appear any more foolish, he forced himself to stroll casually toward the drawing room, opening the door...

"SURPRISE!"

The startling shout made him stumble backwards and collide into Harry.

"What in blazes?" He gawked at the roomful of people.

Polly stood in front of the throng, her face wreathed in smiles. She was wearing one of her new gowns, a delightful pink confection that made him think of her as his own personal bonbon.

"This is your birthday cele—*oh my goodness*," she gasped. "What happened to your jaw?"

"For a scholarly sort, your brother has a mean uppercut." He spoke lightly whilst inside he was reeling. Looking around the packed room, he saw perhaps two dozen guests, wrapped presents covering the tables, and carts laden with refreshments.

Polly had arranged all of this... for him?

She touched a hand to his swollen jaw, and his chest tightened at her gentleness. Her sweetness.

"Harry was supposed to delay you," she said, "not beat you to a pulp!"

At that, he scowled. "Your brother didn't beat me. You should see *him*."

He moved aside so that Harry could step forward and ruefully display his shiner.

"For a posh nob, your husband has a mean jab," Harry informed his sister.

Grinning, he buffeted Sinjin in the shoulder; Sinjin returned the favor.

Rolling her eyes, Polly muttered, "Dear Lord, I've created a monster. I had better separate you two before there's further bloodshed."

"Speaking of bloodshed, I'm going to challenge Violet to a game of cards." Behind his spectacles, Harry's eyes had a trouble-making gleam. "She might be a viscountess and mama now, but she still hates to lose."

The other ambled off, and Sinjin looked into his wife's sparkling eyes. "I can't believe you planned this for me," he murmured, "and on the sly, too."

"It took some maneuvering. I had to ask Harvey for a list of your cronies." Smiling, she slid her arm through his. "Shall we greet your guests?"

They made the rounds. He was relieved to discover that Harvey had exercised discretion in whom he'd recommended to the list of invitees, which included only the most civilized and presentable of Sinjin's acquaintances. As he neared one of the refreshment stands, he was surprised to see Merrick standing there. The stooped, greying man of business was munching contentedly on a plate of canapes.

At Sinjin and Polly's approach, he bowed. "Many happy returns, my lord."

"Thank you, Merrick. I'm glad you are here." Which was the absolute truth, Sinjin realized.

"I was honored to receive an invitation from the countess." The approval in Merritt's expression was unmistakable as he regarded Polly.

"As my husband's trusted advisor, you are always welcome in our home," she returned with equal friendliness. "Isn't that so, Sinjin?"

"Yes, of course," he said.

And nearly keeled over in shock when Merrick *smiled*. It

wasn't a large smile, just a slight lifting at the corners of the mouth... but still. The professional man's next words came as even more of a surprise.

"May I say, it is about time you had a birthday celebration, my lord," Merrick declared.

"I couldn't agree more," Polly said.

Sinjin's throat felt oddly scratchy.

After chatting with Merrick some more, he and Polly moved on.

"What possessed you to invite my man of business?" he said in her ear.

"I asked Harvey who you routinely spent time with, and Mr. Merrick came up. He seems like a very nice man." Her head tilted to one side, the curling wisps around her face glinting in the sunlit room. She'd started wearing her hair in a looser style, one that accentuated the natural sensuousness of her tresses. "Unless you don't prefer to mix business and social activities?"

The fact that she didn't possess an ounce of snobbery was one of the many things he liked about her. Like the rest of her family, she had a tendency to judge people on their own merit rather than their class or wealth. Thus, she, a countess, had invited Merrick, a man who worked for a living, because she'd seen to the heart of the matter.

"I'm glad you invited him." Sinjin thought of the hours the man of business had worked on his behalf, attending to details so that his life would run smoothly. "I owe Merrick a great deal—more than I can say, actually."

"Then we shall have to have him over more regularly. In fact..." Polly trailed off, and he followed her gaze. Ambrose Kent had entered the room and was heading over, his alert air making Sinjin brace.

The three of them tacitly moved to an unoccupied corner.

"Apologies for my lateness," Kent said brusquely, "but I have news."

"You've found Nicoletta's accomplice?" Sinjin's gut clenched.

"Not as yet, but we now know the villain's identity. As you know, my men and I have been canvassing every public house and tavern within walking distance of the docks. Several people recalled seeing our man, but none could tell us much more about him. Today, McLeod met a dock worker who, under the condition of anonymity, identified the scoundrel as Clive Grundell."

Clive Grundell. The name echoed in Sinjin's head.

"The fellow McLeod talked to claimed that he and Grundell had briefly worked together at a shipping company over a year ago. According to him, Grundell wasn't there long before he was caught pilfering cargo. Grundell disappeared before he could be charged, and our fellow hasn't seen him since." Kent's golden brown gaze narrowed. "I just came from interviewing others at the shipping company, and like our first fellow, most didn't want to be involved out of fear. One worker said that Grundell has a devil of a temper and a violent streak. He claims that Grundell once pulled a knife on him over a petty disagreement."

"Grundell sounds like our man," Sinjin said grimly.

"How will you find him, Ambrose?" Polly said, her eyes wide.

"He gave the shipping company a false address in St. Giles. Nonetheless, he might have used that address for a reason. My men and I will go door to door in that neighborhood and see if anyone knows anything about him." Lines deepened around the investigator's mouth. "Admittedly, that strategy is akin to searching for a needle in a haystack. I wish we had more eyes and ears in the stews, for the underworld looks out for its own and mistrusts authority of any kind. But rest assured that we will carry on the hunt until Grundell is apprehended."

Humbled by all that the other was doing on his behalf, Sinjin said, "Thank you, sir. I am in your debt."

"Nonsense. You are family," Kent said.

For the second time that day, Sinjin felt a shift inside him. He'd gotten used to believing that he had no one to rely upon but himself, and now to realize that he had not only Merrick in his corner, but Kent as well...

A spasm hit his chest as he looked at Polly. This was all because of her. She was slowly but surely chipping away at his walls and bridging him to the world that he'd been convinced had no place for him.

Yearning unfurled... and was halted by a sudden cold chill.

You don't know how she'll react to your devils. She may run... or worse. Even as he told himself she was nothing like other women he'd known—that she bore no resemblance to his mama or the current duchess—the thought of Polly's rejection turned his insides to ice. Things were fine and dandy now, but she'd never seen him at his worse...

And she never will, he vowed to himself grimly. It was a necessary reminder that he had to keep his marriage unencumbered by true intimacy. He could only expose those parts of himself that were worthy of Polly; the rest he had to keep hidden.

"Don't worry, Sinjin. Ambrose will find Grundell," she said softly.

He didn't correct her mistaken assumption as to the cause of his unease. "Is there anything I can do to help?" he said to her brother. "I don't like twiddling my thumbs when I could be out searching for this villain."

"As I've said before, it's best to leave the matter to professionals," Kent said firmly. "If Grundell is capable of murdering his lover and co-conspirator, then he may be capable of anything."

"But will you and the others be safe?" Polly asked her brother in worried tones.

"No need to fret," Kent reassured her. "I do this for a living, remember?"

Witnessing the exchange, Sinjin felt a pang. If Stephan were still alive, he would have liked Polly and her family. Like Sinjin, he would have been in awe of the strong bonds of kinship between the Kents...

A sudden hush returned him to the room. His gaze went to the pair of newcomers standing awkwardly in the doorway.

Beside him, Polly whispered, "Oh my goodness, I didn't invite them. How did they know about the party?"

Sinjin couldn't answer her. Because he had no clue why his stepmama and half-brother had come. Or what they wanted from him.

"I am sorry for intruding," the Duchess of Acton said stiffly. "Had I known that you were entertaining, I would have paid a call at a more convenient time."

"What do you want?" Sinjin said.

Polly cringed at his bluntness. The situation was already awkward enough with his family's unexpected arrival in the middle of his birthday party. She'd debated whether or not to invite Sinjin's kin; given their conspicuous absence at the wedding and what he'd shared of his past, she'd decided against it.

Needless to say, the appearance of Her Grace and Lord Theodore had created an uncomfortable moment. Marianne had smoothly suggested that Polly take Sinjin's relations for a tour of the house to show them some of the improvements she'd made. Polly had gratefully accepted her sister-in-law's exit strategy, and now she and the duchess were seated on opposing sides of the hearth in the study, Sinjin and Lord Theodore standing behind their respective chairs.

"There's no need to be boorish," Her Grace said.

Polly supposed that the other lady's fine-boned features and pale blond coloring were quite beautiful, but it was a beauty carved from ice. There was no trace of warmth in the woman's demeanor or aura. Indeed, when addressing Sinjin, the woman emanated frigid animosity—a fact that Polly did not like *at all*.

Neither did Sinjin, apparently, for he said in a tone edged with impatience, "Polly and I have guests to return to, so whatever business brings you here, be quick about it."

Her Grace sniffed. "Trust me, had I any choice I would not have come. But my sense of duty made this visit necessary. This concerns your papa."

"What about him?"

"Acton is... not well."

For the first time, Polly saw a flicker of sentiment beneath the layer of ice, and before she could discern what it was, Lord Theodore spoke.

"What mater means to say is that pater is dying," he said flatly.

Her Grace's lips pressed into a tight line. "There's no need to be so blunt, Theo dear."

"We don't have time to circle around the matter," her son said with a touch of belligerence.

Although Lord Theo shared his mama's looks and haughty manner, his aura differed from hers. Insecurity, not coldness, was at the core of his glow. To Polly, his obvious efforts to appear sophisticated had the opposite effect of making him seem younger than his years.

He addressed Sinjin. "Papa had another coughing fit yesterday. It was so bad that, against his will, we summoned a physician." His throat bobbed above his fussy cravat. "The doctor says Papa has six months at the most. You have a right to know."

Polly's gaze flew to her husband. His face had paled, emotion seething around him. Shock, anger... beneath all of it, pain.

Yet his voice was toneless as he said, "Is the conveying of His Grace's imminent demise the only reason for your visit?"

"That is crass, even for you, Sinjin." The duchess' trickling anxiety, however, suggested that he wasn't far off the mark in guessing that she had an ulterior motive. "In this time of tragedy, I had hoped that we might put aside our differences and come together as a family."

A muscle leapt in Sinjin's jaw. "We are not a family and haven't been since you packed me off to Creavey Hall."

"It was for your own good." Her Grace's hands folded primly in her lap. "You needed discipline, and the school is one of the best in the land for reforming unruly pupils."

"Reforming or abusing?" The words burst from Polly, her voice shaking.

"As you were not even around at the time, I don't see how you have anything to say in the matter," the duchess said frostily.

"Polly can say what she wants because she is my wife. My family. You, Your Grace," Sinjin gritted out, "are not."

"The day I married your papa, I took on two boys as well—I, who had no experience at being a mama. Stephan made the role easy, but you... you have tried me at every turn. With your reckless behavior, your wild moods. I didn't give up, however. Unlike your own mother," Her Grace said pointedly, "I did not run from the problem. Knowing the limits of my own expertise, I found the best solution that I could."

Sinjin's lips whitened. But his stepmama wasn't done.

"Acton and I could not control you, so we placed you in the care of someone who could. The way I see it, Revelstoke, we did our best by you, and you owe us for that, at least."

"I don't owe you a bloody thing," Sinjin snarled. "But I shan't renege on whatever His Grace saw fit to put in place for your care when I am the duke. That is what you came for today, is it not? To ensure your future comfort and security?"

"Acton, of course, made provisions for Theodore and me." The duchess' pale blue eyes narrowed. "I have your word that you will see the terms of those obligations fulfilled?"

If naught else, Polly had to admire the lady's audacity. There Her Grace was, more or less with hat in hand, and yet she managed to make it seem as if Sinjin were the one asking for a favor. As if he were the one who owed her and not the other way around.

"Mama," Lord Theodore said, looking genuinely pained, "can we discuss these matters later? Papa is not yet in the grave. Perhaps if we consult other physicians—"

"Your father is dying. He's been lying to himself for months that it is otherwise, but it is not. Hence, we must look to the future. Well, Revelstoke?" the duchess said imperiously.

"Well, what?"

"Are you going to provide for Theodore and me in accordance with your father's wishes?"

"I'm under no obligation to you or anyone. I will do as I see fit. Now if you'll excuse us—or even if you don't—my wife and I have guests to attend to."

Taking the hand Sinjin offered, Polly got to her feet. The duchess rose as well, her aura fluctuating between resentment and worry. Polly noted that Theodore didn't share his mama's feelings. Whilst some apprehension was there, he seemed mainly... sad. Lost in the way a child feels when he doesn't understand the world of adults.

And there was the wistful way he looked at Sinjin—as if he longed for a connection with his older brother but didn't know how to go about establishing it.

Theodore's yearning made her mind up. Sinjin had too few kin to reject a brother who might act like a bit of a fop but who, at his core, seemed a decent enough fellow. If she could, she wanted to help heal the breach between Sinjin and his half-brother. Thus, as Sinjin marched his relations to the foyer, issuing orders to Harvey to have their carriage fetched, Polly found a moment to speak to the young lordling.

"Would you care to visit us some other time?" she said in a

hurried undertone. "Under less, um, hectic circumstances, when you could spend some time with your brother?"

Lord Theodore gave her a surprised look. "You mean that?" he whispered back.

She nodded.

"I'd like that—" Lord Theo began.

"Your carriage is here," Sinjin said.

His words were controlled, but Polly's pulse quickened at the rage flaring around him.

"Come, Theo, let us not waste another moment where we are not wanted," the duchess said.

After they left, Polly ventured, "Sinjin, are you all right?"

"We'll talk later," he said grimly. "Right now, we have guests to entertain."

———

Leave it to that bloodless bitch to ruin everything.

As Sinjin paced his bedchamber that evening, the memory of his stepmama's unwelcome visit sent a dark undercurrent through his blood. He didn't know what infuriated him more: that the self-righteous harridan had the gall to demand that he support her once he was duke or that she'd treated his father's imminent death with such callous calculation.

Either way, Regina Pelham had destroyed the good cheer of his celebration. His mood had gone from buoyant to irritable, and he'd managed, just barely, to contain himself until the last of the party guests had left. Now everyone was gone, and he was plagued by a question: should he join Polly tonight?

He didn't know if it was his black devil stirring or the normal turmoil that his stepmama always left in her wake. Or the fact that he'd learned his father was dying. Or that Polly—*his* Polly— had been exchanging whispered secrets with bloody Theodore. His gut clenched, and he told himself not to think about any of it now because such ruminations would only ramp up his inner chaos. What he needed to do was to compose himself.

His hand itched for the locket, to hold its comforting weight in his palm until he calmed. He wondered if he could ask Polly if she still had the blasted thing—then he shook his head at his own absurdity. What did some stupid locket matter when he couldn't trust himself to go to his wife's bedchamber tonight?

The very idea of separation angered him. They'd shared her bed every night thus far—and some of the mornings and afternoons as well. And despite the heat burgeoning in his loins, it wasn't just about lust. It also had to do with having her close, knowing that she would be by his side when he awakened. That she would be by his side *period*.

You're in a dangerous mood tonight. You can't risk it, his inner voice said. *What if you expose the disaster that you are?*

He would have to leave, he decided. Go to the apartment that was waiting for him.

Just as he was searching for his portmanteau—where did Strickley hide the damned thing?—the barrier between their rooms parted, and Polly came into his domain. She was wearing her chintz wrapper, her hair loose and damp from her bath. She looked so sweet and uncertain and determined that he went hard immediately beneath his dressing gown.

She stopped a few paces short of where he was standing by a chaise longue. She faced him, her clear eyes taking him in. "May we talk, Sinjin?"

"It's not a good time." *I have to get out of here. I want to fuck you so badly, and I don't trust myself.*

"Clearly, your stepmama's visit has upset you, and you said we would talk about it later," she reminded him.

"I don't want to talk about it now."

"I really think we ought to," she said earnestly. "My mama always said it's not good to go to bed angry."

"Well, I'm not married to your mama," he said, sounding like a right bastard. *Rein it in, man.* "If you'll recall, we promised each other privacy in our marriage. I'm asking you to drop the matter."

She gnawed on her lower lip, her wide, clear eyes searching his face—and, devil and damn, that sent another surge of heat to his groin.

She came a step closer. "I know we agreed to privacy, but I can tell you're upset," she said softly. "I just want to help."

She touched his arm, and that light caress over his bulging bicep snapped his self-control.

"You want to help me?" he said.

She nodded vigorously.

"Then take off your robe."

Her lashes fluttered like a hummingbird's wings, her throat bobbing in the vee of her robe. "I think we ought to talk first—"

"I think we ought to fuck."

Color rose up her cheeks. "Sinjin, that *word*—"

"Is what we're going to do if you stay. If you don't want to get tupped, then get out of here and leave me to my peace," he said flatly.

It was the best he could do to get rid of her. Opposing forces tore at him. He wanted to protect her from his devilish mood—wanted her to leave. He also wanted to stake claim to what was his, to screw his cock inside her snug little hole until she screamed his name...

He stood, tensed and aroused as hell, waiting for her to leave.

Her hands went to the belt of her robe. In a fluid motion, she untied it and shrugged off the chaste covering... and, God Almighty, she wore nothing beneath. Saliva pooled in his mouth as his gaze roved hungrily over her round, coral-tipped breasts, her flaring hips, that tawny nest between her thighs. Her shoulders drew back, and the defiance in her eyes aroused him even more than her other charms.

"Well, are we or aren't we?" she said.

It's over.

"We bloody *are*," he growled.

He tore off his robe, shuddering when her gaze caressed his rampant erection. He yanked her into his arms, groaning as skin met skin, their mouths fusing together. Desire combusted, pulling the air from his lungs, his brain. He became the animal need clawing at his gut.

He swung her into his arms, depositing her onto the nearest piece of furniture—the chaise. Sprawled on her back against the forest green silk, she was a Maenad awaiting his lust. Going down on one knee, he jerked her thighs apart, taking a moment to savor the silkiness of her skin against his palms before he buried his face in her feminine garden.

Her hot, earthy flavor drenched his senses. Her taste, combined with her heavy-lidded eyes watching him as he licked her slit, was a potent aphrodisiac. He wanted her pleasure like he wanted nothing else.

"Pet your tits, love," he rasped. "Help me pleasure you."

She acquiesced, shyly at first, then with growing abandon. As he tongued her pussy, she molded her luscious mounds in her palms. Her slim fingers circled the taut peaks, the sight so enticing that he had to join her in self-pleasure. He fisted his cock, frigging himself slowly, delight ruffling along his spine.

"Yes, that's it, sweeting," he breathed against her damp flesh. "Play with those pretty nipples. Doesn't that feel good?"

She moaned as she plucked at those coral buds in earnest. To reward her boldness, he delved upward to her love knot, tickling it with his tongue and then suckling hard. Her hips bucked, and she cried out, coming in wet surges against his mouth.

When she calmed, he went to the head of the chaise. Putting one knee on the cushions, he speared his fingers through her hair, guiding her lips to his jutting prick.

"Make it wet, love," he whispered.

She did, with an enthusiasm that made him rock back on his heels. Under his tutelage, her oral skills had grown in leaps and bounds. Her tongue circled his sensitive head before she slid him inside her mouth. His fingers tightened in her hair as she engulfed his shaft with moist fire, her cheeks hollowing as she sucked on him as if he were a delicious treat. After several seed-summoning passes, she released him with a pop, the lewd sound making him growl. When her tongue searched out his stones, licking delicately at the seam, he could take no more.

He pulled away, returning to the foot of the chaise. He grabbed hold of her hips, hoisting her onto her hands and knees. He saw her startled look backward at him the instant before he entered her in one deep thrust. A groan tore from his chest at the hot clasp, the dewy slickness of her welcome. He withdrew, loving the way she moaned in protest, then slammed in again, deeper and deeper still. Harder and faster, the rhythm primal, inevitable.

"Aye, love, push your cunny against my cock," he growled. "Fuck me as I'm fucking you."

Her cry echoed his own animal delight. Even as he mounted her tight little sheath, she rode him back, his match in every way. His mate and only his. His balls slapped her lips in a desperate cadence, the first spasms of her crisis making his eyes roll back in his head.

Her bliss summoned his own finish. His body curving over hers, he pounded into her pussy, shouting out as he ejaculated. He nuzzled her nape, feeling her shiver as he continued to slowly thrust, still hard inside her. Their mingled essence overflowed her sex, an erotic trickle down her thigh.

He found her ear with his lips and whispered one word. "More?"

She shivered, and the devil in him smiled.

33

Polly awoke to the watery rays of dawn. Beside her, Sinjin was sprawled on his stomach, asleep... finally. Her well-exercised muscles fluttered as memories of the night assailed her.

Sinjin had been relentless in his drive for pleasure. He'd radiated need, desire flooding his aura, dazzling and limitless. She had never imagined an aura of such intensity... such unrestrained power. He was always a passionate lover, but last night he'd transcended even himself—and in doing so, unleashed a side of her that, in the light of morning, caused a flush to steal beneath her skin.

She'd climaxed so many times, in so many different positions, that she'd lost count.

Yet as potent as their lovemaking was, it didn't take away her worry. Why wouldn't he talk to her? Tell her what he was upset about? The visit with Her Grace had undoubtedly unmoored him, yet instead of sharing his feelings, he'd invoked their clause on privacy.

She bit her lip. She knew what she'd signed on for so she ought to let it be. At the same time, she wanted to ease his troubles—which she could only do if he let her in.

Sinjin stirred, turning over. His gaze found hers, and the slumberous satisfaction in those blue depths melted her insides. Her pulse raced as she saw vibrant energy flaring to life around him.

Good heavens, after last night, he couldn't possibly want more—

Under the covers, his arm snaked around her waist, dragging her flush against his burly warmth. The unmistakable ridge of his cockstand pressed against her belly. His hands clamped over her bottom in a proprietary fashion.

"Good morning," he said in a sleep-roughened voice.

Even as her satiated nerves awakened to his touch, she knew that succumbing to passion wasn't the answer to their problems. She tried to wriggle away. "Sinjin, wait. We have to talk."

"Go ahead and talk." He nipped at her earlobe, his hands wandering. "I'm listening."

"I can't concentrate when you do that," she gasped.

"Mmm, I can feel my seed inside you." The randy light in his eyes made her heart palpitate as did the wicked stirring of his finger. "You're soft and wet—ready for me."

"Sinjin—wait. I'm... sore," she said desperately.

"I'll be gentle."

"But we really ought to talk first—"

The rapping at the door made them both still.

"Why the bloody hell is someone knocking at this hour?" he growled.

She had no idea, but she was glad for the interruption. She jumped out of bed and snatched her wrapper from the floor. Tying it securely, she called, "Come in."

It was Harvey. One look at the normally unflappable butler's aura filled her with apprehension.

"Is something amiss?" she said.

"I'm sorry to bother you, my lady," he said in flustered tones, "but an urgent message just arrived from Mrs. Hunt. She requests your presence at the academy. Apparently, one of the foundlings has gone missing."

Sinjin accompanied his wife to the Hunt Academy. Upon their arrival, they were greeted by a pale Mrs. Hunt, who led them directly into her office.

"We think Maisie left sometime in the night," she said without preamble. "The last time anyone saw her was at lights out. This morning, her bed was empty. Mr. Hunt will be back shortly—he and some men are out in the neighborhood looking for her—but I sent for you because you know her best of anyone, Polly. Do you know where she might have gone?"

"No." Polly's brow furrowed. "But it's unlike Maisie to leave without telling anyone."

Sinjin had awakened feeling on edge, and seeing Polly's concern sent a charge through him. She was his wife. It was his job to protect her from the worries of the world.

"Have all the children been questioned?" he said.

"Yes. And no one saw her leave. Or knows why she would go in the first place." Mrs. Hunt's hands knotted in front of her. "As far as anyone knew, Maisie was content here—"

"Wait—*Tim,*" Polly breathed.

"Tim?" Sinjin said.

"Her older brother. He runs with a band of mudlarks," she explained. "Maisie mentioned that since their leader died, there's been a struggle for power. Tim was trying to protect the younger ones from getting caught in the crossfire. When Maisie was telling me about it, I worried that he might end up in danger. Do you think she caught wind that something had happened and went to him?"

"That sounds like a tenuous situation," Mrs. Hunt said worriedly.

At that moment, Hunt strode in. The brawny fellow had attended Sinjin's wedding and birthday fete, and the two exchanged brief nods.

Mrs. Hunt rushed over to her husband. "Any luck, Gavin?"

"Sorry, buttercup." He shook his head. "No one has seen her in the neighborhood."

"Polly thinks that Maisie's disappearance might have something to do with Tim," his wife blurted.

As Polly recounted her story, the scar on Hunt's cheek tightened. Grimly, he said, "I know the flash house used by the Larks. I'll go have a look."

"You must be careful," Mrs. Hunt said fretfully.

"You can take a man out of the stews, but not the stews out of a man." Hunt's wink was roguish but his touch gentle as he tucked a wayward blond curl behind his lady's ear. "Don't worry, love, I know what I'm about."

"I'm coming with you," Sinjin said.

"But it might be dangerous—" Polly began.

"I can take care of myself, kitten." Restless energy gnawed at him; he needed to get out, to *do* something. "We'll get your Maisie back safely where she belongs."

"Now a nob such as yourself probably ain't acquainted with the likes of a flash house. It won't be a rose garden. So if you'd rather stay in the carriage—"

"I'm going in." Hunt was beginning to grate on Sinjin's nerves.

Somewhere during the journey into the heart of the rookery, the other man had shed his polished manners. He now sounded and acted like a native of the rough enclave. Alert aggression glinted in his tawny gaze as their conveyance pulled to a stop at their destination.

But Sinjin was no lordling with lily white hands. He might not have sprung from these dirty streets, but he knew violence and how to fend for himself. Right now, he *wanted* to fight, his muscles flexing in anticipation of a good row.

"Suit yourself. But take this." Hunt passed him a pistol, shoving another into his own boot. "And try not to get knifed or shot, eh?"

Having dispensed that helpful advice, Hunt exited the carriage, instructing his pair of footmen to keep a discreet watch. He led the way to the flash house, a three-storey building with soot-covered windows and a grimy façade. It leaned crookedly to one side, looking as if a strong wind might send it crashing into the adjacent building. Hunt shoved open the door and strode in like he owned the place, Sinjin taking his cue from the other's lead.

It took Sinjin's eyes a moment to adjust to the gloom inside. The stench of grease and rotted things assailed his nostrils. Three men lay snoring at a trestle table, empty bottles of blue ruin lolling around them.

"*Bloody hell.*"

At Hunt's low utterance, Sinjin followed the other man's gaze. His stomach lurched.

Holy Mother of God.

At the far end of the room, a lad was strung up to a flogging pole, his wrists bound above his head. Even at this distance, Sinjin saw the bloody welts and bruises over the boy's bared torso. He recognized Maisie, the flower girl from his wedding, flanking one side of the injured lad whilst a tow-headed boy stood on the other. The two were trying to coax the wounded boy to drink from a cup and whipped around as Hunt and Sinjin strode over.

"Mr. Hunt. My lord," Maisie squeaked.

"Tell us what's happened, child," Hunt said.

Sinjin admired the other man's controlled tone because, up close, he could see just how badly the boy had been whipped, his own scars tautening in reflex. Rage bubbled up, his fingers curling. He wanted to *kill* whoever had done this.

"They b-beat Tim. Me and Patrick, we've been tr-trying to

give 'im water, but 'e won't ave any." Maisie's voice hitched, tears spilling down her freckled cheeks. "Is 'e d-dead?"

Sinjin was already untying the boy, easing him to the ground. Hunt ran his hands gently over the lanky, battered frame, and a faint moan escaped from Tim's cracked lips.

"His injuries look worse than they are, and his pulse is steady. He'll be fine once we get him tended to," Hunt said.

Maisie gave a relieved sob.

Stripping off his jacket, Sinjin wrapped it around Tim.

"Who did this?" he bit out to the other boy.

"The name's Patrick, guv, and it 'appened like this. Since the Prince o' the Larks cocked 'is toes, a cutthroat by the name o' Crooke fancied 'imself as the next ruler o' the roost. Thing is, Crooke ain't got the Prince's 'eart or 'is brains, but 'e's got plenty o' brawn—or least 'e's got the coin to 'ire some ruffians to do 'is dirty work." The boy shot a disgusted look at the men who remained comatose at the table. "We could 'andle Crooke being a brute and pushing us to comb the tides all 'ours o' the day and night, but we drew the line—least Tim did—when Crooke told us 'e'd made an arrangement to loan us out to Mother Cox."

At the mention of the infamous bawd, blood rushed in Sinjin's ears. He looked at Patrick's dirt-smudged face, topped with a mop of fair hair; the boy couldn't be more than ten. "The bastard wanted to force you into the flesh trade?"

"Aye—and I ain't signed up to bend o'er for no one," Patrick said matter-of-factly. "So Tim, 'e stands up for us larks and tells Crooke that we won't do it, plain and simple. And Crooke 'as 'im beat within an inch o' 'is life and leaves 'im on the whipping post as an example to us all." Patrick's voice trembled for the first time. "I went to fetch Maisie, and we waited 'til Crooke and most o' 'is gang left and that's when you found us."

"Let's get Tim back to the school," Hunt said, his jaw taut, "and I'll handle Crooke later. Patrick, you'd best come with us."

"A king's ransom couldn't keep me 'ere," Patrick said with feeling.

The door swung open wildly, slamming into the wall. A ginger-haired man with piggish eyes and heavy jowls swaggered in. His barrel chest was encased in embroidered maroon velvet, and he held a polished walking stick in one hand. Five beefy cutthroats trailed behind him, some slapping truncheons against their palms in a menacing cadence.

"Crooke," Patrick said, his voice quavering.

"Look, fellows, we found ourselves some vermin," Crooke said with a sneer, "and they're about to scurry away with our goods."

"Give us the word, master, and we'll exterminate 'em," one of his men boomed.

Patrick cowered. Pushing the boy behind him, Sinjin bit out, "I invite you to try."

"We're leaving," Hunt said in lethal tones, "and we'll spare your life if you let us pass."

Crooke sniggered. "Brave words when you're outnumbered. Get 'em, boys."

"Stay back with Maisie and Tim," Sinjin ordered Patrick.

Then all hell broke loose.

Two of the cutthroats charged Sinjin, and his blood roiled. He planted himself, using the first attacker's momentum to flip the other over his shoulder. The bastard flew through the air, landing with a cry of pain. The second came at him, fists flying, and Sinjin dodged the swings, moving in close to deliver rib-cracking blows. The bugger doubled over, and Sinjin finished him off with an uppercut.

His gaze shot to Hunt, who was holding his own against a trio of foes. At that moment, Hunt's footmen burst through the door, charging to their employer's aid. Sinjin honed in on Crooke. Gaze shifting, the bugger calculated his odds, then turned on his heels and made a run for it. Sinjin took off in a sprint after him, tackling the other to the ground.

They grappled. Crooke had the advantage of several stone, but Sinjin managed to gain the upper hand. He smashed his fist into the other's face, energized by the crack of bone. He did it again and again, punches powered by the dark burn of the cane, the sting of the whip, the deep branding scorch of loneliness.

Not this boy. Never again. His blood roared, the euphoric rush blocking out pain.

His arms were suddenly jerked back, and he thrashed in rage at being restrained.

"Revelstoke, enough. You're going to kill him."

The words percolated through his black haze. Chest heaving, he realized that Hunt and a footman had dragged him off Crooke. The bastard's face was a pulpy mess; looking down at his own clenched hands, Sinjin registered the broken skin and leaking veins, knuckles beginning to swell.

"Not that the world wouldn't be better off without the bugger, but being a new bridegroom, you might prefer to spend the night in your wife's bed rather than behind bars," Hunt went on. "Now are you calm enough for me to release you?"

"I'm fine," Sinjin snapped, shaking himself free. He staggered to his feet, aggression still churning inside him. He wanted to take on all the Crookes of the world. He could do it. Right here and right bloody now.

The invincible rush suddenly hit a wall. Even as he soared in his conviction, something in him balked, his gut clenching... in fear? What the hell did he have to be afraid of?

The answer surfaced like a leaf on a dark pond. *Polly.*

He reeled with awareness... which he knew would be ephemeral. Once the devil's claws sank into him, his mind would turn black. He'd lose his head—himself. Bloody hell, somehow he had to get it together before he saw Polly. Had to muddle through until he could make his escape to the apartment.

Hunt hefted Tim into his arms. Maisie and Patrick crowded behind him.

"Let's get the children to safety," he said grimly.

Sinjin led the way out, thinking, *And I have to somehow get myself there, too.*

34

It was dusk by the time Polly and Sinjin made their way home. Thick tension blanketed the carriage. From beneath her lashes, she studied her husband, who was on the opposite bench rather than beside her—or beneath her, as he had a habit of pulling her onto his lap.

None of that playfulness was present, however, and while she understood that—she herself felt as worn as an old apron—the distance between them pressed heavily upon her. Was she imagining the strain between them? She didn't think so. Sinjin was brooding; energetic emotions pulsed around him, yet he didn't see fit to share any of them with her.

So they sat in stilted silence, rattling over cobblestones together, each in their own separate world. She told herself to let it go, that it had been a long day and neither of them was in a place to have a deep conversation. But she could stand it no more.

"Sinjin, what is the matter?" she burst out.

"Nothing."

The immediacy of his reply irked her as much as the word itself, so much so that she didn't watch her tongue. "I'd appreciate it if you didn't lie to me. If you don't want to talk about it, just say so."

"Fine." His eyes smoldered at her. "I don't want to talk about it."

"Fine."

They stewed on. She regretted bitterly that she'd given him the option to choose silence. But just because he'd chosen to hide behind walls didn't mean that *she* had to.

"I am glad that the doctor said that Tim will make a quick recovery," she said in as calm a voice as she could manage. "Maisie's ever so relieved. Her brother's a brave lad for standing up to those villains and protecting the younger larks."

Sinjin stared fixedly at the corner of the carriage, his arms crossed, a booted ankle resting on one knee. His dark energy filled the carriage, yet his lips remained firmly sealed.

Her frustration building, she tried again. "You and Mr. Hunt were heroes as well. From what I understand, Mrs. Hunt is going to try to convince the mudlarks to come to the school, although Mr. Hunt says the boys are too feral to stay anywhere long."

His response? Silence.

Her temper snapped. "Dash it all, Sinjin, I *know* that you're upset. You might as well stop sulking and talk about it."

"*You* know how *I* feel. Are you a mind reader, then?"

His scathing reply churned her stomach. *He's too close to the truth...*

"N-no, of course not," she stammered. "What I meant was... I can, um, sense the tension between us. Why can't we just talk about it?"

"What sweet nothings did you share with that prat?"

She blinked in confusion. "What prat? What are you talking about?"

"Don't play stupid. It doesn't suit you, my clear-eyed goddess." He sneered—actually *sneered*—at her. "You and Theodore made a cozy pair. What were you two whispering about that you didn't want me to hear?"

"You cannot be serious." She stared at him, dumbfounded.

Who *was* this man sitting across from her? Because he surely wasn't the sensual, affectionate husband she knew. In fact, he even *looked* different: his pupils edged out the blue in his eyes, toxic energy rushing like ink into his blue glow, creating an ominous and murky state.

"As death, my love," this stranger ground out. "So tell me: was it a tryst you were planning?"

"I was inviting your *brother* to come spend time with *you*," she exploded. "He longs to be closer to you, the only sibling he has left. He's not like your stepmama."

"And you say you can't read minds," he mocked.

Fear warred with anger. Should she keep pushing ahead? She was flirting with disaster. *Don't take any unnecessary risks. Don't expose yourself further.* At the same time, she couldn't allow his utterly unreasonable behavior to go on.

She drew an unsteady breath. "Look, Sinjin, it has been a trying day. For both of us. Perhaps we should continue this discussion at another time—"

"I didn't want to talk in the first place," he thundered. "You're the one who forced this conversation between us. You're the one who's violating the goddamned rules we set for our marriage!"

"I'm not the one acting like a blessed child!"

"Yes, you're perfect, aren't you? Perfect Polly." With his jeering tone, he might as well have been calling her *Peculiar Polly*, and, indeed, that was what echoed furiously through her mind. "You always know what's best."

"I *never* said that I knew best. What's the matter with you? Why are you being so dashed unreasonable?"

"Maybe that's just the way I am. Maybe you don't know me as well as you think."

"Well, I don't like this you," she shot back.

"Then maybe you shouldn't have bloody married me," he snarled.

The words hung in the air. Their gazes locked, chests surging in unison.

A knock cut into the charged silence like a blast of artillery.

"What?" Sinjin roared.

"P-pardon, my lord." The groom's voice filtered in, and Polly suddenly realized that the carriage had stopped. "We're back as you instructed, but if you'd like us to drive on—"

"Open the goddamned door and help Lady Revelstoke out," Sinjin snapped.

The partition opened to reveal the groom's harried face. Cheeks burning, Polly took the servant's offered hand and alighted down the steps into the cooling night. She tried desperately to calm her inner tumult. She watched as Sinjin vaulted to the ground—only to climb into the driver's seat.

"Wh-where are you going?" she stammered.

His black gaze burned with the devil's fire.

"Away from you," he gritted out.

Through a haze of shock and mortification, she watched the carriage roll away and vanish into the darkness.

35

Three nights later, Polly found herself alone in the Shackleton's garden. She wandered listlessly through the labyrinthine hedges, wishing that she hadn't let Emma talk her into coming. Her eldest sister had said that the distraction would do her good—that it would be better than moping at home, waiting for her husband to return.

During the daytime, Polly kept herself busy at the academy. The one bright spot was that Tim was recovering rapidly, his injuries mostly superficial according to the physician. Yesterday, he'd been well enough to sit up in bed, where he'd been visited by a flow of mudlarks who'd apparently crowned him their new Prince. He'd asked repeatedly for Sinjin, adamant in his resolve to return the favor the other had done him by defeating Crooke.

Inspiration had struck Polly. The mudlarks were the "eyes and ears" of the stews; they were everywhere yet nowhere, blending in perfectly with their environment. Thus, with Ambrose's blessing, she'd given Tim and his band a sketch of Grundell, asking them to keep an eye out for the villain. They were given strict orders not to approach the man but to alert her brother immediately should there be a sighting.

She was rather proud of her idea... and wished she could share it with Sinjin. Looking up at the dark canopy of the night, she wondered where Sinjin was right now, what he was feeling and thinking, and her shoulders hunched. Her despair was only slightly lightened by the fact that he'd sent her a note. In those terse lines, he'd let her know he was invoking their agreement on privacy and would return in a few days.

At least he plans to return. She kicked a pebble out of her path.

As much as she missed Sinjin and regretted that she'd pushed him into a quarrel, she was also beginning to heartily dislike their moratorium on intimacy. They were fooling themselves if they thought they could spend companionable days and passionate nights together and not develop bonds between them.

She couldn't go on this way. She was in love with Sinjin, and she couldn't and didn't want to keep it to herself any longer. The pain of keeping an emotional distance was starting to seem worse than her fear of taking a risk and letting him know about her secret.

How would Sinjin react?

Would he reject her outright... or might he be able to accept her affliction?

Three days ago, she'd had budding confidence that his reaction might be the latter. Then again, three days ago, he'd been an affectionate and wildly passionate husband and now...

Now I don't know what to do.

She reached the heart of the maze, which featured a marble fountain of Bacchus surrounded by his band of merry satyrs and Maenads. *Just perfect.* Now she found herself worrying about what Sinjin might be up to in her absence, whether he would revert to his former rakehell ways.

Don't be a ninny. He said he'd be faithful.

She'd promised not to plague him, to give him space, and she'd broken *her* vow. What if he did the same? She slumped onto one of the benches circling the fountain, tears she couldn't hold back trickling from her eyes.

"Lady Revelstoke?"

She twisted around. *Oh, perfect again.*

"Lord Brockhurst." Swiping at her wet cheeks, she rose, her curtsy perfunctory. "I was just leaving—"

"Please don't go. Not just yet." In the moonlight, his features were beseeching. "I know I have no right to ask, but I wish for a moment of your time."

"What for?" she said warily.

"I want to apologize." He exuded sincerity. "All these months, I've been too cowardly to do so, but I cannot bear it any longer. I know that you must have somehow discovered my... ungentlemanly behavior. Was it Revelstoke who told you about the wager?"

"How I know is none of your business," she said flatly.

Even in the dimness, she could see color spreading over his chiseled cheekbones.

"You are right, of course." He cleared his throat. "I have no excuse except to say that I was an idiot. In my desire to fit in with the popular set, I did something inexcusable. I hurt you, and I humbly beg your forgiveness, knowing that I do not deserve it."

His direct apology surprised her. She hadn't expected him to acknowledge the truth of what he'd done. At the same time, she realized that it didn't matter any longer. The incident, which had once seemed monumental, was in truth naught more than a molehill in her life's journey. A speck compared to the vast, mountainous terrain that was her relationship with Sinjin.

Her husband—*he* was everything. Her heart clenched.

"Forget it. I have," she said.

"You mean that?" Brockhurst came closer, hope rippling over his features. "I've carried the guilt of what I've done for so long that—"

"I said forget it." Just because she didn't hold a grudge any longer didn't mean that she wanted to have some cozy conversation about his feelings. "Now I really must—"

"I never told anyone about your secret," he whispered.

Her heart thudded. She caught a rustling sound, and her panicked gaze swept over the dense, towering hedges. No one there. It must have been the breeze she heard or the blood rushing in her ears.

"You must have wondered why I didn't tell a soul," Brockhurst went on, "why I never revealed what you shared with me. I'll admit I was shocked when you told me that you could, well, *see* people's emotions. You know, their *auras*,"—his hand drew an orbit around his head—"glowing around them. You must understand I'd never heard of such a thing before, and it confused me. I panicked because even though I started courting you because of the wager, I was developing feelings for you."

She stared at him, stupefied. What in heaven's name was he blathering on about? More importantly, how could she get him to promise never to reveal her secret?

"I was afraid to act on my feelings because you were so... different. I waited too long, and Revelstoke snapped you up. But now that I see how unhappy you are, I can't hold the truth back any longer. I love you, Polly," he declared. "I always have."

Before she could react, he yanked her into his arms, his mouth landing on hers. She struggled, trying to get away, shoving her palms against his shoulders—and he went hurtling backwards through the air.

Did I do that? she thought, disoriented.

A large, familiar figure stepped into her line of vision. *Sinjin.* Her joy at seeing him fizzled at the sight of his aura: a bonfire of fury so intense that her heart shot into her throat.

He faced Brockhurst, his hands balled into fists.

"I'm going to kill you for touching my wife," he snarled.

Brockhurst scrambled to his feet, his clothes disheveled, his palms held out in a placating manner. "Revelstoke, we can talk about this—"

Sinjin's swift punch landed in the other's gut, Brockhurst doubling over with a loud groan. The sound snapped Polly out of her paralysis, and she dashed over, grabbing Sinjin's arm before he swung again. His bulging muscles leapt beneath her touch.

"Stop this," she said urgently. "Nothing happened. He—"

"Touched you. Kissed you. *My. Wife.*" In the moonlight, Sinjin's eyes were pitch black. "No one touches you but *me.*"

His vehemence sent a bolt of alarm through her. She held on, insisting, "It was nothing."

"If it was nothing, then why did you lie to me?" he said savagely.

"I didn't lie—"

"You told that fop your *secret.* You confided in him—but you didn't tell me, your own husband!"

Even as Polly's heart drummed in her chest, gasps and whispers made her head swing around. Her panic escalated as she saw the gathering guests, all of them drawn to the unfolding drama. She turned desperately back to Sinjin.

"Let's not do this here," she pleaded. "I'll explain everything once we are in private—"

"What will you explain? That you can *see* emotions? Bloody *auras* glowing around people?" he exploded.

The heat of stares burned into her. Whispers turned into excited titters. *Always said that chit was peculiar... Don't matter how pretty the belfry is if bats are loose in it...* The pyre of social disgrace burst into flame. Heat licked behind her eyes, and she drew a choking breath.

But Sinjin wasn't done.

"You were laughing at me all this time, weren't you?" Anger and despair twisted like snakes around him. "All this time, you could see what a disaster I am. *You could see my bloody moods.* The black devil... the blue. You knew all along, and there I was, a fool trying to protect you from them." He let out a pained howl of laughter. "Did it secretly amuse you, knowing what a pathetic wretch you married?"

In the midst of her soul's darkest night, understanding flashed as bright and ephemeral as lightning. The walls he'd erected, his distant behavior... all because he was trying to hide who he was? To protect her from... what? His *emotions?*

There wasn't time to puzzle it all out. Fear burgeoned—no longer for herself, but for *him.* The guests were looking at him with raised brows, whispering behind fans, not bothering to hide their malicious delight. She could hear the word spreading like wildfire: *mad.*

She had to put a stop to this. Now.

"I love you, Sinjin." Her voice cracked, and she had to swallow before speaking again. "I'm sorry I was not honest with you, but I will explain everything once we are away from here. Please take my hand, my love."

She saw him fighting the darkness that swamped him, blue flickering through black, and her heart swelled at his courage. Her breath held as his hand reached toward her outstretched one...

He jerked back, grunting in pain—because Brockhurst, the *idiot*, had punched him from behind. An attack that reeked of cowardice.

"Don't you touch her, you bastard," Brockhurst yelled.

Sinjin spun around to face his attacker, growling, "You're going to pay for that."

"No. Don't—" Polly tried to grab his arm, but he was too quick for her.

He stalked toward Brockhurst, who held his fists up, his stance belligerent. Sinjin went in, low and swift, dodging his opponent's punch, and feigning to the right. Getting past the other's guard, he delivered pummeling blows to the midsection. Brockhurst stumbled, falling backwards onto the graveled walk, groaning. Sinjin leapt atop him, plowing his fist into the other's face.

Bone crunched against bone. Brockhurst screamed.

Sinjin didn't stop.

Even as Polly dashed forward to help, someone held her back. A trio of footmen rushed forward, pulling Sinjin away from Brockhurst. Sinjin fought wildly as two of them wrenched his arms behind his back, his face contorting.

"Stop it! You're hurting him!" Polly tried to get to him but was kept in a firm hold.

At her cries, Sinjin's head swung in her direction, his gaze honing in on the servant holding her captive. Primal possessiveness surged in his aura, feeding the black flames. With a roar, he flung the footmen off him, surging toward her—only to be tackled from behind.

He landed with an audible thud on his shoulder, tears springing to Polly's eyes as he gave an agonized bellow. She shouted hoarsely for the footmen to desist, but two of them pinned Sinjin down, and the third delivered a punishing blow to the head that took the fight out of him and left him unmoving on the ground.

36

The next evening, Polly paced the length of Emma's drawing room. Her entire family was there, putting their heads together to try to help Sinjin. After the disastrous incident last night, Brockhurst had insisted on pressing charges, and Sinjin had been hauled away by members of the Metropolitan Police. When Polly had rushed to the station house, the constables had refused to admit her, saying it was for her own good. She'd have to wait until Sinjin calmed.

This morning, Polly had returned with Ambrose in tow—only to discover that sometime during the night, Sinjin had been moved yet again. All the constables could tell them was that two physicians had arrived, providing certification of lunacy that had allowed them to take custody of Sinjin. Their attendants had shuttled Sinjin off—to where the constables couldn't say.

"We've checked Bethlem Hospital and the obvious places, but there's no record of Revelstoke's arrival." Ambrose provided the summary from where he stood, his arm braced on the mantel. "So it's likely that he's in one of the private licensed madhouses."

Perched on the settee, Rosie said, "But why was Revelstoke taken to a madhouse?"

"My guess is that the Duke of Acton had a hand in this," her father answered. "He tried the same strategy when Revelstoke was targeted by French and Grundell. But as Brockhurst has actually pressed assault charges, Acton will have to do more than just temporarily hide Revelstoke in an asylum. He'll have to petition for a lunacy inquisition if he wants his son declared legally insane and, therefore, not liable for the assault. I don't know what Acton plans to do, nor do I think this strategy is in Revelstoke's best interests in the long run. When Polly and I went to speak to His Grace, however, we were told the family was not at home."

"Sinjin and his father are not on good terms." Polly paused in her agitated stride to face her family. "In the past, His Grace's brand of discipline has been severe, and although he may think he is helping Sinjin, he *isn't*." Her voice broke as she thought of how her husband might be suffering, the indignities he might be facing this very moment. "Sinjin doesn't belong in a madhouse. He may have powerful emotions and a changeable temperament, but last night was *not* his fault. Brockhurst was the one who started it by making an unwanted advance on me. And then he attacked when Sinjin had his back turned!"

"I've always thought Brockhurst was a cad," Rosie said indignantly.

"Doesn't Polly have a say in Revelstoke's future?" Emma asked from the divan she shared with her husband. "She is his wife after all. Can't she have him released?"

Ambrose shook his head. "Legally, the certification of the two physicians can keep Revelstoke detained until such time as an inquisition is carried out by the Lord Chancellor. If Revelstoke is declared mad by the commission, then his marriage to Polly could be declared null and void," he concluded grimly.

Polly saw the taut looks exchanged amongst her family members.

"Don't worry, Polly, we won't let that happen," Violet declared.

"We'll do whatever it takes to help Revelstoke—won't we, Carlisle?"

"Aye, lass." Her husband, a rugged, dark-haired Scot whose aura glowed with steadfast devotion, engulfed her hand with his large one. To Ambrose, he said, "What is your plan, Kent?"

"As we speak, Lugo is heading the search for Revelstoke. There are around forty licensed private asylums in London, so it's no simple task. Then there's the business with Clive Grundell. McLeod says the man's as slippery as an eel. There have been multiple sightings of him, but he remains one step ahead of us. Hopefully, with the mudlarks on the lookout, we'll net that bounder soon." Ambrose's forehead lined. "My gut tells me that Grundell is the key to all of this."

"We should focus our energies on finding Grundell, then," Carlisle said. "I'll be glad to help."

Polly's heart swelled with gratitude when her other brothers-in-law and Harry also voiced their willingness to help.

"It seems to me that speaking with the Duke of Acton is just as imperative," Marianne put in. "Perhaps we ladies could try him again in the morning."

"Excellent idea," Emma agreed.

At that moment, a knock sounded, and when Em bade entry, the Strathavens' aged butler shuffled in, a scruffy blond boy in tow.

Polly recognized the mudlark who'd accompanied Tim back to the academy.

"Patrick," she said in surprise, "what are you doing here?"

"Brought news, Miss Kent." He doffed his cap in a sprightly bow. "We larks 'ave found the cove you're looking for."

It was past ten in the evening when Polly arrived home.

As much as she'd wanted to be present for the capture of

Grundell, she knew Ambrose was right: it would be too dangerous, and she'd only be in the way. Moreover, when she'd stood up
to leave Em's, she'd suddenly swayed. She was exhausted and
needed a good night's rest so that she could be fresh for the
morrow—when surely Ambrose would have good news.

First thing in the morning, she and her sisters would be paying
a call on the Actons. She vowed to herself that she would not
leave without discovering where Sinjin had been taken and
persuading the duke to pursue a better course of action.

She ached with worry for Sinjin. Why, oh why, hadn't they
trusted each other with the truth? The secrets they'd kept had led
to the present calamity. In hindsight, she knew that they could get
through anything—as long as they faced it together.

I won't give up, my love, she thought fiercely. *I'm going to bring you
home.*

She'd just sent Harvey to bed and was preparing to go up to
her room when a knock sounded on the front door. Strange at
this hour... could it be that Ambrose had sent news already?
Excitement chased away fatigue. She dashed to the door, yanked
it open.

And blinked at the pair of hulking strangers standing on the
doorstep.

Before she could scream, a handkerchief was thrust into her
face. Sickly fumes filled her nostrils and lungs, and darkness
claimed her.

37

"Revelstoke, wake up!"

Sinjin surfaced sluggishly. The darkness sucked at him like a pit of tar, but someone was shaking him, refusing to let him return to the primordial sludge where he belonged. He was no better than the mud on the street, and now the world had seen the truth...

Polly had seen him for who he was.

Anguish crushed his chest like a boulder. He'd been the biggest fool to seek her out at the Shackleton ball. But those three days apart from her had felt like years; in forming his plan to protect his wife, he hadn't taken into account how much he and his damned devils would miss her.

The black one hungered for her. It yearned to pet her silken hair, to feel the sweet clasp of her body holding his. During his self-imposed exile, he'd frigged himself endlessly to memories of their lovemaking—and when that wasn't enough, he'd punched the stuffing out of the practice dummy he'd set up in his apartment.

Even the blue demon, who usually wanted nothing to do with

people—who could barely tolerate even his own presence—
yearned for Polly. To just have her close. To have her snuggled
against him in silence, no need for words, her company a beacon
in the gloom, reminding him that there was a reason to go on.

He'd missed her so much that he'd fooled himself into
believing that he'd had his demons under control. He'd gone to
find her, and seeing her in that bastard Brockhurst's arms had
brought his dark side roaring to life, leading to his disgrace—and
hers.

She'd said that she loved him; he repaid her by exposing her
secret to the world. Her tearful face flashed in his mind's eye, and
he wanted to die.

*I'm sorry, kitten. Sorry that my love brought you low. Sorry that I
couldn't be the man you deserve...*

Groaning, he curled onto his side. Now she was gone, and,
without her, he had no reason to go on. He didn't even care that
he'd been dragged to a madhouse, locked up like an animal.
Prison, lunatic asylum, what did it matter? Nothing mattered...

"Bloody hell, man—*get up.*"

A frigid splash jolted him awake. He blinked blearily, swiping
water from his face. The face hovering over him came into focus.

"Kent?" he croaked. "How did you find me... what are you
doing here?"

"We've searched a dozen asylums looking for you, and I'm
breaking you out," Kent said tersely. "Your father has kidnapped
Polly. I need your help to find them."

"Polly?" The mention of his beloved gave him a surge of
energy. He sat up on the edge of the narrow cot, trying to focus
through the fog in his head. "Why does my father—"

"Acton is behind all of it. We've got Grundell, and he confessed
that the duke paid him and Nicoletta to stage the assault at
Corbett's. To frame you. I'll explain everything later, but right now,
we have to find Polly. Do you know where he would take her?"

Fear cleared Sinjin's head, thoughts slowly crystallizing.

Polly's in danger. The duke has her. Where would he go?

"I don't know." He got to his feet, stumbling across the cell-like room for his clothes. Yanking them on, he growled, "But I'm bloody well going to find out."

"That's absurd, Revelstoke." The Duchess of Acton sat upon the velvet wingchair in her drawing room as if it were a throne, her spine rigid as she faced Sinjin and Kent. "That you would even suggest that your father, one of the highest peers in the realm, would abduct that chit is beyond the pale. Even for you." Her lips curled with scorn as she took in Sinjin's disheveled state. "Clearly, you're in one of your moods again."

It took all of Sinjin's willpower to stay focused, to not give into the blue devil whispering in his ear. *This is all your fault. You're not right in the head. Polly's in danger because of you.*

He evaded the tentacles of hopelessness and self-doubt. *Stay in command, man.*

Polly's life was at stake.

"We have a written confession from Grundell, one of the villains hired by your husband," Kent cut in. "According to Grundell, Acton paid him and his partner, Nicoletta French, five hundred pounds to make it appear as if Revelstoke had gone mad and assaulted French. But when playing with fire, one often gets burned. Grundell and French turned the tables on Acton, blackmailing him to keep his plot a secret. Acton put an end to the pair's greed by shooting Nicoletta in cold blood and framing Grundell for the murder. Fearing that His Grace would go after him as well, Grundell has been in hiding all this time."

The duchess paled, but she clung to her righteous disbelief. "Why would I believe the word of an admitted criminal over that of my husband? And what possible motive could Acton have to see Revelstoke discredited?"

"He wants control... over Sinjin's inheritance." Theodore stood in the doorway, looking stricken. Sinjin had no idea how long the other had been standing there.

"Don't be ridiculous, Theodore," his mama snapped. "Your father is a *duke*. He doesn't need Sinjin's funds."

Crossing over to her, Theodore said, "I am sorry, Mama, but that's not true. I overheard Papa talking to his solicitor last week, making... final arrangements." Swallowing, he went on, "Papa's made some bad investments, and the duchy is floundering in debt. Papa has been keeping the fact a secret from us and the rest of the world."

"My God... we are ruined?" Her Grace sagged against the chair.

Facing Sinjin, Theodore said painfully, "I didn't know of Papa's plan to discredit you. If I had known, I would have said something. Done something."

"I believe you. It is not your fault," Sinjin said.

Theo's chin quivered, and he nodded.

"Now do you have any idea where Papa might have taken Polly?"

Theo's eyes widened. "He took... you mean he *abducted* her?"

"From her home last night," Kent interrupted. "Where would he have gone? Think, my lord. It would likely be a place close by —a temporary place to hold Polly until he could figure out his next move. I don't believe this was a premeditated act on his part; I think he panicked when he realized we had his accomplice in our custody, and it was only a matter of time before his villainy was revealed."

Looking ashen, Theo said, "He... he keeps a cottage in St. John's Wood. I was looking for something in his desk once when I came upon the deed and keys. No one's supposed to know about it; I think it's where he, um,"—he slid a pained glance at his mama, who remained slumped in her chair—"kept his ladybirds over the years."

"We need the address," Sinjin said urgently.

38

Polly's eyelids fluttered open. Her head was pounding, her vision blurry. Where in heavens was she? She was lying on a sofa in a strange room—

"You're awake."

Her head whipped in the direction of the man's voice. She bolted upward, swaying as a wave of wooziness hit her. She grabbed onto the arm of the sofa for support even as she kept her gaze on the stranger sitting in an adjacent chair. His features were harsh and gaunt, his vivid blue eyes startlingly familiar...

"Your Grace?" she said, her voice rusty with shock.

The Duke of Acton inclined his dark, silver-streaked head. His hawkish mien remained impassive, but fury and frustration seethed around him. Fed by underlying desperation, his aura was terrifying to behold: that of a man capable of anything.

The pistol resting upon his thigh underscored his menace.

"I regret the circumstances of our first formal introduction," her father-in-law said, "but my troublesome son and your meddling brother left me no choice. Once I discovered that Kent's men had Grundell in their custody, I knew I had to act."

Understanding struck her. "You... you are the one who tried to frame Sinjin?"

"It was supposed to be simple. Convince Sinjin that he was mad—and what better way than having him believe he'd beaten a woman, committed an act that even he would find unforgivable? And it is not far from the truth. One need only look at his disgraceful behavior and his pathetic inability to control his own moods to see the madness in him. He's not fit for the title, and it was my duty to purge his influence from the line."

"Sinjin is not mad," she said hotly. "*You* are for concocting such a despicable plot!"

The duke's mouth thinned. "Believe what you will, but it was the only way to save the duchy and Sinjin as well. Everything would have been easy if he had only complied with my plan. If he were declared insane, he would no longer have the responsibilities he didn't want anyway. Theodore could have taken guardianship over the money and properties; Sinjin could have lived a carefree life, upon his death leaving the title to my more suitable heir. I did it in the interests of both my sons."

The duke's rational tone, paired with a crazed and feverish glow, made him a sick and dangerous man. Polly calculated the odds of making a run for it. As demented as her captor seemed, he held the firearm in a sure grip... one that conveyed his ability to use it.

Keep him talking. Try to figure a way out.

Humoring him, she said, "So you were, um, only looking out for Sinjin's interests?"

"Precisely." The duke nodded, relief calming some of the agitation around him. "Unfortunately, Sinjin has always been an unruly and uncooperative child. After the plan with Nicoletta and Grundell backfired, and I was forced to... eliminate the problem," —he paused thoughtfully, the hairs rising on Polly's nape—"I had to reassess the situation. I might have let things go on for a while had Sinjin not married you. If he managed to sire an heir..."

Acton shook his head while the possibility flashed in Polly's head: she could, at that very moment, be carrying Sinjin's child. Her determination to escape this madman's clutches was renewed.

"... his bad blood would taint the line forever," Acton was saying. "I *had* to stop that from happening. So I found out as much as I could about you, his unexpected bride, and I learned about a wager involving you and Brockhurst."

She stared at him, pieces falling into place. "You were behind Brockhurst's behavior at the ball?"

"Brockhurst has a *tendre* for you, my dear; he was merely too spineless to act upon it when you were a wallflower. Now that you are the fashionable Countess of Revelstoke..." The duke shrugged. "All I did was have a chance conversation with him at the club. I mentioned that my rakehell son was persisting in his philandering ways after marriage, leaving his new bride unhappy and in need of consolation. Brockhurst took the bait. I had hoped for a scandal, a rift to separate you and Sinjin—but Sinjin gave me so much more." A smile of satisfaction stretched over the duke's lips. "He gave me another opportunity to petition for a lunacy inquisition."

"Why are you so convinced of Sinjin's madness?" Polly whispered. "He is your own son. Your blood runs in his veins."

"Not only mine." The duke straightened in his chair, his blue eyes, so like Sinjin's, shifting eerily side to side, as if he sensed some ghostly presence. "You must understand, I didn't do it purely to gain control of his inheritance or to rid the line of his taint. From the moment he flaunted that damned locket in front of me, I knew he had the power to bring the entire duchy crashing down. *I had no other choice.*"

Did he mean that trifle that Sinjin had tried to charm her with?

"What is so special about the locket?" she said, puzzled.

"No more talking." Acton's expression grew crafty. He rose, pistol in hand. "Now we execute the next part of my plan."

She shrank back against the cushions as he advanced toward her. "N-next part?"

"You're going to write a letter to Sinjin." The duke grabbed her arm, shoving her toward a desk where paper and ink had been laid out. "Tell him that you want him to comply fully with the lunacy inquisition—that your very life depends upon it. When he is declared incompetent, then I will release you, even provide you with a settlement for the trouble of having your marriage annulled. If he fails to obey my wishes—"

A sudden commotion sounded outside. Shouts, the sound of gunfire.

After an instant's paralysis, Polly regained her wits, made a dash for the door—only to be yanked back, her arm twisted painfully behind her. The duke held her immobile, the gun pressed against her temple. The door flung open, and her heart leapt at the sight of Sinjin, Ambrose and his men just behind.

Sinjin's gaze met hers. A thousand unspoken words passed between them. Her pulse raced... and not just because there was a gun pointed to her head.

Sinjin shifted his focus to his father, his aura afire with fury. "Release her."

The duke's grip on her tightened.

"The game is up, Acton," Ambrose said. "We have a signed confession from Grundell; we know you tried to frame your son. That you murdered Nicoletta French. And, outside, my men have in their custody the pair of cutthroats you hired to abduct my sister."

"It's over, Father," Sinjin said, his voice low, "and if you cannot relinquish your hate of me, then at least take me for Polly. She has nothing to do with this."

"Drop your weapons, then. All of you." Acton ground the

muzzle of the gun into Polly's temple, causing her to wince. "Do it now."

Slowly, Sinjin bent, setting his pistol on the ground. Even as Polly gasped, "*No*," he pushed it away, leaving himself unarmed.

Ambrose and the others followed suit.

"I do not hate you, Sinjin," the duke said calmly. "I could have had you killed, but you are, after all, my son. My family. And that, I suppose, has always been my Achilles heel." He removed the pistol from her temple.

To Polly's horror, he leveled it at Sinjin.

"I'm sorry, son. This is the only choice I have left," he said.

Fear spurred Polly to act. On instinct, she jabbed her elbow back as hard as she could. Acton grunted, releasing her, the weapon still within his grasp. She made a grab for it, even as she heard someone shouting her name, but she couldn't let go, couldn't let Sinjin come to harm. She grappled desperately with the duke before he flung her bodily aside. A blast sounded as she flew through the air, her head catching the corner of a table, blackness claiming her once more.

"Open your eyes, love."

It took effort, but Polly managed to lift her eyelids.

The first thing she saw was Sinjin. A dream? But he didn't fade when she blinked, love and worry etched over his beautiful features. When she realized that he was truly there and she was cradled on his lap, she threw her arms around him in joyous relief.

"Y-you're here," she sobbed into his neck.

"Yes, love, yes." His hand moved soothingly over her back, his warmth and scent so comforting and right. "You're safe now."

It all came crashing back. She took in her surroundings: the place where the Duke of Acton had held her captive. She jerked, but Sinjin held her against him.

"Careful, sweeting, you've a bump on your head from hitting the table."

"What happened? Your father—*Ambrose*," she said in sudden panic.

"Your brother is fine. Acton got off a shot, but he missed." Sinjin's expression was grim. "His Grace is in your brother's custody, and the constables should be arriving shortly."

Seeing the pain in his gaze, she whispered, "Oh, Sinjin, I'm so sorry."

"No, love, I'm the one who is sorry." Taking her hands, he said hoarsely, "Can you forgive me for how I acted... how I treated you?"

"It was my fault. I shouldn't have pushed you when I'd agreed not to. And I should have told you the truth about my affliction..." The realization struck her like a thunderbolt, and she gasped, "*Oh my goodness.*"

"What's the matter? Is it your head? Does it hurt—"

"No, no, it's not that. Sinjin," she said, her voice hushed, "you're *not glowing.*"

Ambrose strode into the room and stopped short. Worry radiated from his face... but only from his face, she saw in wonder.

"Are you all right, Polly?" her brother said. "You look as if you've seen a ghost."

"That's just it," she said in astonishment. "I don't see anything extraordinary. The auras... they're gone!"

39

I t was nearing midnight by the time Sinjin and Polly arrived home. Despite his wife's sleepy protests, Sinjin carried her in, and after assuring a worried Harvey that both master and mistress were perfectly well, he continued with his precious cargo up the stairs. He called for a bath but dismissed the maid, preferring to tend to Polly himself.

His throat tightened at the picture she made reclining in the steamy bath. Over the past dark days, he'd feared that this would never be his again: the privilege of being husband to this earthly goddess, the sum of all his desires. Yet somehow, despite everything, she was there with him. And not even the blue devil still hovering at the edge of his consciousness could make him willingly part from her again.

She was dozing by the time he finished his ministrations. He tucked her cozily in bed before bathing himself. After he finished, he came to join her and was surprised to see that her eyes were open.

Shucking his towel, he got beneath the covers with her. "I thought you were asleep."

"I was tired, but now I'm not." Her gaze was shadowed, her voice quivering. "I can't stop thinking... I could have lost you tonight."

"I'm right here." He tucked her firmly against him. "It's over, and we'll never be parted again."

"Sinjin... we need to talk."

Hearing the hesitancy in her voice and knowing that he'd put it there, he felt his gut clench with self-loathing. But she was right: they did need to talk. With reluctance, he released her, and they faced each other curled on their sides.

"Whatever you want to discuss, we will," he said simply.

Her clear eyes searched his face. "What about the rule against intimacy?"

"Gone, kitten. At least for me." Tucking a damp tress behind her ear, he said gruffly, "I insisted upon limits because I was afraid that if you saw me in one of my moods, you would want nothing to do with me. I thought that if I could distance myself when things went to hell, then maybe I could protect you from me. That maybe I had a shot at being a halfway decent husband to you."

"Oh, Sinjin, you are far more than halfway decent," she said tremulously.

"How can you say that after the way I acted toward you?" Anger at himself burned like acid in his throat. "I humiliated you, acted like a goddamned animal—that's what I am when the black mood overtakes me. And when the blue one does..." He let out a harsh breath. "Polly, you've seen my aura. I'm a disaster."

"You're *not* a disaster." She touched his cheek. "You're just you. And I love you."

His chest tightened. "How can you?"

"How can you love me? I mean, you do," she said, biting her lip, "don't you?"

Her uncertainty was so absurd that it drew a hoarse laugh

from him. "God, Polly, of course I love you. More than life. Forever and beyond."

"I'm glad," she whispered. "Now does it change your love to know that I could see auras, that I was what many considered a freak?"

"No. And don't call yourself that."

"Back in the village, they called me Peculiar Polly. I was an outcast there, and here in London as well," she said solemnly. "In some people's eyes, I was so unworthy that they made me the object of a nasty wager."

"Those people are bastards. None of that matters," he said fiercely. "I love *you*, Polly, and nothing could change that."

"And I love you the same way. For *all* that you are, Sinjin. For your strength and resilience. The way you live life fully and with no apologies. For the passion you've taught me, the way your love makes me feel—free and truly myself."

His chest ached at her words, but it was a beautiful ache.

He framed her face with his palms. "I never felt right until I met you. And now I do... as right as I can feel, at any rate." Swallowing, he forced himself to say, "You can't see auras any longer, but my moods—they're here to stay. Are you certain you can handle them... handle me?"

"I'm not afraid of your moods, Sinjin. I'm only afraid of distance between us. If I've learned anything, it is that hiding who we are creates more problems than it solves." Her gaze was earnest, so full of love and acceptance that his eyes stung. "As long as we face all that life brings together, I know we can handle anything."

The only proper answer to her sweetness was a kiss. In the past, his blue devil had dampened his ardor, but the warmth of Polly's lips dissolved the lingering darkness. The knowledge that he was no longer alone sent a hot, joyful rush through him, and before long he needed more than the mating of their mouths.

Laying her against the pillows, he worshipped her. He petted and kissed every inch of his countess and didn't stop until she came, her magnificent breasts heaving, her pussy dripping ambrosia into his greedy mouth. Only then did he position both of them on their sides, tucking her against him, her supple spine aligning perfectly against his front.

Hooking her top leg over his hip, he notched himself to her ready passage and drove home.

Polly moaned at the filling thrust. In this sideways position, Sinjin invaded her completely, his hand trapping her leg over his, holding her steady and open as he plowed her. Nestled against his hard chest, feeling those muscles flex against her back as he worked his big, long cock inside her, she felt utterly surrounded by his strength and power. Utterly right.

His lips found her earlobe, flicking and suckling it, the erotic sensation making her clench in helpless delight.

"I love the way you take me," he rasped in her ear. "You're squeezing my cock as if you don't want to let me go. As if you can't get enough of me."

"I'll never get enough of you."

"You'll take everything I give you, won't you?" He drove in deeply. "Everything that I am."

"Yes, yes," she panted.

He surged, another heavy thrust. "And you'll give me yourself in return?"

"Everything that I am," she breathed. "Always."

He pounded into her, his stones smacking her folds. Reaching in front of her, he searched out her pearl, strumming out a melody of delirious pleasure. Soon the sensations became too much, pushing her over the edge, sending her soaring once again.

Groaning, he buried his face in her neck, his hips pistoning against her, the scorching blasts of his seed saturating her womb.

He cuddled her against him, their bodies still connected, the sounds of their breaths mingling with the crackling of the fire. As spent as she was, sleep eluded her... and apparently her husband as well, for his words rumbled against her ear.

"Tonight would have unraveled me if I didn't have you by my side. Discovering my father's plot..." His voice roughened. "I'll never understand why he hates me so."

His words stirred a memory. Something the duke had said... about why he'd initiated the vile scheme...

"The locket!" She bolted upright. "We have to look at it!"

Sinjin's brows drew together. "Why?"

"Before you and Ambrose arrived, your father mentioned the locket," she explained. "Something about it having the power to destroy the duchy."

Throwing on her robe, she went to her armoire and returned with the locket. She sat on the bed, Sinjin beside her, both of them studying the oval silver charm. It was pretty with its filigree design, but there was nothing remarkable about it.

"What could this locket possibly signify?" Sinjin took the piece from her, pressing on the latch to reveal the empty hollow inside. "Why would Acton care about it?"

Peering closely, Polly said, "See how the inside doesn't fill the entire depth of the locket? Do you think there could be a hidden compartment behind the inner wall?"

"Hmm. Look here at the rim," he said. "It's got a slight dent..."

"Someone might have pried it open there," she said with burgeoning excitement. "Let's try a penknife."

They took the locket to her desk. She lit a lamp, and Sinjin carefully plied the tip of the blade to the edge of the open locket. The interior wall popped off... and Polly's heart thudded as she saw the tiny portrait within: a beautiful raven-haired lady.

Nestled against it was a lock of mahogany hair.

"That is my mama," Sinjin said hoarsely. "And the hair..."

"It could be yours." Polly's voice was hushed. "Open the other side."

When the concave divider separated, he found a slip of paper.

It contained an address.

40

TWO MONTHS LATER

Hand in hand with her husband, Polly trudged up the grassy knoll of a churchyard. It was a sunny late afternoon, autumn crispness in the breeze. In a village near Weymouth, close to the coast of Dorset, they were following their guide, a stout and kindly lady by the name of Mrs. Wakefield.

"... I was surprised when I received your letter," the good lady was chattering. "I never knew my poor Catherine had any relatives—except her brother, of course, who paid for her board and care in my home."

Sinjin's grip tightened on her fingers, and Polly gave a reassuring squeeze back.

After discovering the contents of the locket, Polly had gone with Sinjin to confront his father. The duke had been placed under house arrest pending his trial for murder and kidnapping; all charges of lunacy against Sinjin had been dropped. Perhaps given the evidence of the portrait and the address, or perhaps because Acton knew his time to face the ultimate judge would soon be upon him, he had confessed everything.

Sinjin's mama had indeed run away with her lover, but she had somehow survived the storm that took the ship down. When Acton had arrived in Weymouth, he'd found her in a local hospital —alive but clearly damaged from the near-drowning. She hadn't recognized him or herself. And he, embittered by her betrayals and wild, uncontrollable moods, had seen a way out.

He'd found Mrs. Wakefield's private home for lunatics just outside the port town. Claiming to be her brother, he'd given his wife's name as "Catherine Smith," and left her there, paying for her upkeep but never visiting again. He'd continued on with his life as if she'd truly died and, in doing so, had become a bigamist.

For twenty-one years, the true Duchess of Acton had lived without knowledge of who she truly was. Then, in a lucid moment right before her death, she'd remembered. She'd sent her only memento of her previous life—the locket that Acton hadn't known she'd kept in her possession—to Sinjin.

A week later, she was dead.

"I was separated from my mama when I was young." Sinjin responded to Mrs. Wakefield's unspoken question. "I believed she was dead and was not told of her fate until recently."

"That story is not an unusual one, I'm afraid," the lady said with a sigh. "So many families deal with their afflicted kin in that fashion. And, the truth is, I suspected Catherine might have children."

"Why is that?" Beneath the brim of his hat, Sinjin's eyes were vivid and alert.

"There was a lullaby she liked to sing." Mrs. Wakefield hummed a few bars of *Bye, Baby Bunting.* "When she was singing, her face would grow tender. Sentiment returned to her even if the memories themselves didn't."

Feeling the quiver that ran through Sinjin, Polly clasped his hand tighter.

"Well, here we are." Mrs. Wakefield came to a stop in front of a modest but tidy grave marker sheltered by the bowers of a silver birch. The epitaph read simply, *Catherine Smith, Home with the Angels.* "I'll leave you to your visit, then."

Polly expressed heartfelt thanks to the departing woman. When she turned back to Sinjin, she saw that he'd knelt at his mama's grave, sweeping off the fallen leaves with his gloves, placing the bouquet he'd brought at the base of the headstone.

When he rose, she went to join him. He pulled her fiercely against him.

"My mama remembered me," he said in a voice taut with emotion.

"Yes, she did. Even when her mind forgot, her heart remembered," Polly said softly. "She returned to you every time she sang that song."

"All this time... and I never knew. How could my father do such a thing?" Sinjin shook his head. "Out of fear and hatred, he hurt so many people."

"You've done your best to stem the damage. By allowing His Grace's bigamy to remain a secret, you've chosen the higher road. You've spared Theodore and your stepmama much pain."

Since the duke had, in fact, already been married, his youngest son was a bastard and his present wife an unwitting participant in adultery. Sinjin could have exposed these facts to the world—but he hadn't. Despite the fact that the duchess' behavior toward him was as cold as ever, he'd protected her and his half-brother.

"They don't deserve to suffer because of Acton's actions," he said gruffly.

Her heart swelled with all that she felt for this beautiful, complex man. The rake who'd seen through her wallflower disguise. The god who'd rescued her from an island of fear and self-doubt and who'd let her tame his monsters in return. Her honorable, loving husband and soul mate.

"I'm so proud of you," she said.

His arms tightened around her, and she hugged him back.

They stood together beneath the swaying branches until dusk painted vivid streaks across the sky.

He released a breath and said, "Let's go home."

Arm in arm, they did.

EPILOGUE

"Time to head back, eh?" Sinjin said, reining in his stallion.

"Not just yet." Pulling up beside him, Harry Kent slanted a discreet look at his pocket watch. "I mean, er, I'd be interested in seeing the crop rotations."

Sinjin had been giving Harry a tour of the Acton estate, showing off the improvements he'd made since becoming duke. The excursion had gone on for two hours at this point, thanks to the other's copious questions, and he was ready to return to the house. But this was the third time Harry had stalled the proceedings, and Sinjin knew why.

"Before you try to postpone us further by suggesting an indepth study of the fertilizer," he said dryly, "I know what Polly has planned."

"You do?"

"It's my birthday. I'm sure the guests have arrived and are lying in wait as I speak," he said complacently.

Warmth unfurled in him as he thought of his duchess' sweet scheming, her determination to make his birthday special. Despite the advanced state of her pregnancy, she'd been busy all month making clandestine arrangements for his party. He'd gamely played along, pretending he didn't know. He didn't want to spoil her fun. Or his.

Just this morning, she'd woken him up to give him his present. She was too far along for him to make love to her—he would never risk endangering her or their unborn child—but his kitten had gotten quite creative and bold during their year of marriage. Just thinking of her laughing eyes and frolicsome mouth made his loins stir.

Aye, two hours away from her was long enough.

"I told Polly you wouldn't fall for it." Looking resigned, Harry said, "Could you at least pretend to be surprised?"

Before Sinjin could reply, he saw the rising dust cloud of an approaching rider. He made out Theodore, a frequent visitor to his home these days. His younger brother pulled to a stop; the friendly greeting died on his lips when he saw the other's expression.

"What's amiss?" he said instantly.

"You have to come back to the house," Theo blurted. "It's Polly. The babe's come early—"

Sinjin had already spurred his mount into a gallop, the thundering of his heart louder than the stallion's hooves. The thriving lands of his estate passed by, and he saw none of it. Within him, the devils stirred. For once, they were united, joined in their concern for Polly.

His wife, his love... his everything.

The past year hadn't been perfect. He still had his moods, she her insecurities. But they'd made the commitment to meet all challenges together and head on, and that had made all the difference. Her acceptance calmed his devils; his passionate adoration made her confidence blossom into full, stunning bloom. As Polly had predicted, their love had made them stronger than either had ever been alone. He'd never known such happiness, such pure contentment. If he lost her...

He came to a roaring stop, leaping off his horse and tossing the reins to the waiting groom. He took the steps up to the house three at a time, rushing through the door just as the butler opened it. He didn't pause to greet the guests milling about in the foyer, continuing his path up the sweeping staircase straight to his duchess' suite. He burst through the door, his heart in his throat, prepared for the worst...

Polly was sitting up against a mound of fluffy pillows. She looked tired, but her face was glowing. She held a small, swaddled bundle in her arms.

Their gazes met.

"Surprise," she said with a rueful smile.

He stumbled to the bed, cupped her face with hands that shook. "Are you... is everything..."

"Polly did splendidly." From the other side of the bed, the Duchess of Strathaven smiled fondly at her youngest sister. "Apparently your son has her easy-going temperament for the childbirth took all of a quarter hour. The physician's already downstairs, toasting your heir with the rest of the guests."

Relief rushed through him, the current so strong that he couldn't speak.

In tacit agreement, the others left them to their privacy.

"Would you like to hold your son?" Polly said.

Gingerly, he took the feather-light bundle she handed to him. As he gazed upon the tiny sleeping human, he lost his heart for a second time. Which was strange for the babe looked a bit like an alien creature with his slightly pointed head, red and wrinkled face, a single mahogany curl upon his furrowed brow.

"He looks just like you," Polly said dreamily.

The babe's eyelids lifted, and Sinjin's breath lodged. The unfocused gaze that looked back at him was a clear, brilliant aquamarine. In that moment, he knew that, despite all his faults, he would love, protect, and provide for this child, the miracle that he and Polly had made together, until his dying breath.

"He's beautiful like his mama," he said hoarsely. "What shall we call him?"

"I thought Stephan, if it suits you."

His heart clenched. "Aye. Little Stephan." He pressed his lips tenderly to his son's forehead before placing the babe in the waiting bassinet.

Shucking his clothes, he joined Polly in bed, pulling her carefully into his arms.

"Thank you for my son," he whispered.

"You're welcome." She snuggled up against him, her eyes sparkling with the brightness of their future. "After all, I had to keep my promise to make your birthday unforgettable."

They laughed together.

And then they kissed, with all the love and joy in their hearts.

ACKNOWLEDGMENTS

First of all, to my readers: thank you for your continued support and interest in my work! You mean the world to me. I'm so grateful and humbled to have the opportunity to share the stories in my head with you.

For my writing posse and those who've helped bring this book into beautiful reality: Tina, Diane, the Montauk 8, and Brian. Don't know what I'd do without you. Hugs and heartfelt thanks.

For my family: You are everything.

ABOUT THE AUTHOR

USA Today & International Bestselling Author Grace Callaway writes hot and heart-melting historical romance filled with mystery and adventure. Her debut novel was a Romance Writers of America® Golden Heart® Finalist and a #1 National Regency Bestseller, and her subsequent novels have topped national and international bestselling lists. She is the winner of the Daphne du Maurier Award for Excellence in Mystery and Suspense, the Maggie Award for Excellence in Historical Romance, the Golden Leaf, and the Passionate Plume Award. She holds a doctorate in clinical psychology from the University of Michigan and lives with her family in a valley close to the sea. When she's not writing, she enjoys dancing, exploring the great outdoors with her rescue pup, and going on adapted adventures with her special son.

Stay connected with Grace!

Newsletter: gracecallaway.com/newsletter

Reader Group:
facebook.com/groups/gracecallawaybookclub/

facebook.com/GraceCallawayBooks
bookbub.com/authors/grace-callaway
instagram.com/gracecallawaybooks
amazon.com/author/gracecallaway

Made in United States
North Haven, CT
01 May 2022

18779763R00202